A DRAUGHT FOR A DRAGON

ADVENTURING FOR AMATEURS

SIDE QUEST ROW SERIES
BOOK 3

R.K. ASHWICK

LASKELL

THE SINKING REACH
VINE HEART
TITAN'S NAILS
HART'S FENN
SHABRON RIVER
ELWIG FOREST
THE SCAR
DEEPRIVER
KOLKEAN DESERT
THE DRIFTWOOD
DEEPRIVER DELTA
N
W
E
S

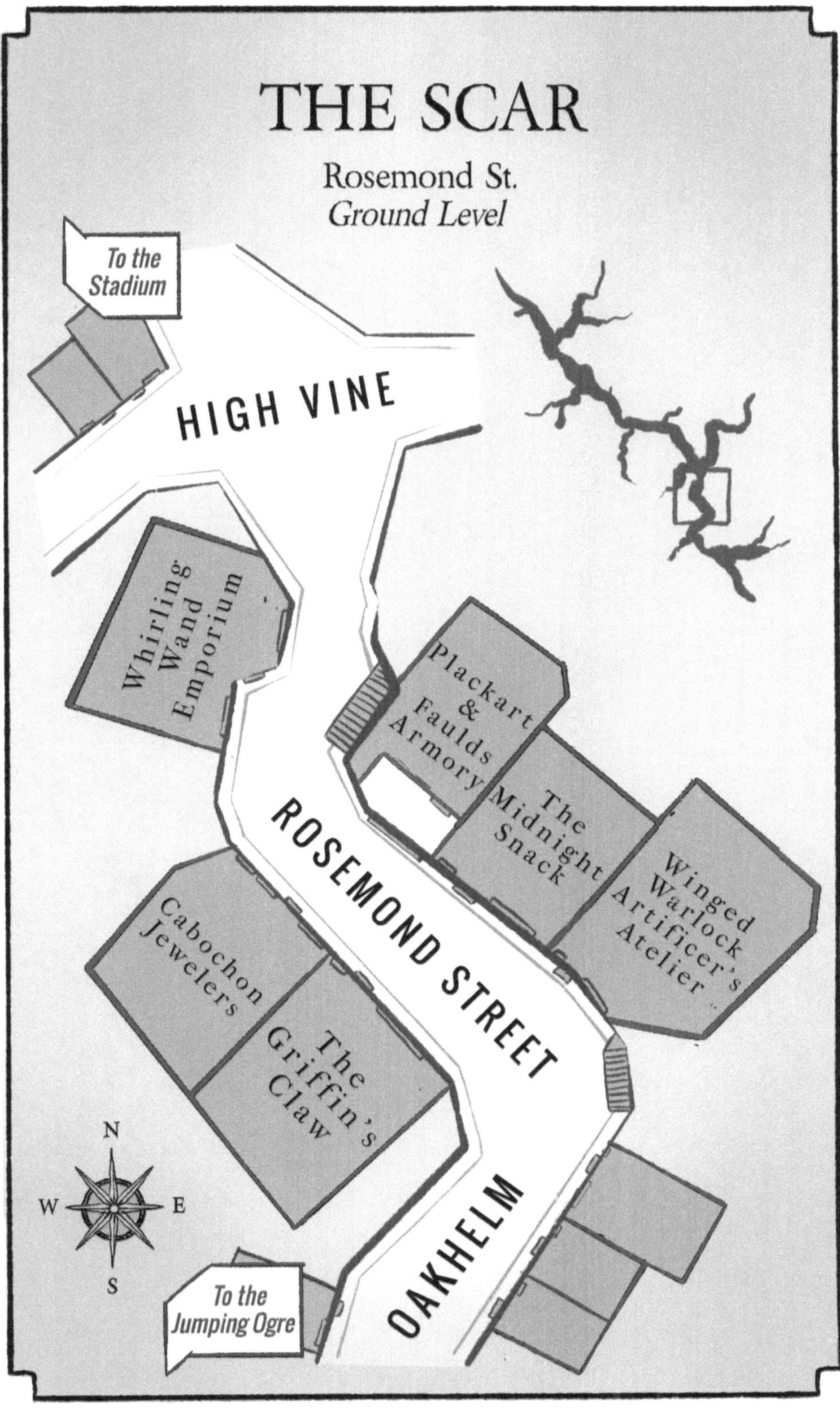

THE SCAR
Rosemond St.
Ground Level
To the Stadium
HIGH VINE
Whirling Wand Emporium
Plackart & Faulds Armory
The Midnight Snack
Winged Warlock Artificer's Atelier
Cabochon Jewelers
The Griffin's Claw
ROSEMOND STREET
OAKHELM
N
W
E
S
To the Jumping Ogre

CONTENTS

TIP 1:

ACCEPT THE QUEST

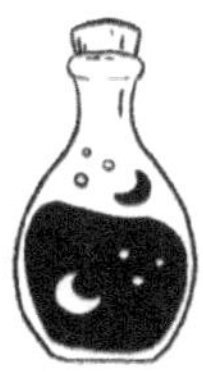

Ambrose

THE GRIFFIN'S CLAW was closed for the day—but that hardly mattered to the other merchants on Rosemond Street.

To them, the *Closed* sign, dimmed lights, and cleaning supplies spelled out an invitation: by all means, intrude. Make as much noise as you like. Destroy the quiet sanctity of his potion shop after a busy day.

Ambrose found he didn't mind it as much as he should have.

"Dawn?" he called to the wandmaker from the top of his ladder. "If you could please pass me that banner by your arm?"

Giggling erupted from the workroom and drowned out his request. Over by the front counter, Dawn leaned toward a riveted Viola, right over the ignored banner.

"So *then* I said that if Rory insists our wedding cake be four tiers, that's fine. But the top tier *has* to be coconut or I'll perish—"

More chatter rose and fell from the workroom; the ladder creaked underneath Ambrose's feet. He raised his voice and tried appealing to a different intruder. "Viola? The banner, please?"

The baker's gnomish ears didn't so much as twitch. "Wait, so what's the third tier, then?"

"Chocolate, obviously."

"The banner—?"

Dawn started counting off on her fingers. "With strawberry buttercream roses, a raspberry drizzle..."

"Hello?"

"Then the second tier is—"

Ambrose rested his forehead against the top of the shelf in defeat. "Someone!" he shouted. "The banner on the counter, if you would be *so* kind!"

A gray blur zipped out of the workroom and grabbed the fabric. He twisted to find a half-orcish young woman standing at the foot of the ladder, the requested decoration draped over her wrist.

"Here you go, Mr. Ambrose." Nat held up the banner and frowned. "Why didn't you say something earlier?"

Ambrose passed a hand over his face.

He mistakenly thought he could finish his festival decorations that day. He had pictured a quiet evening, a cup of tea, a few pennants to hang... But his attempts to decorate his way around everyone else's gossip sessions were measly at best. The front counter lay half-hidden under twisted garlands and tangled bunting. Two of his four banners had already slipped off the shelves and pooled on the floor in bright, shiny mockeries of his work.

And his boyfriend, Eli, was due back any minute.

"Thank you, Nat." He pinned the banner in place with more force than was necessary, then climbed down to his apprentice. "I realize you're off the clock for the day, but if you happen to be free to—"

She brightened. "Finish the Spelltide decorations for you?"

He sighed in relief and pushed the ladder aside. "Only if you have time."

But his relief was naively premature. Nat grinned, the iridescent freckles on her gray skin sparking with the promise of an incoming bargain. It was a habit she had picked up during their time in Aphos two years ago—and she hadn't yet grown out of it.

"I think I can find the time to help." She set her hands behind her back. "If…"

"Oh, here we go."

"*If* you take my catnap potion and talk to Fio today."

He swept past her. "No."

"Sounds like a yes to me!" Nat scampered off to the counter and gathered up a pile of colorful bunting into her arms. "I'll handle these. Dawn, Viola, can you help with those garlands? Mr. Ambrose is going to go talk to Fio!"

Nat rushed back into the workroom without any further explanation. Dawn sifted through the tangle of garlands and pulled out a line of pink blooms that perfectly matched her skirt.

"Fio?" She tossed the decor around her neck like a scarf, the bright flowers glowing against her brown skin, then turned to Ambrose. "You're going to go talk to the dragon?"

Viola froze, her hand hovering over a purple garland. "What? How?"

"There is no *how*. I am not going to talk to the dragon today." Ambrose nodded to the flowers. "Put those wherever you like. I don't care where they go."

He was still rather miserly about the whole thing—gussying up the shop to celebrate the Spelltide festival. He typically never bothered with temporary decorations. They were difficult to put up, difficult to clean, difficult to take down…

But when Nat had eagerly suggested it over a Rosemond Street dinner one night, Eli's face had lit up, and in the few days of rest he had between his quests, he'd churned out six lengths of bunting, a dozen pennants, and a page of discount ideas for the shop.

And in the end, Ambrose could never say no to that face, no matter how much extra work it gave him.

As Dawn and Viola tossed garlands over his shop, turning his stoic, dark brown shelves into a rainbowed garden, he turned to the next order of festival business: his unsorted potion bottles. As Eli's shrewd discount list suggested, Spelltide didn't merely require decorations. Even though the festival itself was twelve days away, the city was already filling up with tourists eager to fawn over his more frivolous brews. Minor illusions, simple levitation, spark evocation... anything harmlessly flashy to celebrate Spelltide. To celebrate magic itself.

Ambrose held up one of his recently brewed levitation bottles, feeling even more miserly as he checked its viscosity in the evening light. Yes, buying such a trifling potion did indeed celebrate magic. But so would buying one of his ground-breaking, high-end psychic resistance elixirs, the latest recipe for which had inspired not one, but *two* separate research studies on—

"These two banners go over there." Nat burst out of the workroom with two more associates in tow, commanding her tiny decorating army with all the force of a general. "Put this bunting up around the bay window. And this"—she held up an earnest yet misshapen wreath Eli had made—"will go...um...on the back of the door."

"Got it." One of her soldiers, a young half-elf with hexagonal glasses, took the decoration. "I'll hide the wreath."

Ambrose hid a smile. "Thank you, Zuri."

Dawn's wand-making apprentice, Zuri, was nineteen going on thirty-two. Her words were as cropped as her straight black hair, and ever since she had arrived at Rosemond Street two years ago, Ambrose got the distinct sense that she knew she belonged here. The same could not be said for Banneker's artificing apprentice, Luka, who had arrived several months later and without the courage to string together more than a dozen words at a time.

"Happy to help." Luka gave Nat a shy smile, his shaggy brown hair hiding his face as he carefully sifted through the tangle of bunting. "Would you like birds or triangles over the window?"

"Birds, obviously. The migration's the best part of the festival."

Dawn glared over a shelf, silk flowers in hand. "That's slander on the dancing and I won't have it."

Viola snorted as she held the ladder underneath Dawn. "Please. As if a few drunken dances can hold up to the games."

They all spread about the shop, arguing over the best part of the three-day festival. The magical shops, magical demonstrations, magical games. Then the magical picnic to watch the magical auroc migration pass overhead on the final day…

Ambrose rubbed his eyes and arranged his bottles on a tiered table. Twelve days until the *magical* festival started, and he was already eager for it to be over.

As he reached for the last bottle on the counter, another one appeared at his fingertips, milky white and swirling with bits of lavender petals.

"Here you go," Nat said proudly. "All cooled down and ready for you to try."

Ambrose slouched. He was proud of her for taking the initiative to brew the potion, of course—he just hadn't realized that *he* was meant to be the test subject once it was done.

"It looks perfectly brewed. Perhaps I could try it…after Spelltide?" he tried weakly.

"But that's weeks away!" She dropped a journal next to the potion with a heavy thud. Its worn leather cover was speckled with dried potion drops and tiny paintings of dragons. "And you haven't seen Fio in at least that much time. See?"

Ambrose did not, in fact, need to see, but she opened the journal anyway, pushing aside the shop's rose statue to make room. He whisked the statue away from her brazen disorder and hid it up in a cubby. The crystal embedded into its polished leaves and petals had been flashing white all day, signaling messages from the other shops on the street, and he had been trying to ignore them in favor of his Spelltide work. In the cubby, however, the statue only blinked brighter. He huffed and tried to hide it with a bundle of herbs.

"Nat, I appreciate your notes, but I am well aware of when I last saw Fio," he said. "Seeing as it was *my* dream—"

But Nat's notes had already attracted an audience. Luka approached quietly, flipping through the pages with a reverent touch. "When was the last time you saw him?"

"Two weeks ago." Nat pointed to her chart. Luka gave a nervous hum.

"And you're…absolutely sure the dragon is starting to wake?"

Standing next to each other, the two apprentices could hardly look more different. Luka's shaggy hair and shrinking posture hid his features as much as possible, while Nat stood straight, decked in clinking orange jewelry against her black clothing. Over the last two years, she hadn't quite grown out of her dark wardrobe—but she had certainly grown. She was no longer a malnourished sixteen-year-old, but a tall, strong, unfortunately self-assured eighteen-year-old, who was confident that she could handle volatile level-six potions when she had only just begun mastering her level fours.

Ambrose blamed Eli for that development. Her lack of caution certainly didn't come from him.

"Mr. Ambrose wrote all his observations down here," Nat continued boldly. "The changes in breathing pattern, scale warmth, his eye movement. Mr. Eli's confirmed all of it, too. Fio's waking up from his hibernation. Which is *why*"—she glanced up at Ambrose—"he should try my sleeping potion and see if he can talk to Fio again."

Zuri soon wandered over, and as Nat showed her the newest pages, the notes within quickly shifted from her chicken-scratch to Ambrose's orderly script. Nat had both named the dragon and started the journal, yes—but both of them had contributed over the past two years, slowly piecing together Ambrose's dreams.

Or, rather, the dragon that had started to appear in them upon Ambrose's rescue from Aphos.

The dreams had been fuzzy at first. Voices calling from a black ether, or the smell of wet rock and moss. At first, Ambrose had thought they were merely unpleasant flashbacks to his kidnapping by the Aphosian crime ring. Of being stuck in their tunneled hideout underneath the city, brewing illegal potions and conspiring with Rosemond Street on his own escape.

But with every dream—two dozen or so, in total—the voices and smells had evolved into shapes, then sights, then places. He kept standing in the same cave every time. He kept seeing the same sleeping dragon he had once found trapped in Aphos, just like he was...

And as soon as the dragon acknowledged his presence and *spoke*, of all things, his theory had shifted. He wasn't simply dreaming about Aphos; it wasn't that simple. His dreams were transporting part of him back there. Back to the dragon—shackled, unmoving, being tapped for its rare, magical plasma...and still hibernating.

For now.

"If the dragon's truly waking, we should keep an eye on it as much as we can." Luka looked up from the journal. "Shouldn't we?"

Zuri shrugged and flipped to another page. "And why say no to a nap? It's a win-win."

Nat pushed her catnap potion closer to Ambrose in victory—that was two votes in her corner. Ambrose pressed his lips into a line and turned to his own allies.

"Dawn, if you kept seeing an irritated dragon in your sleep, would you be seeking it out via sleeping potion?"

"What? No." Dawn shuddered and pointed to the journal with a circling finger. "Whatever you got going on there is creepy. No thanks."

Viola handed Dawn the last garland, her bat-shaped earrings flying all around her folded ears. "I mean, I like spooky stuff, but should we really be trying to talk *more* to the dragon in the cave? What if you get stuck there or something? We can't exactly rescue your astral form, you know."

"Precisely." Ambrose squared his shoulders and pushed the bottle back toward Nat. "The elders have spoken."

Dawn glared at him. "Hey!"

"Now," Ambrose continued, "if you three are all done with the bunting, I could use your help with these—"

Eli's ecstatic voice floated in through the front door. "Decorations!"

An invisible weight immediately lifted off Ambrose's chest. Eli Valenz stood in the doorway, spreading his arms wide at the shop's transformation.

"You put it all up already!" He dropped his pack onto the floor. "You didn't have to do that. I said I was gonna do it!"

Judging by his wet black hair and the scent of soap rolling off him, Eli had cleaned up after his sparring session at the practice pits—but he hadn't fully changed out of his adventurer's gear. Bracers still protected his forearms, his potion belt hung low across his hips. And his enchanted shield pendant—one that Ambrose requested he wear, even when sparring—still winked between his collarbones.

Ambrose took an indulgent moment to admire him. It didn't matter that Eli only sported a plain tunic and pants under his accessories. Against the backdrop of the sparkling, sunlit windows and dramatic clouds of dust kicked up in the street, he looked like a prince.

His indulgent moment went on for another second, then two... then he realized he was well and truly staring, and quickly cleared his throat. "I thought you might like to see it all put together," he said. "We put up everything you made."

"Even the wreath?"

"Even the wreath."

Eli took his time surveying the whole shop, from the bird bunting on the window to the garlands hanging from the shelves, until Ambrose found himself shifting impatiently at the counter. Eli had no right to look as handsome as he did after sparring, yet withhold his greeting kiss for so long. No, he had to smile proudly at the shop first. Compliment everyone's work with gusto. Wander around with his hands at that low-slung belt of his... Gods, it was terribly inconvenient how much Ambrose loved this man—

Then finally Eli made his way to the counter and gathered Ambrose up in a warm, excited kiss, smelling of soap and sand and metal polish. Ambrose couldn't help it—his face tingled at the touch, and he melted into the firm arms wrapped around his waist.

"You like it?" he murmured.

"I love it." Eli pecked his cheek, then his forehead, clearly unwilling to leave his gratitude at just one kiss. "Thank you."

Ambrose smiled at him, dazed by the kiss, the touch, the smile before him...

And Nat took full advantage of it.

"Hey, Mr. Eli." She held up her catnap potion. "You think it's cool that Mr. Ambrose can talk to a dragon, right?"

Ambrose hurriedly shook himself out of his daze. "No. No, he does not—"

"Of course I do." Eli sauntered over and inspected the bottle, his face shining with pride as if she were his own apprentice. "Did you brew this yourself?"

"It's just a catnap potion." Nat feigned a casual shrug. "You think he should take it, right? So he can try to check on Fio and make sure he's okay?"

All eyes in the shop landed on Eli, who smiled blithely. "Yeah, he should totally take it. It's a great idea."

Half the shop groaned; the other half high-fived.

"The elder has decided!" Nat crowed. Eli lowered the bottle.

"Hold on, who's she calling elder—?"

"It's settled. Ambrose will take the potion before dinner." She set the vial on the counter with a definitive clink. But Ambrose couldn't come up with the words to concede her victory—he was too busy rooting around in his pocket for his watch.

"Dinner? Is it that late already?" He always did this when summer rolled around. The lingering sunlight delayed the natural progression of the shadows across the chasm city, tricking him into thinking he had hours left to brew. "I'm sorry, Nat, I've kept you here for far too long—"

He flipped open the watch and groaned. It was, indeed, past dinnertime, and the others scrambled into action accordingly. Zuri and Luka ducked into the workroom to grab their packs, while Dawn and Viola stashed the ladder.

"Viola, you wanna grab something from the sandwich stall before the"—Dawn threw an odd glance in Eli's direction and changed her pitch—"before, um...it gets dark?"

"Sure!" Viola quickly waved to Ambrose. "Bye, Ames! Tell us how the catnap potion goes!"

Ambrose and Eli waved them off—and just as fast as they had arrived, his shop intruders were gone, headed to the closest stall.

Only Luka loitered by the door, letting wafts of summer warmth roll into the cool shop.

"Nat," he called, his quiet voice nearly drowned out by the street traffic outside. "Did you still want to study tonight?"

"For the explosives management seminar?" Nat struggled to close her own backpack against all the study materials inside. "Sure. I can bring the book over to your room after dinner."

Luka's ears went pink. "My—my room—?"

Nat shrugged. "Yeah. I'll bring Zuri, too."

"Oh." He ran a hand through his hair. "Right. Of course. See you later." He nodded to Ambrose and rushed out. "Bye, Mr. Ambrose! Bye, Mr. Eli!"

Ambrose watched the boy hurry back to Banneker's atelier across the street. Luka was what Eli would call a good kid, though socially, he was about as shy as Ambrose had been at his age. A good thing he had Nat and Zuri, then—just as he himself had Dawn when growing up.

Though Dawn wasn't half so bossy as Nat was at times.

"Here's the reversal potion in case anything goes wrong with your nap." She pulled a golden vial off the shelf behind the counter and placed it next to the catnap bottle. "I only brewed the catnap potion to last thirty minutes or so—tell me if it's too short—but it should make your sleep deep enough to reach Fio. And keep the journal by the nightstand so you don't forget to write anything down."

Ambrose bit back a smile and gave a small bow. "Yes, Miss Nat."

"And you're sure you don't need me here to take notes when you wake up?"

"No, I'll be all right." Ambrose gestured to the street. "Please, go have dinner. Is the apprentices' house—?"

Nat nodded, her bag already over her shoulder. "It's chicken and dumpling night!"

Eli looked up. "Can I be an apprentice for the day?"

Ambrose gave him a sideways glance. "And here I thought you enjoyed my cold leftover noodles."

"I..." Eli patted his shoulder. "I love them because you made them."

"Okay, gross." Nat rolled her eyes and pushed past them both. "I'll see you tomorrow! Don't forget to take notes!"

She scuttled off toward the apprentices' boarding house, kicking up dust as she went. How she and Viola stuck so firmly to their black wardrobe while working on the ground floor of a chasm, he'd never understand.

"It seems I'm being sent to bed." Ambrose twined his fingers with Eli's and leaned against his arm. "Will you stay with me?"

He dearly hoped so. That shield pendant, framed just so by Eli's open collar, was so very distracting...

But Eli gave a regretful smile and kissed his knuckles.

"I have to go talk to Sherry about something," he said. "You go on. I'll be there with a hot cup of tea ready for you when you wake up."

Ambrose lifted Eli's hand and returned the gentle kiss. The man truly did know how to seduce him.

"All right," he murmured. "I'll see you soon."

And as Eli headed out once more, Ambrose picked up the catnap potion, sighed at it, and went upstairs to visit a dragon.

Ambrose took his time getting ready for his nap. Not that he doubted Nat's brew, nor their joint theory about deeper sleep leading him to Fio. It was simply that once he was linked to Fio...there was nothing he could do. He could observe, yes. Take notes upon waking up. But his astral form couldn't chase away the dragon's captors nor release him from his prison. All he could do was keep Fio company—and Fio didn't even want that.

But there was no avoiding all that now. He took a swig of the potion, grimaced at its overly floral flavor, then curled up into the pillow.

Fortunately for Nat and unfortunately for him, their hypothesis proved to be accurate—at least, in this particular experiment. He could almost feel the strange pull of the dream as he was falling asleep. An odd ache in his finger, where he had once cut a tiny piece of his astral form against Fio's scales. Then the darkness fell deeper and deeper...

And slowly, the portal back into the dragon's cave began to open for him.

The smell always came first. Rock, leather, moss, and ink, seeping through the darkness. The scent made him tense on instinct. His mind flew back to the dungeons in Aphos, to shadows and tunnels and the fear of being trapped. Every time, he had to remind himself that he wasn't truly entering Aphos again. No one could see or hear his astral form there.

No one except for Fio.

"Hello," he called awkwardly as the dragon's lair slowly took shape around him. The gray smudges of the walls, the large, dark silhouette looming above him. "I'm here. Please don't mind me."

It was his customary greeting to Fio, whenever he found himself in this sort of dream. Sometimes, the dragon was too deep in his hibernation to respond. On those nights, Ambrose merely observed him from afar—or peeked at the artificers' tools and notes while the artificers themselves milled about in ignorance of his presence.

But other times, the dragon was restless. Partially trapped in sleep, partially awake. Awake enough, at least, to send a few sparse words to Ambrose while still appearing dormant to the Aphosians.

Hello? was his most frequent word—always confused, wary, and sharp. An angry *Go away* closely followed, trailed sometimes by a hesitant *How*? Ambrose always tried to respond, but Fio's ability to reply waned after only a few words. A conversationalist, he was not.

And yet a large dragon he most certainly *was*, so Ambrose thought it safest to be polite in his greetings.

"I'm not here to hurt you," he continued as the shapes around him grew in detail. "I'm only here to...well, to see if this worked, I suppose."

And it had: he was napping, and Fio was here. Nat would be thrilled, of course. She'd probably make him take naps every day this week as a result. Which, naturally would cut into his precious Spelltide preparations, which would cut into his normal stocking, and brewing, and advertising, and—

The rest of his surroundings finally came into focus, and Ambrose staggered back in shock.

He was not alone in the cave—not even close. The place was filled to the brim with Aphosians, all of them wearing the same bronze artificer's pin that separated them from the riffraff in the underground city. This made no sense to Ambrose—in all of his past dreams, Fio's lair had been nearly empty. It was always just Fio, one or two scientists, and the assortment of tubes they had stuck into him, depositing smaller and smaller amounts of plasma into oversized glass jars. Every now and then, another artificer would be there —checking the plasma levels, making notes on a chart, testing and replacing the moss that covered the walls. All while Fio curled in a massive huddle in the center of the room.

But the artificers were certainly here now. Every single one in Aphos' employ, it seemed—and none of them sounded particularly happy to be there.

"Look, there's nothing more we can do!" One artificer, a gnome who seemed to visit Fio the most, was shouting to the others, trying to be heard over their dismayed murmurs. "F.10 can't give us any more plasma!"

Ambrose stiffened. *F.10*, the artificers' clinical term for the dragon —and where Nat had pulled his name from. Part of him wanted to correct the gnome, but no one in the room would have heard him, even if they weren't all arguing over each other.

An elf with a clipboard raised her hand indignantly. "But we don't have a working alternative for Madam Mila yet."

"That's right!" another woman said. "The potions team hasn't worked out that blasted potioneer's true illusion recipe yet."

Several other artificers around her grumbled; Ambrose allowed himself a moment of immense pride. Two years had passed, and they still hadn't been able to replicate his achievement.

It was a pity that his illegal potion for Aphos couldn't be mentioned in any of his scientific papers.

"Lucky for you, the *potions* team is about to get a lot bigger," the gnome hissed. "We're transferring. All hands on deck to replicate the potion. Our work with the dragon is done."

The crowd's protests grew louder, but Ambrose could hardly pay attention. They were finally done trapping the poor dragon. His dreams might be coming to a close. If they freed Fio…

He crept closer to the creature, making note of his rapid breathing and the radiant emerald color of his scales. With the exception of the one sharp scale that had absorbed a hint of Ambrose's astral essence, all of Fio's scales burned brighter every day; a sure sign he was leaving hibernation, according to Eli. It was perfect timing, if the artificers were planning to let him go—

"But is sealing him up really the answer?" the elf with the clipboard demanded. Ambrose's gaze whipped over to her.

"We can't just let him fly out, now can we?" the artificer scoffed. "Either he turns and blasts us in revenge, or he flies off and blasts the city in anger. You think Madam Mila wants Mayor Rune on our tail because we went soft and let a damn dragon loose on the Scar?"

Behind the crowd, more Aphosians entered—workers this time, pushing carts of boulders and other chunks of stone.

"No!" Ambrose straightened, his astral words useless in the empty air. "You can't!"

A few of the other artificers echoed him, some of them going as far as to push the workers away—but they were quickly overruled and shoved out into the tunnel.

And as the first boulder rolled into place, one word lashed into Ambrose's mind.

Help!

Ambrose turned to the dragon. "Was that you—?"

You must help me!

The fearful demand was high in pitch, almost childlike—not at all what Ambrose expected from a creature the size of Rosemond Street.

"I..." He looked between the dragon and the tunnel, fists clenched, anger and helplessness lashing his feet to the floor. He had felt this sort of weight before—it had once haunted him in the dungeons not far from this very cave. But he'd had a way out then, through his friends. He had no way out for Fio here. His astral form couldn't hold back the rocks nor stop the workers. "How do I—?"

A second boulder thudded into place. He could no longer hear the artificers' protests in the tunnel, and the workers with their carts paid no attention to Fio. They didn't see the iridescence of his shifting scales, nor the desperate twitching of his tail...nor the opening of his eye. One large, golden eye, staring straight at Ambrose in sharp fear and determination.

Find my family! he said. *Help me fly away from here!*

The rocks piled higher and higher, forming a silent tomb for the dragon who had made them wealthy. The dragon who was trapped in Aphos, like Ambrose had once been. Like Nat had been for most of her life. Giving Aphos everything, and receiving nothing but death in return. It wasn't fair, it wasn't *right*—

He could hardly breathe for his own rage, and it was without all logic or sense or thought when he looked Fio in the eye and said:

"All right. I'll get you out of here."

TIP 2:

GATHER THE PARTY

Eli

As Eli jogged back into the summer heat and veered into Grim's jewelry shop, he pushed aside a twinge of guilt about lying to Ambrose. It wasn't a total falsehood—he genuinely did need to talk to Sherry about something.

But that *something* was also important enough to require the rest of Rosemond Street.

His audience had already gathered in Grim's dark, cozy living room, lounging in wait for him. Banneker hunched over the worn kitchen table in the corner, his bright red hair a beacon as he tinkered with a partially disassembled rose statue. While the artificer made a mess on the table, Grim puttered about their small kitchen, made all the smaller by their large orcish frame. They seemed determined to get out of the way of the ladies, who had snuck into Grim's just before Eli and now held court on the squashy, oversized couch, discussing the details of Dawn and Rory's impending wedding.

"I've narrowed the list down to seven possible venues," Dawn explained to Viola and the gray-haired armorer, Sherry. The trio presided over a thick pound cake and a thicker wedding planner, its pages tabbed in brilliant pinks and purples. "Rory and I are going to narrow down our options this week."

Viola flipped through the planner and hummed over a collage of newspaper clippings. From Eli's spot by the door, he could barely make out illustrations of wedding arches and vaulted ceilings. "And how many guests do you need to fit, exactly?"

"Over a hundred," Dawn said proudly. Sherry gasped, startling the little companion on her lap: an automaton made of a beer mug, a broom head, and pointy little utensil arms.

"Sorry, Tom," she cooed to the automaton, then turned back to Dawn. "So many guests! A far cry from mine, back in the day. Please tell me your family's helping with the planning."

"Oh, of course." Dawn waved a hand, her bright pink engagement ring flashing. "Mom's handling the dinner, my brothers are taking on the welcome events, and Auntie Max and Rory's dad are coordinating the ceremony."

Viola divvied up the pound cake on the coffee table. "And you've worked out all the traditions?"

Dawn turned to another tabbed section of her planner. This part alone was half as thick as the slice of cake she now balanced on her free hand.

"Four traditions for the ceremony, four for the dinner. Evenly divided between families." She brightened. "First, my mom adds a lily to my bouquet for luck, then—"

Eli gently cleared his throat. As he'd hoped, Tom leapt out of Sherry's arms and wheeled over to his feet, gracefully cutting Dawn's list short. Not that he didn't love wedding traditions, of course, but Scarrish weddings almost weighed them above the vows themselves. If he let Dawn keep going through her list, they'd be here until midnight.

And his own announcement was already making him jittery.

"Oh! Sorry, Eli. Just excited." Dawn quickly closed her planner and patted it with a smile. "You ready for us?"

Now that the wedding court had adjourned—for now, at least— the full group gathered together before the hearth. Grim finally emerged from the kitchen and tapped Banneker's shoulder. The artificer waved a wand over his mess, reassembling the bits of wood and crystal back into the floral shape of the statue, then flopped over an armchair. For Eli's part, he wanted to keep holding on to Tom for encouragement—but as soon as she spotted all the open laps on the couch and chairs, she whirled her little fork arms in a silent command to be put down.

"Hey, hey, all right!" He set her down and straightened his tunic as she wheeled back over to the couch. Yes, he had practiced this several times—but some emotional support from his own automaton would have been nice.

"Whatcha got for us?" Banneker asked. Eli straightened and took a deep breath.

"Thanks for agreeing to meet up. I have to say this quickly before Ambrose wakes up from his nap."

Sherry immediately leaned forward, her frown deepening the wrinkles on her forehead. "Is he all right?"

"Oh, he's fine."

"And you?" Grim pressed. "Are you all right?"

Eli held up his hands. "I'm fine!"

"And Nat, is she—?"

"We're all fine! Everyone's fine!"

Gods, he really did need to do this quickly. He accelerated through his words, his nerves leaking into them in a way they never had during his rehearsals.

"It's Kolkean tradition that if you're partners with someone, you have to go to the family first. To sort of—declare your intentions. And you're all basically his family, so..." He set his sweaty palms behind his back and ignored his heart pounding against his ribs. "I'd like to marry—"

The room erupted into ecstatic chaos.

Sherry burst into tears. Tom spun in circles around the coffee table. Dawn gave an ear-splitting shriek and launched off the couch, sweeping him into a crushing hug. Banneker was beside her seconds later, somehow lifting both of them off the ground with his twig-like arms. Through the embrace, Eli could barely see Viola flying into a tizzy over the untouched slices of pound cake.

"This isn't nearly enough!" she declared. "We need more. Something *big*, something celebratory, something..." Her face lit up. "Hold on, I've got just the thing back at The Midnight Snack!"

She rushed toward the door, stopped to squeal and shake Eli's arm, then continued on to her bakery in pursuit of a bigger dessert, her prosthetic leg clinking down the stairs to punctuate her excitement. Grim was apparently of the same mind—they duly handed Sherry a handkerchief and shuffled right back into the kitchen. "Well, can't have all this hubbub without some bubbly," they said, their voice gravelly as they withheld tears. "Think I've got a bottle here somewhere..."

Eli melted in both relief and utter confusion.

"Wait!" He squirmed his way out of Dawn and Banneker's grasp. "Hold on, hold on. You're not supposed to make it that easy! Come on, you're supposed to ask me questions. You know, demand to know my plans for the future, how I intend to support my spouse—"

Grim turned and folded their arms. "All right. What are your plans for the future, Mr. Valenz?"

Eli readied himself and began to count off on his fingers. "Marry Ambrose Beake—"

"Excellent. And does Ambrose Beake need financial support?"

"Not exactly—"

"Good. Sounds like we're all set, then."

As Grim retrieved a bottle and poured overflowing glasses of sparkling wine, Dawn similarly overflowed with excitement.

"I can share my wedding planning templates with you!" She did a bouncy little dance next to him. "You'll love them, it'll make the whole thing *so* easy. I've got charts, notes on this year's trends, my list of venues if you want to use that as a starting point—"

Eli's relief quickly muted, and he took her hands. He had been burning for weeks to declare his intentions to them—but he hadn't exactly been looking forward to saying this particular bit.

"Ames...doesn't want a wedding."

Dawn froze mid-dance. "He *what*?"

Behind her, Sherry was still dabbing at her eyes with Grim's handkerchief. "No wedding? Are you sure?"

Even Tom had stopped spinning in confusion—but Grim didn't lose a beat as they brought over the tray of glasses.

"Of course the kid doesn't want a wedding." They shrugged. "All eyes on Beake at an event with, what, a hundred people? Unless your venue is the Potion Con debate stage, you'll never get him up there."

"Aw, but it's only one day." Banneker helped them pass out the wine. "We can make it a quick shindig."

"Oh, surely we can do something small." Sherry clutched her soggy handkerchief to her chest. "Rent out The Jumping Ogre for the night, at least? You both must be celebrated, after all."

A twinge went through Eli as a few of the bubbles leapt out of the over-full glass and fizzed against his fingers. *He* didn't need to be told twice. He loved any excuse to celebrate anything—particularly Ambrose Beake.

But Kolkean weddings were much like Scarrish ones. They were designed to be overwhelming. A massive descent of family members and friends into a single space, sometimes for multiple days. There would be games, gaudy decor, nearly double the number of family rituals Dawn had mentioned...

He loved it—but when he had described it to Ambrose over dinner once, the poor man looked like he was going to throw up his meal. And when he'd asked in an unnervingly small voice if they could avoid that sort of thing, Eli hadn't thought twice about agreeing. No wedding was better than a miserable wedding.

"Don't worry." He squeezed Sherry's hand. "We'll find a way to celebrate in a small way once we're ready. I still gotta propose to him before we think about all that."

The room's excitement churned back up at the mention of the proposal, and Dawn firmly guided Eli to the couch to further interrogate him on the subject.

"So, how will you propose?" she asked eagerly. "Fireworks over a river?"

Eli gave her a look. "Dawn, I'm not gonna copy Rory."

"It worked, didn't it?"

He shook his head and sipped on the wine; the bubbles on his tongue were just as giddy as Dawn's expression.

"I've got a plan," he said as everyone else gathered back around. "I'll do it on Spelltide. The third day, while the auroc migration's going over the city. I've already got the ring, and I'm gonna tie it to a potion—"

Over on the kitchen table, Grim's rose statue flashed white. Banneker squinted at it.

"Sorry, Grim. I thought I had fixed that. I'll take another look at it later." He waved off the glow. "You were talking about a potion?"

"Yeah, for Ames. See, there's this sort of memory potion I want to make—"

The statue flashed again. Banneker groaned and stood. "Hold on."

He loped over and checked its base with a frown. After finding no issues there, he unrolled the scroll—and his eyebrows shot up. "Uh-oh. The dude of brew's ears must be burning." He looked over his shoulder. "Ames is calling for a street meeting."

Eli stiffened. "When?"

"Now."

Eli crossed the room in two strides and reached for the scroll.

Ambrose: Emergency street meeting. Rory already contacted. Convene at Grim's.

Eli cursed. He knew he should have stayed with Ambrose and waited for another time to—

"Act normal!" Sherry flapped her hands. "Everyone, act normal!"

Dawn spun around, Tom in one hand and her glass in the other. "What do we do with the wine?"

"Chug it!" Banneker shouted and immediately downed his drink. As he grimaced at the bubbles, Viola burst through the door, a giant cookie cake in her arms.

"Look what I've got—!"

"No!" Sherry shooed her back down the steps. "Go back, go back! He's coming!"

Viola yelped and rushed off. Grim swept up the empty glasses. Dawn yanked Eli back onto the couch and smoothed out her skirt.

"Quick, let's talk about something else." She wiggled both hands, as if willing the words to manifest themselves. "Let's talk about, um—"

Eli glanced around, his mind struggling to get away from the proposal. Potions, rings—

"Spelltide?" he offered.

Dawn straightened. "Yes, Spelltide!" As footsteps echoed up the stairs toward them, she raised her voice. "Boy, how I'm looking forward to the festival about magic. Magic is the best—oh, hi, Ambrose!"

Ambrose stopped in the doorway, his brow furrowed in confusion. "Hello," he said slowly. "You're all...already here?"

"Yes! We were just, ah..." Sherry tapped her fingers on her glass, then realized it was still in her hand and quickly hid it behind her back. "Talking about the street decorations for the festival! Weren't we, Banneker?"

"Absolutely." He stretched across his half of the couch. "You know, lights and stuff."

Grim cleared their throat. "Probably some bunting."

"Flowers are great." Dawn beamed. "Love a good flower."

Ambrose stared at them. "I...see." He took the spot Eli had been standing in earlier—the spot in front of the hearth, where Grim typically held court for street meetings. "I apologize for intruding on such short notice, but I—"

"Ames?" Rory's voice echoed up the steps, her words nearly muffled by a cascade of younger voices. A moment later, the investigative journalist herself appeared, with an empty-handed Viola and Rosemond Street's three apprentices gathered like ducklings behind her. Even amidst the gaggle, Rory was easy to spot, with her purple undercut, tailored jacket, and signature saunter.

"Got here as fast as I could." She squirmed her way onto the couch next to Dawn, kissed her fiancée's cheek with a cheesy smack, and jerked a thumb at the apprentices. "Ran into these rascals on the way from the press office. I tried to tell them they didn't need to come, but they wouldn't listen."

"Oh. Well"—Ambrose fidgeted with his sleeve—"I don't want to burden them unnecessarily."

"It's a street meeting, right?" Nat sat cross-legged on the faded rug and pulled Tom onto her lap. "We're part of the street."

Viola, Zuri, and Luka filled in the remaining spots around the makeshift circle of merchants. When Sherry offered the newcomers pound cake, Rory eagerly took a slice.

"Honestly, I gotta thank you for calling me over," she said, stabbing at the cake with her fork. "I'll take any sort of break from covering the city's Spelltide preparations."

Eli leaned back, trying to look like his heart wasn't still pounding from his earlier announcement. "Lotta crime over by the food stalls? Noodle embezzlement?"

"I *wish*." Rory rolled her eyes. "Normally, I'm happy to lend a hand off my usual beat. But if they ask me to interview one more traveling bard, I'm gonna take their noodles and embezzle 'em up their..." She held up a hand. "Sorry, sorry. Ames, you said this was an emergency."

Zuri jotted something down in her journal.

"No apologies needed," she said dryly. "Your off-topic discussion just earned me a square."

Ambrose sighed; Eli grinned. He had almost forgotten about Street Meeting Squares.

It was something he wished *he* had come up with back when he was regularly attending the meetings as a rival potioneer to Ambrose. He glanced over at Zuri's game board—a simple grid scribbled in her journal—to see what today's winning phrases were. He spotted *Sherry Serves Tea, Dawn Wears Pink, Banneker Tries to Get Out of Cistern Inspection...*

Desserts, naturally, filled the free space in the middle.

"Well?" Grim said, unfazed by the game. "What is it, Beake?"

Luka crossed off a square on his own paper. Ambrose ignored that and shuffled in place for a moment, as nervous and rigid as Eli had been minutes ago. Eli's own nerves spiked—he hoped Ambrose hadn't suddenly decided to propose himself. He was so excited about his potion idea for Spelltide.

Ambrose finally cleared his throat. "I spoke with Fio tonight and I...I may have promised him that I'd help him escape Aphos."

Nat straightened. "It worked! My potion *worked*!"

Ambrose gave her a weak smile, but no one else acknowledged her victory.

"I'm sorry. You promised to free a trapped dragon into the *city*?" Viola squeaked.

"Not into the city!" Ambrose retorted, his cheeks going pink. "Ideally, into the, ah...sky..."

"Oh, right, the sky." Zuri stared at him. "The sky *over* the city. That sky."

Even Eli had to agree with the others, his own words of reason tasting sour. "Ames," he said gently, "you can't promise that the dragon won't set the whole place on fire in revenge for being trapped for so long—"

Ambrose held up a finger. "I believe he spits acid, actually."

"—and even if you could, he's stuck down in Aphos." Eli ran a hand through his hair. "We could barely get *you* out of Aphos."

The air in the room drew taut at the memory—of Ambrose's kidnapping, his descent into the underground crime ring, the weeks of effort it took to snatch him from Madam Mila's iron grip—but even as Ambrose paled, he didn't waver.

"I wouldn't have made the promise if it weren't of utmost importance," he said. "As we speak, Aphos is sealing up the tunnel that leads to his cave. Either we get him out of there, or he never gets out at all. Angry as he might be, he deserves to be free of them, just as I am, and I've already left him down there once." He swallowed. "I cannot in good conscience do it again."

The room went quiet again, and Eli slouched. He was right; of course he was right. But such a task could go wrong in hundreds of ways, only half of which he could predict as an adventurer. Aphos' security, for one. Then there were the small matters of the dragon's anger, the dragon's teeth, the dragon's talons...

Nat broke the reluctant silence.

"We're getting him out, then," she declared loudly. "How do we start?"

Her determined gaze landed on each of them, a silent dare to contradict her. And Eli couldn't bring himself to do it.

"If Ames can keep talking directly to Fio," he ventured, "maybe he can force out a promise from him not to retaliate on the city. Maybe."

Banneker drummed his fingers on his knees. "Well, if he can do that, we might not need to make a whole thing of the rescue," he said. "Fio's cave isn't that far from us, right? We could just walk over and blast the top off. Let him fly out on his own."

Zuri crossed off another square on her grid. "Questionable idea from Banneker. Got two squares in a row, now. Keep 'em coming."

Banneker pouted, but Grim didn't argue against her judgment.

"Aphos won't take kindly to us blowing up part of their lair," they said. "We're already lucky they haven't tried to retaliate after Beake's rescue. I'm not giving them another excuse to get angry at us." They shifted. "Best that we keep this whole business as quiet as we can."

"What if we snuck in again?" Dawn asked. "We've done it before."

Eli turned to Rory—their resident expert on Aphos and the estranged daughter of Madam Mila herself—but the journalist only grimaced at the idea. "I wouldn't. Their guard rounds have gotten harder to predict in recent months. I swear they set the schedule using interpretive dance these days."

"Then we use the hole already in the cave chamber," Viola offered. "We could rappel down it to help Fio out. I mean, *I'd* rather not"—she gestured to her prosthetic leg—"but I can make a mean floating pastry to help out. Or a nice sedation cupcake for the dragon, if he doesn't agree to be on his best behavior."

The others began to murmur at that, offering similarly enchanted wands, potions, jewels, and hand cannons—but off to the side, Luka raised his hand.

"I'm sorry, but are we..." He trailed off, waiting for the room to quiet. When both Banneker and Nat nodded to him in encouragement, he gathered himself once more. "Mr. Ambrose, are we quite sure Fio can handle magic like that?"

Rory frowned. "What do you mean?"

But Eli understood instantly.

"Some creatures react differently to magic," he said. "Red-winged gulls, for example, just absorb it like nothing happened—you can't so much as hex them. Some rock phoenixes have learned to reflect spells back in a fight. And others..."

He considered telling them all about an orange-fanned lizard exploding at a simple light spell, then decided against it.

"Others can be, um, allergic," he finished. "Luka's right. We should check how Fio might handle enchantments."

Ambrose nodded. "It's a fair point. But I'm afraid I'm not an expert on dragon allergies—"

"Oh, we've got people for that." Sherry waved a hand. "Just go see Marlin!"

Nat twisted to look at her. "Marlin?"

"A dragon expert from the Folded Wings Foundation out west. A dear, dear friend. I've known him for ages." Sherry brightened at her own idea. "He's set up a booth in the market for Spelltide, gathering donations to build another reservation. If anyone's going to know the magic tolerance of a dragon like Fio, it'll be him."

But Ambrose wasn't convinced. "Sherry, I can't simply walk up to him and inform him about the dragon sleeping underneath the city," he said. "If word like that gets out—"

Rory shrugged. "She never said you have to tell him everything."

Zuri leapt out of her chair. "*Squares!* Rory encouraging mild crimes, that's square three! I got squares!"

Nat groaned. "Come on, lying doesn't count as a crime."

Luka checked his own paper and slouched. "Oh. I completely

forgot to cross off Grim being the voice of reason. Do you think I could come in second?"

Ambrose pinched the bridge of his nose and gave a long sigh. "Sherry, will Marlin be at the market tomorrow?"

"He'll be in town all through the festival."

"Good. I will endeavor to be...creative with the truth." Ambrose steeled himself, then nodded to Nat. "And you'll be coming with me."

TIP 3:

STOCK UP

Nat

NAT WOULD NEVER TELL Ambrose this, but her favorite place in the Scar wasn't his potion shop.

She loved The Griffin's Claw, of course, but in truth, her heart belonged to the markets. The open-air Elwig market in the northern quarter, the orcish grocery market on the second level, the weekend flower market that took over the top ramps... The type didn't matter. She loved them all. Back when she was a servant in Aphos, she had assumed—or rather, forced herself to assume—that the markets aboveground in the chasm city were no different than the markets below. Smelly, probably. Loud, definitely. Full of hagglers and shouting merchants and people who walked too slowly.

And they were all of those things, yes. But no one had told her about all the *colors*.

Down in the underground tunnels of Aphos, color was hard to come by. The darkness muted it, and even in the torchlight, everything took on the same muddy orange hue. But here in the upper markets, colors didn't have to hide. They basked in the summer sunlight, so vibrant they were almost painful for her to look at. The flower stalls exploded in pastels; the fruit vendors peddled rainbows of near-garish hues. More than once, Nat had lost track of time just staring at the lemons, until she'd had to buy several out of sheer embarrassment.

In her opinion, the markets couldn't contain any more color than they already did—but Mayor Rune and his Spelltide preparations were rapidly proving her wrong.

According to Ambrose, the Scarrish festival department dragged out the same decorations every five years when Spelltide rolled around. Floating crystal lights, gem-hued banners, patterned cloth that stretched from one side of the chasm to another... Nat couldn't tell whether they were enchanted or simply well-painted, but all the decorations had a delightful sparkle to them, mimicking the aurocs that would soon pass overhead and molt their icy, shimmering feathers in a cascade of glitter.

And today, Mayor Rune was in the markets himself, ensuring his own glittering decorations were being arranged to his satisfaction.

"No, no." The orcish mayor waved to a harried assistant holding a large, floppy piece of paper. "Let's keep that poster for the square. Put the smaller sign by the ramp instead."

The assistant dutifully pasted up a sign on the chasm wall, advertising Spelltide's coming attractions for the festival. Nat only got a brief glance at the sign as she followed Ambrose into the markets. *Bellz the Bard, The Great Leaping Jugglers, The Scar's Magical Showcase...*

"Dad, Dad!" A young orcish girl ran around the mayor in a circle, her shoes and dress just as purple as the banner hanging above her. "Will you get me a dragon this year?"

Rune sighed. "You said you wanted a llama parade, so I'm getting you a llama parade."

"Can we have the llama parade go underneath the migration, then?"

"The parade will be on the second day, dearest. The aurocs are flying by the day after."

Beatrice stamped her foot. "But then how will the llamas become magical?"

Nat smothered a laugh, envisioning llamas floating up out of the lavender fields upon receiving the aurocs' magical blessing. That line of thinking was how the festival had begun, after all. All the birds were really doing was shedding their protective layer of ice as they flew north, where they'd build it up all over again. But the Scarrish citizens of old, in their ancient wisdom, had interpreted the sparkling display as a gift of magic to the world. A renewal of sorts, enchanting the very earth.

Or in this case...llamas.

"We will make the llamas magical in other ways, I promise." Rune rubbed his forehead, and as Ambrose and his trail of Rosemond Street apprentices passed, he gave Ambrose a weary nod. "Master Beake."

"Good morning." Ambrose nodded back and continued on his way, leading Nat, Zuri, and Luka deeper into the market. Nat trailed behind them, watching Rune in curiosity until he trudged down the ramp with Beatrice, his assistant, and a stack of posters. Madam Mila always had plenty to say about the aboveground mayor—none of it good, of course—but he didn't seem all that bad. Tired, maybe. Very dedicated to signage.

In the mayor's defense, his dedication to the advertisements was already paying off. As soon as his signs went up, market-goers crowded around them, eagerly gossiping about the bards and merchants coming into town. And the market itself had already capitalized on the fervor—several of the stalls Nat passed were already selling flower crowns and little white auroc statuettes.

In all the colorful excitement, it was easy to forget that a dragon lay trapped underneath the city.

"Mr. Ambrose!" Nat caught up with him at a stall peddling all manner of vials, corks, and twine. Between Ambrose's height and his shock of light blue hair, it was easy to find him in the crowd. "If Marlin says Fio can handle magic, can we start brewing some stuff for him tonight?"

Ambrose gave a half smile as he inspected a thick square bottle. "I appreciate the enthusiasm, but we hardly know what to brew for him yet."

"We can figure it out tonight, then." She patted the journal in her backpack. "I've some pages set aside for—"

"Mr. Beake!" The stall vendor approached, their beefy hands raised in greeting. "My favorite customer!"

Nat was fairly certain that *every* customer was this vendor's favorite, but they did seem to save the particularly nice bottles for when Ambrose came around.

"I've got some new vials in stock," they continued. "Tempered with winged ironfish scales. Very durable—could survive a lightning strike! If you'd like to see them...?"

Ambrose generally maintained a passive stance against up-selling —but there was no mistaking the intrigued sparkle in his eye. Nat reached for the shopping list in his basket.

"You look at the bottles. I can handle the rest. If—"

"Nat, you know there's no need for an *if*." Ambrose handed her the list. "We'll discuss the dragon brews later today."

Victory achieved, Nat rushed off with the list and quickly worked her way down the stalls. Ambrose's supply list rarely changed from week to week, and she had rapidly mastered a routine to fill her basket as quickly as possible. Not that dallying in the markets would be punished, like it would have in Aphos. She just wanted to show how efficient she could be.

But her efficiency ground to a halt when she reached the music stall.

Zuri and Luka were there; Zuri slowly wandering off, while Luka remained to leaf through sheet music. Banneker had hired Luka because of his enchanted instruments, and Luka would often ramble to the vendor about what he was making next, or what song he had just learned to play. Normally, Nat loved listening to him ramble— but today, she found him flipping through the wares silently, chewing his lip while the vendor attended to a lutenist nearby.

"Luka?" Nat said. He yelped and jumped into the air.

"Gods—!" He clutched his chest and gave a sheepish laugh. "I'm sorry, I didn't hear you coming."

"You see anything good?" she asked. He turned back to the pile of sheet music with a frown, as if he had forgotten they were there.

"I, ah..." He finally shrugged. "Wasn't really paying attention. I was just thinking..."

"Sorry?" She leaned forward; his words, thoroughly dampened by the noise of the crowd, barely made it to her scarred ear.

"Oh." Luka hurried over to her other side. A smart move—his voice was already so quiet, it was almost impossible to hear him in the markets.

"I was just thinking," he continued, leading them both away from the music and back toward Zuri. "Do you really think Mr. Ambrose can actually get Fio out of Aphos?"

He tried to push his shaggy brown hair off his furrowed brow, only for it to fall back over his face. He had been anxious ever since the impromptu street meeting. Well, technically, he had been anxious ever since he arrived at Rosemond Street, and before then, ever since he was born (his words)—but Nat didn't think it'd help him to bring that up now.

He just needed a little confidence—and she was always happy to lend him some.

"'Course he will." She bumped his shoulder with hers. "He got me out of Aphos, didn't he?"

She had been walking in the sunlight for two years now, thanks to him and the rest of Rosemond Street. Gone were the days of scuttling around underground tunnels as a servant for crime lords. In one fell swoop, Rosemond Street had teleported her and Ambrose away, and even let her get a good punch in on her former boss Cassius first—

Ahead of her, Zuri snorted, cutting into her cherished reverie.

"Sure, he got *you* out," Zuri said. "But you don't breathe acid."

"He doesn't breathe it, he spits it." Nat paused. "Maybe."

Fio didn't seem to align perfectly with any modern dragons in the Scar, nor even those in the surrounding plains, forests, or mountains.

Sherry estimated that he was *quite old*, in her words, and had his origins in a sub-species now extinct. As a result, most of Ambrose's notes on the creature's abilities and characteristics were...educated guesses at best.

And Fio's temperament was another matter entirely.

"Breathing it, spitting it..." Zuri stopped at a crystal and herbs stall and held a chunk of amethyst up to the light, inspecting its edges. "Doesn't matter. If the acid comes out, Eli or someone will have to risk their life to take him down."

Luka swallowed in fear; Nat merely huffed. Zuri was just as skeptical as Luka was anxious about the whole affair—but if Nat had learned anything from her rescue, it was to never, ever underestimate Ambrose.

Or the whole of Rosemond Street, for that matter.

"Mr. Ambrose will *talk* to Fio and make sure he won't attack anyone once he's out," Nat said firmly. "Then we'll take him away and get him somewhere safe. He deserves to be free from them."

She didn't have to clarify who Fio was escaping from. She had told them about Aphos, and Cassius, and overlord Madam Mila before. On nights when studying for seminars had pivoted to cheap wine, stale snacks, and divulged secrets.

"You're right." Luka slowly absorbed a smidgen of her confidence. "Of course, you're right. We can't just leave him down there." He tried to gather himself and smiled at Nat. "We won't."

His smile warmed her more than the summer sun—see, all he needed was a nudge.

"Okay, okay," Zuri relented and held out the amethyst. "Mr. and Ms. World Peace, how much would you pay for this?"

Nat tore herself away from Luka and squinted at the crystal. Market haggling and appraisal was one of the first things their mentors had taught them. Nat didn't need the practice when it came to haggling, but she was still getting the hang of estimating the value of magic ingredients.

"I dunno. Maybe, um..."

Luka barely had to glance at it. "Twenty-three and a half talons."

To their collective benefit, Luka had rapidly memorized the value of every scrap of copper, quartz, and wood—but the mere thought of negotiating a price turned him as pale as an albino bat.

Which is where she came in.

"How many do you need?" she asked him. Luka checked his list.

"Three."

Zuri held up two fingers. Nat pushed her way forward, checked her own list, then leaned against the counter—a tactic she had seen Eli use many times before.

"Good morning." She smiled to the vendor—Jasper, a man she had met a few times before at a sign language class. "How much for these five—"

"Ah." He held up his hand, then switched to sign, speaking as his hands moved. "Have you remembered to practice?"

Nat straightened. Since she was still a beginner in the language—particularly in potioneering speak—she couldn't both lounge casually *and* sign at the same time. She'd have to use Eli's tactic some other time.

"How much for these five?" she signed instead.

"Thirty each."

"Oof." She took Luka's list from him and grimaced at it. "I love the purple..." She tried to correctly emphasize the sign *love*. Flattery rarely failed her here."But I don't think I can pay that. How about eighteen each?"

The vendor hesitated, his hands hanging in the air for a moment. "Giant migration is making these hard to come by."

"Twenty and..." Nat rapped her fingers on the table in thought—then her eyes caught sight of the bundle of dried lavender behind the quartz display. Weirdly, Eli had been snooping around for lavender just that morning. "That dried lavender for ten."

"Done."

Nat grinned, trying to look casual about her double win: a decent deal *and* some lavender for Eli. Not that she knew what an adventurer was going to do with the stuff—maybe try to freshen up that smelly leather armor or something.

The vendor quickly bundled up her purchase, even throwing in a fresh lavender stalk for each of them to celebrate Spelltide. Zuri tucked her stalk behind her dully pointed ear. Luka carefully placed his in his waistcoat pocket. Nat tried to imitate Zuri, but having both fine hair and no glasses to keep the flower in place, the bloom kept falling out.

That was all right—purple didn't go with her outfit, anyway.

"Here." She turned to Luka. "Take mine."

"Oh." Luka blinked. "That's, um—"

She reached forward and tucked her flower next to the first one in his waistcoat pocket, the purple standing out brightly against the dull forest-green fabric. It looked quite nice there—just like the blooming lavender fields above the chasm.

"Thank you." Luka's ears burned red as he smiled at the flower. "Very kind of you."

Nat smiled back. It was only what he and Zuri deserved for being her friends. They couldn't be further from her old Aphosian co-workers. They never once tried to play mean tricks on her, or steal her stuff, or get her in trouble...

Neither of them would last one second in Aphos—but it was nice having real friends for a change.

"Nat!" Ambrose waved to her from further down the street, his basket now filled with glass bottles of all shapes and sizes. "Come along—Marlin's over this way."

The three of them hurried along and caught up with him at the Shimmering Circle—a round plaza dug into the side of the chasm to house merchants who had traveled from afar. To better attract customers, each merchant adorned their stalls and tents in any shiny thing they could muster. Pearls, shells, and paintings from the coast. Polished bone and gems from Hart's Fenn. Ore from Titan's Nails, delicate jewelry from the Driftwood...

Nat fiddled with her necklace, which was already loaded with trinkets and charms she had picked up in the markets. It never felt like enough when she looked at these merchants, and every week, it was a monumental effort not to spend her whole stipend here.

(Zuri was often her impulse control—unless Zuri found something *she* wanted, then they were all in trouble.)

She took in a deep breath, steeled herself against all the shininess, and joined Ambrose at a new booth in the circle. This one hadn't draped itself in finery—merely a painted sign:

The Folded Wings Foundation:
Giving Our Fiery Friends a Fresh Start!

Only one person manned the booth: a round, bald human with a friendly smile and even friendlier dragon stuffed animal affixed to his shoulder. Both leaned over the table in eager conversation with Ambrose and the traveling merchant next door, Jae.

"And how's the mister?" she asked Ambrose. In such balmy weather, the gnome wasn't wearing her signature patchwork cloak, but Nat could see it hanging in the back of her stall, surrounded by a myriad of chests and jars. "Is he back from his quest in Elwig?"

"He returned safe and sound last week." Ambrose straightened with pride. "And he took down the diseased phoenix himself. Saved his party and, I daresay, the entire village nearby."

Jae lifted her waterskin in a toast. "Tell him to come by later. I wanna hear all the juicy details."

All told, the exchange was perfectly cordial. Nat had a hard time believing that Jae had once banned Ambrose from trading with her because of a scuffle with a rival merchant.

(It took Eli telling his side of the story over drinks for her to learn that the other merchant had been, well...Eli.)

"Oh!" Jae sipped from her waterskin. "Did you find that material for those potion robes you were—?"

Ambrose loudly cleared his throat; Jae glanced over at Nat and straightened.

"Right, right. Well, uh—don't mean to keep you from Marlin! Have fun!"

Ambrose gave a strained smile, then turned to the man at the Folded Wings booth. "Marlin, if I may—?"

"Mr. Beake!" Marlin rubbed his hands together. "How's the street? How's Sherry?"

"All's well. No phoenix fights to speak of here." Ambrose nodded to the little tent behind the booth. "If I could ask for a private conversation?"

"Sure, sure!"

Nat nodded to Zuri and Luka, then followed Ambrose and Marlin into the tent. Amidst all the finery of the other merchants, the interior was quite plain—simply a tiny square of blank space butting up again the chasm wall. A few crates of merchandise pretended to fill the corners. Pamphlets, books on dragon rehabilitation, a smattering of other stuffies... But for the most part, it remained empty, smelling faintly of charcoal and straw and humming with the sound of the crowd outside.

"So, how can I help?" Marlin asked, gesturing to the crates like they were chairs.

Ambrose took one glance at them and remained standing. "I have a question about dragon reactivity to magic, and Sherry informed me you are an expert on such topics."

"Oh, of course!" Marlin patted the stuffie on his shoulder. "Peanut Butter and I have spent years studying that very topic. But tell me, what sort of dragon are you asking about?"

Nat wanted to ask what sort of dragon Peanut Butter was, but Ambrose remained disappointingly on topic.

"A Scarrish one," he said vaguely, glancing at Nat. "Acid, most likely. Possibly a distant relative to the snub-nosed dragon."

"I saw it out by the lavender fields," Nat added, as they had planned. "Near where we test out some of Dawn's bigger wands and staffs. We want to make sure the leftover magic aura won't affect it."

"Well, thanks for thinking of our scaly friends." Marlin folded his arms in thought. "But the snub-nose has all sorts of cousins in the area. Do you remember the size, color, wingspan, anything like that?"

Ambrose shifted. "It's...large. Wingspan is—*was*—unclear. And the scales changed color."

Something in Marlin's expression shifted at the mention of color. "And how big was it, exactly?"

That was not a casual question, but Nat had already said she'd seen it—and lying about Fio's size wouldn't get them the information they needed.

"Big, like Mr. Ambrose said," she started, then in a mumble: "Maybe...maybe A-class, according to Eli."

Marlin's demeanor flattened, and he set his hands on his hips like a disappointed father. "Now, I don't know what you two are on about, but I'm very busy here and I don't appreciate tricks—"

"It's not a trick!" Nat blurted out. "We really did see it!"

"Please." Marlin looked at Peanut Butter in a *can you believe her?* gesture. "You're telling me you saw the lost greater acidwing? Just flouncing about in the lavender fields?" He sighed. "If you could please leave, I really am very busy here—"

"What if that's precisely what we're telling you?" Ambrose cut in, his voice startlingly level. "What if there is one such dragon left?"

His gaze bore into Marlin's, as if daring him to call him a liar one more time. Marlin blinked first.

"But—that's not possible—"

"If I'm to explain myself," Ambrose continued, "you must swear to keep this a secret."

"I..." Marlin glanced nervously between him and Nat. "All right. I swear."

Ambrose gestured to the nearest crate. Marlin sat.

"There is a dragon down in Aphos," Ambrose explained quietly, his voice only barely skating above the commotion of the market outside. "One that used to be deep in hibernation. Aphos has been harvesting an ingredient from it. Some sort of plasma."

Marlin's hands immediately balled into fists. "*What*? How—how *dare* they—" He caught Ambrose's expression and relented. "Sorry, sorry. Continue."

Nat stepped in here. "But the dragon's waking up and can no

longer give Aphos any plasma. Yesterday, they abandoned it and started sealing up the tunnel leading to its cave."

At that, Marlin leapt to his feet. "Abandoned it? Gods, the last of its—?" Then his gaze narrowed. "Wait. How do you know all this?"

Nat looked at Ambrose, who pressed his lips into a line.

"I may or may not be...psychically linked to it."

Well, so much for being creative with the truth.

Marlin stared at him. "Oh, come on, this *has* to be a—"

"It's not." Nat quickly grabbed her backpack and pulled out the journal she had made. "Mr. Ambrose can visit the dragon in his dreams sometimes. This is all the information we've put together based on what he's seen." Imitating Ambrose, she drew herself up and handed it to him. "If you could please review it."

Marlin hesitated, then did as she asked, flipping through each page carefully. And the further he read, the more he slouched.

"Oh, dear," he murmured. "The poor thing."

Ambrose ventured one more tidbit. "If this is a greater acidwing, as you said—the dragon mentioned some sort of family to me. Is there...?"

Marlin's voice faded into reverence. "I'm sorry, Mr. Beake. If he really is an acidwing—and gods above, it looks like he could be—he truly is the last of his kind. His flock was chased out of the Scar by other creatures over three hundred years ago, and they mingled with other sub-species after that. Across the plains, all the way up to the Elwig Forest. You can't find any of them here anymore, not even half-blooded. This...Fio...would be the only one left." He closed the pages in brief, silent mourning, then looked back up. "Why were you asking me about his magic sensitivity?"

"It was a genuine question." Ambrose gestured to the journal. "We're trying to free him with magic."

"And you don't want to hurt him," Marlin finished. His thoughtful expression had returned, this time with more urgency. "You're right to ask, but a dragon of his kind should be able to absorb magic handily. Problem is, for a dragon this *big*, your potion will have to be far more potent than what you can safely make."

Nat shrugged. "So...what, we gotta shrink him?"

Marlin gave a small chuckle—but Ambrose furrowed his brow in thought.

"Well..."

Nat gave a nervous laugh. "Mr. Ambrose, I was joking."

"Oh, surely you can't shrink a dragon of that size." Marlin paused. "Can you?"

But Ambrose had started to pace around the tent's tiny footprint.

"I can make it work," he countered almost indignantly. "Shrinking him would make him far easier to carry out of the cave. My ingredient needs would just be...a little *different* than what I typically use. More potent, as you said."

Nat brightened as she took the journal back from Marlin. "Can we get them here in the market? I can help you start on it today—"

It was Ambrose's turn to laugh. "No, no, they cannot be found here. Not at the potency I'm referring to." He gave Marlin a small bow. "Thank you. I won't take up any more of your—"

"Wait!" Marlin held up his hands. Peanut Butter nearly fell off his shoulder; he took a moment to steady it. "The dragon—Fio," he corrected himself. "He'll need a place to stay once you get him out. My foundation can help make space for him, I'm sure of it."

Ambrose blinked. "That's quite generous of you—"

"But I'll need far more data than what you have right now." He nodded to the journal in Nat's hands. "Information to confirm his sub-species and details on his habitat."

That sounded easy to Nat. "Of course!" She looked at Ambrose. "We can just make you more catnap potions and visit Fio more often. He'll need a place to live, right?"

Ambrose hesitated. "I'm afraid Fio doesn't entirely *enjoy* my presence—"

But Marlin was already scribbling out a list for him on the back of a pamphlet.

"Here's all the information I need. You send those data points back to me, and I'll make sure Fio has a safe place to call home once he's aboveground." He handed the pamphlet to Ambrose and nodded quite gravely for someone with a dragon stuffie on his shoulder. "On my honor as a dragonkeeper."

Ambrose looked between Marlin and Nat, then sighed and pocketed the pamphlet.

"Right. Data points," he muttered. "For Fio's sake, I will...retrieve them efficiently."

TIP 4:

GET BREWING

Ambrose

AMBROSE WASN'T PARTICULARLY eager to spend more of his sleeping hours with a dragon, but Nat was far too excited to let the brewing wait even a day. As soon as the shop closed, she took control of the cauldron, bubbling away while the rest of Rosemond Street clogged the rose statue scroll with messages about evening plans.

"Remember, it's three turns clockwise—" he began.

"Then four turns counterclockwise, lower the heat, add the lavender, let it simmer," Nat rattled off without so much as looking at her notes. "I got it. And I'll keep an eye on the light in case anyone comes in."

Ambrose nodded. About a week after her arrival, he had asked Banneker to install a small light above the main cauldron—a simple crystal that would flash whenever someone entered the shop. Not that Nat had much trouble hearing most things over the bubbling cauldrons, of course, but the added support seemed to help her relax.

"I shall let you brew, then." He removed his goggles. "I'll be off smashing that rose statue into pieces."

"Tell the others I say hi!"

Ambrose sighed, wandered over to the counter, and unrolled the scroll at its base, thankfully muting its incessant white flashes.

Banneker: I hear a few of the Spelltide bards are practicing their sets over at The Jumping Ogre. Anyone else in?
Viola: Me! Me me me!
Sherry: Yes, please.
Dawn: Just in time for happy hour!!

As Ambrose rolled up the scroll to hide Dawn's lopsided drawing of a wineglass, the bell above the front door rang, and the artist herself strode in. Today, the elven wandmaker had aligned all of her dozen earrings to match her engagement ring and her floral dress. Given how much she had elevated her fashion in the months following her engagement, Ambrose was almost afraid to ask what she had planned for after the wedding.

"Excuse me, miss." He pretended to stand stiffly at the front counter. "If you're seeking happy hour, The Jumping Ogre is just down the street."

Dawn hopped to sit on the counter, eyes narrowed at the potion robes he still wore. "*You* don't look like you're ready for happy hour."

Nat popped her head out of the workroom; the light must have successfully signaled Dawn's entrance. "Who's—? Oh. Hi, Dawn!"

She waved and ducked back into the workroom, where the sound of bubbling liquid and clinking glass rose.

"As you can see, our to-do list never sleeps." Ambrose turned and began arranging small signs on the tall shelves behind the counter. To his amusement, Eli had scrawled little birds in the corners of the labels when he wasn't looking. "You look lovely today. Did Rory pick out that dress for you?"

Dawn primped her curly mohawk. "She sure did."

For a woman who rarely wore anything other than purple, black, and silver, Rory certainly was attuned to Dawn's vibrant style. Not that Ambrose could blame her—there was a very specific joy in dressing a partner with clothes they sparkled in. Ambrose himself had added several well-tailored waistcoats to Eli's wardrobe, and in his view, they were worth every talon.

"I'm thinking about wearing this to our cupcake tasting at The Gingersnap Cafe tomorrow," Dawn continued, toying with a fold of her dress. "You and Eli wanna come?"

Ambrose smiled. "I've seen your planning journal. Do you even have room for two more opinions?"

"Of course I do! *Please*, will you come?" Dawn begged. "Deciding is going to be so hard! I know I want strawberry, which will go with Rory's lemon, but my mom really wants a chai cupcake, and my dad refuses to eat any dessert that isn't chocolate..."

She rattled off several other equally strong opinions on cupcake flavors, all from various family members. Ambrose stared at the little bird doodles on the sign in his hand. He didn't need to be at the tasting. What was his opinion, compared to family's?

But this was Dawn, and he was no match for her clasped hands and wide eyes. He placed the sign, turned around, and forced out a cordial smile.

"What sort of friends would we be to let you drown in cupcake flavors by yourself?" he said. "Just send me the time, and Eli and I will be there."

Dawn squealed and clapped. "Yes! Oh, it'll be *so* much fun! I'm going to go tell Rory. Keep an eye on the scroll, I'll send you the details before I head to the Ogre!"

The doorbell tinkled once more, and a quiet queasiness settled in Ambrose's stomach. But before he could fight it off, he turned—and found Nat sitting on a stool by the counter.

"Gah!" He jumped and held the edge of the counter for support. Her ability to suddenly just *appear* was one Aphosian habit he could never get used to. "Gods preserve me. Are you done with the potion already?"

"All done." She held up a vial in one hand and flipped through a recent potioneering magazine with the other. To Ambrose's dismay, his academic rival Xavion Demachel was on the front cover again. An illustration of their toothy elven smile and gold-dusted cheeks sparkled above the headline: *Demachel in the Driftwood! Traveling Potion Showcase!*

Ambrose made a mental note to unsubscribe from the magazine at the next opportunity.

"Thank you for brewing so quickly." He reached for the potion—but she pulled it away, eyes narrowed.

"Why don't you like wedding stuff?"

Ambrose stiffened. How did she know? He had never told Nat he didn't want a wedding; he had only ever confided in Eli. "What?"

"Your face." She waved a finger in a circle. "Gets like that every time Dawn talks about her wedding."

Oh.

His queasiness briefly swelled into something more—dread, shame, guilt—but he pushed it down.

"I'm allergic to wedding bouquets," he said quickly and grabbed the sleeping potion before she could take it back. "Thank you for this. I'll report back to you in the morning."

"Ames, it'll be fine."

"The dragon has told me to *go away* at least five times." Ambrose pointed to the journal. "Literally. I wrote it down."

Eli dropped his head onto the pillow and held the blanket open for Ambrose to join him. "If you just explain it to him—"

"Ah, yes. Explaining data collection to a dragon. That's what I excel in." He gently pulled Tom off the bed, climbed under the blanket, then lifted Marlin's pamphlet off the nightstand and flapped it around. "I mean, look at this—twenty different data points? I have a shop to run. An apprentice to train. A festival to—"

Eli pulled him into a firm, overly warm cuddle. At the far edge of the bed, Tom scrambled back up the duvet and plopped down by their feet.

"And who was the one who told Fio they'd get him out?" Eli said, his words muffled by Ambrose's hair.

Ambrose took a swig of the potion, then grumbled incoherently into the pillow. Eli kissed the back of his neck.

"Just focus on one thing at a time," he reassured. "And who knows —maybe the sleeping potion won't last that long, anyway."

Ambrose snorted. "Excuse you. My apprentice made it. Of course it will last."

When he fell asleep and his dream quietly opened into the cavern, the place seemed almost peaceful compared to Ambrose's last visit. The artificers were gone and the blocked tunnel muted the room, leaving behind the sound of water trickling down the walls and a thin shaft of moonlight drifting in from the ceiling.

Fio, for better or for worse, had made progress in waking during his time alone. Both of his golden eyes were open now, glowing in the silver light. His claws shifted, his wings rustled—but he hadn't yet gained the strength to move far beyond his current position in the middle of the room. Not that it would take much longer, Ambrose guessed. Deep claw marks already raked the ground around him.

Even though he couldn't be harmed in his astral form, Ambrose kept a safe distance away from the gouges, standing in a stream of water that poked and tickled his shoulder.

"Hello," he started, as he always did. "I'm here."

He almost added his customary *don't mind me*, but unfortunately, the dragon did need to mind him this time.

In response to his call, Fio arched his back, the long points along his spine flaring in surprise—then when his gaze landed on Ambrose, he slowly settled back down.

You.

The word formed in Ambrose's mind like smoke—not heard, exactly, but its meaning came across as clearly as if they had been spoken aloud.

Are you here to get me out now?

Ah—it seemed Fio's wakened state had unearthed more conversation from him as well. Ambrose tentatively stepped toward him, away from the water. "Yes. I mean, not quite. I'm working on a plan—"

Then leave me alone and work on your plan.

With a snuffle, the dragon shifted his weight and stretched out his bat-like wings. The cavern wasn't wide enough to fit his full wing-span, and the gesture forced Ambrose back under the water. While he swatted uselessly at the stream, Fio peered down at him, his golden eyes rather smug.

"I *am* working on the plan." Ambrose tried to ignore how much the droplets tickled. "I thought you might like to know what the plan is."

Keeping his wings out, Fio extended his front legs next, his claws curling to deepen the stretch. *What is it, then?*

"Well, I'm afraid you're too large to fly out of here or sneak out, so my friends and I thought we'd, um..." Ambrose swallowed. There was no way to make this sound elegant. "We'd shrink you."

Fio's nostrils flared. *Shrink me? Are you one of them? Those—those artificers?*

The word *artificer* was muddled, as if Fio had mispronounced it—but the venom behind it was unmistakable.

"No, no!" Ambrose held up both hands. "I'm a potioneer up above. I make potions. Magical...liquids. I'm not one of them." He tried smoothing out his voice. "I promise, we're only trying to get you out safely. We wouldn't propose shrinking you if it wasn't the best way to do so."

Best way to do so, Fio repeated, as if trying to toss the words away. But a moment passed, and without any better idea materializing between them, he pivoted to stretching his back legs. *Shrinking. Fine. Then what?*

"Then we're working on a place you can live in once you're free," Ambrose continued quickly. He wasn't sure what would run out faster—the catnap potion or the dragon's patience. "I simply need to, uh..."

Fio's claws curled again, ripping deep lines through the dark earth. Ambrose looked around for something far away from those claws—ah. The wall. Marlin had wanted information on the moss that grew there, hadn't he?

"I simply need to get our ally some...information on your food," he continued. "The moss you've been absorbing for nutrients."

He did his best to stride confidently—and rapidly—over to the mossy wall and memorize the types that grew in the crevices. But the weak sliver of moonlight muddied all their colors together, leaving him with guesses that would fade even further in his mind after he woke.

Marlin was not going to be impressed with this data.

While Ambrose struggled, Fio stretched his neck in slow, careful movements—but his tail flicked quickly, and his narrowed eyes followed Ambrose's every move. *And who is this ally?* he asked. *A human?*

"Yes, actually. Marlin's a—"

A long, fearful hiss filled the air, making Ambrose jump.

I won't be trapped by another human! Not again, not ever—

Ambrose turned away from the moss. "He won't trap you, I promise! I have several friends helping me get you out. Yes, they're all humanoids, but—"

Fio lunged and snapped his jaws at him with a great *crack,* heat and acrid steam blasting into Ambrose's face. Ambrose leapt backward and pressed his body against the moss. He wasn't here, he told himself. Not really. Those teeth couldn't hurt him, even if each one was as long as his forearm.

"We won't trap you," he repeated steadily, pushing aside how his heart rattled within his chest. "And apart from Aphos, we're the only ones who know you're here. Please let us help you escape and—and find you a safe place to live."

One very, very far away, he silently hoped. Fio regarded him for a long moment, blocking the moonlight with his towering form, his eyes briefly the only source of light in the room...

Then he slowly retreated, his movements weary and sluggish after such a whiplike attack.

Should never have asked a two-legged creature for help, he muttered, settling on his haunches and laying his spines flat. The iridescent swirls of his green scales made it look as if grumpy storm clouds blazed inside him. *It's not becoming of a guard dragon.*

Ambrose cautiously turned back to the dull puffs of moss, trying to coax his heart beat to a normal rhythm. "Guard dragon?"

Yes, Fio said, as if it were the most obvious thing in the world. *Guard to my family. And when I get out, they'll smell that I'm back and come find me.* He tucked his claws underneath him, his neck arching in a proud swoop. *Then I won't need your safe place. They'll take me back home.*

His declaration did nothing to help settle Ambrose's heart rate. Marlin had said that the acidwings had abandoned the Scar a long time ago, before humans had even made a home there. How Fio had remained in hibernation for so long before Aphos found him, he wasn't sure—but this family of his was most certainly not going to find him. It was years upon years too late for that.

Not that he was going to mention that particular fact to a dragon who had snapped his teeth inches from his face moments ago.

"Right," he agreed vaguely. "Well, Fio, let me just look at this moss one more time and I'll—"

Fio?

Ambrose blinked. Oh. Of course, Fio didn't know he was Fio. Nat had made up the name, after all.

"Apologies." He looked over his shoulder. "We didn't know your name, so we made one. Do you...have a name you'd like for us to use?"

Not one a two-legged creature is worthy of using. Fio tried to sharpen the words to a fine point, but his eyes were already closed in exhaustion. *Fio is...fine. Do your work quickly and I won't have to hear it much longer.*

Ambrose set his jaw. Never in his life did he think he'd be taking orders from a dragon.

"Understood." He turned back to the moss. "One shrinking potion, coming right up."

TIP 5:

TASTE TEST

Eli

ELI HAD every confidence that Rory was the one for Dawn.

He'd known that for a while now, of course, but what really clinched it—what truly sealed the deal—was that Rory had taken one look at the politically fraught cupcake tasting, with all its heated family opinions and complex flavor tiers...

And had decided to up the ante by making a game of it.

"Master Beake," she announced boldly, pointing one finger at Ambrose while looming over the cafe table, "your second choice, please."

Ambrose stared in confusion at the paper before him. "Must I?"

"Yes." Rory's navy eyes shone fiercely in the light of the game. "Your fantasy cupcake draft will *not* be complete until you've selected your second champion. Now, what will it be? Vanilla raspberry or caramel chai?"

"I...um..." Ambrose flipped helplessly between the front and back of the cupcake roster. Eli leaned over to look at the list.

"Caramel chai," he advised sagely. "Dawn's cousin and aunt have both picked it, and it's an interesting dark horse against the fruit flavors. The odds are lower, but the payout will be better."

Said payout only consisted of another cookie from The Gingersnap Cafe, but Eli wasn't going to pass up such a meaningless competition. He *lived* for meaningless competitions.

And, clearly, so did Rory. She gestured to Eli and grinned. "See? Someone here gets it."

But they weren't the only ones fully invested in the game. Dawn cleared her throat, her wedding planner open before her like a holy book.

"Keep in mind," she proclaimed, one finger raised, "that the cupcakes not only need to gain everyone's favor, but they also need to match the atmosphere of the wedding venue."

Eli raised an eyebrow. "Which is?"

Dawn checked her book. "We've narrowed it down to four places." She paused. "Maybe three, once we check out the Guild-house reception hall tomorrow."

Everyone at the table groaned.

As Eli reevaluated his choices and Rory applied fictional stats to each flavor—intensity, moistness, sultriness—the cafe's waiter floated out with their first array of cupcakes. Dawn had requested they start with the classics first, but the waiter had tossed a few glittering delicacies into the mix.

"Two complimentary Spelltide cupcakes from the baker," he explained. "Just testing out some recipes before he sets the festival menu."

Eli's stomach grumbled, even as he braced for an impending headache.

"Between Viola's test batches and this baker"—he grabbed one of the sparkling cupcakes and sliced it into quarters—"I don't think I'm gonna wake up from this sugar coma."

Ambrose yawned as he neatly carved a chocolate cupcake for the group. "After last night, I will gladly accept the sugar coma."

Normally, Rory would rib him for his choice of words—but this time, she had mercy and spared him.

"You talked to Fio last night?" she asked. "How'd it go?"

"I don't want to talk about it," he muttered. Dawn glanced over at Eli, who gave her a look and held up a finger. Three, two, one…

Ambrose threw up his chocolate-stained hands. "If I have to keep enduring a"—he reluctantly lowered his voice here—"a dragon snapping its *teeth* at me in my dreams every night, I'm going to take Banneker's initial idea and blow the top off that cave chamber myself."

Rory shrugged. "Look, he's been a science experiment in Aphos for who knows how many years. If all he's doing is snapping his teeth at you, that's pretty good."

"I'd still rather he grow out of the habit before I try to sneak him out of Aphos." Ambrose rubbed his under-eye circles. "And he keeps mentioning his family. That they'll find him and take him away to their home."

Dawn frowned as she passed a slice of lemon cake over to Eli. (This one was Eli's first choice on the draft. Favored by four family members, including Rory.) "Family?" she repeated. "But I thought Marlin said the other dragons were all gone?"

"Precisely." Ambrose tried a bite of the vanilla cupcake, shook his head, and handed the rest to Rory. "And I'm going to let *Marlin* inform him of that when the time comes."

A second tray of cupcakes arrived to punctuate Ambrose's statement. Rory stood and cleared her throat.

"Finish your notes on the first round, everyone," she declared. "Be detailed, please. This is a cake-or death-situation."

Eli did as he was told, expounding as outrageously as he could.

Lemon: sharp as dragons' teeth, with a bouquet of summer and an aftertaste of mellowed citrus. Pair with a tear-jerking ceremony and chase with an awkward toast from a second cousin.

Chocolate: smooth like wand oil with a hint of coffee on the nose. Guaranteed to get Meemaw up on the dance floor. Not guaranteed to pay for her medical bills after.

He glanced over at Ambrose's notes.

Lemon: Fine.
Chocolate: Good.

He gave Ambrose a look. "Ames."

Ambrose shot him a weary look right back. "Do not test me."

The second round of cupcakes dared to be a little bolder. Here was Ambrose's caramel chai, along with Eli's second choice: raspberry mocha. He took a bite of it and reeled back. If the coffee in *that* didn't wake Ambrose up, nothing would.

"Here, try this." He set a slice in front of Ambrose and rubbed his back. "You know, I don't have training for the next few days. If Nat's busy, I could help you pull together the ingredients for Fio's shrinking potion."

Ambrose grimaced. "You mean you know someone in the Scar who sells *kaolin agaricus saphira*?"

"Hold on." Dawn stopped with an orange sherbet cupcake halfway to her mouth. "Are you serious?"

Ambrose nodded miserably. Rory looked between them in confusion. "A what now?"

"Blue clay mushroom," Dawn explained. "And it's rare. *Stupid* rare."

Eli's mind whipped back to flashbacks of college, where he had broken into a sweat simply handling a tiny jar of the dried stuff. The oddly moldable mushroom had limited uses—but for those poor potioneers who *did* need it for a brew, a few ounces cost them as much as three good cauldrons.

"What about Jae?" he asked. "She's gotta have some of it. She's got everything."

"Everything from Hart's Fenn," Ambrose corrected. "The mushroom grows in the Driftwood. And with Spelltide coming up, none of the other merchants are venturing back into the forest until after the festival." He took a bite of the mocha icing, coughed, and passed it back to Eli. Rory tapped her pencil against the table in thought.

"Dawn, isn't our wedding florist from the Driftwood?" she asked. "Think she would know anything?" She turned back to them. "Love this florist. You should see what she does with floating succulents. If we can make them part of the decor, my family'll flip."

Ambrose stiffened; Eli placed a cinnamon cupcake in front of him in an attempt to lift his mood.

"You've already locked in a florist?" he asked.

Dawn brightened. "Of course! Mostly for the flower exchange during the ceremony, but we may use those succulents here and there."

Eli sifted through what he knew of Scarrish wedding traditions. "Flower exchange. It's...not a jewelry exchange?"

"Not in the Scar, no." Dawn brushed crumbs off her planner and eagerly flipped to another section, this one filled with sketches of lilies. "Here, the parents of each family will go up and hand each other flowers. The moms usually arrange the bouquets themselves—"

Ambrose stood abruptly.

"Tea," he declared, looking anywhere but at the table. "Tea will help wash down all this sugar. Would anyone else like anything to drink?"

Rory blinked. "Uh, sure. Can I get a coffee?"

Ambrose took everyone's orders and hurried off to the counter, his shoulders only rounding down once he was in the long, sluggish line.

All those remaining at the table leaned in.

"I'm sorry," Eli whispered. "He gets like this around wedding talk."

"Did you ask him why?" Dawn peeked over at Ambrose.

"I..." Eli hesitated. He had wanted to, certainly—but part of him was terrified that any well-intentioned prying, no matter how gentle, could be taken as a hint. A nudge toward something Ambrose didn't want. Something he had looked so terribly guilty about when asking to avoid it.

"I haven't," he finally said. "But it's probably like Grim said. The party, the dancing, the crowds—it's just not his thing."

"I don't think it's that." Dawn pointed her fork in Ambrose's direction. "Really, it isn't. I've gone to weddings with him before for some of our oldest clients. He never minded any of it then." She paused and waved around the fork. "All right, he minded the dancing part, and maybe the part where I tried to push him into the middle of the dancing circle when I was drunk, but this"—she set the fork down— "this is different. This is weird, even for him."

Eli gave a reluctant hum. Ambrose had reassured him several times that his qualms about a wedding in no way indicated any qualms about marriage. In fact, it had been hard for Ambrose to stop smiling after the first time they had discussed the idea of forever. But something about weddings always wiped that smile away, something Eli couldn't begin to—

Dawn squeezed his hand, drawing him out of his thoughts.

"Don't worry about it," she said. "You just work on your proposal potion. I can try to dig into the Ambrose-ness of it all. He'll open up eventually. He always does."

"I know, I know." That wasn't a lie—he fully understood the consequences of not being patient when trying to coax words out of Ambrose. He'd just have to focus on his own potion while Ambrose focused on his.

Just like old times.

When Ambrose finally came back with a tray of cups, the three of them were wrapping up their final cupcake notes. Eli specifically was finishing up a diatribe on the orange sherbet cupcake. *Sweeter than true love itself, made for a reception hosted in the heavens...*

"A coffee for Rory. Hibiscus tea for Dawn..." Ambrose carefully placed the drinks around the table while the others passed back their notes to Rory. "And the green Driftwood blend for Eli."

Eli took a long, satisfying whiff of the tea. In all honesty, he ordered the Driftwood blend mostly for its scent: rich and woody, with a lovely hint of hazelnut. It almost made him want to go back to the Driftwood, as dangerous as the place was. He almost had, in fact, back when the Guildhouse had posted a quest about…

An idea bolted into his head.

"Ames." He straightened. "The Guildhouse."

Ambrose sat down. "What about it?"

"You don't have to hunt down merchants or florists for that blue mushroom you need. You can get it delivered right to you." He gestured eagerly out the window. "Just head to the Guildhouse and post a request for it, and one of the adventurers will go fetch it for you. It'll be easy!"

Dawn tore her gaze away from her wedding planner, where she was rapidly crossing out cupcake flavors. "Oh! You can come with us to the Guildhouse tomorrow!" She elbowed Rory, who jumped.

"Right!" Rory said quickly. "We'll be checking out the reception hall as a wedding venue. We can help you post it while we're there."

Ambrose hesitated. "Won't that sort of quest be expensive?"

"I bet I can pull some strings," Eli reassured him. "Just tell them I sent you, and they'll give you a discount."

"And you promise it will be easy? No quest paperwork in triplicate?"

Eli squeezed his hand. "An easy win, I swear."

"Good. Ames is gonna need all the wins he can get." Rory grimaced at Dawn's wedding planner. "Because this fantasy cupcake draft is not looking good for him."

TIP 6:

CONSIDER A FETCH QUEST

Ambrose

BETWEEN ELI'S reassurances and Dawn's excitement, Ambrose struggled to find an excuse not to join the Guildhouse wedding tour —so, the next morning, he found himself on the top level of the Scar, walking up to one of the most extravagant buildings in the city.

Much like the government square, the Adventurers' Guildhouse had spared no expense when it came to carving the stone wall around its double-doored entrance. Chiseled columns stretched from the walkway to the upper edge of the chasm, their tops hidden by dripping foliage. Around the columns wound all manner of snarling, gnashing creatures: dragons, griffins, great river eels. The artist had taken extra time in carving their sharp teeth and claws, making sure they truly popped against the striped chasm wall.

Ambrose suppressed a grimace. It was not a place *he'd* pick for a wedding, but he wasn't about to mention that to Dawn. She and Rory already stood by the doors, introducing themselves to an orcish woman holding a clipboard.

"I'm Clem, the event manager for the Guildhouse." When Ambrose joined them, she gave the trio a cheery smile and held the door open for them. "I'll take you through a tour of our reception space."

Naturally, the Guildhouse had taken care to make its lobby as imposing as the monsters at the entrance. Thick wooden beams latticed the ceiling, heralding a massive stone hearth at the far end of the stretched room. Above the hearth, razor-tipped alcedon antlers presided over a scattering of heavy, warm furniture. A welcoming place for adventurers—as long as they didn't mind the sharp spikes hanging above them.

"Hey." Rory nudged Ambrose and nodded over to the clerk. "Did you want to go ahead and submit your mushroom request? Judging by the crowd, you might get some bites today."

Ambrose glanced over at the smattering of bored people lounging by the hearth, some of them half-heartedly dressed in leather armor. Ah, yes, just what every glory-seeking adventurer wanted, he thought. A quest to forage for mushrooms.

He did consider it—scuttling over to the clerk, submitting his request, and leaving before wedding talk resumed. But next to Rory, Dawn was bouncing on her heels in anticipation of seeing the space. He couldn't simply abandon her now.

"Later," he said, trying to muster a smile. "After the tour."

As Clem led them down a hallway, he tried to reassure himself about the whole visit. With any luck, the venue would prove too... adventuresome for the brides-to-be. He imagined taxidermied griffins above the altar. Claws and furs draped over the seats. It would be a brief peek, a quick *no thank you*, and an easy check off Dawn's list—

Clem opened the door at the end of the hall, and Dawn gasped in delight.

The Guildhouse hadn't been satisfied with merely carving out a space for themselves within the chasm wall. Much like Aphos and their Oasis, the Guild had decided to claim a neighboring sinkhole as their own as well. But while the Oasis' garden-like charm was merely an illusion, the Guildhouse had infused every speck of the place with real, tactile beauty.

The glass ceiling struck him first: a complex, tessellated structure of iron and glass, refracting joyful rainbows across the stone floor below. But that wasn't nearly enough color for the Guild. Flowers in every hue cascaded like waterfalls down the sinkhole, giving the walls a pillowy appearance. At the far end, the flowers converged and melted into a grand archway, hewn of rippling wood from the Elwig Forest. Even from here, Ambrose could catch a whiff of its scent: pine, cinnamon, and cool breezes on a spring day.

"Oh my gods," Dawn breathed, gripping Rory's arm tight with both hands. "It's *everything*."

Rory beamed and kissed the rainbow that fell across Dawn's forehead. "It really is, isn't it?"

Clem glowed in her easy victory.

"You can see it's partially set up for a wedding right now," she said, her boots clicking on the stone floor as she led Dawn and Rory toward the altar. "The space can fit up to two hundred people, with modularity to include both a ceremony and a feast afterward. Depending on when you're booking, we might also have the sweetheart balcony finished by that time. I can show you what it looks like now, but please pardon our dust..."

Dawn and Rory eagerly followed Clem up the carved staircase to a half-finished balcony above—but Ambrose remained where he was, staring at the flower-laden altar.

Gods, Eli would love this place, wouldn't he? The sky beyond the glass, the perfumed air, all this space for his family and then some. Ambrose could see him standing at the altar now, in a dozen dreamy variations. A flower crown, a tailored coat, Kolkean wedding robes... His outfit didn't matter. It only mattered that he stood there and smiled at Ambrose.

The sun-dappled visions dug deeper into his heart, dredging up thoughts that scarcely saw the light of day. Thoughts of him standing with Eli under the foliage, declaring a love that had once frightened him, and now carried him. He had imagined this sort of thing as a young boy a long time ago. What was so terrible about it now? What was so frightening about simply demonstrating what everyone already knew? In a brief, almost desperate surge, he wanted Eli to be with him right now. He wanted to hold his hands, he wanted to—

Clem's voice cut into his thoughts, echoing down the staircase as she descended. "And of course, I'm well-versed in wedding traditions all across Laskell, should you need any assistance in implementing them."

"I'll see if I can stump you with some of the Deepriver ones, then," Rory said, then in uncharacteristic anxiety, tucked a strand of hair behind her ear. "Though...it'll, um, be just my dad's side of the family in attendance."

"Of course, of course." Clem smiled. "We can accommodate that."

Ambrose fidgeted with the button on his shirt cuff, wondering how far a lack of family could be accommodated—but he didn't have the fortitude to ask until the end of the tour. Clem led the three of them back into the Guildhouse, rattling off details about timelines and package options, then handed Dawn and Rory a neat little folder.

"Please take your time to review everything," she said sweetly. Dawn turned to Ambrose, her excitement barely veiling an under-lying curiosity.

"Would you like to go through this with us?" she asked, holding up the folder. Ambrose glanced back at Clem, then lowered his voice.

"Perhaps in a second," he said. "I have a question I'd like to ask her first."

"Oh!" Dawn's eyes went wide, and she nearly started bouncing again. "Okay! Yes, absolutely! Go for it! And if you have any, you know, questions for me, I'm here!"

She smiled far too wide, punched his arm, and went off to huddle with Rory and the venue folder. While the brides huddled on a couch by the hearth and giggled over signature cocktail names—things like *Vodka Vows* and *Having the Lime of Our Lives*—Ambrose summoned his courage and approached Clem.

"I was wondering," he began quietly, "if you're familiar with... alternate Scarrish wedding rituals. For non-family members."

"Alternate rituals?" Clem tidied up a stack of brochures on a side table, all advertising various local Scarrish businesses. Ambrose tried not to look impatient, but he could feel Dawn glancing at him from the other side of the room.

"Well, those are entirely up to the couple, of course," Clem continued. "That said, I've organized several weddings with non-traditional rituals. You know, bringing in second cousins, a great-aunt twice removed..."

"No, I mean, um..." Suddenly, Ambrose's voice felt too loud in his throat. "If there's no family at all." He spoke faster, as if to hide the statement. "But if there's anything involving friends or neighbors—"

Clem laughed in disbelief, the sound a cold tinkle in the echoing space.

"A Scarrish wedding without any family?" she said. "None at all? My dear, it's about families joining *together*. Intertwining for generations to come. I'm not familiar with any traditions that don't involve them in some way. But"—she plucked a different brochure, dull and faded, from the pile—"there are more compact venues I can recommend if you have a, um...*smaller* audience."

Her smile remained bright, but the condescension in her voice dissolved all his tentatively happy visions. He had gotten so swept up in imagining the vows that he'd nearly forgotten about the people who would be there to watch them—or, rather, wouldn't be. He didn't have a mother to bring flowers to the ceremony. He didn't have a father to give opinions on cupcake flavors. He didn't even have a second cousin to fill in as an awkward, stilted substitution.

His vision of Eli at the altar returned, but his groom stood far away now, just one of a crowd of family members seated on his side of the room. And they all *whispered*. Gossiping about how alone Ambrose stood. At how empty his side of the altar was. How many beloved traditions they had to skip, knowing the exchanges would be one-sided. What sort of groom was he, they wondered aloud, to not even merit a single family member in attendance?

Pain flared deep in his chest—the same pain cradled there since he was eight, that had torn open and healed over and torn open again more times than he could count—and he weakly tucked the brochure into his pocket.

"Of course. Thank you."

As soon as Clem turned around, he looked around the room, avoiding eye contact with Dawn and Rory. He needed something else to do, something else to think about—

At the other end of the hall, a clerk hummed and filed papers behind a desk. Ambrose did his best not to break into a run on his way there.

"A quest," he blurted out to the clerk. "I'm looking to add a quest to the signboard. What do I need to fill out?"

He'd never posted such a quest before. The Scarrish markets and Potion Con always had what he needed, and unlike the Guildhouse, they didn't require any sort of filing in advance. But for the first time in his life, he silently begged for long paperwork. Complex forms, questionnaires, indecipherable instructions—anything to make him focus on something other than Clem's laugh echoing in his ears.

"Oh, there's not much paperwork," the clerk happily reassured him. "Mind if I ask the nature and the location of the quest, to get us started?"

Eli had already supplied him with the proper terminology, and he duly rattled off the words. "A foraging mission in sector A2 of the Driftwood. Would require a senior adventurer with at least two prior completed quests in that sector, for safety. And here." He slid Eli's wooden adventuring card across the desk. "I'd like to request the Guild discount."

The clerk broke into a grin as soon as he saw Eli's name on the card. "Oh, you're Valenz's guy! Ambrose Beake! You know, just this week, I recommended The Griffin's Claw to at least three new swords in town. Can't tell you how many folks here mention your potions on a weekly basis."

Ambrose accepted the compliment as a weak balm. "Thank you so much. Would any of those...swords...be willing to take on a quest to the Driftwood?"

"Let me see..."

Ambrose tried not to tap impatiently on the desk as the clerk rifled through a thick ringed book, filled with tabs and magically shifting notes on adventurers. Rory had been right at the cupcake tasting—he needed some sort of win today. Just a small one would do.

But the clerk's grimace did not spell victory for him.

"Valrina's on medical leave, Benedict's currently in the Vineheart..." He reached the end of the book and looked up. "Afraid I don't have anyone available for two months. Can your request wait that long?"

Ambrose's palms started to sweat. He had promised Fio a quick rescue. Two months was not a quick rescue. "I'm afraid I'd need the delivery as soon as possible."

The clerk gave a dismaying hum and reached behind him to take some forms from a tray. "Mr. Beake, I'll be honest with you. I can try to post a rush job for you, but it's Spelltide. If anyone's interested, you're probably looking at paying extra talons for the holiday, on top of the distance fee and hazard pay."

Ambrose nervously tapped his fingers on the table. The hazard pay alone for the Driftwood would likely be steep, given the forest's literal inability to stay still—not to mention all the monsters that had learned to hunt within the moving trees. "How many talons, exactly?" he asked.

The clerk pushed the forms across the desk. "Maybe three thousand. Four if you want a larger party."

All of the color drained from Ambrose's face.

Spelltide was not cheap for merchants. There were the special potions, the extra supplies, the Spelltide gift he had bought Nat... With any luck, his budget would be happy at the *end* of the festival, but it was certainly not happy now. At least, not to the tune of four thousand spare talons.

"After Spelltide, then," he said quickly. "It'll just have to wait."

Fio would just have to wait. Such a delay wouldn't be disastrous, exactly—according to Marlin, the nutrients in the cave moss could last another few weeks before a proper hunt was required. Ambrose would just have to take another damn catnap potion that night and talk to Fio about it. Reassure him that they were working on the rescue, but it would take a few more days than he—

The ground beneath him shook.

It wasn't a long quake—more akin to a rug being pulled out from under his feet—but it made him stumble anyway, and the clerk behind the desk gave a yelp.

"The hells was that?" Rory and Dawn both stood up, while Clem grabbed a taxidermic phoenix to keep it steady. But neither the events manager nor the clerk nor Ambrose himself had an answer. The Scar never experienced earthquakes, not in all his years here.

His mind leapt to the worst. Ramp collapses, shop explosions—

"The shop." He hurried for the door. "I have to go check on the shop."

Quest forms and venue paperwork forgotten, the three of them rushed back down to Rosemond Street, cautiously favoring the side ramps over the narrow, shaky bridges that criss-crossed the chasm. Ambrose tried to ignore the people he passed—all spooked and gossiping loudly from doorways and windows—but when he reached Rosemond Street, the atmosphere was much the same. The merchants had gathered in the middle of the road along with a frightened gaggle of customers, all of them tossing out possible causes for the quake.

"Don't know of any construction in this area," Grim was saying to an elf clutching a canvas shopping bag. "Not until next month, at least."

"Just asked my husband about it," another customer said as she pocketed a speaking stone. "He didn't feel a thing in the northern district, but blast if it didn't almost give me a heart attack here."

Banneker ran a hand through his bright red hair. "I'm telling you, man, it's just like the horoscopes said. It's the alignment of the stars."

Zuri looked up at him. "No, it isn't."

"Zuri!" Dawn rushed over to her. "Are you all right?"

Her apprentice jerked a thumb toward Banneker. "I've been injured severely by this man's theories."

"Hey! Luka will back me up." Banneker looked around. "Wait, where'd he—?"

The door to The Griffin's Claw burst open, and Tom whirled out, wheeling as fast as she could to hide behind Ambrose's legs. Luka's voice soon floated out behind her.

"Nat, if you could—"

"I'm *trying!*"

As a string of curses followed Nat's response, Ambrose sprinted into the shop, a dozen terrible visions filling his head. A bottle had fallen on her—no, a whole shelf—no, a bubbling cauldron had tipped over and—

He yanked open the door, and a bundle of shining feathers slammed into his face.

"What the—?" He jerked back and batted it away; the bundle careened back into the shop, joining its brethren.

"Mr. Ambrose!" Nat shouted nervously. "We've got it handled, don't worry!"

The vision before Ambrose was not the bloody mess he was fearing—but it most certainly was not handled. One of his more expensive Spelltide illusion vials had broken on the counter, releasing a thick, silvery liquid and the illusion itself: a dozen miniature aurocs, flying and screeching about the shop like panicked pigeons. Their white wings molted icy crystals, just as their real counterparts would during the migration, leaving a shimmering trail in their frantic wake.

Lovely, but it was not the time to admire his own handiwork.

"Why won't they just"—Nat batted away the fading crystals with one hand and wielded a reversal wand in the other—"stay *still?*"

Ambrose ducked and dodged his way over to the counter. "Hand me the wand, I can—"

A sharp whistle cut into his words. On the other side of the shop, Luka had his hands cupped around his mouth, perfectly imitating the aurocs' cries while he moved toward Nat. With each trill, more of the birds flocked toward him, briefly distracted from their panic.

Nat took advantage of the distraction and leapt over the counter.

"Nat, wait!" Ambrose tried, but it was no use.

"I got it!" She ran forward and pointed the wand. "I got 'em—!"

The spell shot forth in a sunshine-like ray, banishing the mass of birds gathered above Luka in one fell swoop. But neither of the apprentices' momentum could be stopped—they crashed into each other in the middle of the shop and fell in a clumsy heap onto the floor.

"Sorry!" Nat looked down at Luka, half-straddling him. "You okay?"

Luka could only blink up at her, his ears scarlet. "Um."

Ambrose quickly helped both of them up. "Are you all right?"

Nat ignored the question.

"It was my fault!" she babbled as soon as she stood up. "I broke the bottle and lost a sale. I was holding it out to a customer when the quake happened and it shattered and got everywhere and—"

Ambrose waved all that away. "But are you all right?"

She finally blinked at him. "Yeah, I'm fine."

"You know you can be honest with me if—"

"Ugh, I swear I'm *fine*," she said, with all the huffiness her eighteen years allowed her. Then she softened, and a spark of fear crossed her gaze. "Will you...will you let me keep covering the till?"

Ambrose frowned. "What? Of course I will."

Now, if this had been his old mentor, Master Pearce, speaking, the answer would have been quite different. Admonishment for such foolishness. A dock in stipend matching the cost of the bottle. Banishment to the supply closet for at least three days.

Just the thought of it made his voice soften.

"It was an accident," he said gently. "And one broken bottle is hardly a problem."

Nat let out a relieved sigh. "Thanks, Mr. Ambrose."

While Nat went off and babbled additional apologies to Luka, Ambrose set about mopping up the spill on the counter. The cleaning wasn't pleasant, exactly, but he'd take anything to distract from his experience at the Guildhouse. The sooner he could forget about all that, the better—

But sadly for him, Nat hadn't forgotten about his mission.

"Did you find an adventurer for Fio's potion stuff?" she asked brightly. "Who signed up? Any adventurer I might recognize?"

Ambrose deflated. He had run off and left the request forms blank on the desk. Given his luck today, the cost will have gone up another thousand talons since he stepped out of the Guildhouse.

"No one yet." He set aside the cleaning wand. "I'll need to...make another visit. But why don't I make us some tea first?" He glanced at Luka, who looked like he needed tea as much as Ambrose did. "For all of us."

The contained chaos of the apprentices in his kitchen didn't exactly ease his nerves, but the tea most certainly did. Once Nat resumed her place at the counter and Luka scuttled back to Banneker's shop, Ambrose dove back into Spelltide restocking. The repetition of organizing bottles on the shelves always helped him think, and today was no different.

There had to be other ways to secure the mushroom. The Guildhouse and the markets had nothing to offer, and universities were closed for the holiday—but they weren't the only ones with access to magical ingredients. He could reach out to a few more Potion Con associates in the distant corners of the country. Some of the more reclusive potioneers had ingredient collections larger than his entire shop. Surely one of them had a few ounces of fresh blue clay mushroom lying around...

But his peaceful brainstorming didn't last long. The jarring earthquakes returned only an hour later—little jolts without any predictable rhythm or cause, cutting into his thoughts every time they surfaced. The stability spells on his shelves all held up perfectly well—of course they did, Banneker had applied them—but that didn't matter. The customers were so on edge that one by one, each shop on Rosemond Street gave up and closed early. Ambrose himself was flipping the store sign to *Closed* when Eli suddenly appeared at the door.

"Eli—!" Ambrose jumped back with a shout, then shook his head at himself and opened the door. "Apologies. Not the first time we've been spooked today. Do you know what's causing the—?"

"No clue." Eli slipped inside, his expression grim. He still had his sparring gear on, and judging by the dust on his greaves, had clearly run here after the last quake. "No one at the practice pits has any idea, either. They all went home. Is everyone all right here?"

His gaze swept over Ambrose in a rapid check for injuries. Despite the circumstances, Ambrose grew warmer the longer his eyes roved over him.

"We're all fine." He kissed Eli on the cheek, already unwinding at his mere presence. "Just closing early, along with everyone else."

"And where's the gremlin?"

"Over here!" Nat stepped out of the workroom, hoisting up her backpack of study books. Banneker had made her the bag, and Nat had adorned it with so many charms that it clinked and rattled with every step. "Mr. Ambrose said I could go home for the day."

Yes, he had indeed said that—but something about sending her off into the city amidst these strange quakes made him uneasy.

"Only if the apprentices' house is safe," he added. "If it's taken any damage, I can always ask Sherry to set up her spare room—"

"I know, I know. See you later!"

She waved and left, joining Luka and Zuri in the street before heading north. Behind Ambrose, Eli started to unbuckle his sparring gear.

"Sorry I didn't come back sooner," he said. "None of us thought the quakes were going to keep going, and Oren wanted us to practice our—"

Ambrose didn't wait for him to finish undressing—he gathered Eli into a tight, grounding hug, ignoring the sweat and dust that still clung to him. It didn't matter that he was a far cry from Ambrose's foolish vision of flower crowns under the altar. He was here, and real, and the best thing Ambrose had laid eyes on that day.

"I love you," he murmured into Eli's hair. Eli hugged him tight in return, allowing Ambrose to close his eyes and relax against his pauldron.

"Love you, too." Eli kissed his cheek, though Ambrose could hear the frown lingering in his voice. "The quakes really got you, huh?"

The earthquakes weren't even the worst part of the day, but Ambrose didn't feel like talking about it. He'd have to first skip over the wedding venue bit, then explain the clerk's ridiculous fees for his Fio quest...

He groaned internally at the thought of Fio. He could likely feel the quakes, too, and it wouldn't do to have an irritable *and* confused dragon underneath the city. Ambrose would have to check on him when he went to sleep.

But that was still hours away, and if he was being perfectly honest with himself, there was a half-undressed, sweaty adventurer standing before him who could distract him from his terrible day in a manner of ways.

"I'm just glad you're back." He lowered his voice and began to tug at the buckles of Eli's pauldron. "Here. Allow me to help."

There was no fooling Eli—he immediately grinned and set his hands low on Ambrose's waist, his thumbs drawing circles against his hip bones. "Impatient, are we?"

"After the day I've had?" Ambrose hooked a finger around one of the straps, tugged Eli forward, and pressed a long, hard kiss against his lips, willing his memories to disappear with the gesture. "Yes."

***

Fortunately for Eli and unfortunately for Ambrose, impatience seemed to be the order of the day.

When he found himself standing in Fio's cavern that night, something about the place strangely soothed him. He stepped forward, both cautious and confused. Nothing seemed to have changed. Water still dripped down the walls. All the artificers' equipment still lay here, dusty and broken. And Fio was still curled in the middle of the floor, his scales shifting green and silver in the bright moonlight, nearly too bright to look at. Wait, the *light*—

Ambrose squinted up. What had once been a small sliver in the ceiling was now a large, jagged crack, letting in a brilliant beam of moonglow rather than a pinprick. Under normal circumstances, he would have enjoyed the silvery sight—but his brief sense of peace fell away instantly. This change was no accident; massive claw marks lined the jagged edge of the hole, and on the ground, debris formed a rough circle around Fio.

"Fio?" Ambrose pointed upward. "Did you do this?"

The dragon let out a long, tired huff, his tail draped over his head to shield his eyes from the light.

I tried to make it bigger, he said, every word underlined with frustration. *Tried to get out.*

Ambrose gauged the distance from the ground to the ceiling. To make those claw marks, Fio would have had to jump quite high. Several times, at least. And without space to use his wings, his landing would not have gone unnoticed. Not by Aphos and not by…

He cursed silently. The quakes in the Scar. Fio wasn't going to be confused or upset by the quakes because the damn dragon had *caused* them.

"Fio." He picked his words carefully. "I know you want to fly out of here, but—but you won't be able to fit through that hole—"

Course I won't. Fio's tail twitched, enough to reveal one surly eye glaring at Ambrose. *The humans took my acid. Or some part of it, at least.* His eye swiveled over to the dusty glass jars in the corner, now empty of his plasma. *Can't melt a single thing anymore. But if I can make the hole bigger with my claws, my family will be able to smell me and help get me out.* He curled up tighter and laid a paw over his face. *Even if I am a bad guard dragon.*

Ambrose tentatively moved closer. Marlin and his data points had never clarified the significance of Fio's words. "What do you mean, guard dragon?"

You mean humans don't have any? Fio gave a condescending sniff. *I'm not the only one. We take turns, you see. Sleeping until we're needed. When the others need us, we wake up ready to fight.* He gave a great yawn, every one of his long teeth flashing in the moonlight. *Usually.*

"I...see." Ambrose looked around uncertainly. "Well, I'm sure you're not a...bad guard dragon..."

But even Ambrose's clumsy reassurance seemed to rile him up. He reared back his head, teeth bared, voice ringing loud in Ambrose's head. *How can I not be? I can't claw, can't spit. Got trapped by two-legged creatures. I'll never make it beyond a novice guard at this point!*

The word *novice* blurred in Ambrose's mind, as if the magic had trouble translating the term from dragon-speak. Even so, he had a hard time believing Fio could be anything like a novice. What with the claws, and the teeth, and his massive size...

Water dripped down onto Fio's horns, and as the dragon hissed and batted the drops away, Ambrose looked closer at their shape. That particular element *had* been in Marlin's notes. For many dragons, their horns' length and twist betrayed their age. Fio's horns curled once, twice...

Only three times—they seem to have stopped growing during his hibernation. He was young, then, only six or so years old before he'd gone to sleep. A true novice of his kind.

And his family had never woken him up.

A pang shot through Ambrose's heart, but he shoved it aside. There were more immediate threats to attend to. Fio carving out that hole in the ceiling wasn't going to attract his family—it was going to incite enemies. Humanoids, specifically, spooked in both Aphos and the Scar. If Mayor Rune began to search for the cause—or if Madam Mila decided it wasn't worth the risk to leave Fio to rot in peace...

"I'm sorry they haven't come yet, but..." He searched for the right words to work around Fio's anger. They didn't exactly cover this type of bargaining in potioneer training. "But when we get you out, we can look for—for other dragons. It'll be easier for them to smell you if you're not stuck in this cave. And—*and*"—he held up a finger—"there are plenty of other dragons at Marlin's foundation. Perhaps they've seen..." He swallowed. "Dragons who know you."

The lie burned his throat, but it worked. Fio stopped snarling, and a modicum of hope veiled his tone.

Really? he said. *When can we talk to the dragons?*

The hopeful question sent another jab through Ambrose's chest. He couldn't bring himself to say two months, as the Guildhouse clerk had advised. Fio wouldn't be able to stay still for two months. There had to be another way.

"Give me a few days to find what I need for the potion," he said. "It won't take long to brew once I have everything."

Fio shifted. *And then I'll be out of here?*

"And then we'll get you out of here. I promise."

Fio stared at him, unblinking, his emerald scales silently swirling in the moonlight...then he drew back and curled up again.

Fine, he said petulantly.

Ambrose slouched in relief. *Fine* was a sight better than snapping teeth, or snarling, or further demands...

Then moments later, the cave faded, and he hurtled from sleepy relief into panicked wakefulness.

Days? Why in the hells had he said *days*? He couldn't get the ingredients that quickly. Even if he scrounged up the coin for rush mail, magic messages to and from reclusive collectors, city-to-city teleport delivery... It was Spelltide. Getting a response from these sorts of potioneers took weeks on a normal day, often with excuses like *I was catching up on my reading list* or *I forgot my mailbox existed.*

(Every year, it was a miracle they even made it to Potion Con before it ended.)

Ambrose sighed and hugged his pillow. "Eli, I—"

He glanced over and stopped himself. Eli normally stayed up at least an hour later than him, but tonight, he was already asleep, splayed out over three pillows. He hadn't bothered to wear a tunic to bed, which left his scars on full display. Old ones from his days as a griffinkeeper remained scattered over his arms, but his career change had added more to the pile. The burn mark on his shoulder blade from a rock phoenix, the dual bite mark on his ribcage from a two-headed bat...

A desperate thought crossed Ambrose's mind. The Guildhouse had no adventurers to offer him, but he shared a bed with one. And he knew for certain that Eli had no quests lined up until after

Spelltide. He had experience in the Driftwood, too. Knew how to find and handle potion ingredients. Likely wouldn't charge thousands of talons—not for lack of Ambrose trying to pay him, of course...

Ambrose tossed back his pillow and flopped heavily onto it. No. No, he couldn't endanger Eli like that.

But...how dangerous would it be, exactly?

He flipped over onto his other side. *No.* He wouldn't risk his own boyfriend for such a venture.

But then he was risking Fio. Risking potentially the whole Scar, if the dragon got out on his own.

He turned over and over again like a roast chicken, silently arguing with himself for hours. When dawn finally broke, he gave up and shuffled into the kitchen for coffee. The aroma eventually woke Eli, who wandered out, blanket draped over his shoulder, eyes half-open.

"How's Fio doing?" he asked, his voice creaky. Ambrose handed him a cup of coffee.

"My dear, I have a terrible idea."

TIP 7:

WHEN IN DOUBT, GO TO THE TAVERN

Nat

THE DAY AFTER THE QUAKES, Rosemond Street did its best to soldier forth with Spelltide cheer.

To help them along, no shudders or jolts plagued them that morning, allowing Eli to finish decorating the shop and Banneker to hang up a few lights above The Griffin's Claw sign. Nat used half her break just to admire the glittering crystals; Ambrose ignored them with a grumpy grimace. She wanted to ask what was bothering him —yes, he was a humbug about Spelltide, but not *this* humbuggy— but the answer came to her soon enough, just after she had left the shop and settled in her room for the evening.

As much as she loved being outside—in the sunlight, with the other apprentices, with *friends*—she adored her room in the apprentices' boarding house. It was hers and hers alone, free to fill with whatever she wanted. Pillows, rugs, and thick, knitted blankets from Sherry. Stacks of books from her countless trips to Widdershins'. Tiny glowing crystals affixed to the walls at different heights for a starlike effect. Hells, she was even considering begging Banneker for a defunct cannon just to see if she could fit it into the corner—

"Nat?" Luka knocked on the door, interrupting her measuring of said corner. "Sherry's inviting us to dinner."

"What?" She stashed her measuring tape on the cluttered shelf above her bed, next to her growing collection of pretty potion bottles and funny-looking rocks. Compared to Ambrose's lucky shelf, it wasn't much; compared to her collection back in Aphos, it was a treasure trove. "I thought Sherry and Banneker were getting dinner tonight."

Luka hesitantly opened the door a crack and peeked through. He and Zuri knew better than to come into her sacred space, so he remained firmly in the hall when he said: "They told us we should join. All of us."

Zuri poked her head in above Luka's. "She's not exactly... asking."

So, the three apprentices wandered back down to Rosemond Street, then past the shops to The Jumping Ogre.

"Evening, council of apprentices." Rory strolled up at the same time and held the tavern door open for them. "You three have any idea what this dinner's about?"

"Oh, sure," Zuri said. "The magic that fuels the core of the earth is dying."

Rory froze. "...Really?"

Zuri walked inside. "No."

The merchants had taken over one of the longest tables in the tavern, tucked away in a cozy, well-lit alcove. Nat arranged her seat so that her good ear faced Luka, Ambrose, and the troupe of bards performing on the other side of the tavern. Next to her, Luka watched the bards with a serene smile, his shoulders wound down for once. Music seemed to be the only thing that calmed him—and what drove so much of his work. After all, it was his enchanted, hand-carved flute that had first caught Banneker's attention.

"Thank you, thank you!" the bard finally called from the stage, bowing to the crowded tables. "We'll be here all through Spelltide!"

Luka gave them some quiet applause and reluctantly turned back to the table. Zuri passed him a basket of steaming bread rolls.

"So, when are you gonna go up and play for us like that?" she asked. Luka gave a small laugh and took a roll.

"Never." He passed the basket to Nat. "I don't need to play in front of people like that."

Nat frowned. "But you play for us all the time."

"Well, that's you. You're not..." He fumbled with his words. "You're my friends."

"I dunno. Those guys are friends with the whole bar." Zuri jerked her head toward the bards, who had joined the bar's patrons in their carousing. Laughing, swapping stories, clinking drinks together... Already, several people were batting their eyelashes at the musicians, jostling for more than just a chat. Nat took a piece of bread and rolled her eyes. That sort of flirtation was a dance she could never understand. The bards were pretty, sure, but in the same way Banneker's sketches were pretty, or crystals were pretty, or Luka's music was pretty.

"I don't think Luka wants to be in the middle of all that," she said, waving her butter knife at the bar.

"Doesn't mean he can't still go onstage," Zuri nudged Luka. "Come on, I bet you can do it. I'll even handle the costumes for you."

Nat snorted as she slathered butter onto her roll. "Costumes?"

"I've got a vision." Zuri pushed up her glasses. "Gilded instruments. Half-capes. Fully open shirt."

Luka blushed. "Um—"

"Sequins."

"I don't—I don't think I need all that—"

Nat laughed as she tried to imagine it: Luka standing up on stage, lute or lyre or flute in hand, winking and smiling at the crowd.

It didn't fit him. Of course it didn't fit him, poor Luka would have a heart attack in such a situation. But for a brief, vivid instant...he looked good up there. Really good. Like, her cheeks were growing weirdly warm sort of good. With Zuri's half-cape and the open shirt and the dimples that only appeared on his face when he smiled—

She quickly shook her head and stuffed her face with her bread roll. Stupid thoughts. She was probably just hungry.

"—Nat?"

She blinked at Luka, half a roll still hanging from her mouth. "Hm?"

"Can you sing?" he repeated the question, his words nearly carried off by the surrounding tavern chatter. "If Zuri's sending me to the stage, I can't go up there alone."

"Oh. I, um..." She swallowed the hunk of bread. "You don't want me up there."

Zuri pointed her fork at Nat. "Didn't answer the question."

"Really, I can't sing! You don't want me on stage with you, I'd ruin it."

"I don't know." Luka's voice went soft and low, and one of his dimples made an appearance. "I love hearing your voice."

The visions suddenly returned with a vengeance—of Luka singing not to the crowd, but to her from the stage. Cheeks pink from performing, hand outstretched, eyes wide and sincere as they looked down at her. He had such a beautiful voice, it would be impossible to hear anything else—

She resisted the urge to slap the giddy warmth out of her own face. This was *Luka*, her *friend* Luka. What in the hells did The Jumping Ogre put in their bread rolls—?

"Sorry, sorry!" Banneker slid into the final seat at the table. "My last customer wandered around for a half hour after closing and didn't buy anything. Classic." He took a mug of cider from Viola and downed half in one swig. "All right, what are we yapping about today?"

Grim cleared their throat, quieting the remaining table chatter and drawing all attention to them. Nat gladly took the opportunity to turn away from Luka.

"Thank you all for coming on short notice," Grim said gruffly. "Beake has an update on our"—their gaze shifted to the nearby tables —"dragon...statue...predicament."

Sherry leaned toward Rory. "I trust this can be off the record to avoid statue-related panic in the streets?"

Rory nodded, one arm draped over the back of Dawn's chair. "You got it."

All eyes fell on Ambrose, who sat ramrod straight in his chair.

"I'm afraid we must remove the statue more quickly than previously thought," he said carefully. "Its attempts to escape caused... certain unusual events yesterday. If it continues, I fear it will attract the wrong sort of attention from the societies near it. Above *and* below."

Nat shrank in her seat. She hated to think what Aphos—what Cassius and Madam Mila—might do if they decided Fio was too much of a threat even while trapped.

"I spoke with the Guildhouse about securing the ingredients I need for statue removal," Ambrose continued. "Unfortunately, there are no adventurers available until after Spelltide."

Eli leaned back in his chair. "So we're going ourselves."

"What?" Nat jolted back up. That wasn't possible. Did Ambrose ever actually leave the Scar? She'd never seen it, and he never talked about past vacations or trips. As far as she knew, the farthest he had been from home was...well, Aphos.

Not exactly an ideal getaway.

On the other side of the table, Dawn was just as slack-jawed. "Wait, *both* of you are going?"

"Yes," Ambrose said flatly. That didn't seem to clarify things for her.

"You." She pointed at him. "Ambrose Beake. Going on a quest."

Eli grinned and slapped his back; Ambrose merely winced.

"I cannot let Eli go by himself, and the ingredients are *extremely* specific." He sighed. "I must go along with him. We've planned the trip so it will only take a few days. We'll be back before Spelltide."

"Spelltide?" Banneker shot a pointed glance at Eli, who returned it with a short nod.

"We'll be back with time to spare," he said. "Nat will cover the shop, and Tom will provide her moral support." He grinned at Nat. "If Nat's up for it, that is."

If Nat could have gotten up and run a lap around the table, she would have.

Her? Being trusted to run the potion shop herself? Arranging all the shiny Spelltide displays, giving sage advice to big, important adventuring customers, brewing whatever she wanted—okay, maybe not whatever she wanted, but still. She could do this. She could truly be a part of Rosemond Street.

"I'll do it!" she said with a burst, then tried to reel herself back in. "I can cover for a few days, I can handle it."

But the rest of said street hadn't yet accepted the plan.

"What, just the two of you going into the Driftwood?" Sherry pursed her lips. "No, that simply won't do. Normal adventuring parties would have at *least* four people. You must take someone else with you."

"No," Ambrose said quickly. "Sherry, I will risk as few people as possible—"

Dawn's hand shot up. "I'll go!"

Rory's head whipped toward her. "You'll *what*?"

"We just booked our wedding venue, and Zuri's got the shop all prepped for Spelltide," Dawn said brightly. "And you were *just* telling me I should take a break."

"By break, I meant—you know, take a nice spa day, not"—Rory gestured toward the door—"run off into a dangerous forest!"

But apart from Ambrose, Rory seemed to be the only one against the suggestion to expand the party. Across from her, Banneker downed the rest of his cider and gave a hum. "Well, if you really need four people, it might be a good chance for me to field test my new hand cannon builds."

Eli's eyes flashed in excitement. "New builds?"

Luka froze. "You'd leave?"

"Only a few days, my guy." Banneker squeezed his shoulder. "I'll be back before you know it."

"No." Ambrose held up both hands, his face pale. "Dawn, Banneker, please—"

But the conversation had already spiraled out of control.

"If Banneker's joining you," Grim said, "I need to ensure he doesn't blow any of you up."

"And if Grim's going, I'm most certainly going," Sherry demanded.

"I'm packing your rations, then," Viola declared. "Good ones, too. Not those twice-baked rocks the Guild likes to call food."

Zuri held up a hand. "Can I come?"

Firm refusals resounded across the table.

"Well, that's it, then." Sherry cheerfully passed around a plate of crispy potatoes. "A party of six is far better than a party of two, don't you think?"

Ambrose got to his feet, almost knocking his chair to the floor. "Gods dead and alive, Sherry, if *all* of us are going, who's going to look after the whole street?"

The table went silent. The merchants blinked at each other.

Zuri raised her hand once more. "Hi. We're still here."

Zuri looked at Nat to second her motion—but Nat's thoughts were already barreling ahead. This was perfect. What better way to prove herself on the street than to run the entire place?

"Yeah," she said, then more eagerly: "Yeah! We'll cover all the shops for you!"

Luka now looked as pale as Ambrose. "Hold on, all of them—?"

But it was too late for his hesitation.

"We'll set up a rotation plan and cover them, half a day each," Nat said. "If you're back before Spelltide, we might not even need to restock before you return."

"But," Ambrose tried weakly, "but what do we tell the customers?"

Dawn waved a hand at that. "Short sabbatical. Half the nearby towns are hosting magic seminars for the festival. Just say we're at one of those."

Rory let out a breath and straightened. "All right, then. While you're off at your seminar, I'll keep an ear out for any whispers about the dragon statue. In cities above *and* below." She nodded to Viola. "Make sure the street's always informed with the latest."

Ambrose could only watch in defeat as the street planned the rest of his quest for him.

"Dude of brew'll need a way to keep Fio informed, too." Banneker tossed a bread roll between his hands. "Bet Luka and I can make an amplifier for that. You know, boost the psychic connection so it can cover the distance."

Grim nodded along. "Something flexible enough to work around the magic of the Driftwood."

Next to them, Sherry was already scribbling something on a napkin. "Before we go, I'll need to measure you all for armor. Ambrose might fit into some old leather pieces I have in the closet..."

The table buzzed anew, throwing around ideas on supply packs, rations, and sturdy boots. Nat high-fived Zuri and piled potatoes of encouragement onto Luka's plate.

Ambrose sank into his chair and set his face into his hands.

"I can't believe I'm saying this," he muttered, "but when can we all be ready?"

TIP 8:

THE EARLY BIRD GETS THE WYRM

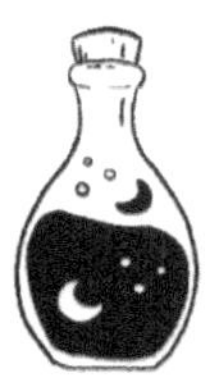

Ambrose

As Ambrose suspected, Fio didn't entirely understand nor appreciate the travel implications of a quest.

Leaving the city? the dragon repeated, his spines flared in confusion. *Now?*

"Tomorrow, if we can."

But you said you'd get me out with your potion—

"And I have to leave to find the potion ingredients," Ambrose clarified once more. "I can't make the brew until I get what I need from the Driftwood. I'll return in a matter of days."

Judging by Fio's narrowed eyes and downward-pointing ears, the term *potion ingredients* wasn't completely translatable through the astral magic that connected them—but he settled back anyway, his tail twitching over a puddle on the floor. *Fine. I will wait until then.*

But the dragon's rare moment of patience didn't last long. As Ambrose walked under his shadow, carefully counting his own steps to estimate the width of the cavern for Marlin, Fio watched him intently, his claws flexing with unspoken questions.

Are there other dragons near the Drift Forest? he finally asked.

"The Driftwood," Ambrose corrected. "And yes, I believe so." Not that he was particularly keen on observing such inhabitants for himself.

Then you can ask them if they've seen my family, Fio commanded. *They all have green scales like me. Longer horns, though. Bigger wings, too.*

Ambrose stopped walking. "Fio, I—"

But the dragon had grown excited over his own question, his tail now splashing in the puddle. *I look just like my father, you know. Except he has a broken horn on his left side. And my mother doesn't have any—* the word *iridescence* bloomed fuzzy in Ambrose's mind, a poor translation of Fio's intent—*on her right claw. And my sister, she—*

"Fio," Ambrose reluctantly cut in. "I'm afraid I can't talk like this to other dragons. Only you."

He braced himself for snarling or teeth, but received neither. Fio's ears simply drooped, and his tail slithered away from the puddle to curl against his legs.

Oh, was all Fio said. Somehow, Ambrose thought, he'd prefer the teeth.

"I'm sorry," he found himself saying. "But—but I can ask the other...two-legged creatures...if they've seen any dragons matching that description."

He turned on his heel and resumed measuring the length of the cavern, slowly making his way back toward Fio. The dragon set his great head on his claws, but didn't yet leave Ambrose in silence. *There are others like you in the forest?*

Ambrose fought not to lose track of his steps. "Certainly. And plenty of other creatures, too. Not that I hope to see them, you understand."

Fio hummed and narrowed his eyes again—but in evaluation, rather than suspicion. *You don't look like you'd taste very good,* he mused. *But other creatures will eat all sorts of things. You are taking guards of your own, aren't you?*

Ambrose bit back a smile. In a way, he was. Eli would most certainly guard him. Sherry and Grim would do an admirable job.

Banneker... Well, as long as his new cannons didn't backfire, they would be fine.

"I won't be going in alone." He stopped in the dragon's shadow. "Are you concerned?"

Fio huffed too quickly and flopped his tail over his eyes in feigned sleep. *Concerned I won't get my shrinking potion*, he answered.

When Ambrose woke, he brewed his tea extra strong and readied himself for quieter, more civilized company—but to his dismay, his customers relayed a similar sort of petulance.

"You're...going on a trip?" his first shopper repeated after he broke the news. "*All* of you?"

Ambrose couldn't claim he was surprised by his customer's... surprise. This particular patron was Gary, an archer who bought night vision potions every other week. He likely had never seen Ambrose take so much as a sick day.

"Merely a short sabbatical," Ambrose reassured him as he rolled his potions in paper, trying to sound casual. "We'll be back before Spelltide."

"But who's gonna run the shops?" Gary jerked a thumb toward Nat, who was cleaning a shelf at the back. "The kids?"

Ambrose sighed. "The *kids* are adults who are more than qualified to handle the shop for a few days. Now, if that's all?"

As soon as Gary left, Nat rolled her eyes and hopped off the ladder. "I don't care what discounts you set while you're out, that guy's not getting any." Then, in a low mutter: "Call it the asshole tax—"

"Nat."

"Sorry, Mr. Ambrose."

But reassuring his customers was far from the only task on Ambrose's list. At lunch, the rose statue on the counter pulsed with a steady white light, its message scroll filled with frantic messages about travel preparations.

Viola: I'm baking the rations right now!! Leave room in your packs!!
Banneker: I'm gonna need a second bag, these hand cannons aren't
all fitting as it is
Grim: We do not need hand cannons.
Banneker: well, my wheeled cannons aren't gonna fit, are they?

The conversations through the statue continued late into the night, until Ambrose could still see its white flashes when he closed his eyes. He tried to sleep despite the frenzy, but Eli barely bothered. The following morning, his side of the bed was cold already, and Ambrose wandered out to find him attaching a coil of rope to his pack while bouncing on his heels.

"Good *morning!*" He bounded up and kissed Ambrose's cheek, then pressed a mug of coffee into his hand. "Come on, everyone else is up already!"

While Ambrose sipped the coffee and blearily made scrambled eggs, Eli ran through every vial he had packed in their matching bags.

"I put in four different types of healing potions," he rattled off. "Then we've got invisibility, climbing, floating, fire-breathing—"

Ambrose looked up from the pan. "That one's experimental, why did you pack that—?"

Eli ignored him. "Psychic resistance, warming, cooling, hydration —okay, that's just water—and night vision." He fastened the packs and patted their tops. "Not that we'll need all that, of course."

Ambrose continued to stir the eggs, but he had little appetite for them. His mind kept brainstorming all the terrible ways he might actually need those potions. Falling off cliffs, wallowing in summer heat, getting lost in the forest in the dark of night—

Then Eli hugged him from behind and broke through his thoughts.

"Don't worry." He pressed his lips against Ambrose's neck. "I'll protect you out there."

Ambrose leaned back against his solid chest and closed his eyes. Of that particular fact, he had no doubt.

But even after the coffee and eggs, he couldn't summon half of

Eli's energy for the voyage. As a result, he was the last one to trudge out into the street, where everyone else had lined up in the cool morning air to receive Viola's ration packs.

"Biscuits for you!" Viola crammed a wrapped package into each of their bags. "Biscuits for you, and you..." Once she reached the end of the line, she raised a commanding finger. "And I expect you to *eat* all of them. No just taking one bite and calling it a day! I don't care how tired you are, you're gonna eat something on that trail!"

A weary chorus of *Yes, Viola* floated up into the air.

Viola's biscuits weren't the only handouts. Dawn had brought out a roll of wands, each bearing a uniquely painted handle, and was passing them out like peppermint sticks.

"I'm pink, obviously." She tucked the pink-handled wand behind her ear. "Banneker, you're red. Grim, you're purple. Eli, you're orange."

"What are these?" Ambrose asked as Dawn handed him the blue wand.

"Fireworks! Think of them like unique distress signals, in case we get separated."

Ambrose stowed his wand and quietly stepped closer to Eli. In a place like the Driftwood, he wasn't going to stray more than an arm's length from any of them. The soil would swallow him up otherwise.

By the time everyone had taken turns stuffing random bits of equipment into each other's packs, Rory and the apprentices had arrived to wave them off.

"Now, don't do anything *too* cool without me." Rory gave Dawn a long kiss and a crooked grin. "I'll get jealous."

"And don't pick the final cupcake flavors without me," Dawn countered. "I swear, if your cousin tries to slip tutti-frutti back onto the list—"

Rory held up her hands. "You'll never see a tutti-frutti cupcake again in your life, I promise."

While they kissed again and promised each other they'd stay safe, Banneker pulled Luka aside and unfolded a piece of paper.

"I took the liberty of writing down your horoscope for the next few days," he said, "since I won't be here."

"Mr. Banneker, that's very kind of you, but—"

"Ahem." Banneker cleared his throat and held up the paper. "It says..." He folded it back up again. "That you're the best apprentice to ever live and you're going to do just fine."

Luka went red and gave a nervous laugh. "Thank you, sir."

"Just remember your breathing exercises and to keep it simple. Only—"

"Only pick-up orders and waitlist additions." Luka nodded. "Understood."

Someone feigned a scoff at Ambrose's shoulder.

"Best apprentice," Nat muttered and elbowed him. "You gonna take that sitting down, Mr. Ambrose?"

Ambrose smiled. "If I inform Banneker he's wrong before we set out, he may turn his hand cannons against me."

"Fair point." Nat straightened. "Don't worry. I've got the to-do list and the stocking list and the cleaning list. When you come back, the shop'll be better than ever."

He didn't doubt her on that—but nerves overtook him all the same, and he turned back to The Griffin's Claw behind him. He stared at the paint around the door, already flaking after the anniversary coat. At the bright, clean windows, the perfectly organized shelves, the welcoming workroom door beyond.

He had never voluntarily strayed from the shop. Not once since his arrival in the city. The very idea of it closed his throat.

But he had to have faith—a little, at least—in his plan. In Rosemond Street. In Nat.

Eli squeezed his arm. "Time to go," he said gently.

Ambrose placed his hand over Eli's. "One moment."

He ducked into the shop, smoothed down his potion robes hanging by the counter, then picked up a parcel sitting next to them: layers of thick black cloth, carefully decorated with threads of gold and orange.

"Nat?" he called. "I have something for you before I go."

She jogged into the shop. When she stood before him, it occurred to him that he should have thought of something more profound to say in this moment. This was supposed to be a bit of a ceremony, after all.

"These are, um…" A knot formed in his throat. "I meant to give these to you on Spelltide, but I'd rather you have them now. I took care to make sure that these have the—the utmost of protective enchantments, because it is my duty as a mentor to—to…"

His eyes watered. He wiped them and held out the parcel.

"Your first official potion robes," he finished. "I hope you like the colors."

Eyes wide, Nat carefully unfolded them and held them out. The garment was similar in cut to Ambrose's, but embroidered in a wilder, more looping pattern, fiery colors against jet cloth with just a touch of shimmer. Nat slipped them on.

They fit perfectly.

"Mr. Ambrose, I…" She sniffed. "I, um—"

Something tapped against the glass behind her. She turned to find all of Rosemond Street watching them through the window.

"Oh, gods," Ambrose muttered and quickly pulled himself together. "Well, you have the discount notes?"

Nat hurriedly wiped her eyes. "Yup. Got 'em."

"And the keys?"

"And the keys."

"Right. Well." Ambrose gave her a short bow. "I'll be back very soon."

He walked out, shrugged on his pack, and began to follow Rosemond Street down the road. No use for emotions now. He'd just leave the Scar, run about the Driftwood, come back with some mushrooms, and—

"Wait, Mr. Ambrose!" Nat ran out of the shop, her new robes flowing behind her.

"Yes?" He turned around. "What is it, did I forget something—?"

She tackled him with a hug, arms wrapped tight around his waist.

"Please be safe," she said, her voice muffled against his vest. He set his jaw to keep himself steady.

"With this adventuring party?" he said weakly. "I could not possibly be safer."

TIP 9:

DON'T LOOK DOWN

Eli

ELI ADORED nothing more than Ambrose Beake—but if he were being honest, a close second would be the sight of the Scarrish airfield early in the morning.

To him, everything about it promised adventure. The ashy smell of dragon scales and their leather saddles. The misty silhouettes of the griffinkeepers getting ready for the day. Even the dewdrops sang of the journey ahead, paving Eli's path like tiny gemstones. He had to keep himself from running toward his mount in excitement. Taking flight, after all, was a close third to his love for Ambrose Beake—

But when he happily reached out to take the hand of his *first* love, he found only empty air beside him.

"Ames?" He stopped and turned. Ambrose had abandoned him several paces ago, staring stiffly at the griffin ahead.

"That?" he said. "We're taking *that* to the Driftwood?"

In Eli's professional opinion, *that* wasn't the proper way to address the lovely whippet griffin before them. The species was built just as narrow and quick as the canine they were named after, with long legs that made them tower over the bulkier cargo mounts on the field. Eli had organized three such griffins to bear them to the forest, and the others in his party were already boarding eagerly. Sherry and Dawn on a green-breasted one, Grim and Banneker on a proud mount with a purple sheen...

But Ambrose just stared at his griffin, his grip white-knuckled around his pack.

"I thought we were going over land," he said. "On a *horse*."

To be fair, Eli had informed Ambrose that he had arranged mounts for them. He had just...failed to mention the type.

"I promise you, this'll be faster and more comfortable than riding a horse." He grabbed two helmets from the stand by the griffin, then handed one to Ambrose. "Just put this on and follow what I do."

His love was not reassured; Ambrose remained where he was, frowning at the thick, paneled leather helmet in confusion. "Must I wear this?"

"You wanna squint into the wind and swallow bugs the whole day?"

Ambrose grimaced and put it on without further question. In the shadow of the leather, his unenthused blue eyes were almost luminous. Eli tried not to let it distract him as he checked the helmet's fit.

"Perfect." He patted Ambrose's cheek. "Very handsome."

The headgear muffled Ambrose's grumbling response. Eli chose to ignore whatever he had said and took his hand.

"Now, let me get you up in front so you understand what's going on. First, you approach from the griffin's right side..."

Together, they climbed a set of portable wooden stairs and slid onto the saddle, Ambrose seated in front of Eli. Ambrose glanced back at the stairs and immediately stiffened, both hands gripping the width of the saddle horn tightly.

Eli also tried not to let that particular pose distract him.

"It's all right," he said in a steady voice. "We're not going anywhere yet—"

"But it's quite..." Ambrose peered over the griffin's flank and swallowed. "Tall."

"Ames, we're only a few feet off the ground. You live in a chasm. You take the elevators almost every day."

"I live at the *bottom* of a chasm," Ambrose hissed, "and the *elevators* do not have wings or minds of their own—"

"Valenz?" Grim called from behind them. "We're about ready over here."

The griffin shifted under them in anticipation of a command; Ambrose yelped and held on tighter.

"Hey, hey." Eli slipped both arms around his middle. "Look, you're gonna be just fine. Just keep your shoulders over your hips and don't grip too hard with your legs. The saddle's enchanted to help keep you on. You feel it?"

He himself had grown accustomed to the feeling—the low thrum coming from the leather, quietly pulling him level on the griffin's back no matter the angle. After so many flights with his own party, the sensation was reassuring to him—but often unsettling for new riders.

"I feel it," Ambrose muttered, then after a sigh, quietly repeated Eli's instructions. "Shoulders over hips, don't grip with the legs..."

Eli selfishly let his hands settle on Ambrose's hips as the man shifted between his legs, telling himself that it was simply to steady his boyfriend and most definitely not feel every tiny movement of his body. When Ambrose finally settled, Eli kissed his shoulder and silently resolved to do far more than that once they reached the inn for the night.

"Very good." Eli squeezed the spot he had kissed. "We're almost done. Now you're gonna practice dismounting."

Ambrose perked up. "And then we'll take a nice carriage to the Driftwood?"

"Then you'll get back on with you behind me."

Ambrose deflated.

Once they were in the air, Eli had hoped he could point out some of the sights to Ambrose to distract him from his fear—but the whippet's famed speed and efficiency hardly allowed for it. The Scar retreated into the distance far too quickly. Lakes and rivers flitted by underneath them, barely more than sparkling stripes and specks against the hills. If he were with his own adventuring party, he might have guided them to lounge at one or two of the natural attractions. Checked for evidence of monsters, or caught up with other adventurers taking a break. But Ambrose's tight dragon-rescue schedule was too harsh for that, and after only a few brief stops to eat and stretch, they landed at an outpost just outside the Driftwood. In the setting sun, the forest itself stood in an ominous silhouette, its stark, shifting tree line looming on the horizon.

Not exactly a welcoming view for the start of their quest—but the other merchants didn't seem to care.

"That was amazing!" Dawn shrieked as she disembarked; within seconds, she had rushed up to Eli and was shaking his arm. "I could almost see all the way to Elwig Forest! And did you catch all those rivers we passed? They were so *gorgeous*—!"

Banneker and Grim passed by them, rambling at an equally fast pace. "I studied its wing movement the whole time, and I think I can replicate it in one of my whirligigs." Banneker waved his hands. "Just as a test, you know? I mean, the motion is incredible..."

Even Sherry was all smiles as she tugged off her helmet, her wispy gray curls flying every which way. "Well, griffin travel's sure come a long way since I last had to take one."

"How long ago was that?" Dawn asked.

"Oh, let's not get into all that." Sherry patted Ambrose's shoulder. "How did you like it?"

Ambrose pulled off his helmet, his expression and hair both utterly flat. "Where are we staying?" he asked briskly.

"Over at the airfield inn, the Tree and Feather." Eli pointed to the closest building. "The rooms are under Grim's name, since the innkeeper owes them a favor—"

"Excellent." He stuck his helmet on the post and strode off quickly. "I am never doing that again."

"Ames," Eli called after him with a grin. "How are we gonna get back, then?"

Ambrose didn't respond.

The following morning, the group gathered in Sherry's room to prepare for their venture into the forest—and whether Ambrose knew it or not, he wasn't done distracting Eli.

"Sherry, is this all really necessary?" he asked weakly as she pushed a bundle of clothing into his arms.

"Quite." She evaluated a bracer, then added it to his pile. "You're not conditioned to wear armor, but I'll be a hobgoblin's aunt if you wander into that forest without *something* on. Now go on, my dear— try it all out. Dawn, come along. You're next."

As Dawn eagerly hopped up and Ambrose shuffled off behind a folding screen, Eli raised his voice to address the group. He had promised he'd get them all into the Driftwood safely—and as he had often learned the hard way with his own party, safety began long before stepping outside the door.

"I lined up a wisp guide to Tolvale," he explained to the room. "He'll take us down the main forest path and right to the city. As long as we *stay on the path* and *stick close to the guide*, we'll be in Tolvale by nightfall and can start searching for the mushroom tomorrow morning."

Banneker nodded along with Eli's words and unfolded a pamphlet the innkeeper had provided upon their arrival. The paper was doused in colorful, magically copied ink, shouting the praises of various towns in the Driftwood. The city of Tolvale, naturally, was on the cover. Its expansive markets, tree houses, and dancing fairy lights made for a spectacular illustration to draw in tourists and adventurers alike.

"I have a few contacts from Potion Con in Tolvale's upper

markets," Ambrose called from behind the folding screen. "If they don't have the blue clay mushroom, we should be able to hire someone who can find it in the surrounding area."

Banneker slapped the pamphlet against his knee. "But I brought all my finding gear! Come on, where's your sense of adventure?"

"Back in the Scar, I'm sure," Grim grunted. "If we can make it easy on ourselves, we will. Upper markets are a good starting point, Beake."

"I've never been to Tolvale before," Dawn said brightly, lacing up a wandslinger's jerkin as if she were merely dressing for a nice day out. "Do you think I'll be able to find a good Spelltide gift for Zuri there?"

"Oh, absolutely." Banneker flopped so he hung upside down off Sherry's bed, still reading the pamphlet. "I already hid a stash of chocolate in the shop for Luka, but I was hoping to get him something in Tolvale, too. Something cool. Like a half trumpet, half harpsichord, half violin."

While he and Dawn debated the merits of such a monstrous instrument, Eli cracked open his own copy of the pamphlet and scanned the exaggerated description of Tolvale's attractions. Markets, gardens, town squares, all anchored within the shifting forest by magic. If Ambrose shopped in the upper markets for a few hours, Eli could likely do his own hunting for his proposal potion ingredients. He'd already secured lavender from the Scar, thanks to Nat, and he had bought a few bits and bobs himself. But he still needed a handful of forget-me-nots, and the Driftwood was known for its unique floral varietals. Surely, he could find what he needed here, then sort out a way to brew the potion back home—just in time for Spelltide.

Then he could finally, *finally* dig out that ring he had been hiding and get it on Ambrose's finger.

"Sherry, I am *loving* all this space for wands." Dawn twirled in her wandslinger outfit, poking at the array of loops sewn into the sides— then knocked on the folding screen. "Ames, how are you doing?"

Ambrose shuffled back out, his voice as monotone as Dawn's was bubbly. "Ready as I'll ever be."

When Eli turned to look at him, he immediately lost all thought.

Sherry had dressed him in gear fit for a field medic. Simple leather jerkin, a potion bandolier, bracers covering his slim forearms. As much as he might have disliked it, the ensemble looked good on him. Natural. Like he was strong and smart and could take care of Eli if he were ever injured on the field.

Eli's mind immediately dove into absurd fantasies. Of Ambrose hovering above him, pouring liquid onto his wounds, backlit heroically by the sun. Of his beloved boyfriend carefully wrapping his injuries, pressing his lips to his torn and bloody knuckles, cradling Eli's head just so as he leaned down for a kiss tasting of love and relief...

Ambrose approached him, the leather emphasizing his every movement in fascinating and infuriating ways, and Eli kept staring. Perhaps he didn't need to put together a proposal potion. Perhaps he could just ask the big question here and now. That would be fine, right? That wouldn't be weird at all—

"—Eli?"

Eli blinked. "What?"

"Could you help tie this, please?' Ambrose held out his unlaced bracer.

Several thoughts crossed Eli's mind. *It would be my honor* was one and *I should actually untie everything you're wearing* was another. Then he recalled he was both in a crowded room and on a deadline, and he yanked himself back to dull, unsexy reality.

"Of course." He cleared his throat and laced up the bracer with ease, not at all imagining tearing it off and kissing the wrist that lay underneath.

By the time Ambrose was fully dressed, Sherry had already thrown armor on the others—real armor for Grim and herself, and a few small metal pieces for Banneker—and was ushering them out like ducklings to go meet their wisp guide.

"Hey, you think our guide might want some extra cookies?" Dawn asked Eli, tugging a cinnamon-scented bag out of her pack. "Sherry put too many in my backpack."

Eli hid a grin. "That's a nice thought, but I don't think he'll take them."

"What do you mean—?" Dawn looked ahead and stopped. "*Oh.* I see."

The guide waited for them by the path at the edge of the forest, just as grumpy and impatient as all wisps generally were, in Eli's experience. He was little more than a sentient blue flame, a being intrinsically connected to the changing currents of the forest—and deeply tired of having to navigate through them every day.

"All here?" he said, his flame flickering impatiently as his voice manifested from nowhere. "Good. We'll arrive at Tolvale in eight hours, breeze willing."

Dawn looked like she had a dozen questions—but without further preamble, the wisp floated off into the trees, leaving them to scurry along behind him.

"Fine," Dawn whispered to Eli. "More cookies for me, I guess."

The wisp guide led them down the wide forest path in relative silence, too familiar with his surroundings to admire or comment on its beauty. But that didn't mean Eli couldn't take a moment to drink it in. At first glance, the forest appeared to be a beautiful, perfectly normal swath of deciduous trees. Flowers within the undergrowth bloomed in the summer sun, while heavy green branches formed a golden, dappled canopy above. And all around, scores of birds and bugs kept them company with their songs.

If this had been a normal forest, Eli would have tried to identify some of the birds, or rustle up a good story to tell about one of his past adventures in the Driftwood. But this was no ordinary woodland, and as soon as the canopy shadows deepened, he shifted to the back of the group and slipped into his training. He quietly tracked every movement, every shift in the restless forest. The magical presence of the wisp guide ensured that their path remained anchored in place, but farther off, Eli could see the natural currents of the forest changing its shape at will. Boulders shifted out of the corner of his eye; trees appeared and disappeared in a blink. Each movement was a constant, silent, dangerous reminder that for all the magic they could control and understand, there were forces at work here far beyond their current grasp of the science.

And ahead of him, Banneker couldn't get enough.

"Here, check this out." He nudged Grim and pointed to a watch-like device in his hands. "Absolutely no pattern in the readings. Can you believe it? Man, if I had just brought a few more of my things…"

He dug into his pack, and harsh clinking sounds filled the air. In other forests, Eli might have tried to silence him—but in a place like this, the loud sounds more likely chased off potential threats. Red-fanged deer, territorial Driftwood foxes…

Eli kept his eyes peeled for all of them, but his ears kept tugging back to a conversation starting ahead of him.

"You know…" Dawn glanced back at Eli, then slipped her arm around Ambrose's. "After all the earthquakes, I totally forgot to ask you about the Guildhouse. What did you think of the venue?"

Eli strained to hear Ambrose's response over Banneker's rummaging. A forest trail wasn't exactly a relaxed, gossipy lunch at The Gingersnap Cafe, but Dawn's words had been able to coax Ambrose out of his shell a hundred times before. There was no reason she couldn't work her magic now.

"The reception space, you mean?" Ambrose said. "Not that you need my approval, of course, but it was beautiful. I'm not at all surprised you and Rory fell in love with it." He gave her a small smile. "It's very you."

Dawn couldn't help but giggle and squeeze his arm—but she hadn't lost sight of her goal.

"Well, it helps that the event manager cut us a deal on that sweetheart balcony," she said. "Speaking of which…what did you two talk about?"

Eli made his footsteps as quiet as possible. He had no idea that Ambrose had spoken privately with the manager; he hadn't said a word about it.

And clearly, he wasn't planning to now, either. As soon as Dawn asked the question, his shoulders bunched up.

"Oh." His voice lowered, nearly muddled by the birdsong overhead. "She... It was nothing. Nothing interesting, anyway. Merely a question about the brochures on the table."

Dawn could sense Ambrose's discomfort. She quickly lightened her tone into faux loftiness, sticking her nose high into the air. "I see. For a moment, I thought you were trying to influence our event manager. Fix the cupcake draft in your favor, perhaps."

Ambrose laughed, and slowly, his shoulders rounded down. "Me? Stand between you and your cupcakes?"

"In pursuit of a free cookie?"

"As if Eli would ever let me eat a cookie without begging for half of it."

Eli gave a reluctant smile and drew his attention back toward the forest. Dawn's best friend tactics had been deflected—for now, at least. But she could always try again, perhaps when they were truly back in the cafe, plying Ambrose with all the cookies he could want.

The thought of cookies—and his ensuing stomach grumbles— kept him occupied until they were halfway to Tolvale, feet sore and backs hunched under their packs. They had stopped to nibble on Viola's rations, of course, but the open forest was no place to relax for long.

"How much farther to the next way station?" Grim called to the wisp guide as they checked the weight of their waterskin.

"A few minutes," the guide grunted. "It's just up ahead. We can stop there for a rest. A *short* one, mind you," he added haughtily. "When the sun sets here, it sets, and nighttime hazard pay is not something you want to add to your costs—"

Over to Eli's right, the trees shifted.

To the others, it may have seemed that the trees were always jostling a little, and that this particular movement was no different. But this change was far too close to the path—to the wisp's anchoring magic and the magic embedded in the road—to make any sense.

"Hold," he commanded. Everyone stopped in their tracks as Eli visually inspected every tree on that side of the path. Normal bark, normal leaves, normal teeth...Wait—

"Mimic!" he shouted. "Tree mimic!"

The wisp cursed and disappeared in a puff of smoke. The group immediately tried to huddle together—Ambrose to Eli, Sherry to Grim, Dawn to Banneker. Eli quickly shoved them apart.

"No, spread out! It'll make it harder to catch us—"

As if demonstrating his wisdom, the tree mimic lurched out onto the road and raised a long, branch-like claw above its conveniently clustered victims. This mimic had mastered the lock of a birch tree, with peeling white bark and yellow-green leaves poking out of its limbs—but the open, glistening maw splitting the trunk in half could no longer be mistaken for anything arboreal.

Rosemond Street shrieked and scattered just in time; the mimic's arm crashed onto the path in a flurry of leaves and dust. Eli leapt in front of Ambrose, every muscle tensed. He could keep them safe. He had trained for this, he had packed them all equipment for this. What did these sorts of mimics hate most? Lightning was too risky, as was the area effect of fire or acid. His hand whipped to the axe strapped to his belt. Classic and simple would have to do here—

"Keep scattering!" He held up the axe. "I'll scare it off!"

But over on the other side of the path, Banneker had other ideas.

"Wait, wait!" He scrambled in front of Eli, digging into his pack for something. "I've got a new hand cannon that could work for this!"

Eli froze. "Banneker, now is not the time to field-test—"

But Banneker kept going.

"It's a confusion ray," he babbled excitedly, affixing a copper contraption to his arm. "One blast and it'll send the big guy lumbering back into the forest! See?"

He aimed for the mimic, pulled on the copper lever—

And nothing happened.

"What the—?" Banneker pulled back his arm with a frown. "Hm. Okay, fascinating interaction with the forest magic. I gotta jot down the exact failure conditions—ope!"

The mimic lunged for the artificer; he leapt neatly out of the way. Eli rushed forward. Hand axes weren't meant for combat, exactly, but a few quick chops at the bark could be enough to spook the creature—

Sherry burst through the whirlwind of leaves with her great axe. Eli held up his free hand. "Sherry, it's okay, I've got this!"

"You get *away* from them!" Sherry brought her axe down with a mighty swing. Eli held his breath. The metal swooped and flashed in the summer sunlight—

And buried itself into the mimic's bark, sending chips of wood flying every which way. The creature roared and twisted in surprise.

"That's great, Sherry!" Eli shouted. "Now come this way, quickly!"

Instead, Sherry rested her axe on her shoulder and rubbed her hip.

"Gods above, I haven't made a swing like that in ages." She squinted through the leaves. "Grim, you packed those potions for my hip, right?"

Eli dove forward and yanked Sherry away from the mimic's next attack, only to get tangled in the creature's branches.

"No one else come near it!" he shouted desperately through the leaves whipping around him. "Just let me handle it!"

But Dawn didn't seem to hear him over the rustle of foliage.

"I'll save you, Eli!" In a panic, she grabbed at the first wand on her belt loop and pointed. "Get out, you freaky shrub!"

A burst of flames careened wide over the mimic's shoulder and whiffed into the sky.

"Not fire!" Eli hacked a branch away from him. "Dawn, we are *in a forest*—"

"Got it!"

She pulled out another wand. Lightning reeled past the creature's head this time, charring part of the canopy above it. Eli groaned and chopped faster. If he could just get free of these branches, he could land a good swing at the trunk and—

A meaty orcish hand reached in and yanked the branches apart.

"Grim!" Eli stumbled out into the air. Finally, a companion with some sense. "Look, if you still have that hatchet on you, we can take it on together—"

But Grim's attention had already snapped to something else. "Don't move, Beake!"

Eli held his breath and whipped around.

The mimic had ducked away from the smoking canopy and set its gaze right on the potioneer. Ambrose stood stock-still, eyes wide in fear. Eli's heartbeat roared in his head.

"Ames." He shifted his grip on his axe, taking slow, silent steps toward the mimic's exposed back. "Don't make any sudden moves—"

The mimic took one step forward, and Ambrose panicked.

With Eli hidden directly behind the creature, he made for the closest ally—Sherry, in this case—but his movement proved too predictable, and the mimic crashed its leafy arm directly in his path. With a yelp, he scrambled back and turned the other way, only to trip on a root. He flipped onto his back, the creature's black maw opening wide, dripping thick, sap-like saliva...

Then in a blink, he had sprung to his feet and sprinted into the trees.

"Ames, *no!*"

The mimic loped after, as if eager for a chase; Eli had no choice but to spew curses and follow both of them. There was no point telling the others to stay behind—they were all on his heels already, clambering through undergrowth, shouting after Ambrose—

Until the trees shifted before them, forming a jagged wall where the deer trail once was.

"Stay close!" Eli ordered, sweat trickling down his brow. They were all off the path now, and that damn wisp guide had run to save his own hide. If the mimic caught Ambrose before they did, it would run off with him, forcing them even deeper into the—

Blue fireworks appeared in a panicky splatter above the canopy. "Ames!" Dawn pointed. "Those are my fireworks—"

"Keep shooting!" Eli shouted, then followed the sparks as best he could. Over boulders, past a stream...

And onto another path, where Ambrose hung off the low branch of a tree, kicking sharply at the mimic.

"Don't you dare eat me!" he commanded. "The glass potion bottles"—another kick—"would be very crunchy—"

The mimic reached for Ambrose's leg; Eli grabbed the fire wand off Dawn's belt and shot.

The narrow blast of flame landed perfectly on the back of the mimic's head, setting the green leaves alight in a contained burst of red and orange. The creature shrieked and staggered away from Ambrose, instinctively raising its arms to its crown—then when its arms singed in turn, it retreated into the forest, toward the nearest stream. Within seconds, the trees shifted to close its path behind it, leaving behind only the scent of sap, a gauzy trail of smoke, and the distant sound of hissing water.

Eli let out a sigh of relief and handed the wand back to Dawn.

"Here, Ames." He stepped forward and held out his arms. "You can let go, I've got you."

He had imagined something like this being a little more heroic—Ambrose draped dramatically over his arms after a bard-worthy battle—but instead, his boyfriend dropped clumsily into his grasp, covered in leaves and spouting apologies.

"I know you told me to stay still, but that blasted thing was going to *eat* me—"

"It's all right." Eli set him down on the ground, then plucked a twig out of his hair and kissed his cheek. "That's why you've got me. It's not like you get a lot of hungry tree mimics coming into your potion shop."

Nor the wand shop, armory, jeweler, or artificer's atelier, judging by everyone's performance.

After making absolutely sure Ambrose had suffered no more than a scratch or two at the hands of the forest, Eli left Sherry and Dawn to fuss over him and turned to assess their new surroundings. The area beyond the clearing shifted and changed constantly, but their little meadow seemed relatively stable. After poking around in the brush, he found the reason why: an old path still clung to life here, bisecting the meadow in half. It was thin and scraggly, hardly more than a deer trail compared to the main path—but its soil must have retained a few anchoring enchantments, and that was what mattered.

"I'm not sure where this goes"—he toed the path—"but it'll lead to some sort of town. Follow me, listen carefully, and stay close. *Please*."

They continued walking for hours, tensing at every little sound and movement in the forest, until more structural silhouettes appeared on the horizon. A skewed chimney, a moss-covered roof... Eli quickened his pace. It wouldn't be Tolvale, that was for sure, but a nice village or a bustling town could likely direct them to where they needed to go—

He turned a corner and stopped in his tracks.

This was neither a nice village nor a bustling town. This was a single building—an ivy-covered, wattle-and-daub inn—that looked like it had been cobbled together by a toddler. The roof leaned left, the porch leaned right. The flagstones in the courtyard lay scattered, as if they didn't want to talk to each other. Even the gate that heralded the courtyard—clearly once a well-kept, artistic piece of twisted iron and stone—sat a little to the left, its pillar partially blocking the pathway.

This was a far cry from Tolvale. In fact, this was a far cry from anything else Eli had seen in the Driftwood. The place barely looked *anchored*.

But that didn't matter to the willowy man standing in the courtyard, wearing a checkered vest and beaming at them in delighted surprise.

"Oh! More friends!" He gave a little clap and spread out his arms. "I'm Chester. Innkeeper, birdwatcher, and pal. Welcome to the Skipwallow Inn!"

TIP 10:

TAKE INITIATIVE

Nat

FOR THE FEW hours that The Griffin's Claw was open, Nat couldn't get enough of running the shop.

Yes, the place did require constant attention. Handling the till, keeping the shelves clean, talking to customers, checking the supply closet...

But for those precious few hours, the potion shop was all hers. She was the one keeping it shiny and welcoming. She was the one answering customers' questions, suggesting options, showing off everything she had learned from Ambrose. As long as the shop was open, it was hers. Her work and her home—and her old life in Aphos was but a distant memory.

Then the rotation kicked in, and she was off to face the consequences of her own idea: joining the circus of other apprentices darting from shop to shop to cover the whole street.

Sherry had banned them from touching the forge, of course, so she headed over to handle the waitlist for helmets and greaves. Then across the street to Grim's to wrangle pick-up orders and deliveries.

Then the next day, it was back to The Griffin's Claw, the artificer's atelier, helping Zuri clean the wand emporium...

When she finally dragged herself back into the potion shop for lunch on the second day, the rose statue flashed white with a message. It had been recalibrated by Banneker to reflect the current communicators, and Viola made sure to keep that line of communication open every day, no matter how busy her bakery was.

Viola: How are we doing, everyone? Sound off if you're not dead.
Luka: I'm here! Thank you for checking, Viola!
Zuri: Alive.

Nat set aside her half-eaten sandwich and scribbled out her own response.

Nat: I think this sandwich bread is the only thing keeping me going right now.
Viola: Knew you'd like it. You need more, just come on by.

Nat had initially assumed her lunch breaks would be a quiet, relaxing reprieve from all the chaos—but instead, she found herself hugging Tom and watching the striped rock next to the statue in tense silence. Ambrose had set up the speaking stone just before he left, promising daily updates on his progress. But there had been no updates yesterday, and none yet today. If her estimates were right, they'd be in Tolvale by now. Probably headed to the fancy tree markets or something. It should be easy for him to activate the speaking stone, right? Give a quick call, reassure her none of them had died—

The bell above the door jingled. Nat leapt a foot off her stool, and Tom went leaping with her.

"Sorry, sorry!" Rory held up her hands. "Just checking in."

Gods, how many people who weren't Ambrose were going to check in on her today?

"I've got my sandwich," she replied dully. As if to reflect her mood, Tom wheeled back and wearily plopped down next to the stool. In response, Rory held up a bag of greasy goodness.

"And I've got your snack." She tossed a bag of garlicky roasted almonds on the counter. "Any word from our daring heroes?"

Rory tried to make the question sound casual, but Nat could see right through it. Dawn was out there, too, after all. Rory must not have received an update from her, either.

"Nothing yet," she said, restraining herself from diving right into the almonds out of stress. "I know Mr. Ambrose said not to call him, but—"

The speaking stone rippled to life, light running along the rock's wavy striations. Nat lunged for it, nearly knocking over the rose statue in the process. "Mr. Ambrose?"

"Sorry, gremlin, it's just me," Eli responded.

Well, that was all right—Ambrose never strayed far from Eli.

"Are you in Tolvale yet?" she asked. Eli cleared his throat.

"Not...exactly. We got a little sidetracked, but I think we can make it work."

"Sidetracked?" Rory leaned over the counter. "Is Dawn with you?"

"Of course! She's fine, I promise. See?"

"Hi, Rory!" Dawn called more distantly. Rory's shoulders rounded down in relief.

"Dawn, what happened?"

"We almost got eaten by a—"

"*Hey*, hey, we're all good!" Nat heard rapid footsteps, as if Eli was hurrying away from the others. "Real quick, Nat—do you know if variegated forget-me-nots grow in the Skipwallow area of the Driftwood?"

Nat pulled out her map from under the counter, stored there so she could peruse it multiple times a day. She had just learned about forget-me-nots from Ambrose: they were typically used for perfume and memory potions. Neither brew was a favorite of the shop's adventuring clientele, but Ambrose had still taught her where the ingredients grew naturally.

"Northwest?" She squinted at the map. "Uh, I think so. They

should grow all around the Driftwood, especially in the unanchored places."

"Good, good."

She looked up from the paper. "Wait, what the hells is a Skipwallow?"

"That's what I'm gonna find out." Eli paused, then his voice returned. "Okay, bye! Talk later!"

"But—!"

The lines on the speaking stone went dull.

"Ugh." Nat tossed it back onto the counter, then shoved a handful of roasted almonds into her mouth. "Won't tell me anything."

"I'm sure they'll call back when they're settled," Rory tried, but something in her voice was also on edge. "How's the shop been?"

"Fine."

"Even with the quakes?"

Nat shrugged. Despite Ambrose's plea to Fio, the dragon still seemed to be causing one or two quakes each day. She couldn't bring herself to be upset with him, not even a little bit. She knew being trapped in Aphos sucked.

Part of her wanted to sneak over to the cave opening and wave down, maybe throw him a snack—but then she recalled that she'd be waving down into Aphos, to a dragon who had no idea who she was, and thought better of it.

"I've got the shop handled," she said. She had to. She was part of the street now, and anyone worthy of being on the street should be able to handle this sort of thing.

But Rory didn't seem to share her confidence.

"Remember, it's not like Aphos here. It's okay to ask the others for help." She peered over at the to-do list sitting next to Nat's half-eaten sandwich. "If you're underwater, you've got Viola and me and Zuri and Luka—"

"Yeah, sure, I'll ask 'em," she said quickly, folding up her list before Rory could analyze it further. "I talk to Zuri and Luka all the time."

The journalist leaned back, a different sort of smile slowly crossing her face. "You know, Luka's a real nice kid."

"Yeah, he's a good friend."

Rory just stared at her, smile unmoving. Nat sighed. Not this again—Dawn had done this last week.

"What? He's a *good friend*! I don't like people like that." She shoved her to-do list under the counter. "Most of the time, at least."

Before she could defend herself further, the message statue flashed, and she yanked open the scroll.

Luka: I'm closing for lunch. Is anyone else around?

Nat grabbed her bag of almonds and pushed past Rory. She had to tell Luka what Eli had said, anyway. "Gotta go, thanks for the almonds!"

"Wait, what are you—?"

"I'm telling my *friends* that our bosses got lost!"

She shoved another handful of almonds into her mouth as she strode over to the artificer's atelier. Rory and Dawn had it all wrong. Zuri was a friend; Luka was a friend. Best friends, actually, and she was quite proud of that fact. Friendship of any kind had been hard to come by in Aphos.

Not that she hadn't tried, of course. One needed allies down there. But as soon as she considered someone a friend, then thought that maybe, perhaps, there could be a spark of something else if the friendship deepened—

The backstabbing would surface. Or the gossip, or the snitching, or whatever else was required to preserve oneself against her old boss, Cassius. Then that tentative spark would vanish, and so would the friendship.

Nat shook her head and opened the door to Banneker's shop. No point in over-thinking all that, anyway. She had actual friends now, and it was easy to wave away the rest. All that romantic nonsense about love at first sight, mooning over strangers—that was just for books with bare-chested men on the cover. Never mind how Rory and Dawn had met or whatever. Banneker had the right of it: romance, shmomance.

"Luka?" Nat called, her voice bouncing around the vaulted ceiling. "How are you doing? Eli called!"

In response, music drifted in from the far corner of the shop—a shadowy back section, tucked away behind crates and cannons.

Nat picked her way over to the corner. Ever since Luka had moved onto Rosemond Street, this little spot had been exclusively his. Over the past two years, he had gradually filled it with instruments, both functioning and broken. Nat had watched him revive over a dozen such devices, selling some, keeping others. The one he played on now was a horizontal row of thin little blocks, each one connected to strings hidden inside a polished wooden box. Luka called it a harpsichord. Nat had never seen one in Aphos—it looked terribly unwieldy. Not something a bard would ever want to drag down into the tunnels.

But here, the vaulted ceilings gave the sound new life. Luka barely touched the blocks and they sang for him, forming a melody Nat had never heard before. Not that that was uncommon—Luka rarely played with sheet music, opting instead to experiment with the notes and find the song for himself. According to Banneker, that was part of how he had found Luka in the first place: sitting in a little seaside inn, improvising music on an enchanted flute he had carved himself.

He hadn't yet noticed Nat's arrival, so she quietly took a seat on one of the crates and watched him play. Every now and then, he'd reach up and test a knob on the box, or a button, or a switch. Each one made the sound float a little differently. More echoey here, more muted there. But none of the little enchantments could impede with the beauty of his music.

Sherry had once lovingly compared him to a little bird—attentive, soft, the prettiest song. Nat had never gotten much experience with birds while living underground, but from what she had seen of them up on the surface, she could imagine it. Everything about Luka seemed feather-soft. His hair, his expressions, the way he set his hands on the instrument. Almost like he was apologizing for bothering the keys, then gently coaxing the sound out of them.

For a brief moment, she forgot all about Eli's call. And the bag of almonds in her hand, and her long to-do list sitting back in the potion shop. She just watched Luka's movements, wondering absently what his touch would feel like against her hand. Would it be like touching feathers? Or would she even feel it at all—?

The music suddenly stopped; she jolted as if being woken.

"Oh, Nat!" Luka brightened and pulled his hands off the keys. "I'm so sorry, I didn't hear you come in. Are you terribly busy?"

She shoved aside the strange thoughts about his hands and held out the bag of almonds. "Nah, I'm never too busy to visit. Want some?"

He took the bag and carefully poured some of the treats into a napkin. "Have you gotten many customers today?"

"Loads. You?"

"Too many, if I'm being honest." His brow furrowed. "A few demanded answers about the quakes. Tourists, mostly. I had no idea what to tell them."

"I know what to tell them." Nat crunched on an almond. "You tell 'em to come over to me and I'll show them where they can stick their demands."

Luka laughed, his brow smoothing back out. "I don't think Mr. Ambrose would like that."

"Mr. Ambrose isn't here to complain about it." Nat tried to shift the conversation back to something that relaxed him. "I liked the song you were playing. Do you think you'll write it down?"

"Oh, no." Luka folded up the napkin. "I don't think it was good enough. If it's worth playing again, it'll come back to me later."

Nat rolled her eyes. That was always his response.

"Well, I enjoyed it. It was"—she paused to pick through the almonds with the most garlic dust—"it was soft."

Luka tilted his head. "Soft?"

"Yeah. Soft like you." Nat froze—did that sound bad? "I mean, soft like birds! You know, like—like feathers? I mean—"

Her cheeks blazed with heat—gods, what was she even saying?— but across from her, Luka simply laughed.

"I'll accept soft," he said, his voice as gentle as the notes he had played. "Thank you. And thank you for visiting." He paused. "Perhaps I'll need to make a song that sounds like *you* next."

His eyes crinkled with his smile, and a fluttery warmth spread in Nat's chest. She had never gotten anything like that in her old life.

Before she could come up with some casual response, worry crossed Luka's face again. "Has Mr. Ambrose called, by any chance? Did they all make it to Tolvale?"

The words were a cold bucket of water on the nice warmth she had just been feeling.

"Not exactly." She sighed and headed over to Banneker's rose statue. "Hold on—I should get Zuri over here first."

She scribbled a quick message on the scroll at the base of the statue.

Luka: ZURI, COME OVER, LUKA'S HARPSICHORD IS SUMMONING DEMONS — Nat

Moments later, Zuri appeared at the doorway, soup bowl in hand, utterly unfazed. "What's up?"

Once Zuri was settled on a stool—Luka quickly handed her a napkin before her soup dripped on Banneker's floor—Nat ran through Eli's paltry update. No, their bosses were not in Tolvale. They were in Skipwallow, wherever that was. Eli had *said* everyone was fine. Nat definitely doubted that.

"Skipwallow..." Luka repeated. "I've never heard of it. Do you think they need any supplies? Should we try to send them something?"

Zuri snorted. "With their luck, the shipment would get sidetracked and end up in Tolvale. But they brought plenty of stuff. They should be—"

The bell above the door tinkled. Luka quickly jumped to his feet and brushed crumbs off his apron; Nat stood, ready to tell off the customer for interrupting his lunch.

"The sign says—" she began, then quickly swallowed the rest of her words when she saw the newcomer. "Oh. Um. Mayor Rune?"

The mayor looked almost as befuddled as she did. His gaze wandered over the whirligigs by the ceiling and the wheeled cannons on the shop floor. When he caught sight of the apprentices, he cleared his throat and regained his mayoral posture.

"Afternoon," he said, his voice gravelly. "I am...seeking a device."

Luka hurried behind the counter and opened an oversized catalog. "Of course, sir. I can help you find anything in Banneker's inventory or write up a custom request if we don't have what you're looking for."

Rune blinked at him. "Is Banneker not in today?"

"Not today." Luka gave him a queasy smile. "But—but I assure you, I can assist with whatever you need."

Rune gave a slow nod and looked around again. "I was going to ask about a device that can track...well, ogres, perhaps."

Luka flipped through the catalog. "Ogres...perhaps?"

"Or trolls." Rune bit his lip. "Or rock movement?" He waved a hand. "Anything that might be causing these quakes. I have a duty to ease the minds of the city and our visitors so close to Spelltide."

"Oh! I see." Luka flipped through the catalog with a shakier hand, not meeting the mayor's gaze. "Banneker doesn't have any creature-tracking devices on hand, but I'm sure I could...adapt one of his general tracking devices in storage. As for rock movement, that would have to be a separate device. But if you allow me a few days, I'm sure I can, um, tinker with—"

"No, no, that's all right." Rune's gaze had already turned to the street. "I'll try Grim. They might have something more immediately in stock."

Luka swallowed. "I'm afraid Grim's out as well, sir. But I can—"

"Out as well?" Rune frowned. "What about Mr. Beake?"

"Not available today," Nat said quickly.

"Ms. Kerighin?"

Zuri slurped her soup. "Away."

Rune's frown deepened. "What, all of them? Where are they?"

"Short sabbatical," Nat cut in, parroting the words they had been instructed to tell the customers. "At a magic seminar up north in Remington. But they'll be back soon!"

"Well..." Rune wiped his hands on his robes in thought. "Remington is only a day's ride. Call them back today, then. Inform them this is an urgent request directly from the mayor's desk."

Nat froze. The little white lie had worked for all her other customers—but apparently not the mayor or his desk.

Over by the counter, Luka had gone pale, and his hands shook as he closed the thick catalog. "Well, you see, um—"

He glanced over at the other apprentices in fright, but Nat's thoughts were already sprinting for a cover. Mayor Rune was the last person Ambrose would want to tell about the dragon underneath the city. If there was even a sliver of a chance Rune wouldn't let Fio live, they couldn't risk it.

"You see," Nat began loudly, searching for a lie. What else did the mayor care about? What else might distract him? Oh, of course—

"We can't call them back just yet," she declared. "They're out... getting something together for Spelltide."

It worked; Rune lit up.

"Really?" he said. "For the magic demonstrations?"

Nat swallowed. "Yup. Those. For sure."

"Well." He rubbed his hands together in delight. "Do you know what they have planned?"

Zuri gave Nat a warning look and elbowed her, but Nat was too far in now. The merchants had trusted her with Rosemond Street, hadn't they? She could handle this tiny issue.

"Something special!" she said. "That's why they've been so...secretive about it. Didn't want to spoil the surprise."

Rune hummed. "I've never seen Rosemond Street participate in Spelltide's opening demonstrations before. Incredible—I'll have to add them to the attractions list." He turned to Luka and gave a perfunctory bow. "Do check Banneker's storage and contact me if any of his devices match my request. I will see what else I can do in the meantime."

He swept out as quickly as he had come in, striding on to other mayoral tasks. Zuri and Luka turned to Nat.

"Something special?" Zuri repeated flatly. "For Spelltide?"

Luka ran both hands through his hair. "But they all just landed in the middle of *nowhere*. What if they're not back in time for the festival? Rune will see right through it and demand to know where they are, then I'll get fired and Banneker will lose his shop and all of Rosemond Street will—"

"Will be fine." Nat held up both hands. "They'll be fine—because we're going to figure this out."

TIP 11:

FIND ALLIES

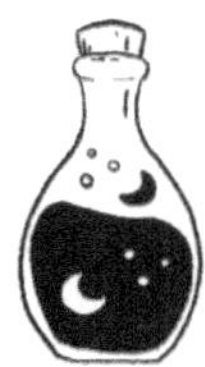

Ambrose

AFTER TAKING three steps into the Skipwallow courtyard, Ambrose understood why this inn hadn't made an appearance in the Driftwood's advertising pamphlet.

The lopsided building couldn't have been further from Tolvale if it tried. It wasn't built gracefully into the trunk of a tree, nor did it have string lights drifting gently in the breeze—unless one counted the dead branches hanging off the roof. It simply squatted in the clearing, quietly ready to crumble in several different directions at the slightest provocation. The only piece that seemed remotely well-kept was the statue in the middle of the courtyard: a metal platypus standing on its back legs, surrounded by broken stones, weeds, and a single, sagging bench.

Dawn tilted her head at the display. "A, uh...a platypus?"

"Ol' Skipwallow himself!" Chester the innkeeper bounded up to the statue, his orange hair flopping over his forehead as he went. "He houses our anchoring mechanism."

He lovingly patted the statue's bill; something rattled within.

"He's been working like a charm for five years and thirty-three days now," Chester continued brightly. "Except for, um, a small incident last week."

Given the state of the place, Ambrose could distinctly imagine what had happened last week.

"Of course, y'all aren't the first *drifters* to come to my town." Chester elbowed Dawn, thoroughly amused at his own turn of phrase. "Nor the last."

As he led them up the creaky porch and into the inn, they found their fellow drifters: waylaid merchants, adventurers, and musicians, all having claimed various corners of the inn. Off to Ambrose's left, a pair of bards tuned their instruments in the light of the hearth. Over to his right, a trio of tinkerers had set up a card game, trying to ignore the fact that their table floated in three separate pieces.

"That's why the Skipwallow Inn's here, after all." Chester proudly set his hands on his hips. "To catch the unlucky folks in this part of the forest and send 'em back out with the next wisp guide."

Eli perked up. "You get wisp guides here? Do any of them go to Tolvale?"

"Sure, sure." Chester kept his lanky, leisurely pace to the front desk. "Plenty."

He began flipping through a logbook; behind him, a lovely painting of a meadow creaked and tilted.

"Are there any guides here now?" Sherry asked nervously.

"Oh, no," Chester replied, his tone unerringly cheerful. "Not for another week or so."

Ambrose's grip on Eli's hand tightened.

"A *week*?" He leaned toward Eli. "What if we just walked to Tolvale ourselves? Surely there's another anchored path that goes there—"

"Oof," Banneker cut in with a grimace, tapping a second wrist device strapped to his other arm. "Given the season and the alignment? That'll take at least four days."

Ambrose began to sweat under his leather jerkin. "And you're quite sure we can't teleport out?"

"I don't have anything calibrated to Tolvale." Banneker shrugged.

"A few other cities in the south, but nowhere that would save us time."

Ambrose hurriedly dug into his pack for his map of the Driftwood. He couldn't spare four days on simply walking. He hadn't even prepared Nat for a trip longer than four days. Gods, he hated this forest...

He unfolded the paper and held it against a splintery wooden pillar positioned by the front desk. His markings for the location of the blue clay mushroom were more densely concentrated near Tolvale, yes—but he had drawn a few smudged Xs near the pinpoint that was Skipwallow. If he found the mushrooms here, there'd be no need to hike to Tolvale at all. Then all they'd have to do was...find a way out of the forest.

"Are there any foragers staying here?" he pressed. "Anyone local who might know where to find Driftwood potion ingredients in the wild?"

Chester slapped his logbook shut with a grin. "Potions! Why, yes, as a matter of fact, one of our current guests is a potioneer. Got sidetracked on the way to Leaf Harbor and will be taking the next wisp guide out that direction. Come along, I'll introduce you two!"

Ambrose could have melted with relief as Chester handed Eli a few room keys and led them all upstairs with a bouncy gait. Another potioneer, stuck here with them? If they were local, there was a small chance they could have some of the mushrooms in their own supply. Ambrose hadn't brought much coin with him, but he could surely figure out how to barter for it—particularly if the potioneer recognized him from Potion Con. Perhaps he'd even met them before, at a panel or a demonstration. How wonderful it would be to have a friendly face in an inn like this—

"Pardon?" Chester rapped smartly on a door, this one actually aligned within its frame. "I've got a—"

An annoyed sigh cut him off from within the room. "I already said, I have no desire to join your ghastly fireside singalongs—"

The door swung open, and there stood Xavion Demachel.

If it hadn't been for their unmistakably haughty voice, it would have taken Ambrose a moment to recognize them. Gone were the gauzy, sparkling robes and gold sheen of make-up over their cheeks. They were dressed for travel, not Potion Con—and their travel experience had clearly gone as well as Ambrose's. The hem of their coat was spattered with mud and rips, a layer of road dust hid the flashy embroidery on their tunic...

And their expression was both parts disbelieving and mortified.

"Beake?" they said. "What in all the fiery hells are *you* doing here?"

"Think we just walked into a fiery hell," Eli muttered to Dawn. Ambrose was inclined to agree. A friendly face, godsdammit, he had asked for a *friendly* face.

"I—I could ask you the same," he shot back, holding himself together with the mental equivalent of twine and glue. "It seems neither of us is where we want to be."

Beside him, Chester merely beamed.

"Looks like you two already know each other!" He slapped Ambrose on the back. "Well, I'll just be moseying along to check on the guests downstairs."

"And we'll check out our rooms," Dawn said quickly, glancing between Xavion and Ambrose. "Let the, uh, potioneers talk."

"Talk?" Xavion recoiled. "Excuse you, I will not be *talking* to this nincompoop—"

But Rosemond Street was already hurrying away behind Dawn, save for Eli, whose hand lingered against Ambrose's in a silent question. Ambrose shook his head, and after a warning glare to Xavion, Eli followed the others.

Ambrose turned back to his professional rival; they stood there for a silent moment, glaring at each other, both covered in dirt and dust.

Finally, Xavion shifted uncomfortably. "I won't tell anyone at Potion Con if you don't."

Curiosity got the better of Ambrose. "What sent you here?" he asked. "Red-fanged deer? Cairn cat?"

Xavion scoffed. "As if I would be waylaid by anything so inconsequential."

"Tripped over a root, then?" Ambrose tsked. "In your home forest, too—"

"My home forest treats me far better than it treated you. Clearly, it has good taste."

"Then why do you have a leaf stuck in your hair?"

Xavion instinctively raised a hand to their head; when they found nothing, they scoffed and turned on their heel, their traveling coat doing a poor job of twirling in their wake. "Good *day*, Amby."

They started to close the door, and for a moment, Ambrose willed it to close faster, to cement his small victory—then recalled that Chester had brought him here for a reason.

Xavion was a potioneer. Xavion was native to the Driftwood. Xavion would, unfortunately, know what to do about the blue clay mushroom.

Ambrose set a hand on the door before it could close.

"Wait," he said wearily. "Chester brought me here for a reason. I have a…question about a rare ingredient. A valuable one."

That last addition was the right move. A flash of intrigue crossed Xavion's face, and after a moment of thought, they opened the door once more.

"Fine," they said. "You have ten minutes of my *valuable* time."

Ambrose tentatively stepped inside the room. Judging by the set-up within the cottage, Xavion was continuing his work for the tour even while stuck in the inn. A tiny cauldron bubbled in the fireplace, while stacks of magazines, signed and unsigned, took up the desk.

No rest for the wicked, he supposed.

"I won't waste your time," he said, remaining close to the doorway. "I'm searching for a large quantity of fresh kaolin agaricus saphira. The Scarrish markets had none, and I couldn't send any adventurers to fetch it for me."

The intrigue on Xavion's face muddled into confusion. "Blue clay mushroom?" they repeated. "Valuable, certainly, but I can't imagine it's worth an excursion yourself. What on earth are you using it for?"

"I..." Ambrose stopped. "I can't tell you."

Xavion rolled their eyes and sighed. "Amby, you came to me—"

"I didn't come to you," Ambrose hissed. "I was led here by—by a *birdwatcher*—"

"Whether by choice or by fate, you are now seeking my wisdom." Xavion reached for their supply cabinet, then paused to glanced over their shoulder. "Which is infinite, by the way."

Ambrose snorted.

"And I happen to have a dried sample with me," Xavion continued, plucking out a small vial of shriveled blue discs. "If it is at all helpful to you."

Ambrose tried to look disinterested—but it would indeed be helpful to him. Banneker had said he'd brought his tracking materials. If he could use the dried sample to find a path to fresh mushrooms...

"Perhaps," he hedged—but Xavion wasn't fooled.

"Then I shall make you a deal," they said. "I will most generously bestow upon you this sample if..."

It was Ambrose's turn to roll his eyes. Between Nat and Xavion, he was never going to escape these deals.

"*If*"—Xavion handed him a piece of paper—"you agree to write a quote for my next magazine article."

Ambrose balked. He had been prepared to pay an absurd amount of talons or split the foraging with Xavion.

But a blasted *quote*?

"And say what?" he demanded. "Shall I sing your praises?"

"To the heavens, ideally."

Ambrose scoffed as he scanned the handwritten paragraphs on the anti-gravity properties of griffin feathers. Xavion didn't need his praise for this article—they had enough fame and followers for that. No, this was a blatant attempt at humiliation. At proving something to all the Potion Con readers who had ever watched them debate. All of Ambrose's hard-won victories against this fool, muddied by a coerced magazine quote...

The dragon, he staunchly reminded himself. There was a dragon under the city and he needed those mushrooms yesterday.

"Fine." He clenched his jaw. "I'll do it. I'll use your dried sample to track down where it grows."

Xavion shook the vial with two fingers. "How adventurous of you, Amby. Do note the silt saurians this time of year."

"Silt saurians?"

"Your adventuresome beau would call them mudmires."

Ambrose shifted. He wasn't familiar with them, but after the tree mimic, he'd already had more than enough of Driftwood's flavor of danger. "Are they dangerous?"

"Only when they're not sleeping."

"And...are they sleeping now?"

"Gods, no. It's mating season. I wouldn't take a single step away from the path this time of year." Xavion dropped the bottle into his palm with a mock smile. "Do try not to die. I'm afraid your death would quite overshadow your illustrious quote."

Ambrose folded the map with a sharp gesture. "I will take that into consideration. Do you require the quote now?"

"Please, take your time with it." Xavion wandered back over to their cauldron and gave it a stir with a smug, satisfied grin. "After all —it's not like you're leaving anytime soon."

As Ambrose stalked out of Xavion's room, he soothed himself by imagining all the possible misfortunes Xavion could come across in the Driftwood once they left the inn. Perhaps their next wisp guide would lead them straight to a mudmire. Or that burned tree mimic his party had faced. It would be both angry and hungry, at this point. Perhaps still aflame! That would be a nice touch—

Something gently tugged on Ambrose's arm and nudged a piece of metal against his fingers. He jolted and looked down—there was suddenly a rusty key in his hand, placed there by a...wooden stool.

An automaton, he realized. A stool with legs that bent in odd ways, and ropes that levitated to form arms. Just like Tom, it didn't have eyes, but someone had pasted pieces of paper with crudely drawn circles on the edge of the stool as an approximation.

Chester whistled from downstairs. "Heckley! Here, boy!"

The automaton's drawn eyes stared at Ambrose for a moment, then it scuttled down the stairs at an unnerving, spiderlike pace. Ambrose swallowed and decided that he vastly preferred Tom to... whatever that thing was.

Before the inn could find new ways to be unsettling, he took the key and slipped into room four, where the others had already laid out their speaking stones. With everyone talking over each other, Ambrose had to take a moment to recognize the voices on the other end of the devices. He immediately relaxed upon hearing Nat demanding details of their journey. Zuri made a dry comment now and then, and Luka whispered in the background. Then there was Rory asking after Dawn, Viola asking after the rations, and a new voice somewhere in there—

"And how's our Fio doing?" the voice said.

Ah. Marlin.

"I must say, this is all very exciting," the dragon expert continued, sounding like he was bouncing on his heels. "I've told the other folks at the foundation—bending the truth a bit, of course—and they are simply over the *moon* to meet Fio! We're setting up a habitat for him using the data you've sent so far, Mr. Beake. We've got a nice, mossy bed for him, and a huge pond, and a—"

"We appreciate your attention to detail, Marlin," Sherry gently cut him off. "And I'm sure Fio will be just as excited to meet you."

She glanced over at Ambrose, who grimaced.

"We'll bring him to you as soon as we can," he said, trying to sound positive. "I was able to secure an opportunity from an... associate."

The words tasted sour, but he continued with them anyway, explaining his plan for the dried mushroom samples and the threat Xavion had warned him of.

"Mudmire?" Nat repeated. It sounded as if she was standing at the front counter of the potion shop; her voice bounced against wood. "What the hells is a mudmire?"

Grim leaned against the wall of the inn, their expression darkening. "Not exactly something we want to see in person."

Next to him, Eli grunted in agreement. "If we can't handle a tree mimic, there's no way I'm taking anyone up against a mudmire."

"Cart before the horse, my dudes," Banneker said, hanging upside down off the bed. "Now that we've got a sample of the shroom, I just gotta hook it up to my gear and track down where it grows. It might not be anywhere near those mud guys."

"How long will that take?" Zuri asked. "Not sure if Nat told you, but Fio's still doing jumping jacks down in Aphos."

Ambrose groaned. Of course the dragon hadn't listened to him.

"Apologies, I thought I had gotten through to him. I'll try again tonight."

So long as Banneker's astral amplifier worked. Ambrose rubbed his forehead. As if he needed to amplify a dragon admonishing him for being too slow with his rescue...

But while he worried about what the night would bring him, Luka's worries projected further ahead.

"So...." Luka ventured, his voice warbling out of the speaking stone. "Spelltide is only six days away. Will you still be back by then?"

The whole room winced at that—especially Eli.

"I don't see how we can be." He ran a hand through his hair. "Even if we find the mushroom tomorrow, we'll have to wait for some sort of wisp guide to lead us out of here. If Chester was telling the truth about their arrival, we'll..." He slumped. "We'll still be here at the inn on Spelltide."

Everyone protested at that, but their dismayed words couldn't magically summon a solution. Ambrose grabbed a scrap of paper from his pack and scribbled down what he recalled of his shop's inventory. It was only enough to cover a few more days, as he and Nat had planned. But to have her run the shop—no, not just the shop, the entire *street*—on the biggest and most magic-related holiday of the year? His apprentice was going to need an apprentice at this rate.

He reached for the speaking stone to talk to Nat, his palms sweaty —but Dawn snagged it first to do some damage control of her own. "Zuri?"

Judging by the shuffles and bumps heard over the speaking stone, Zuri was wrestling the speaking stone from Nat.

"Yes, captain?" she finally said.

Dawn straightened, her gaze firm. "You're the wandmaker now. Keep the target practice loft closed to customers, don't bother restocking the upper back shelves, and just churn out those sparkle wands like we practiced." She gave a commanding nod to the stone. "You've got this, soldier."

"Aye-aye, captain."

Dawn tossed the stone to Banneker next, who bounced it in between his hands a few times before talking. "Luka, you still there? Haven't run away yet, have you?"

Judging by Luka's wobbly tone, the poor young man could have been halfway out the door. "Still here, sir."

"Glad to hear that. When you're back in the shop, go check the left closet door in the workroom. There's enough inventory and cleaning spells to last..." Banneker checked the freckles on his wrist. "Two weeks. I made sure of it. You're all set, no extra work needed."

"Really, sir?"

Everyone else in the room stared at Banneker. Banneker stared back at them. "What?"

Sherry set a hand to her chest. "Banneker, you *planned*?"

"Why, is that weird?"

While the others recovered from their shock and Ambrose tried to grab the stone from Banneker, he caught snippets of Nat and Luka whispering to each other.

"See? Banneker said you're all set!"

"No, it's not that. What do we do about the mayor and the—?"

"Decorations for the street?" Nat finished loudly, drowning out the rest of his question. "I'm sure we'll figure something out. Grim did leave the boxes of decorations in their shop, after all."

They spent another hour passing the speaking stone back and

forth—first, to Ambrose to plan a minimal re-stocking list with Nat, then to Dawn to discuss wedding invitations with Rory, then to Marlin to finish describing Fio's new habitat. As Marlin waxed poetic about all the pools he had dug and the moss he had gathered, Ambrose glanced over at Eli. He was still slouched against the wall; Dawn offered him a sympathetic smile and squeezed his hand.

"It's all right. We can figure out an alternate—"

Eli quickly shook his head. "I know, I know."

Ambrose stood to join Eli at the wall and gently pry into the matter—but Banneker tapped him on the shoulder first.

"Hey, I got that amplifier for you," he said, digging into his pack. "Let me show you how it works."

The artificer took his time setting up the oil lamp-esque device on the nightstand, showing Ambrose the ins and outs of the settings: activated, deactivated, and highly unnecessary options to project star shapes on the ceiling or the sound of ocean waves toward the bed. By the time he had made Ambrose pick the colors of the stars—blue— and calibrated the ocean sounds to his preferences—silent—nighttime had fully blanketed the Driftwood. Fireflies drifted eerily between the black trees, while crickets chirped into a low, continuous symphony. After the others left for the night, Ambrose took a moment to stare through the window, at the utterly foreign surroundings. Eli had once said the sounds and sights of the forest were peaceful—but all Ambrose could think of were the monsters shifting somewhere out beyond the fireflies. His window back on Rosemond Street never promised anything scarier than mail-delivering dragons and the occasional pickpocket.

He tapped his fingers against the windowsill. He shouldn't have done this—planned this ridiculous quest, only to get thrown off course, put everyone in danger, ruin the festival for everyone. Ruin the festival for *Nat*.

He could only rip his eyes away from the midnight silhouettes when Eli gently pulled on his wrist. "Bed?"

Ambrose closed the curtains against the view and turned back to Eli, who seemed as quietly unsettled as Ambrose felt: his reassuring smile didn't quite meet his eyes, and his rumpled tunic didn't sit right on his shoulders.

"Are you all right?" Ambrose asked.

"Yeah, I'm fine," Eli said too quickly. "Just thought we'd be back in time, you know?"

Ambrose tilted his head—he knew Eli had been excited about Spelltide, but not *that* excited. But before he could open his mouth to ask about it, Eli yawned and pulled him close. "Come on. Time to get you into bed."

Eli's hands tightened around his waist. Ambrose stiffened. He knew this particular move. "No, wait—"

Too late. Eli picked him up, whirled him around, and tossed him onto the bed—then, as if subduing a baby griffin, he wrapped the duvet around Ambrose and shoved a pillow under his head.

"Okay, good night!" Eli made an exaggerated snuggling motion on the other side of the bed. Ambrose's helpless grin was hidden by the pillow.

"Eli!" He tried to move his arms; no use. "Release me at once!"

"Excuse you, I'm trying to get some sleep."

"Elias Valenz—"

"All right, all right!" Eli unwrapped him until he was settled under the covers as normal, staring up at the glowing blue stars Banneker had provided. "Goodnight, Ames."

He leaned down and gave him a soft, lingering kiss. A goodnight kiss—perhaps one of Ambrose's favorite kinds.

"I demand another one," Ambrose said, his command losing all its teeth in the faint light of the stars. "For accosting me."

Eli's eyes went dark, and his goofy grin shifted into a knowing smirk. As he bent down to bestow another kiss, he ran his fingers along Ambrose's scalp, gently coaxing him into relaxation until he had melted into the pillow.

"Another?" Eli murmured against his lips. Ambrose ran his hands along Eli's back, closing his eyes against his comforting weight. Now it truly was far too late; Ambrose couldn't move—and even if he could have, he wouldn't have done so for the world.

"Please," he murmured. "As many as you can give."

———

When Ambrose finally closed his eyes, he clustered at the edge of the bed, as close to Banneker's amplifier as he could. But there was no need—as soon as he fell asleep, the magic device caught onto his astral form like he imagined a net entangling a fish, pulling and tugging against the normal current of sleep to drag him into the desired dream. Not that he minded the visit tonight—when the cavern finally appeared in his mind's eye, the striped Scarrish stone on the cave was welcoming in its familiarity.

And, oddly enough, so was the dragon.

There you are! Fio jumped to all fours—a motion far less sluggish and unconcerned than Ambrose expected. When Ambrose blinked up at him in surprise, Fio quickly settled on his back haunches. *I...see you made it through the forest unhurt.*

Ambrose didn't much feel like correcting him on that point. "Only a few bruises to my dignity," he muttered. "But yes, we're all unhurt."

One of Fio's ears pointed upward. *Did you see any other dragons on your way there?*

The hope in Fio's words drew a solid, steady line to the fresh claw marks around the hole above him.

Ambrose swallowed. "None, I'm afraid. The skies were clear the whole way there."

Skies? I didn't know you could fly.

"No, no—we rode on griffins."

Rode? Fio's ears flattened once more, and his next words came as a disgusted mutter. *Can't believe there are creatures out there that will let humans ride on them. Like those twiggy little animals that like running about the plains. What are those called—*

"Horses?"

Yes. Fio's tail twitched. *They don't taste very good.*

Ambrose raised an eyebrow. "Yes, well, with all the jumping

you've done recently, I'm sure you've chased all the unpleasant horses away."

Me? I didn't—!

Ambrose didn't blink. Fio eventually lowered onto his front paws, not meeting his gaze. *I only jumped a little.*

"We already established you won't be able to fit—"

I know, I know.

Ambrose hid a smile. In that moment, he sounded very much like Nat.

"All I ask is that you save your energy for the rescue and"—he glanced back at the blocked tunnel—"stay quiet so your neighbors don't catch on. Now, do you mind extending your wing as far as it can go? Marlin requested I do my utmost to measure your wingspan for the habitat he's building for you."

With an indeterminate grumble, Fio reluctantly extended one wing to the far wall, allowing Ambrose to approach the expanse of moonlit scale and membrane. He expected Fio to remain surly and silent through the inspection—but instead, the dragon bent down his neck to better see Ambrose while he worked.

This habitat Marlin is making for me, he said. *What exactly is it?*

"It's your own place to stay," Ambrose said, trying to channel Marlin's upbeat tone. "Your own home—"

But Fio's lip curled.

My own home? he repeated, the spines on his neck flaring up. *I had a home, and the humans down here kept me from it. Why can't I just go back?*

Ambrose stumbled on his response, forgetting where he was in his measurements. "Well, there are...quite a few humans up there as well. Would you like to live with them?"

Fio shuddered, and the spines on his neck flattened back down.

Fine. What is Marlin putting in this habitat, then? He folded one paw over the other, his tone haughty. *He doesn't even know what my favorite moss is.*

"On the contrary. He's stocking it with twenty types of Scarrish moss."

Hmph. And how thick will it be? My younglings always needed thick moss. They were so clumsy at flying.

Younglings blurred in Ambrose's head—a word imperfectly translated. Ambrose straightened in confusion.

"Fio, you've had children?"

Children? Fio repeated, as if that word had also transferred poorly. *No, not mine. The younglings I guarded. They were my responsibility as a novice.*

Ambrose wanted to ask more about these younglings—but Fio had already barreled forth, eager to pick out more flaws in Marlin's plan.

And this Marlin probably hasn't thought about waterfalls in sinkholes, has he? For baths and such? I don't even know if humans bathe. Some certainly smell like they don't.

Ambrose brushed aside his complaints—thankfully, it was getting easier to do so with every visit—and leaned forward to inspect the thickness of his wing membrane. Up close like this, Fio seemed more vivid. Ambrose could count the subtle swirls of color in every scale, feel his warmth pulsing underneath...

And a pool doesn't count as a waterfall, Fio said loftily. *They are very different things, as I'm sure you know.*

But Ambrose was too distracted to respond to him. That warmth coming from the scales—he shouldn't be able to feel that sort of energy, not in his astral form. And he certainly hadn't felt it on any other visit. Was there anything different tonight? He was in the Driftwood, he had no sleeping potion—

And he had Banneker's amplifier.

While Fio continued railing against the shallowness of ponds, Ambrose stepped back and extended his hand to the closest trickle of water down the cave walls. Yes, there it was. Coolness, a fine spray, and the distinct slip of water down his fingers. Banneker's amplifier had not only connected him to Fio across a great distance, but it had solidified his presence here. He could feel the mist, the stream, the slippery rock behind it...

He turned back to Fio's wing in curiosity.

Though I suppose a waterfall spilling into a pool would be acceptable, Fio said, now half ranting, half thinking aloud to the moon above. *A pool surrounded by moss.*

Ambrose took a breath and slowly reached out his hand again. Fio likely wouldn't feel a tiny touch, but if he could test it out, just once...

Soft moss, mind you. I'll need somewhere nice to rest after a good bath—

Ambrose set a light finger on Fio's wing.

As soon as they touched, the dragon sprung into the air on all fours. When he landed, every scale and spine had flared, and he held his wings high in surprise.

What was that? He looked wildly around him. *A bug? A rat?*

Ambrose reeled back, both hands raised. "Apologies, it was me!"

You?

Fio retracted his wings and circled him, blocking out the moonlight. Ambrose had nearly forgotten how large he was and stood stock-still while he moved.

But you're not here, Fio continued. *Not really.* He stopped lowered his head until his large eyes were level with Ambrose's. *Aren't you?*

Fio hadn't been this close to him since he had snapped his teeth right in his face—and those teeth were only inches away now. In the face of them, Ambrose forgot how to breathe. Surely if he could touch Fio, the opposite was now true. What if the dragon decided to eat him after all? Would he just disappear from the bed next to Eli? Oh, gods, what if he only ate an arm or a leg—?

Fio inched even closer, his hot, moss-scented breath now blowing over Ambrose's hair. Ambrose screwed his eyes shut. This was it, this was the end—

Fio set his head down on the floor right in front of Ambrose.

This scale right here. Could you scratch it?

Ambrose opened one eye. "I beg your pardon?"

Fio huffed. *Middle of my nose. If you're really here, I thought you could help. But if you can't—*

"No, no, I, um…" Ambrose shook off the vivid thoughts of his untimely, bloody death. "I can help. I think."

He tentatively reached out toward Fio's snout. Every instinct in him screamed to do the opposite, to draw his hand away from the giant maw that could take his fingers in one bite. But Fio merely watched him move, and when he carefully scratched the scale in the very middle of his nose, a great thrum rippled just under the dragon's skin, low and steady and content.

A purr, he realized. Fio was purring.

Ambrose throat's tightened, though not with fear. Under his fingers, Fio felt both incredibly powerful and terribly young. The vibration of the purr alone was strong enough to shake the ground under his feet—but here Fio was, eyes closed to a human, enjoying the first friendly touch he might have felt in years. Decades. A century, even, after only six years of being alive—

But the purr was over as soon as it had begun. As soon as Fio's itch was sated, he pulled away, quickly trying to adopt the stance of a dragon that hadn't just asked for help from a lowly two-legged creature.

That was it. He folded his wings in tight, his voice wound tighter. *Thank you.*

"Of course." Ambrose cleared his throat. "And…if you're that insistent on a waterfall, I'm sure I could make a request of Marlin. I think he'd be happy to provide one for you."

I appreciate the thought, but that won't be necessary. Fio's words grew distant once more. *I shouldn't have asked about it. My family would never let me stay there anyway. They'll take me somewhere far nicer.*

He glanced up at the hole, his ears briefly drooping. The purr still lingered in Ambrose's palm, the echo of its vibration cracking his heart further.

"Yes." He gave Fio a weak smile. "I'm sure they will."

TIP 12:

COVER YOUR PARTY

Nat

THE DAY after Rosemond Street's terrible tidings, the apprentices gathered in the loft of Dawn's wand emporium. Zuri had wand gems to charge, and according to her, she wasn't about to let Nat's improvised scheming get in the way of her to-do list.

"It'll be fine," Nat tried to reassure her as she helped spread out the crystals on the table. On the other side of the table, Luka spluttered.

"But we promised the mayor—the *mayor*—something we don't have!" he said, holding on to Tom like an emotional support pillow. "He'll be expecting our bosses at the festival with something magical and big—and we don't have any of those things!"

Zuri picked up her charging wand and waved it over the crystals. "He's right, you know. We're screwed."

"We're not—"

"Nat?" Rory's voice floated in from the front door, urgency tinging the single word. "You in here?"

Nat didn't exactly want to say yes, but Rory was already halfway up the steps to the loft.

"Just spoke with someone from the mayor's office," she continued. "Getting quotes about Spelltide attractions. Why"—she set a hand on the top stair post—"is the mayor saying that Rosemond Street is bringing something special to the festival?"

Luka gulped; Nat froze.

"That...isn't in the paper yet, is it?" she asked warily.

Rory folded her arms. "It's printing right now for tomorrow's issue. What's going on?"

As Tom leapt out of Luka's arms and wheeled over to Rory to greet her, Nat's instincts told her to remain tight-lipped. Don't admit anything, ever, even on pain of death—

Rory raised a brow. Nat threw up her hands in defeat.

"Fine. The mayor came into Banneker's shop wanting to figure out the cause of Fio's earthquakes. When he told us to bring the merchants back to help him, I covered, okay? I said they were out getting something special for the festival."

Rory stared. "But they're not going to be back in time."

"I didn't know that then!"

"And you don't have anything to bring—"

"I know *that*!" Nat huffed. "Look, I just didn't want him finding out about Fio. We can figure something out."

She'd been in worse situations, she told herself. The entirety of her time in Aphos, for example. She'd come up with a way out of all this and Rosemond Street wouldn't have to worry about a thing—just like she had promised them.

Rory passed a hand over her face. "I...*appreciate* you trying to cover. I'll see if I can help, but I don't know if I'll have the time. I'm trying to make sure Aphos isn't making any moves toward Fio." She handed Zuri a bag. "And here. Dawn ordered me to get you provisions for the business hours ahead."

Zuri paused, wand balanced delicately between her fingers, and peered into the sack. Nat got a whiff of candy—the chewy, sour kind from Elwig.

"Provisions received." Zuri took the bag and resumed her wand charging. "I will survive the winter."

Luka nervously straightened the line of gems for her. "Does it look like Aphos is planning something?" he asked Rory. "Against Fio, I mean."

"Eh. Lotta talk, no action yet." Rory shrugged. "Pretty typical. Just means I'll need to keep listening in on their chatter. Might need to ask Viola for some disguise cakes. Make my way into a few other Aphosian taverns to get the good gossip..."

If it weren't for the whole Aphos part of things, Nat would have eagerly volunteered to join these outings. She had wanted Viola to bake her some disguise cakes ever since she learned they existed. To go around for a day looking like someone else entirely...

She almost dropped the last gem in her hand.

"Disguises," she blurted out. "Rosemond Street won't be back in time for the festival—but we can pretend like they are."

Zuri looked up. "What, you mean disguise ourselves to look like our bosses?"

"Just for a few hours!" Nat scrambled for a Spelltide brochure on the table. "The magic demonstration is in the afternoon, right? All we have to do is disguise ourselves, roll in for the event, and run back out. We can even come back to the festival later and enjoy it just as ourselves once the magic's faded away."

Luka paled. "No. No, we can't." He looked to Rory for moral support. "Right?"

But he had looked to the wrong person. Rory—a woman who scuttled around criminal hideouts for fun and profit—tilted her head and considered the idea.

"Look, if it keeps Mayor Rune from asking any more questions about Rosemond Street, it's not the worst thing in the world. And if it's really just for an hour or two..."

Zuri reached for her wand notes. Her journal was neater than Dawn's, but given the number of tabs and extra notes she was already adding, it was only a matter of time before it rivaled her mentor's falling-apart monstrosity.

"I think I can make us some disguise wands," Zuri said as she flipped through the pages, eventually landing on a blueprint. "Yeah, here. I've made a few with Dawn before."

"But the enchantments won't be in a controlled environment," Luka tried to counter. "How will it interact with all the other magic at the festival?"

"It'll be fine if I build it with the right type of handle."

Luka fidgeted. "And you're certain we can't just tell the mayor that our bosses...fell ill?"

"You heard Rory." Zuri gestured to her. "The news is printing as we speak. If we pull out now, the mayor will ask why."

"Violently ill, then," Luka pressed. "Contagiously ill."

"What, and have to close the shops?" Nat said. "The merchants want the shops open and the mayor wants some magic. We can do both." She did her best to give Luka a confident smile. "Do you trust me?"

He let out a long breath, then steadied himself and nodded. "I trust you."

Together with Rory, they slowly pieced together what sort of magic they would debut at the festival. The display couldn't be just any old cantrip. It needed to be *big*—big, impressive, and quick. Just a short dazzle, then they'd scurry off stage.

They finally settled on the Whirling Winged Griffins: a mash-up of their three shop names. They'd present a flurry of griffin illusions that squawked, sparkled, and felt soft to the audience's touch. It was what Banneker would call a heavy illusion—three components in one, each of them contributing a part—but it was the sort of thing the audience would expect from Rosemond Street.

"Well, it's only our jobs on the line if we fail," Zuri said, gathering up her charged gems. "I'll get going on the disguise wands."

"And I'll work with Nat on the griffins," Luka said quickly, then went pink. "If—that's all right?"

Nat grinned. "Of course. Zuri, we'll bring a test over once we've got our part nailed down."

Rory stood and made for the stairs. "And I'll tell Dawn next time I—"

"No!" Nat scrambled to her feet. If Dawn knew, she'd tell Ambrose, and Ambrose would never agree to something like this. Her mind spiraled thinking about what his reaction might be. What if he got upset? Refused to teach her level-five potions? Told her she could never run the shop again—?

"Don't tell her yet," she continued, her throat tight. "I...I want to make sure we have a working prototype first."

Rory's eyes narrowed. "You want me to lie to my future wife?"

"Not lie! Just...um, not...say anything about it yet. There's a difference."

Rory tapped her fingers on the railing. "Nat, they've got to know sooner or later."

"Yeah, of course." Nat tried to sound nonchalant. "After the test."

TIP 13:

NEVER TRAVEL WITH A BARD

Eli

THE MORNING after the speaking stone circle with the rest of Rosemond Street, Banneker wasted no time in turning the inn's courtyard into his new workshop.

"So if I set it up like this, and feed it this paper..." He shoved a map under a whirling maze of gears and copper bits, half overshadowed by the Skipwallow statue. "Hand me the little shroom guy?"

Ambrose handed over the glass vial from Xavion. Banneker plunked it into a metal slot with a satisfying clink, then stepped back.

"And there we go!" He pushed his goggles to his forehead, revealing pink imprints around his eyes. "This'll grab the essence of the sample, search for a match in the area, and draw out where it is on the map. Dawn and Grim helped get it going." He rapped his knuckles against the platypus statue. "Amped up the power, too, to work around ol' Skipwallow's anchoring magic."

Both Ambrose and Eli tilted their heads to assess the contraption before them. Eli couldn't pretend to understand even a quarter of what Banneker had built; most of it looked like its primary function was to spin and emit steam while incidentally moving a pencil around a map.

But this mess of a device was their best shot at safely finding the mushroom—so Eli grabbed his own copy of the Driftwood map and began to follow along with the crooked gray line it was drawing.

The map Chester had provided was tiny—after all, he could only reliably track what remained anchored in the area—but thus far, the pencil seemed to be wiggling somewhere north of the inn. Eli marked the spot on his own map with charcoal. Good—it wasn't too far away. He could do his due diligence before risking the others' necks out in the forest again. Scout out the area, check for monster tracks, curate their supplies—

Someone crouched down next to him. "What's this thing drawing?"

On Eli's other side, Ambrose barely suppressed a sigh.

The newcomer was one of Skipwallow Inn's current residents—one of a pair of bards. For once, Eli couldn't begrudge Ambrose his dismay. He had met more than his fair share of bards along the road with his adventuring party. Good bards raised one's spirits. Gave one courage for the road ahead, or a welcome distraction when failure struck.

These were not good bards. And the only thing worse than a bad bard...was a bored bard.

"Doesn't look like it's drawing a mushroom," the crouching bard continued, while her partner lounged under the Skipwallow statue with his lyre. "Looks like it's drawing a..." She tilted her head. "Half note."

"No sheet music here!" Eli said quickly. "Just, uh—tracking some mushrooms out in the wild. For foraging."

Over on the ground, the lyrist brightened and strummed a jarring chord.

"Oh, no," Ambrose mumbled under his breath—but it was too late.

"Going on a hunt for a mushroom!" the bard warbled loudly. *"Better be careful around their...fumes!"*

A few other guests lounging about the porch wrinkled their noses and hurried inside. Over in a secluded corner of the courtyard, Xavion rolled their eyes and kept reading their magazine in the sun.

Eli winced and tried to return his focus to Banneker's device. The pencil had veered west, then south, headed right through a smudged icon on his map: a guard tower. Likely ruins, given the population of this part of the forest, but any kind of landmark would be better than wandering through the woods. Landmarks meant anchored paths, possible signage, maybe even other foot traffic to help deter wildlife...

"Ames, you see this?" He waved Ambrose over and pointed to the smudge. "Looks like there's an old tower over here. If it houses some sort of garden or grove, it's possible the mushroom is growing somewhere close to—"

"*Sneaking through the forest gloom!*" the bard proclaimed, every note flat. "*Better hope you don't meet your doom!*"

"Darling," Ambrose muttered. "Please take your dagger and kill me."

If Eli was going to murder anyone here, it would not be Ambrose —but Chester didn't give him the chance.

"Doom? Who's singing 'bout doom?" He made his cheerful way toward the statue, his voice muffled by the bunting loaded up in his arms. "Why don't we get a happier song going? It's almost Spelltide!"

Chester wasn't alone in bearing decorations—Sherry, Grim, and Dawn walked out behind him, each carrying banners and bundles of flowers. Heckley the automaton trailed after, his rope arms dragging across the grass.

"We're...decorating the inn now?" Ambrose asked.

"My dear, it's only five days until Spelltide, and poor Skipwallow here doesn't have a lick of festive cheer on him." Sherry smiled, fully bought into Chester's attitude. "If we're going to be here for Spelltide, we might as well make the most of it, don't you think?"

"Oh, we'll do our darnedest, Miss Sherry!" Chester piled on, tossing bunting haphazardly over the metal platypus. Once he appeared satisfied with the lopsided paper triangles, he hopped up onto the bench, his shadow falling directly over Eli's map.

"Uh, Chester?" Eli squinted at the pencil hidden under Banneker's machine. Had it gone east or west? "You think you could gussy up the platypus some other time—?"

A shrill bird call jolted Eli, Ambrose, and the nearby bards. Eli looked up—Chester had paused in his decorating. He held a telescope in one hand and a bird whistle in the other, his gaze focused on a few bright specks crossing the clouds.

"You see those?" He pointed cheerily. "Our first harbingers of Spelltide!"

The others in the courtyard—save for Xavion, of course—eagerly clustered around Chester to stare up at the specks: the first aurocs of the northern migration.

"These early birds'll be first to shed their ice and first to grow it back up in the mountains," Chester said proudly. He blew the bird whistle once more, but the aurocs made no response. "Would love to get one of them to roost near the inn one day."

Next to Eli, Ambrose was still rubbing his pointed ear against the grating sound of the whistle. "Aren't they rather...large?"

Eli gave a quick glance up at the clouds before moving his map back into the sunlight. Ambrose wasn't wrong; the distance made them look like hawks, but on the ground, they were almost as large as griffins.

"Oh, they're gentle giants." Chester waved a hand. "Wouldn't hurt a firefly."

Next to him, Banneker nodded sagely. "They've got great auras."

One of the lines of bunting fell across Banneker's device; Ambrose flicked it away. "Are you all quite done with your decorating—?"

"Oh, that's right!" Chester hopped off the bench. "Not nearly done, sir. Dawn, Grim, if you could help me with these bouquets?"

A pang went through Eli as pops of color slowly appeared all throughout the courtyard. Sure, he was up for making Spelltide fun no matter where he was—but he couldn't propose here, could he? In the middle of a dangerous forest, far away from almost everything

Ambrose found comfort in. He couldn't do it. He didn't even have those forget-me-nots he needed for his proposal potion.

His chest feeling like sludge, he tightened his grip on his charcoal and tried to track the map line once more. For some reason, the pencil was still moving, slowly headed south. He'd have to ask Banneker what it meant—multiple sources of mushrooms, perhaps, or some sort of triangulation—

Next to him, Ambrose suddenly stiffened.

"You're getting married, you say?" The second bard brightened as she hung out with Dawn by a lamppost. "What's the lucky beau's name?"

"Rory."

"*Dawn and Rory!*" The lyrist strummed. "*A legendary love story!*"

Dawn giggled and continued gossiping through the music; the bard mercifully cut into the next jarring chord with a gasp.

"The Scarrish Guildhouse? Are you truly getting married there?" She clapped in delight. "My friend played there for a wedding once. Said it was the most beautiful place she'd ever seen. Tell me, what will you be wearing?"

The lyrist cleared his throat. "*Full of love and glory—*"

The first bard lightly slapped his knee. "Stop it, Jerry." He turned back to Dawn. "I hear flower crowns are traditional in the Scar, are they not?"

"My mom preserved hers," Dawn said proudly. "So I'll be wearing that for the ceremony."

"*A wedding so very flory!*" Jerry desperately tried. In a quick, jerky motion, Ambrose got up and left the device.

"I'm going in for a nap," he muttered. "Feel a headache coming on."

Eli somehow doubted that. He hesitated—the pencil marks were slowly drifting south, closer to the inn—but Grim just strode over and took the charcoal and map from him.

"You go on with Beake," they said quietly. "I'll keep an eye on the tracker and tell you when it's stopped moving."

"Thanks, Grim." Eli jogged after Ambrose in relief. "Ames, I'll go up with you!"

He followed Ambrose up the stairs to their room. Once inside the inn, he could no longer hear the bard's warbling, but that didn't seem to help Ambrose at all. He ascended the stairs stiffly, hardly cognizant of Eli behind him.

"Some luck to get stuck with those bards, huh?" Eli tried.

"Hm?" Ambrose briefly looked back. "Oh. Yes, atrocious."

So, it wasn't the bards, then. Eli thought through it as he sat on the edge of the bed and pulled off his boots. Spelltide didn't truly bother Ambrose, and Banneker's tracker was already pointing to mushrooms nearby. If the bard's singing didn't...

He paused, his boot hanging off his foot. Oh, of course. The bard's singing. The bard's singing about *weddings*.

Dawn never had quite cracked Ambrose's shell regarding that topic. She said he had seemed perfectly fine during the Guildhouse tour. He had even chatted with the event manager for a moment— then the quakes had struck, then the quest to find the mushroom... and all thought of broaching wedding topics further had been put on hold.

As Ambrose slipped under the covers, Eli opened his mouth, almost ready to ask the question himself. But Ambrose had come here to escape the topic, not face it head-on. Eli wasn't going to trap him in here with such questions, not now.

Instead, he slipped under the covers with Ambrose and pulled him close, burying his face into the back of Ambrose's neck.

"Nap well," he mumbled, then grinned to himself. "And if you need a lullaby... *Sneaking through the forest gloom...*"

"Oh, gods."

"*Better hope you don't meet your doom—*"

"You're going to meet your doom with this pillow, Eli."

Eli didn't normally dream. Sure, there was the occasional *I'm late for my first college class* nightmare, and now and then he'd dream about a giant dragon chasing him around his family's house. But today, he had anticipated a dreamless nap—until he opened his eyes and found a very real dragon staring back at him.

He yelped and leapt back, his shoulder blades meeting with a rocky wall. Don't run, he told himself, his adventuring instincts kicking in even while asleep. Running would only entice it, activate its prey drive...

But this dragon didn't seem enticed. In fact, it didn't seem like it was really even looking at him. It was looking to his left, at Ambrose.

"Afternoon, Fio," he said, walking forward. "Apologies if my appearance is a bother. I forgot to turn off the amplifier before I fell asleep, and I can't very well turn it off now."

Eli slowly peeled himself off the wall in fascination. That was *Fio* sitting before him. Oh, he was such a beautiful dragon close-up. And Ambrose hadn't been exaggerating his size. A-class was an understatement. He was likely monstrous class, once properly measured. What Hickory and the others in his party wouldn't give to see a powerful creature like this. And Marlin! Marlin was going to lose his *mind*. But how was he even here to see Fio? How could he have connected with them—?

Eli looked down at his transparent arms—the ones currently holding Ambrose Beake in his sleep.

"Ames?" he called. "Hey, Ames!"

Ambrose turned with a frown. "What was that?"

Fio looked somewhere past him, and a voice jarred into Eli's mind, half the words muddled. *I don't see anything.*

"You didn't hear anything?" Ambrose looked up at the dragon.

No.

Eli almost shrieked in excitement. Fio's voice, he could hear the dragon *talk*—

Then Ambrose walked toward him, looking in his general area like he was squinting through mist. "Eli?"

"I'm here!" Eli grinned. "Can you see me?"

"I—sort of, yes—"

What is it? Fio demanded. Eli smothered a laugh. He understood now about the dragon's attitude; for all his massive size, he sounded like Nat when she was annoyed.

"Nothing," Ambrose said quickly. "Merely a...side-effect of the dream, it seems."

"Hey, I don't mean to upset him." Eli lowered his voice. "You go ahead and talk to him."

Ambrose glanced back. "I suppose I could take some data on his claws while I'm here..."

"I won't get in the way, I promise."

Eli backed away, admiring both Ambrose and Fio from afar while Ambrose in turn inspected the dragon's back claws. Fio did his best to appear as regal and detached as possible—surely the right of any dragon deigning to interact with a human—but Eli couldn't help but laugh at him. Every time Ambrose looked away or turned, Fio would blink his warm, golden eyes at him—then as soon as the man turned back around, it was back to being as aloof as possible.

I had thoughts, he said, pointing his snout upwards.

"Did you, now?" Ambrose asked. "About what?"

The habitat. Marlin's habitat, I mean.

"What else do you think Marlin should include?" Ambrose said. "I can inform him of what else you like about the Scar, but I can make no promises as to the architectural integrity of his creation."

I require birds to watch, Fio said.

"You and Chester both," Ambrose muttered, then waved a hand. "What else?"

Flowers to decorate my nest.

"Those sound reasonable."

Once Ambrose straightened, Fio maneuvered to the very middle of the sunny patch in the cave.

Most birds are too small to eat, you see. But they make nice sounds. And sometimes they drop nice feathers I can add to my nest.

"I have every confidence in your nest decorating skills, Fio."

And if Marlin has dragon younglings that are being unruly, Fio added,

I...suppose I can allow them into my nest. Strictly to teach them proper behavior, of course.

Eli grinned. In that moment, Fio sounded an awful lot like Ambrose.

"Ames has a youngling," he called, knowing only Ambrose would hear his tease. "He tries to teach her proper behavior, but it doesn't always work."

Ambrose turned. "Nat is not a *youngling*."

"Actually, now that I think about it, it never really works—"

Nat? Fio repeated, catching on to Ambrose's response. *Oh, you've mentioned her. She made that book of notes about me. Does she have a habitat?*

"One much like yours, I understand," Ambrose said. "She enjoys collecting shiny things."

And you? Fio bent down toward him, trying and failing not to sound too curious. *What do you like about your habitat?*

"The Scar?" Ambrose reached out and scratched the center of the dragon's nose. "I, ah...well, truth be told, I didn't actually like it when I first arrived."

Not enough birds, Fio said sagely, a deep thrum running through his words.

"No, not that." A smile flickered across Ambrose's face, but his voice went distant. "When my family brought me here, I thought it was...too crowded. Too loud, compared to where I'd been."

Then why did they bring you?

"I...I don't know."

Fio tilted his head—one ear pointing up, the other drooping down. *Well, why don't you ask them?*

A pang went through Eli's chest, a mere echo of what he knew Ambrose was feeling.

"I can't." Ambrose's tone tried to be matter-of-fact. "They left me in the Scar and then..."

Fio stared, waiting for the rest.

"And we don't really see each other," Ambrose said quickly, a weak smile crossing his face once more. "They...aren't all that interested in me, I suppose."

Fio recoiled, his neck arching. *Are all humans like that with their younglings?*

"No!" Ambrose held up a hand. "No, of course not. Some—most—are more than decent. Normal parents." He cleared his throat and pointed to his back claw. "Apologies, could I take one more look?"

As Ambrose ducked down in the dragon's shadow, Eli set a hand to his own chest, rubbing the pain that hadn't fully healed there. No, Ambrose didn't have normal parents or a traditional family. But he had Rosemond Street. He had Eli.

And he could have Eli's family, too. He just needed to propose.

Eli straightened. That was it—he'd propose on Spelltide, no matter what Spelltide looked like. He'd make sure Ambrose had more family members than he could count. Parents, grandparents, cousins, siblings, the works. Ambrose hadn't met all the Valenzes yet, of course, but they'd love him just like he deserved—

Then a roar slashed through the dream, ripping both of them away from the cavern and back into the daylight.

TIP 14:

IMPROVISE WEAPONS

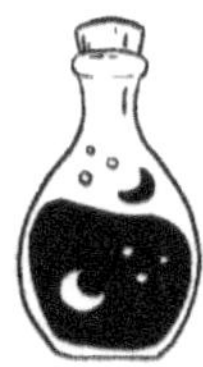

Ambrose

"What was that?"

Ambrose jolted awake, clutching his chest. Beside him, Eli bolted up and reached for the dagger on the nightstand.

"Stay here." He shoved on his boots. "I'll go check it out."

Ambrose couldn't help it; despite his heart crashing against his ribcage, he threw off the blankets and followed Eli into the hallway.

"You were supposed to tell me I dreamt it!" He stumbled. "That it was nothing—"

"No, I *told* you to stay there!"

Eli flipped his dagger to his left hand and yanked open the doors to the courtyard with his right. As soon as he looked outside, his shoulders dropped. "Oh, gods dead and alive, are you serious?"

Ambrose dared peek over his shoulder—and found the inn had attracted an unruly guest.

At the far end of the courtyard, a shambling mass of mud, moss, and foliage stood on its hind legs, its murky shadow stretching over the Skipwallow statue and its new Spelltide decorations. The monster's beady eyes, half hidden by a fringe of vines, glared right at Banneker's tracking device.

And Banneker still stood right next to it.

"Uh, nothing to see here, big guy!" He ducked, frantically trying to turn off the mass of gears and steam. "Don't mind me—"

The mudmire roared and swiped at the device with a long, sludgy paw. Banneker grabbed the contraption and leapt out of the way.

"Banneker!" Ambrose wedged himself behind the door and shouted around its edge. "What in the hells is it doing?"

"I don't know! Admiring my craftsmanship?"

To Ambrose, it looked more akin to a jealous artificer trying to sabotage Banneker's work. It pounded the earth and reached for the device, while on the other side of the statue, Chester was doing his best to evict his unwanted guest.

"Shoo!" He waved at the creature. "Get!"

The mudmire roared once more—a terrible gurgling sound that made Ambrose's skin crawl—and snapped its gooey jaws at Chester. Grim picked up the innkeeper and set him down outside of the resulting mud puddle.

"Did you take the proximity of the anchoring magic into account?" they shouted to Banneker.

"Of course I did!"

"And you calibrated the strength?" Sherry called from the other corner.

"Obviously!" Banneker lifted the device to check his gears. "It's all attuned to the Driftwood anchoring specs from this year's reports!"

Next to Sherry, Dawn snorted. "Does that statue *look* like he was tuned up this year?"

"Aw, don't use the word *tune-up* in front of old Skip," Chester tried. "He gets very sensitive about it—"

The mudmire slammed a paw down, swatting the metal out of Banneker's arms and onto the cobblestones. Mud and gear shards splattered all over the artificer.

"Aw, dude, *really*?"

"Not to worry!" One of the bards—the lyrist from earlier—vaulted onto the bench. "I shall distract it!" He gave a valiant strum. "*OHH—*"

The mudmire shrieked and hurled a glob of mud at the bard. It hit him square in the mouth, and for a brief moment, Ambrose considered asking Chester to let the mudmire stay a while.

"That's it, everyone inside!" Eli shouted, throwing open both doors and ruining Ambrose's hiding spot. "Get in and I'll chase it out of here!"

Dawn picked up her skirts and rushed for the door. The mudmire's next roar hurled a whirlwind of mud spittle all around her, and she slipped on the wet flagstones. "Not my skirt, I *like* this skirt—"

"I've got you!" Sherry took Dawn's arm and helped her along. Behind her, Grim was doing their utmost to wrestle a pitchfork away from Chester.

"But I can take him!" the innkeeper tried.

"Kid, you couldn't take a fanged rabbit if it rolled over on its belly for you!"

Unlike Chester, Xavion had no qualms about listening to Eli. With a lip curled at the mud, they packed up their magazine and hurried inside.

"So much for getting a bit of *sun,*" they muttered, carefully picking their way through the mud right behind Dawn. "Clearly, I can't have a moment of peace without getting accosted by idiotic creatures in my own damn forest—"

Whether the mudmire understood their language or not, they didn't seem to appreciate it. Vines shot out from its foliage-covered back, yanking Xavion off the ground. Within seconds, they hung by their feet above the Skipwallow statue, mud dripping from the vines onto their immaculate boots.

Ambrose barked out a laugh. Xavion glared at him with all the power their beloved sun had to offer.

"Will your boorish adventuring party deign to assist me?"

Ambrose ventured beyond the door, extending an arm to Dawn to help her across the now dirty porch. "Perhaps my *boorish* adventuring party will deign to leave you up there—"

His victory was short lived. As he guided Dawn toward the doors, he failed to notice the vines snaking around his own feet. By the time he caught sight of the slivers of green, it was too late—a cold, slimy lasso yanked on his ankles. He grabbed the edge of the stairs, but the splinters there couldn't help him. Within seconds, he hung upside down next to Xavion, his dignity smarting as much as his scraped palms.

"Eli!" Ambrose shouted at the upside-down inn. "Get me down from here!"

To his adventuring party's credit, Eli leapt into the courtyard, and the others all converged with him. Eli sliced and hacked at vines holding Ambrose, while Sherry and Banneker rushed underneath the creature's victims with a wheelbarrow filled with straw.

"Yes, that's it!" Ambrose tried to reach for the vines around his ankles. "Just—just stay below us—"

But the mudmire had no interest in letting either of them be rescued. It shrieked against the attacks and swung right, leaving the wheelbarrow stuck in the mud. By the statue, the blinded bard knocked into Eli, and behind the looming creature, Chester had recovered his trusty pitchfork and was poking ineffectively at its butt.

"Aye!" he yelled. "Avast!"

The vines around Ambrose's ankles started twining to his knees. "Help!"

"Eli!" Dawn crouched behind the platypus statue. "My firework wands might help! I left them to charge by the fence post!"

"Hold on, hold on!" Eli shoved the bard off him and dove for the pile of wands glowing faintly in the sunlight.

"What, a wand with a few little sparks?" Xavion scoffed. "Amby, what good is this beau of yours if he can't even rescue us from a pile of mud—"

Ambrose tried pushing on the vines. "See, I was rather hoping he'd let you get eaten."

Somehow, Xavion managed to fold their arms. "And *I* was rather hoping your last paper on brimstone extracts would demonstrate a lick of sense, but we all can't get what we want, can we?"

Ambrose stopped struggling with the vines to glare at him. "You mean the paper you quoted four months later in your article on gatling flower solutions?"

"Ah, so you admit that you read it!"

Below Ambrose, Eli leapt over a sweeping gale of vines and, with one hand, lifted the wheelbarrow out of the mud. "Sherry, roll this under Xavion! Banneker and Grim, you get under Ambrose! And Chester!" Eli lined up three of the wands in his hand. "On three, you take that pitchfork and poke its front toes!"

Chester pointed. "But the butt—"

"Mudmires don't *have* a butt, Chester!"

The creature bent its neck and snapped at Eli's head; he dodged neatly and pointed the wands. "Okay, on three! One!"

Sherry pushed the wheelbarrow forward; Grim and Banneker jostled into place. "Two!"

Xavion flicked mud at Ambrose. Ambrose shoved him with his shoulder, sending him swinging right into the dirt-soaked vines.

"*Three!*"

Brilliant sparks of blue, orange, and pink shot straight at the mudmire's eyes in a torrent of light. With a shuddering shriek, the creature reared—and the vines slithered right off Ambrose's ankles. He held his breath, hoping one of his party had managed to find their way underneath him. Air rushed past him for one second, two—

He landed in Grim's arms just as Chester gave a wild shout, ran to the front of the monster, and stabbed at its toes with his pitchfork.

Between the blinding sparks, the pain, and the righteous fury of Chester's war cry, the mudmire decided it no longer needed to check in to the Skipwallow Inn. It reeled away and lumbered through the tilted archway, seeking the cool comfort of the forest. Ambrose wiped mud off his face as he watched it go, its back an overgrown riot of foliage. Red, orange, green, blue...

Blue?

He squinted—and his heart dropped. Banneker's device hadn't attracted the mudmire itself. In a reversal of its original purpose, it had attracted what grew on its back. What Ambrose was looking for.

The blue clay mushroom, growing in bright, plentiful clumps all along the monster's back.

TIP 15:

WATCH THE FIRE

Nat

VIOLA HAD OPTED to keep The Midnight Snack open after-hours in case anyone else on Rosemond Street needed a quick stress-relieving cupcake or a calming cookie.

And as Rory, Viola, and Nat gathered around the dessert case to hear Ambrose's latest update, Nat found she needed at least a dozen of each.

"You fought a *what*—?"

"It was nothing," Ambrose said quickly. "Just a small mishap."

Viola's gaze narrowed. "Eli said the mudmire nearly ate you!"

"That was merely an—an exaggeration."

Ambrose's voice trailed off, as if glancing in the direction of the other merchants. According to Ambrose, they had all gone to claim a table for dinner before the bards could beat them to it, leaving him with the speaking stone to address the others' questions—or, in this case, assuage them with lies.

"Are you sure we can't send you anything to help—?" Rory tried.

"I appreciate the offer, but I can assure you we're all fine."

Ambrose quickly veered away from the subject of the mud monster. "By the way, has Fio continued jumping? I did tell him again to stop."

Nat sighed, and across from her, Rory and Viola rolled their eyes. They weren't going to get any further details on that mudmire tonight. Nat would have to press Eli for details once he was back.

"No, no more jumping," she said, reluctantly allowing him to change the subject. "Not a single earthquake today."

It was more of a victory than she wanted to let on: the quakes settling had gotten Rune off their collective backs. The apprentices hadn't seen him come back during her rounds, not to the artificer's atelier nor any of the other shops.

"Well, at least Fio listened to me," Ambrose muttered. "I cannot in good conscience hand Marlin a misbehaving dragon."

Nat fidgeted with the corner of her dragon journal. She had tried to update it herself with the data Ambrose had been collecting, but she couldn't match the precision of Ambrose's notes—nor did she particularly like what the information meant.

"Does Fio really have to go all the way to Marlin's habitat?" she asked. "He's a Scarrish dragon. What if he just stayed in the Scar?"

Selfishly, she wanted to see Fio. Wanted to watch him thrive in the sunlight above Aphos, like she had.

Ambrose went quiet for a moment.

"He doesn't have any family here." He cleared his throat. "And Marlin's habitat will be...healthy for him. Allow him to recover properly. We should do whatever Marlin thinks is best."

Something else lingered behind the words, but Nat didn't see the sense in trying to pry it out now. If he refused to say anything about the mudmire, he certainly wasn't going to—

"About Spelltide," Ambrose said, deftly changing the subject once more. "I hear it will be particularly special this year."

Nat immediately broke into a sweat. Viola and Rory exchanged a glance—then Viola covered the speaking stone with a flour-dusted hand. "Did you not tell him about your plan?"

In truth, Nat hadn't even told *Viola* about her plan; that had been all Rory's doing.

"I said we'd tell him after we have a working prototype," she babbled in a whisper, "and we don't have one yet—"

"Nat?" Ambrose called. Viola quickly retracted her hand and gestured to the stone, eyebrows raised.

"What have you heard about Spelltide?" Nat squeaked.

"Well, I..." Ambrose said in confusion. "I heard you all decorated the street yourself."

"Oh!" Nat slumped on the stool on relief. "Yeah. Rory and Viola helped us. It looks real nice."

That part wasn't a lie. The street was sparkling just in time for the festival. Purple, blue, and green bunting ran down from The Whirling Wand Emporium to the edge of The Griffin's Claw. Shimmering banners hung from all their second-story windows. Luka had even dug up a few floating whirligigs in a rainbow of colors and set them in a slow, mesmerizing pattern up and down the street. Aside from distracting the occasional mail dragon, they were quite effective in slowing down foot traffic and attracting more customers.

"Wish you could see it," Nat added quietly. She wished all of them were here—and not simply so she wouldn't have to go on stage in disguise and briefly lie to the entire city. It was just that such an empty street was not very befitting of the holiday.

Ambrose gave a small sigh, and behind him, the sound of chatter and clinking bowls slowly grew. "I do apologize for this mess," he said. "We should be there with you."

A chorus of voices echoed around him in agreement. Rory leaned in. "We miss you!"

Viola leaned in as well. "I'm setting aside some cookies for you all!"

As the faraway merchants all cheered at that, Nat raised her voice to be heard over the chatter. "I'll just have to get you some souvenirs, then. How do you feel about a feather boa?"

Ambrose laughed. "A what?"

"Yeah, someone up in the Elwig market's already selling 'em. I could get you and Eli matching ones."

"No. No, please, he'll insist on actually wearing them—"

"Wear what?" Eli cut in.

"Nat's terribly busy, she must go," Ambrose blurted out. "Goodbye, Nat!"

Nat laughed. "Goodbye, Mr. Ambrose. And start thinking about which color boa you want!"

Eli gasped. "*Boas*—?"

As soon as the lines on the speaking stone went dull, Rory looked at Nat, not nearly as distracted by the concept of feather boas as Ambrose and Eli were. "You have to tell them soon. When will you have a prototype?"

Nat gulped. A prototype? Possibly tomorrow. A *working* one? Possibly never.

She stuffed the rest of her fernberry cupcake into her mouth. "Luka's coming over to work on it tonight," she said. "Give me a few days and I'll tell them. I promise."

Nat tried to hold on to the little joy the conversation with Ambrose had brought her, using it to push down her nerves about the prototype—but by the time Luka arrived to test their Spelltide illusion, she was pacing behind the front counter.

"Come in!" She jumped to open the door for him. "You got my message about—?"

"About the mudmire? Yes, I saw it." He shifted his pack on his shoulder, his face pale. "I went through Banneker's books and looked up what they were. In hindsight, I shouldn't have done that. Did you know that they can fully absorb their prey in under a minute and leave absolutely no trace?"

Nat deeply wished to erase that newfound knowledge from her mind.

"You know, maybe we don't look at Banneker's books for a few days." She ushered him into the workroom. "Let's, uh, get set up for the prototype."

As Luka opened his pack and pulled out an array of metal bits and bobs, Nat gathered her courage and opened her recipe book. Today's experiment was only a test, she told herself. They'd make just one griffin illusion, to ensure their combined potions and devices could capture the shape, lightness, and feel they wanted. Sure, their intended effect was high above her current level, not to mention far above anything she had ever done with Ambrose before.

She glanced over at Luka, who had his devices perfectly arranged and assembled, his hands moving deftly about them like he could do this work in his sleep. She smiled. She was with Luka—she would be fine.

"Show me what you got," she said, leaning over the worktable. Luka cleared his throat and held a punctured metal disc to the lamplight. Oddly shaped offshoots were screwed into the sides, some shaped like handles and others carved with runes. Nat had no idea what those did, but the carvings in the center were clear: tiny griffins, hewn so uniformly that they almost looked stamped into the metal.

"The process will be straightforward," Luka explained, flipping the disc so she could see both sides. "You'll pour the smoke into the center here, the griffin will appear directly below, and Zuri's wand will enchant it with flight. I've taken the liberty of enchanting the illusion to hover, so we can more easily check its shape and texture. This metal I used made it easy. If you look at its edge, you can see how special it is..."

As he continued, his eyes and voice softened, reminding Nat of the warmth of buttery sunlight. He always looked like this when discussing his work or his music. He didn't get that bounce in his heels like Eli, or that patina of confidence like Ambrose—but his love poured through all the same, enchanting her until it was hard to look at anything but his face.

"And what about you?" Luka finally set down the disc.

"Hm?" Nat blinked; she had set her chin in her hands, fully mesmerized by his voice. Luka tilted his head.

"Your...potion?"

She'd rather listen to another hour of him speaking than cut in with some nonsense about her potion—but there was no procrastinating further.

"For our test, it'll have to be brewed right before we pour," she said, lining up the vials and spoons she had already set out on the table. "I only have so many bottles that will preserve smoke well enough for the demonstration." She looked up from the tools. "But if you'd rather not get involved with all the brewing—"

"Please." Luka smiled and reached for the goggles hanging on the wall. "I'm here to help."

While he reviewed her recipe, she shrugged off her jacket and slipped on her new potion robes from Ambrose. She still loved them just as much as the first time she had put them on: sturdy, comfortable, an array of pockets. And the embroidery, the looping, fiery swirls up and down the sleeves... She could stare at the pattern forever.

And apparently, so could Luka.

"Okay, so the recipe is..." She turned to find him staring at her, wide-eyed. "What?" She looked down at her robes. "Did I spill something on them? I *knew* I shouldn't have brought my coffee in here—"

"No, no!" Luka's cheeks went pink. "They're—the robes, they're just so lovely. May I take a closer look?"

Nat looked up. "Sure."

She held out an arm as he approached, letting him touch the cuff with careful reverence. He ran a finger over the abstract swirls of yellow and gold, and for a brief second, she held her breath, wondering if his finger would trail back to her hand.

"The enchantments?" he asked. It took her a moment to realize he had asked a question.

"Shield, mostly," she said. "A cooling spell around the neck, too. The tailor tucked a little card into the robes so I had a list of what's what."

A part of the cuff had folded back on itself; Luka carefully unfolded and smoothed it out. His fingers brushed the hem, then her wrist—

Nat's breath hitched, and a flash of warmth shot up her arm. But before she could pull her hand back or logic away the feeling, Luka straightened, looked her in the eye, and made it worse.

"Beautiful," was all he said—and her mind went blank.

There were no thoughts in her head anymore. Only fluttery feelings that made no sense. It was just because—because no one had ever used that word for her before. That was all. No one in Aphos had ever called her beautiful. To be honest, she'd probably punch them if they did, assuming it was an insult or a trap or both.

But Luka—well, he couldn't be punched. Not in a million years. He did not insult or trap. He was kind. He *meant* it.

She pulled her hand back and cradled it against her chest for a moment. "Thanks," she mumbled, then tucked her hair behind her ear. "Mr. Ambrose picked out a nice pattern. Should we, um—should we get started?"

"Yes." Luka stepped back, his gaze suddenly focused hard on the cauldron. "Yes, of course. Let me just..."

He dug in his pack once more and pulled out a tiny box with a tinier silver handle. He turned the handle a few times, then set it on the worktable. Music tinkled out of the little thing—a calm, unobtrusive melody that danced somewhere in the back of Nat's head. Luka often had these playing near him when he was working, but she had never thought to bring one here.

"Good idea," she said. "Did you make this one?"

"No, found this one in the market. Recorded by a troupe well-known in Kolkea, apparently."

Nat hummed as she gathered wood under the cauldron. "Madam Mila had a bard visit from Kolkea once. Didn't like him much, though. Pretty sure she threw him into the deep tunnels where the big spiders live."

She looked up; Luka was staring at her again, and not in admiration this time.

"Is this..." Nat bit her lip. "Is this one of those things I think is normal but is actually—?"

"Terrifying?" Luka nodded. "Yes."

Don't mention the spider tunnel murders, she noted. Got it.

"First step," she quickly read aloud from her recipe book. "Preheat the cauldron."

As they worked together on the smoke potion and watched murky gray shapes form in the bottom of the cauldron, Nat's nerves slowly evolved into excitement. She knew what to expect from parts of the recipe, of course, but other steps felt more like discovery. Following her intuition on what worked and what didn't, digging up old tips and advice to gradually patch together a deeper understanding of what was brewing. She stoked the fires and stirred the liquid with increasing energy, waiting eagerly for that next shift in the potion's color or texture. Did Ambrose feel this way when he made new potions? He never looked particularly excited or bouncy while brewing. Then again, he had been doing it for almost his whole life. And he wasn't a bouncy person. Unless he was drunk—then he just silly-smiled at Eli the whole time.

"Ready for the silverweed?" Luka held up a bottle, and Nat's excitement dimmed. All told, the smoke potion had almost been beginner's work—up until now.

"Ready." She steeled herself. "In it goes."

Once the silverweed had been added and the brew reached a boil, it would be time to harvest the smoke. Ambrose had shown her a trick a few months ago, one that gave the smoke a tangible, soft texture—like fur floating on the breeze. Normally, this sort of smoke was then strained to include in another potion, but in Nat's case, this smoke was her end goal.

And harvesting it was easier said than done—even for someone like Ambrose.

She handed Luka a large lid made of wood planks and riveted metal. "I'm going to throw this in"—she held up a bottle filled with a sticky green solution—"and it's going to ignite the potion."

Luka swallowed. "All right."

"And you have to put the lid on immediately."

"Understood."

"Like, *right* away."

His head bobbed. "Okay."

"Like, the very second I—"

"All right, I get it!" He tightened his grip on the lid, face pale. "I can do it."

Nat paused. "Are you sure? Because we can switch—"

"No, I can do it."

Nat checked her goggles and gloves for safety, then carefully uncorked the bottle. "On three. One...two..."

She held her breath and poured in the potion. Emerald flames erupted instantly from the cauldron, blazing across the surface like cobwebs above a torch. For a second, Luka flinched, and Nat raised her arms, prepared to grab the lid and shove it down for him—

Then, with a shout, he dropped the lid onto the cauldron and snuffed out the flames.

"There!" He jumped back, gloved hands held high. "Did it—did it work?"

They both stared at the cauldron for a tense moment. If the lid held, the brew would fade into silky gray mist, ready to bottle. Nat just needed it to hold, to keep the alchemical process in—

Flames licked up the sides of the cauldron, and the lid began to rattle.

"Luka!" She rushed forward, her heart lodged in her throat. "Luka, get away—!"

She wrapped her arms around his waist and whipped him toward the wall. In a violent hiss of steam, the lid burst off the cauldron and careened toward her—

But the spells in her robe didn't falter. A flash of white whirled out of the embroidery, and the lid slammed off the newfound shield. She held Luka tightly as the lid settled on the floor with a clatter. He was fine. He was protected.

But behind her, the cauldron bubbled over with angry flames and steam.

"Stay here!" She pushed Luka away from the cauldron and scrambled for the lid. One of her gloves slipped off as she moved, but there was no time to turn around and retrieve it now. The fire couldn't spread. Not here, not in Mr. Ambrose's shop—

She grabbed the lid, gritted her teeth against the brush of hot metal against her fingers, and slammed the lid back down. It had to hold, it *had* to hold...

And it did. The potion didn't have enough energy to fight her this time. The flames whiffed away, the bubbles sulked off. The lid remained still, forcing the brew into its next stage of transformation.

Nat exhaled and staggered back, away from the heat. The coolness of the surrounding air rushed across her face in relief, then down her neck and arms...

But her hands still felt like they were welded to hot metal.

"Nat." Luka took her shoulders with trembling hands. "Nat, please stay still. I can help you."

She blinked down at her fingers. Her gray skin had gone a strange purple-red where she'd grasped the metal bands on the lid. The wounds lay in stripes, puffy and swollen and—oh gods, it *hurt*.

"It's fine," she said automatically, numbly, her body shaking. "It's fine."

The words came out on instinct. She'd been through worse before. Worse that she'd had to hide from people. In Aphos, pain was weakness. Pain was a disadvantage to exploit. Pain would go away on its own, eventually, probably—

But Luka was already guiding her to a stool. Pouring something into a cloth. Setting a hand back on her shoulder.

"I'm going to place these on your fingers, all right?" he said, his tone as soothing as the cool air around her. "It'll cool the burns. This part won't sting, I promise."

He delicately draped the cloths over her fingers. The effect was instant, sending an uncontrollable shiver through her. The pain was still there, of course, its pulsing making her dizzy. It was all she could do to stare at the cloths, willing them to work faster.

"Now for the rest of the medicine." Luka readied himself and dumped another potion into a spray bottle. "Learned this part from Banneker. I don't want to know how he figured this out." He gave her a weak smile. "Please forgive me for this."

He removed the cloths and sprayed the medicine all over her hands.

A stream of curses immediately left her lips.

"I know, I know, I know," he babbled, continuing to spray even while he flinched. "It'll be over soon, I swear!"

Luka never made promises lightly, and this one was no different. He must have fetched Ambrose's strongest potion in the cabinet, because by her fifth curse, the angry splotches were fading, and by the tenth, the pain had shriveled away.

But when Luka wiped her fingers down, she still flinched.

"I'm so sorry!" He yanked his hands away. "Do they still hurt?"

She could only stare at him in turn. He was supposed to be... upset. Angry. She had messed up. She had nearly botched the potion, set the place on fire. Anyone would be angry at her for that. Aphos would have thrown her to the spiders for it.

"You're not...mad?"

He gave her a genuine smile in return. "Nat, why would I be mad at you? I'm just glad you're all right now."

As he folded up the cloths and moved away, she stared at her hands, willing herself to get up. To move like normal. Continue with cleaning or preparing for the bottling of the potion. The danger had passed, after all. The pain was gone. She was all right; she was *fine*.

She burst into tears anyway.

"Nat." Luka reached instinctively for her hand, then stopped himself. "It's all right."

"I *know*," she forced the word out through tears—the horrible kind that made her eyes sting and her breathing hurt. "Why? Why am I—?"

Luka hesitated, then held out both arms in a silent gesture.

She should have been ashamed for how quickly she accepted his embrace. Her old thoughts shouted something about weakness. About traps. About how dangerous this sort of care was.

But that was how she survived Aphos. Not Rosemond Street.

She fell into him, and they both found themselves on their knees, Nat clutching Luka's shirt as if the slight breeze in the room would buoy her away. She wasn't even sure why she was crying anymore. Pain, fear, shame, gratitude—all of it stained the fabric in her hands.

And as she sobbed, Luka began to hum.

It was soft, like he always was. The music box had stopped playing a while ago, leaving him no accompaniment. But the sound made his ribcage vibrate, thrumming against her palm, her cheek. As he hummed, he stroked her hair, his eyes closed. And slowly, her tears dried, her chest empty of anything but the little song.

"How do you feel now?" Luka eventually murmured. "Any pain?"

She shook her head and pulled away from the poor, sopping mess that was his shirt. "I'll pay for your laundry." She sniffed. "Sorry about the—"

"No apologies." He wiped a tear off her cheek. "Please."

She expected him to pull away, for them to get back to work—but he stayed there, his hand remaining on her cheek. He was so close now. Close enough to see the freckles that dotted his nose. The deep brown of his eyes. The lips that had turned up in a gentle, relieved smile. Were they as soft as his hands, she wondered—?

Suddenly, the emptiness in her chest was home to that fluttering again. Warmth, too, as she always felt toward her friends, but marked with a giddiness she couldn't place. A giddiness she only felt with Luka.

Somehow, she doubted that friends often thought about kissing other friends. Wait, did they? No, she didn't think so. Oh, gods—was *this* what Rory and Dawn were talking about?

"Nat?" Luka frowned and dropped his hand. "You...look like you're thinking about something."

Not kissing you, Nat almost said. Definitely not that, for sure—

She scrambled back.

"Water," she said, her throat doing her a favor and creaking right at the end of the word. "Just thinking about how I need water."

TIP 16:

STEALTH NEVER WORKS

Eli

ON ANY OTHER QUEST, Eli would have loved the idea of adventuring to an old guard tower in the Driftwood.

He would have had his whole adventuring party with him, naturally—armed to the teeth with weapons and good stories to swap on the way there. They'd case the tower in minutes, get in within seconds, and get back home within a day. The quest would practically be a picnic for his party.

But the five merchants trudging behind him were most certainly not his normal group, and no matter how much food Sherry tried to pack, this was most definitely not a picnic.

"Look." He turned around and walked backwards along the thin path, addressing the group as if he were a Driftwood tour guide. "That mudmire went easy on us yesterday. But those things have good memories, and we're not exactly here to make its day any better. If we're going to harvest the mushrooms off this thing, you have to focus. You have to stay on task. And you have to listen to me the *first* time I say something."

Yes, Eli, they chorused back.

"And let me take the lead on the fighting," he pressed. "No charging in yourself."

Sherry raised her hand.

"Even if someone's in trouble."

Sherry pursed her lips and lowered her hand.

Whether they listened or not, he had no more time for further lecturing. He turned back around and inspected Banneker's map—or, at least, the little of it the artificer had recovered from his wrecked tracking device. The pencil had been circling near the smudged tower before following the mudmire's path to the inn. If Chester's instructions were right, once they turned this corner, the tower should be...

He looked up and lowered the map. "Lovely."

As he had suspected the day before, the old tower did indeed lie in ruins, its anchoring magic just barely keeping the structure together. Worn stones floated inches away from the walls, and mossy roof tiles hung below the eaves, as if the whole thing was caught mid-crumble. Given its state, letting the forest take the poor thing apart would have been a mercy.

But something within must have still been intact—or at least, intact enough to entice the mudmire. One of the windows on the second floor had been broken open, and a thick, slimy trail of mud led from the ground to its sill. Clearly, the mudmire had never bothered with the door when entering its ruinous home.

"My time has come!" Banneker proudly whisked a device out of his pack. "Stay back. Old places like these tend to have their trap and alarm spells still lying around. But I can get around 'em."

Everyone dutifully took a step back while he strapped on goggles and pulled on the device's levers. The tower door shook and clicked as he spoke. "Let's see...bypassing a broken trap mechanism... neutralizing an old curse...analyzing the lock..."

The door slowly creaked open. He pushed his goggles to his forehead with a grin. "And *that's* how you get through a locked door."

Dawn bent and picked up a rock by the entrance; a rusted key lay underneath.

"What about this?"

Banneker waved a hand. "Aw, where's the fun in that?" He tucked away his device and made a loping stride for the door. "Welp, time to go in—"

"Hold on, hold on." Eli grabbed his collar. "I'm going in first, and you're following. *Quietly.*"

Despite Banneker's device, he ran through every precaution and then some. Wiping the hinges with oil, testing the floor around the door, assessing the draft within for any movement or unusual airflow... Then he finally snuck inside.

For something as imposing as a guard tower, the inside wasn't particularly impressive. A cold hearth, a few bare, dust-covered shelves. Everything else had been taken away from the room; all the old guards had left behind were empty boxes and the faint smell of stale beer.

Eli signaled for the others to follow him inside. The path up to the mudmire was obvious—the stairs were covered in mud where they met with the second-story window, and the trail continued up to the open loft on the second floor. He moved forward without a sound, assessing his options. If he enchanted the stairs with one of Dawn's silence wands, they could strike at the mushrooms before the mudmire even realized they were—

Behind him, wood creaked against wood. Eli whipped around and glared at Banneker, who had his arm halfway into an old crate.

"What?" Banneker whispered. "I'm just looking!"

Grim leaned over his shoulder. "Anything good?"

"Nah, just some sandals and rags or whatever—"

Eli passed a hand over his face. "You don't need anything here, just get out of the crate and focus!"

"Okay, okay!"

He crept up the stairs first, using Dawn's wands to painstakingly clean and silence each wooden plank as he went. Gods help them if one of them slipped or hit a creaky step. If this didn't go right, there was every chance one of them could meet a terribly muddy death.

Or, well, injury, at least.

Once he neared the loft, he held up a hand to the others and peeked over the top step. There was the mudmire: napping in the middle of the wooden floor, splayed out in a sunbeam, its stubby tail twitching lazily. All in all, it wasn't a bad spot to sleep—the creature had clearly made a nice little nest up here. In addition to the mushrooms growing on its back, all manner of plants flourished both on its body and around the loft. Ivy along the walls and around its arms. Then moss around its claws, pale blue flowers on its tail...

Eli squinted. Those weren't just random wildflowers on its tail. Those were variegated forget-me-nots. And good ones, too—strong color, shiny leaves. They would be perfect for his proposal potion—

"Eli?" Sherry whispered. "Is the mudmire up there?"

Eli yanked his focus back. He couldn't think about flowers now, not with the monster right in front of him. "Sure is."

"And we're still going for the legs first?"

Eli assessed the mudmire's position. The tail twitched again, longer and heavier than he remembered from yesterday. The flowers lured him, yes—but that limb was also a threat.

"Here, you take the leg," he whispered. "I'll take on the tail."

"I thought you were taking the front?"

"Change of plans. That tail can wipe us all out if we're not careful."

They quietly circled the creature with wands and devices in hand, while Ambrose positioned himself near its shoulder with an open jar. The plan was ostensibly simple: paralyze the mudmire until Ambrose could harvest a few mushrooms from its back. Then a short flash-bang, a quick retreat back to the Skipwallow Inn, and—

Over by the mudmire's chest, Sherry's armor clanked in the loud, echoing screech of metal against metal. The mudmire cracked one beady eye open; everyone groaned.

"Aw, Sherry—"

"I thought we agreed not to bring the shield!"

"What?" Sherry lifted her shield. "I couldn't just leave it behind!"

The mudmire pushed itself to all fours and gave a great, gurgling hiss. Everyone instantly scattered.

"The legs!" Eli raised his wand. "Go for the legs, now!"

He shot at the tail and paralyzed it in a flash of light. Ahead of him, the others' weapons struck true, pinning its legs to the ground.

"Okay, Ames!" Eli shouted. "Go up and—!"

But the mudmire refused to be so easily downed. The ivy on its back leg shriveled in response to the magic, absorbing the spell and releasing the limb. Eli tried dodging, but it was too late—the freed leg immediately lashed out and kicked him in the side.

"*Eli!*" Ambrose shouted. Eli staggered back but remained on his feet.

"I'm fine!" he called back. It was mostly true—nothing was broken, but the resulting bruises would only slow him down. Keeping his wand aimed at the mudmire's leg, he grabbed a potion off his belt and shook it.

"What are you doing?" Ambrose demanded, the jar in his hand completely forgotten. Eli flicked the cork off the bottle.

"Trying to aim at the other leg in a second—"

"No, with the potion!"

"What?" Eli shrugged and gulped the frothy, spearmint-tasting liquid in one go. "They work faster when you shake them!"

Ambrose clutched his hair. "That's not how they're designed to be *used*, Eli!"

Eli flicked his wand; the spell shot directly into the mud this time, and the leg before him froze mid-kick. "Never mind that, just get on its back!"

Face wrinkled in utter disgust, Ambrose clambered up onto the mudmire's back with squelching steps. "Do not think I'm going to forget about your potion misuse so easily!"

"What? It's fine!"

"It's not fine, the effect of such churning has not been properly tested in a controlled setting—"

With all of its legs now frozen, the mudmire tried to shake its back in protest against the assault; Ambrose yelped and grabbed a handful of vines to stay on.

"Everyone, get in front of it!" Eli ordered. "Keep it distracted!"

While Sherry, Banneker, and Grim all crowded awkwardly near the stairs, Eli kept one eye on the flowery tail and one eye on Ambrose. He had half a mushroom now. Okay, a full mushroom…

The mudmire writhed once more; the mushroom fell out of the jar.

"Banneker!" Ambrose shouted. "You're supposed to distract it, not piss it off!"

Over by its head, Banneker staunchly continued dancing.

"What do you want me to do?"

Dawn stared at him, firework wand raised. "*Use* your *stuff*, Banneker!"

"I *am* using my stuff!"

"We're all going to die," Eli muttered, then grabbed the forget-me-nots on the tail and yanked. It worked; the creature's attention was pulled from Banneker's dancing, and the flowers were in his hand.

Very efficient, if he did say so himself.

"Ames!" he called, stuffing the flowers into the pack at his belt. "How you doing up there?"

"I've got two samples! Hold on, I'm almost…" Another squelch and a roar from the mudmire; Ambrose straightened. "Three, I have three!"

"Great!" Eli reached out with both arms. "Now jump to me, I'll catch you!"

Ambrose took two steps down the creature's spine—then froze. Eli waved to him.

"Really, I promise I'll catch you—"

"I know that!" Ambrose tried to pull his leg out of the mud with both arms. "I'm stuck!"

With a terrible gurgle, the mud on the creature's back began to bubble—and Ambrose started to sink into its mossy flesh.

"Oh, no." Dawn reached wildly for Ambrose's arm. "No, no, don't you dare get eaten—!"

"Hold on!" Eli pulled out his axe and slashed at the creature's flank, hoping to meet whatever lay underneath the mud. Nothing—

the blade came away covered in goop and nothing else. Who else had a clear shot? Grim, standing by the stairs—

"Grim, your ring!" Eli yelled. "Aim for its shoulder!"

The orc twisted their ring and shot. The purple beam of concentrated force landed perfectly on the monster's shoulder, shriveling the mud into plates of parched earth...

Which fell away, revealing fresh, angry goo underneath. Above the injury, Ambrose kept pulling uselessly at his legs.

"I don't think—I can emphasize"—he stopped pulling with a tired gasp, now up to his knees in mud—"how much I do not want to die like this!"

Sherry hefted up her shield. "No one's dying today!" She strode forward, elbowing Grim and Banneker out of the way, and began banging on her shield, hammer against metal. "Let—our—boy—*go!*"

Dawn and Banneker covered their ears; the air around the shield shimmered, as if reverberating from the impacts. Within seconds, the mudmire was shaking its head in pain and confusion—and around Ambrose, the mud began to ripple and fall away.

"That's it!" Eli leapt up onto its flank, grabbed Ambrose's arm, and pulled. With one good yank—and a shudder-inducing sucking sound —Ambrose slid out of the creature's back and down into Eli's arms.

"We're leaving," Ambrose said shakily, shoving the jar into his backpack. "We're leaving *right* now—"

"You got it. Everyone, down the stairs!" Eli waved the group along. "We've got five more minutes on the paralysis spells. Keep going and don't stop until you get to the inn!"

As Eli held a one-man line on the loft, the others started clambering down the stairs. Grim bounded down in two strides. Ambrose and Dawn hurried off arm in arm, as if helping each other get out faster.

But Banneker glanced behind him and frowned.

"Hey, are those mushrooms supposed to be doing that?"

Eli turned. It was no longer just the air reverberating from Sherry's magical shield—the mushrooms on the mudmire's back had begun to vibrate at the same resonance. Their caps puffed up, and smoke began to wisp from their spots. He knew those mushrooms. Skullcaps, how could he have missed the *skullcaps*—

There was no time to duck or grab a shield. The mushrooms exploded in rapid succession, a concussive burst of spores and heat, shoving him backwards. He hoped to hit the railing, hit the floor— but the dilapidated loft had no railing, and the floor disappeared underneath him. He kept falling, and falling, and falling—

His last thought before he hit the ground was that if he lived to tell his adventuring party about this, he'd never hear the end of it.

When Eli next awoke, he braced himself for the pain.

He expected throbbing in his skull. Rough stone against his shoulders, the cold draft of the tower, the reverberation of the fall in his bones. Everything he deserved for not noticing the damn skullcap mushrooms on the damn mudmire.

But instead, everything around him was soft and bright—so bright, he could hardly do more than squint. Sunlight assailed his eyes, moss cradled him from below...

And all around him, Rosemond Street scurried.

"Use that bandage." Ambrose pointed Dawn to something off to the side. "No, that one, I already soaked that one. Banneker, will that plank work as a stretcher?"

"Once I get it floating! Grim, can you pick up that end and angle it toward me?"

"Thank you both. I—" Ambrose met Eli's gaze and slouched in relief. "Oh, thank the gods you're awake." He grabbed Eli's hands, his grip clammy with nervous sweat. "If you ever scare me like that again, I'll kill you myself."

"He's awake?" Sherry leaned into his vision, holding up a blurry, backlit hand. "How many fingers am I holding up?"

Eli squinted. "What?"

"Let me give him this first." Ambrose held up a bottle and

checked its level. "Apologies for the fuzziness. Dawn's healing wands can have that effect. This should help speed it along…"

Eli tried to crack a smile. "You're not going to shake it first?"

Ambrose glared at him and uncorked the bottle. "I'm going to pretend you didn't say that."

In a motion that sent a delirious thrill through Eli, Ambrose slid an arm under his head, then held the bottle to his lips. This healing potion tasted slightly better than the last one—green tea, with a hint of licorice—but within a few blinks, his mind had cleared. Some of the fuzziness remained, as if the healing magic had clustered at the back of his head to keep the pain at bay, but the rest of his senses quickly returned to him. The scent of soil and wood struck his nose. The sunbeams streaming from the canopy rapidly warmed his limbs.

And Ambrose—his touch, his face, his presence—sharpened into delightful focus.

"How's he looking?" Dawn leaned in alongside Sherry, blocking one of the sunbeams. Eli smiled dreamily.

"He's never been more handsome than he is now."

Ambrose glared at him, mud dripping from his hair onto his cheeks. "My potion was clearly inadequate. He's still talking nonsense."

"You're my hero—"

"Someone put this man back to sleep." Ambrose wiped his hands and face with a cloth, then started to bandage Eli's other arm. "Grim, is the stretcher ready? Good. I'll sedate him for the walk back."

Eli was so fixated on the seductive movement of Ambrose's hands that he almost didn't register what he had said.

"Sedate me? No, I"—he tried to reach for Ambrose with his other arm—"I wanna kiss you—"

"You absolutely do not. Now drink this."

"No."

"*Eli.*"

Eli grinned. "Keep saying my name like that."

Ambrose huffed and set the bottle to his lips. Eli didn't remember anything after that.

TIP 17:

TAKE A REST

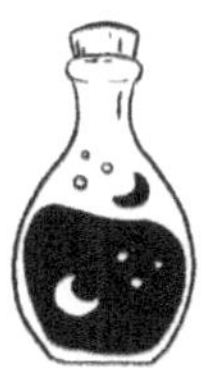

Ambrose

THE MOMENT ELI fell fast asleep in his bed at the Skipwallow Inn, Ambrose turned to his blue clay mushrooms for solace.

He sat by the hearth, chopping the rare mushrooms, while Heckley curled up by his feet and his table floated stubbornly off the ground. With a glower, he ignored the annoying quirk of the furniture and continued his ingredient preparation. These mushrooms didn't require immediate chopping, exactly—this particular species wouldn't degrade for at least eight hours—but he needed something to do. Something to occupy his mind other than the squelching sound of mud and the stomach-flipping sight of Eli falling off the ledge.

Thank the gods the others had been there. Eli's shield pendant had sputtered after the first skullcap impact—but Grim's other ring had cushioned the fall. Then Dawn's healing wand was out a mere second after impact, and Banneker's makeshift stretcher didn't so much as tilt the entire walk back...

Leaving Ambrose with nothing to do but worry and fret the whole way home.

He would have continued fretting through the night, but Sherry had insisted she cover Eli's bedside for an hour or two, so…here he was. Sitting next to Dawn with an automaton draped over his foot, dipping mushrooms in a preservative solution, and hoping to forget about the whole ordeal.

To Ambrose's chagrin, everyone else in Skipwallow Inn wanted the very opposite.

"What was the old guard tower like?" Chester sat across from them and set both elbows on the floating table, grinning eagerly. Beside him, a sleepy Heckley reached out with one rope arm and poked the mushrooms.

"Empty." Ambrose swatted away Heckley's arm. "Empty and muddy."

One of the bards leaned against the mantle of the hearth and hummed. "Muddy, ruddy, buddy…no decent rhymes. Come on, what else you got? Was the place spooky? Mysterious? Cursed?"

Heckley slowly dragged a mushroom off the table. Dawn snatched it back for Ambrose.

"Walk over there and find out yourself," she muttered.

"Oh, no, I couldn't possibly go that far from the inn," Chester said cheerfully. "Not when we're just so dang busy. Am I right, Heckley?"

He patted the automaton, while behind him, the resident adventurers and tinkerers were beginning to peer over in curiosity at Ambrose and his bright blue mushrooms. Sensing more questions on the way, Dawn nudged his arm.

"Think we need to go check on Eli."

"Right. You're absolutely right." He bundled up his work and stood. "Excuse us."

Technically, neither of them needed to check on Eli—Sherry had at least another hour left on her watch duty—but if anyone else asked Ambrose questions about his adventure, he was going to summon the mudmire again just to get out of answering them.

"The hearth was rather busy," he grumbled to Sherry as he opened the door to his room. "How is he?"

"Just fine." Sherry smiled and flipped through a magazine. "Sleeping like a baby."

Ambrose stared at the cover of the magazine, where Xavion Demachel's smug, illustrated face stared back at him. "*Sherry.*"

"What? Oh." She half-closed the magazine to glance at the cover. "I'm sorry, but it was the only reading material around."

"I cannot be caught with that in my room!"

"All right, all right." She stood with a creak. "It's past my bedtime, anyway. The boy's bandages are all checked, but make sure you check them one more time tonight."

"I appreciate it, Sherry."

As Sherry folded up the magazine, Dawn squeezed his arm. "Hey. Try to get some sleep yourself, okay? Just watching him won't make him heal any faster."

Ambrose scoffed. "As if I would just sit and watch him."

That was precisely what he ended up doing.

Too afraid to jostle the mattress, he pulled his chair up to the edge of the bed, then rested his head on his arms and idly counted Eli's breaths. Eli was all cleaned up now—no armor, fresh bandages, his plain tunic open at the neck. According to the others, there was no doubt he'd make a full recovery from both the impact and the heat rashes. But with each breath Ambrose counted, the less he thought about that day's quest, and the more he thought about all the others: the countless quests Eli went on for work, the constant journeys out into the dangerous wilderness.

How often had Eli been truly injured while away from the Scar? Did anyone else in his party watch over him while he recovered? Did they make sure he was cool while he slept, that he had a pillow under his head and at his side? Did they check his wounds regularly, or did they just shake up potions and hope for the best?

Ambrose rubbed his eyes. The day had exhausted both him and his poor grasp on positivity. He had to think about something nice for a change, something hopeful. Something that didn't involve mud, mushrooms, or bandages...

He yawned and gently wrapped his fingers around Eli's hand. His left hand, currently bare of any jewelry...but would eventually, some-day, have a ring on it.

He rubbed the back of Eli's hand with his thumb. Dawn would make fun of him for it, but he didn't dare think about what sort of ring he would get Eli. Not yet, anyway. Part of him didn't want to jinx it—and another part of him wanted to match what Eli had bought him.

(And Eli most definitely had already bought it. He hadn't been nearly subtle enough about hiding the box in the sock drawer, nor had he been able to hide his goofy grin all day.)

But now, in the quiet safety of his mind where no one could judge him, Ambrose started to build the ring in his mind. A gold band with a shield enchantment. A ruby with a shield enchantment. A diamond with a shield enchantment. Or perhaps he should just nix the ring and tattoo a damn shield enchantment on this reckless man's hand—

Eli's fingers weakly squeezed back; Ambrose bolted upright. "You're awake!"

Eli looked up at him and pouted. "You changed."

But Ambrose was already diving for the bandages on the night-stand. "Sherry says I have to check you one more time. It shouldn't take long, and then you can..." He paused. "What do you mean, I changed?"

"Your armor." Eli reached for Ambrose's arm, his voice raspy. "You changed out of it."

His sleepy gaze trailed up and down Ambrose's body, as if he was hoping the leather jerkin would magically reappear. Ambrose gave a tired sigh.

"That armor was covered in mud. *I* was covered in mud—"

Clearly, that didn't matter. As soon as Ambrose sat on the edge of the bed, Eli pulled him down by his shirt and muffled his words with a kiss. A jolt ran through Ambrose, thrilling and bright and almost—almost—wiping the day's bad memories entirely from his head.

"You were taking care of me," Eli murmured, the sweet rasp in his throat like golden honey over toast. Ambrose gave him a weak smile and pushed his hair back from his forehead.

"I'll always take care of you. You know that."

Eli lowered his voice. "Then let me take care of you."

With a surprising surge of energy, Eli wrapped his arms around Ambrose and dragged him onto the bed. Ambrose knew he shouldn't give in—he had bandages to check, pain medication to measure—but he couldn't bring himself to move away. Half-collapsed against Eli, he tightened his grip on his hair and let his kisses travel, across his cheek, down his neck, right to the exposed spot between his collarbones—

Eli winced; Ambrose shot up. "Sorry, sorry—!"

"No, no." Eli gave a breathy laugh and held his hips firmly in place. "I'll just take care of you...more slowly."

<hr>

After the events of the day—and the events of the evening—Ambrose fell asleep the moment he blew out the candle and curled up against Eli's fortress of pillows. The wall of softness was such that when he woke in the cave, the vast emptiness of the place unsettled him.

"Good evening, Fio," he said with a yawn. "You'll be pleased to know that I finally got what I need for the shrinking potion. You won't be pleased to know what I had to do to get it. Safe to say I could have used a guard dragon out there."

No response from Fio's silhouette.

"Fio?"

Ambrose stepped forward into the moonlight. Fio was staring up at the hole in the ceiling—a jagged circle now wide enough to give him a clear view of the stars and moon hanging above the Scar. But he had nothing haughty to say today. No questions about Marlin or Driftwood dragons or waterfalls. He simply watched the stars, both ears drooping.

So, Ambrose stood with him, watching the sky until a white blur flitted overhead.

"Oh." He tried to brighten his voice for Fio's sake. "An auroc. Did you see it?"

An auroc?

"That bird that went by. An early one, it seems. You'll see more of them flying over soon as part of their migration." Ambrose hesitated. "But perhaps you were too young to have seen them before your hibernation—"

I've seen them.

There was a knife hidden in the words, a sharp edge that Ambrose didn't dare touch. He fell silent again until Fio's tail swished heavily against the earth.

I watched them with my family, he finally said. *Flew alongside them with my family. Not to eat*, he added quickly. *Too much ice. We flew to play. To enjoy.*

Each word sharpened the knife—until it dropped. As if Fio was tired of holding it.

I can't smell them. I can't smell my family out there. I can't smell anything I recognize. He slowly turned and bent his head down toward Ambrose, his golden eyes glowing in the light. *They're not out there, are they?*

Ambrose's next words were like hot coals within his throat. "No. They're not."

Fio lowered his body, muscles tense, wings held high—but he made no move to fly. He simply crouched with nothing to hide behind.

They left me, he said, his words broken as they tumbled over each other, louder as they went. *They said they'd be here after I woke up. I didn't want to. I didn't want to sleep for so long, I was scared and they promised me they'd be here and then they abandoned me—*

"They didn't abandon you," Ambrose said quickly. "They—they were here in the Scar for a while, and then they... They moved on."

The sentence cut a slash in his chest—and the words seemed to be just as comforting to Fio. His spines flared, and he curled further in on himself.

They're not here! he said once more. *The air isn't right, nothing is right, I don't belong here—*

He cut himself off, his breath coming in sob-like gasps.

Where do I go?

Ambrose had nothing to offer. Yes, there was Marlin's habitat. But it was far away from the Scar, filled with strangers both human and dragon. A foreign, mocking facsimile of a home.

"I don't know," he said quietly; in response, Fio grew even louder.

I'll—I'll melt it all, then! His claws gouged the earth, and his cries roiled into a growl. *I'll melt my way out of here and take to the skies and never come back!*

He cleaved at the wall, hissing and snapping at the moonbeam. No acid came, not even a drop, but that didn't matter. He kept just clawing, again and again. Ambrose fell to the ground, the stone floor freezing underneath his palms. He should end the dream now. Should get out of the cavern that housed an enraged dragon.

Instead, he stood.

"Of course you're angry," he said. "I know it. I know all of it. The abandonment. Not having family. Nothing being familiar."

Old rage built inside him, and part of him suddenly wanted to grow claws and gouge the earth himself. To berate the dragons for not staying, for not caring for their *son*—

"Of course you're angry!" he repeated, his own voice rising until he couldn't control it anymore. "Of course you want to melt it all down! Why wouldn't you, after all those years of being alone? Of waiting for them to return? Of looking for them out the window until you were grown, knowing and *knowing* they didn't even care enough to come back and explain why they did it, or to see if you were even still alive, let alone successful, and—and in love, and pretending like you never even needed them in the first place—"

His words broke with a gasp, his hand clutching his own chest. Tears stained his cheeks, dust marked his hands.

And Fio had lowered his head level to Ambrose's.

"I'm sorry," Ambrose breathed. "I'm sorry, I don't know what—"

Then Fio nudged his snout underneath Ambrose's hand and began to purr.

It wasn't a contented purr—there was too much underneath the rumble for that, and Fio's eyes remained wide open. But Ambrose set a hand on Fio's nose anyway, on his smooth, shimmering scales, and let the vibration thrum through his bones. It didn't melt the grief—nothing would—but it shook him loose from it. Let him step out and stare at it for a moment.

Then he set his other hand on Fio's scales.

"I don't know where you should go," he said, quiet and exhausted. "But wherever it is, I will make sure you get there safely."

A Beake CPM ← and Nat!
Shrinking Potion
(at 150x scale)

and Nat.

apply wax
for travel

round or
square?

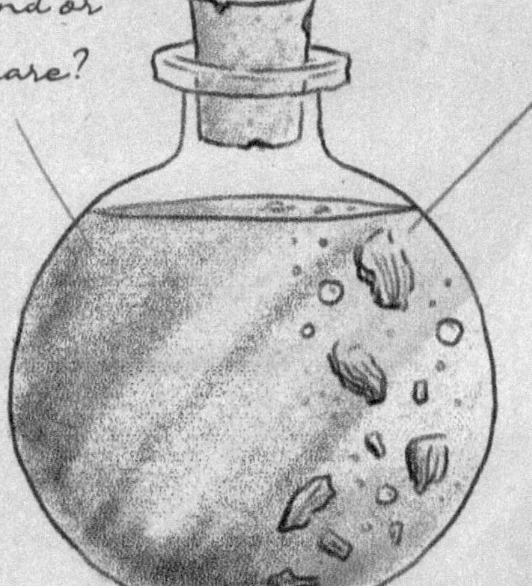

Kaolin Agaricus
Saphira

- chop and preserve
  within 8 hours
- do not over-handle
- will dissolve within
  brew in a day

Procedure

1. Preheat cauldron to
   level 200.

2. Prepare mushroom by
   chopping into talon-size
   pieces, then dipping into
   preservative. (see pg 5.)

Observations

175 better?

will need to prepare
preservative in
advance

Pg. 1

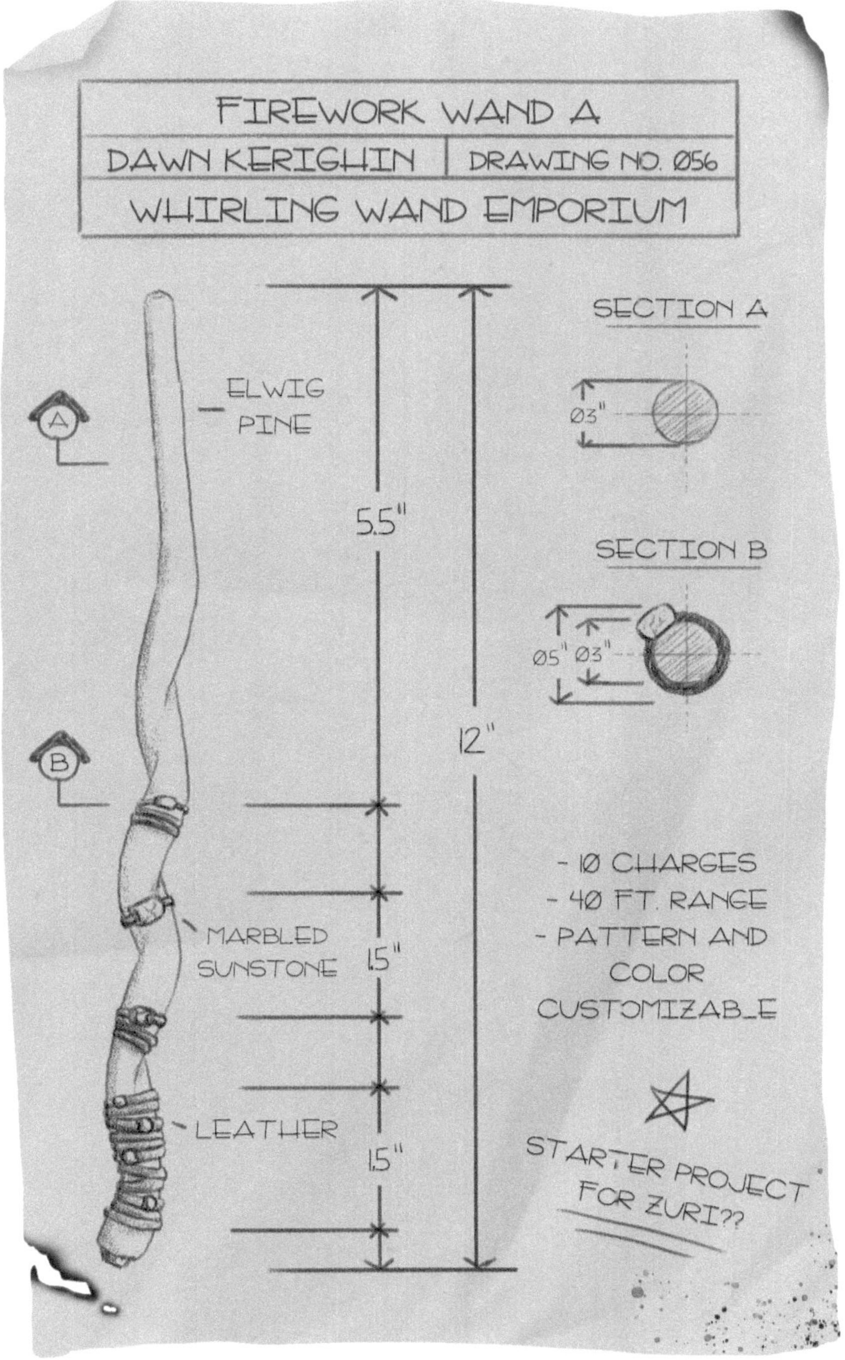

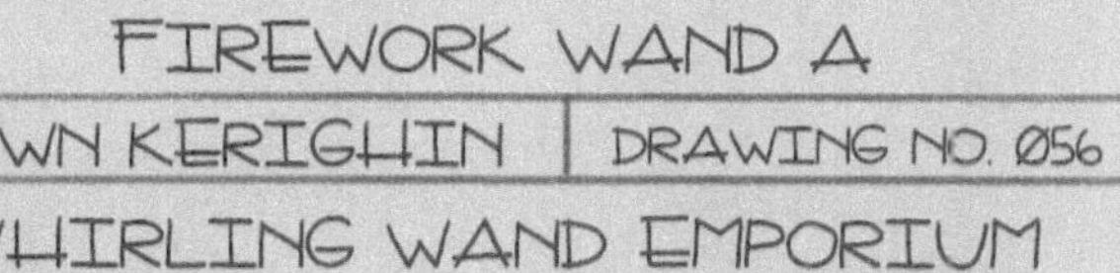

FIREWORK WAND A
DAWN KERIGHIN
DRAWING NO. 056
WHIRLING WAND EMPORIUM

A
B
ELWIG
PINE
5.5"
12"
MARBLED
SUNSTONE
1.5"
1.5"
LEATHER
SECTION A
Ø3"
SECTION B
Ø5" Ø3"
- 10 CHARGES
- 40 FT. RANGE
- PATTERN AND
  COLOR
  CUSTOMIZABLE
STARTER PROJECT
FOR ZURI??

WINGED
WARLOCK
ARTIFICER'S
ATELIER

PLATE 1

TITLE: ASTRAL AMPLIFIER

INFUSED GLASS
FOR STABILITY
IN DRIFTWOOD

CHARGES:

15, CAN MOD TO 20
NOTE: LUKA WANTS TO
ADD MORE SOUNDS

TRAPPED PSYVINE
ESSENCE

SET STAR LIGHT COLOR

SET
OCEAN SOUNDS

CLEANSED COPPER
WITH
ATTUNED SILVER
INLAY

SLIDE TO ACTIVATE
ASTRAL AMPLIFICATION

Banneker

PLACKART & FAULDS ARMORY
SHERRY
DRAWING NO. 09
STUN SHIELD (var. C)

FIG. 1
STEEL BASE
CHARGE
(STUN SILVER;
STRIKE TO ACTIVATE)

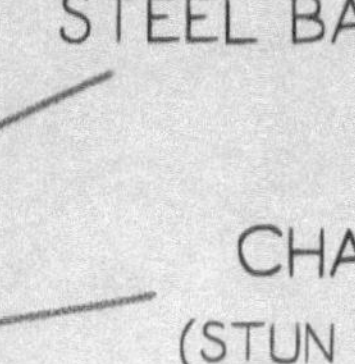

FIG. 2
BACK
ADJUSTABLE GUIGE
AND HAND STRAP
(INFUSED LEATHER)
POSSIBLE INFUSIONS:
STRENGTH, SPEED,
HEALING

WEDDING RING SET

NESTED SET

VAR: CUSTOM
CLIENT: ELI VALENZ

FIG. 1

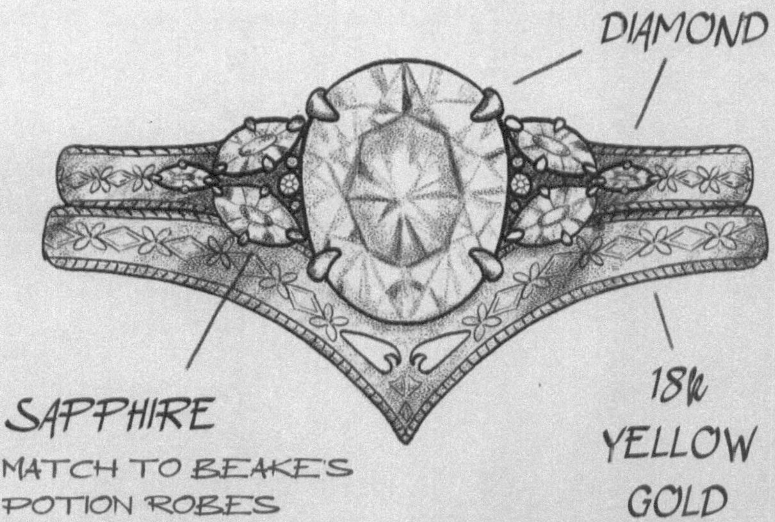

SAPPHIRE
MATCH TO BEAKE'S POTION ROBES

VALENZ ASKED FOR NO ENCHANTMENTS.

WILL ADD SOME ANYWAY. BEAKE WILL LIKE THEM.

Grim

~~The Twirly Whirly~~
~~The Winged Whirl~~
The Whirling Winged Griffins

that looks nice, nat
thanks, Luka!

Smoke Potion

girl what kind of
potion drawing is that

I can't draw bottles
as well as Ambrose, Zuri!!

ILLUSION SIEVE

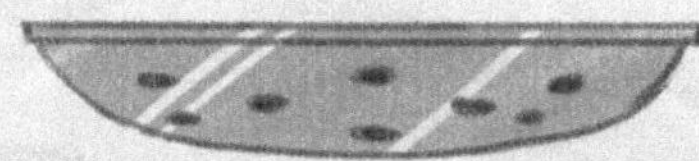

Smoke will pour through
the sieve and adopt carved
griffin shape.

See pg 3 for full griffin
drawing and possible variants.

levitation wand.

I know what
I'm doing.

zuri youre supposed to write stuff

you didn't leave me any room.

we have an entire notebook...

Page 1

TIP 18:

GET BACK TO THE CAULDRON

Eli

WHEN ELI NEXT WOKE, he had clean bandages, a growling stomach, and a post-magic headache the size of the entire inn.

It was the only downside to an entire street of magical merchants shoving healing potions and spells at him in rapid succession. He was perfectly healed, yes—the bandages revealed unburnt skin, and he had hardly more than a bruise on the back of his head—but the lingering daze made him feel like he had been out drinking for several days straight.

And when he trudged downstairs to find some breakfast, Ambrose looked like he had been out drinking alongside him.

"No, Heckley..." he mumbled, shooing the automaton away with his foot while he stirred a cauldron in the hearth. With shoulders rounded and eyes underlined with dark circles, he balanced a wooden spoon in one hand and a notebook in the other. "Next question," he said more loudly. "What is your favorite place in the Scar?"

Next to the hearth, the rest of Rosemond Street had dragged a table close to the fire and was picking through a platter of eggs, rolls, and fruit. Sherry took an orange and consulted the ceiling.

"Must I pick just one?"

"Just one, please. My dreams with Fio don't last that long."

Eli fought through his haze and made his way toward the table, the sight of Ambrose, breakfast, and his friends boosting his strength. He knew how he *could* answer Ambrose's question—naturally, it would be Ambrose's bedroom—but if such an answer would get him barred from that plate of bacon on the table, he'd have to reconsider—

"Eli!" Dawn jumped up with a grin. "You're alive!"

Ambrose whipped around, but the others were too fast. They clustered around Eli first, then dragged him to a seat right in front of the food, shoveling toast and scrambled eggs onto a plate for him.

"It'll help with the headache I'm sure you've got," Grim said as they supplied him with extra slices of toast. "Beake, you sure you don't want any?"

"Quite sure, thank you." Amidst the commotion, Ambrose managed to plant a light kiss on Eli's forehead. Even so, Eli didn't fail to clock the half-eaten toast sitting by Ambrose's potion ingredients: a clear sign that the potioneer had something else on his mind.

"What's with the survey?" he asked, pointing to the notebook with one hand while shoveling eggs into his mouth with the other.

"Fio," Ambrose answered. "Last night before I left him, he started asking questions about my guards—er, you all."

"Guards?" Eli grinned. "We're your guards?"

"No, of course not—"

Eli grabbed his hand and kissed the back of it. "No, no, I'm your guard now."

Ambrose bit back a smile as he rolled his eyes. "I thought I would gather some answers to pass along next time I see him," he continued, moving back to the cauldron to stir it a few times. "If I don't return with something for him, I'll never have a peaceful night's sleep again."

Eli scarfed down another piece of bacon-loaded toast. Grim was right: the food was rapidly helping chase away his headache, and thoughts were beginning to fight their way to the surface.

"That amplifier Banneker made," he ventured. "It was strong enough to accidentally let me join the dream that one time. Any chance it could be modified to include another visitor on purpose?"

Dawn gasped. "I could meet *Fio*?" She grabbed Banneker's arm and shook it. "Do it, I wanna meet Fio—"

"Okay, okay!" Banneker laughed. "Give me a few days and I'll see what I can do."

Ambrose rubbed his forehead. "More people in my dreams. How lovely."

Eli ignored his pessimism—something he had practice with by now—and leaned over to peek at the next question in Ambrose's notebook.

"All right, everyone," he called. "Favorite food, let's go."

Heckley was quite clear in his answer; he reached again for the mushrooms in the cauldron, forcing Ambrose to swat his arms away with his spoon. "Heckley, you aren't even capable of eating these—"

"Come here, Heckles!" Chester bound forward with a plate of sausages. In one smooth motion, he set the sausages on the table and scooped up the automaton with his free arm. "Sorry about that. He loves to be a part of things."

Clearly, so did Chester, because he also peeked at the notebook and brightened.

"Favorite foods!" he said. "Well, I love a good fernberry pie. Or an apple pie. Or a lemon pie. Or a—"

"Thank you for your response," Ambrose tried in a strained voice, but Chester wasn't done.

"Oh! And honey pie!" He bounced on his heels a little, rustling the pack on his shoulders. "I usually set out these honey stalks for the aurocs, but they make a mean galette if you chop 'em up right."

Eli frowned at the bamboo-like sticks poking out of the pack. "Do the aurocs actually come by and eat them?"

"Not if I put them too close to the inn. But you never know!" He took one of the stalks and chomped on the end. "They'll pick my courtyard to roost one of these days, I know it. They like the anchored spots in these parts. It's easier to rest if they know the forest won't up and change around them."

Eli wanted to comment that the courtyard was barely anchored, and maybe old Skip needed that tune-up he was so sensitive about, but Chester was already bounding out the door, waving the bitten stalk at them.

"You let me know if you need any more breakfast!" he shouted, made his greetings to a pair of adventurers by the door, and loped out into the courtyard to place honey stalks around its perimeter. Heckley followed eagerly, two stalks in his rope arms. Ambrose shook his head and picked up his quill.

"All right, I need at least one question answered before tonight," he said. "Actual favorite foods, please?"

While the group debated between Viola's baked goods and Sherry's baked goods, Eli glanced over at the simmering cauldron. His headache had lifted, allowing him enough energy to think about his own brew. He had the lavender, the violets, and now the forget-me-nots from the mudmire. There was technically nothing stopping him from brewing his proposal potion.

And as long as Ambrose couldn't move from his own brewing spot, now was a good time to do it.

"You keep going with the questions." Eli stood and kissed Ambrose's cheek. "I'm going to nap. See if I can kick the rest of this headache."

As he leaned in, he quietly nicked an empty potion bottle from Ambrose's tools, then headed upstairs in quiet victory. But one member of Rosemond Street didn't miss the theft: Dawn quickly finished the last of her toast and followed Eli up the steps.

"Hey! Are you brewing the"—she glanced behind her—"the proposal potion?"

"Trying to." Eli held up the bottle. "If Xavion will let me use their space for a second."

Dawn recoiled. "*Xavion?*" she repeated. "You can't use their stuff. What if they try to blackmail you or something?"

"Well, I can't brew it in the hearth. Ames already claimed that."

"What about Chester's kitchen?"

Eli paused at the top of the stairs. "You really think Chester's gonna be able to keep his mouth shut?"

"Fine, fine." Dawn stepped aside. "I'll guard the hall and let you know if Ames is coming."

While she ducked away, Eli took a breath and knocked on Xavion's door.

"Xavion?" he called. "It's Eli Valenz. I know you don't want visitors, but—"

Xavion gave a loud sigh and opened the door. "Did Amby get eaten by that mudmire?"

"No."

"Good, he still owes me that quote." They set a hand on their hip. "What do you want, then?"

Eli swallowed; he hadn't exactly formulated a good argument for this on the way up the steps.

"I'd like to use your cauldron to brew something small," he said. "A...slightly magical potion."

Xavion frowned. "A...slightly magical...potion."

"Yes."

"What makes it slightly magical?"

"It's low strength," he said vaguely. "Look, I just need access to a cauldron for less than an hour—"

Xavion's gaze narrowed. "Why would I give you access to mine, knowing what happened to your last shop?"

Eli winced; that was, unfortunately, a fair question.

"I swear I'll use all the safety equipment you have." He held up both hands. "It's just—it's an important potion."

"It's not that mushroom brew Amby's trying to make, is it?"

"No."

"Then what is it?"

He definitely couldn't tell Xavion that. He stiffened, trying to think of a reasonable substitute on the fly. Enchanted perfume, maybe, or—

"Gods, you two and your strange little secrets." Xavion started to close the door. "Have a good day—"

"Wait!" Eli checked the hall to make sure it was empty, then sighed. "It's...it's a proposal gift for Ambrose."

Xavion raised their eyebrows and stared at him for one long moment. Eli bit his lip. He *knew* he shouldn't have said anything—

"Fine." Xavion swung the door open once more. "As long as you let me send Amby a wedding gift."

They stepped aside; Eli remained right where he was.

"That's it?" he asked.

"That is all."

"No other trade?"

"No."

"No catch?"

"No."

"You're not gonna mess with the potion behind my back and make it explode in Ambrose's face when I—?"

"*No.*" Xavion sighed. "Ambrose Beake is an arrogant, proud, infuriating man—"

"Obsess over him less," Eli grumbled.

"*But*"—Xavion glared—"he is not undeserving of whatever happiness you give him. The kindest of beings I am not, but I won't stand between...whatever it is you two have going on." They gestured toward their room. "My early congratulations."

They led Eli to the corner, swept clean of everything except a floor cauldron, a fume pull, and a fold-out chest of ingredients. For being a hasty travel set-up, it was similar to Ambrose's in terms of quality and cleanliness.

Ambrose would hate to learn that.

Eli pulled his flowers out of his bag and worked quickly, double-checking the heat of the flames and his handwritten notes to soothe his simmering anxiety around lit cauldrons. This potion would be easy—easier than most of what he'd had to brew as a potioneer. All he had to do here was boil the ingredients together, then infuse his own memories into the brew. It couldn't encapsulate everything Eli wanted to say to Ames—nothing could, really—but he had to try.

He worked quickly and carefully, ignoring Xavion's presence in the room while the floral scent of the potion filled the air. As soon as the liquid reached the right color—a light, springtime green, bordering on a sunny yellow—he ladled the potion into his stolen bottle, cooled the glass, and took a deep breath.

Infusing the potion with memories was, in theory, straightforward. All he had to do was close his hands around the potion and think of Ambrose. Easy—he already did that all the time.

But here in Xavion's room, with the minutes ticking by and his Spelltide proposal deadline looming... His mind went blank. He could only vaguely picture their first date, their first kiss. The potion was supposed to turn a rich, dark green when filled with memories, but it had been fifteen minutes now, and the hue had hardly changed—

"Caw!"

Both Xavion and Eli frowned at the door.

"Caw *caw*!" Dawn tried again, more frantically—then as her footsteps retreated into another room, a new set of steps approached the door. Eli froze, willing whoever it was to keep walking, to disappear down the hall...

Someone knocked on the door. Xavion cast a glance over at Eli, then slowly ambled over and opened the door a crack.

"You again," they drawled. "What do you want this time?"

"A favor, if possible." Ambrose's voice floated in from the entrance. "I seem to be missing a small bottle—"

"So I take it to mean you're ready to brew your little mushroom tea?"

Ambrose huffed. "Not quite. I'm trying to prepare the solvent for one of the steps, and I've run out of sanitized bottles. I was wondering if you had one I could borrow."

Eli gave a silent curse and scrambled to cork the potion. Xavion could ruin it all, gleefully, in this moment. They could open the door, lead Ambrose right over to him, spoil the whole thing—

"Perhaps." Xavion leaned against the doorway. "What kind do you need? What glass thickness, cork type, shape—"

"Nothing special, just the standard."

"How so terribly dull of you. Not even considering reaching beyond your boring horizons."

Behind their back, Xavion waved impatiently to Eli, who spun around in a circle. There were no other doors to this room, not unless he counted the—*ah*, the window—

He shoved the window open and slid onto the narrow balcony just as Ambrose bristled.

"I am *practical*, unlike some people I know. Now, please, I truly only need the bottle for an hour. I can even pay you for it if you'd like."

Xavion flicked a glance backward; Eli ducked down under the sill.

"No, no. I shall be magnanimous for once." Xavion opened the door. "Here, take your pick."

Eli assessed the distance between the balcony and the ground—jumpable, for sure—while inside, Ambrose assessed a row of bottles in Xavion's travel cabinet.

"This is a nice cabinet," he half grumbled. "I recognize the filigree. Did you purchase it from—?"

"Druther's in the Scar? Why, yes," Xavion said smugly. "Two years ago after Potion Con. I believe he's the same carpenter who supplies your wand-making friend with her cabinets. I daresay she has far better taste—a shame her brilliance hasn't rubbed off on you."

Eli snorted; Ambrose glanced toward the window. Xavion, in a gesture of true generosity, stepped in to block the sill.

"You know, I hear she's engaged," they continued.

Ambrose plucked a bottle from the cabinet. "She is indeed."

"And *you've* been with your beau for several years now. Will the Potion Quarterly soon have your wedding portrait emblazoned across it?" Xavion inspected their nails. "That will be difficult to compete against, you see. I must plan for it."

"No, you don't have to worry on that front." Ambrose headed for the door. "I will not have a wedding."

Xavion paused in a moment of genuine confusion.

"Really?" They quickly pulled themself back together. "But—but you at a Scarrish wedding, Amby! Must you deny your Potion Con fans the dashing image of you in a flower crown and a half-cape?"

Ambrose's voice went flat. "I thought you didn't want to compete against it."

"Oh, please, don't start going easy on me now." Xavion opened the door for him. "What's victory without a little competition?"

"And what's a wedding without a family?" Ambrose snapped.

Eli stopped breathing.

Oh gods, that was it. Of course that was it, how had he not seen it? His mind raced through every conversation he'd ever had with Ambrose about weddings. Every time he had described family traditions, gushed over family members attending... And Ambrose had just sat there, quietly knowing he had no father to stand with him. No mother to walk him down the aisle. No siblings, no cousins, no...

He clutched the still-warm potion to his chest, words building up on his tongue until they almost sent him straight out of his hiding place and back through the window. He didn't brew this potion to have a wedding. He brewed the potion to have a *husband*. Someone he could cook dinners with, and come home to, and care for, and just be with—

Memories of their days together flooded his mind. Simple moments, none of the grand gestures he had been trying to think of. He imagined Ambrose reading by the fire. Walking down the street with him. Laughing at The Gingersnap Cafe, holding Tom, falling asleep in his arms...

The potion under his fingers turned a deep green, as richly hued as the forest outside. And back in the room, Ambrose cleared his throat.

"Apologies," he said to Xavion, his words clipped. "That was untoward of me. You've been uncommonly generous. It's...it's just the deadline this potion is under."

For once, Xavion didn't have a witty retort nor cutting insult on hand.

"I understand that well enough," they said stiffly. "Clean that bottle before returning it. I will be here, lovingly daydreaming about that magazine quote of yours. And do consider keeping *uncommonly generous* in your phrasing, yes? I rather liked the sound of that."

The door closed with a click. Eli stared at the potion bottle, then slid to the ground and slipped away into the courtyard.

TIP 19:

PREPARE YOUR SPELLS

Nat

MUCH TO ROSEMOND STREET'S relief and Nat's chagrin, Rory and Viola never missed checking in on the apprentices each evening after the stores closed—and today, the ladies had cornered Zuri and Nat in The Whirling Wand Emporium.

"Good news on the Aphos front," Rory said, leaning against the railing of the loft while Zuri cleaned. "Now that the earthquakes have stopped, Aphos is dragging their feet on the whole Fio problem. Apparently, no one feels like going head-to-head with a giant dragon if no one's complaining about it."

"Good." Nat helped Zuri run a repair wand over the straw targets in the back. According to Zuri, an adventuring party had been particularly enthusiastic in testing out some blast wands that morning, and the targets had the blackened scars to prove it. "That buys us more time to get him out. Has anyone heard how the mushroom hunt went yesterday?"

Everyone shook their heads. That didn't surprise Nat—but they only had three days until Spelltide. If Rosemond Street was going to try to make it out right after the festival, that only gave Ambrose so many days to brew the potion.

When she said as much, Viola grimaced.

"They're cutting it close, but it's Ambrose. He's done more in less time, I'm sure." She brightened. "How did *your* brewing go the other day?"

Nat shifted. It was bad enough that Rory and Viola knew all about their Spelltide plan; there was no way in any of the hells she was going to admit to them she had almost burned her hands off. They'd throw a fit. Rosemond Street would lose their heads. Ambrose would probably wrap her in a padded duvet cover and ban her from looking at a cauldron ever again—

"Fine!" she said, her voice far too high-pitched. "Got our part of the prototype all ready to test."

Zuri shot her a frown over her hexagonal glasses, but Viola simply nodded along.

"And you'll tell the others about your plan?" she asked.

Nat bobbed her head, focusing very hard on repairing a straw target with its head burnt off. "As soon as we have it working."

Rory checked her watch. "Well, as much as I'd like to stay and watch your test, I'm late for an interview with the guy heading up the Spelltide llama parade."

Viola scrunched her nose. "What do llamas have to do with magic?"

"Guess that's what I'm going to go find out." Rory paused at the top of the stairs. "You got all your safety gear? Goggles, reversal wand, fire foam, all that nonsense?"

Zuri popped up from behind a target. "Got so much nonsense prepared, you wouldn't believe."

"Good." Rory straightened her jacket. "Because if anything backfires on you, it's me Dawn'll kill first. Then you. Then whatever did the backfiring. Basically, she'll go on a rampage."

"What if I want to see the rampage—?"

"No, you do not."

After she jogged down the steps, Viola followed, claiming she had both Tom and a batch of Spelltide cookie dough waiting for her in the bakery. As soon as the chime above the shop door faded away, Zuri turned to Nat and folded her arms.

"Okay, what happened last night?"

Nat gulped and slotted her repair wand onto the rack. "Nothing!"

"Liar. Both you and Luka have been jumpy for the past two days. Tell me what happened."

Nat fidgeted with the charms on her necklace. Zuri was not the rest of Rosemond Street. Zuri wouldn't wrap her in a duvet if she admitted what happened. Probably.

And she had to tell *someone* about her stupid Luka-related thoughts.

She screwed her eyes shut and ran through the confession in words so fast they blurred. "I may have burned my hands a bit—okay, maybe a lot—and Luka healed me and now we're fine and everything's fine and I sort of thought about kissing him after he healed me."

A taut silence followed. She tentatively opened one eye. Zuri stared flatly back at her.

"You only just *now* started thinking about kissing Luka?"

Nat opened her other eye. "What do you mean?"

Zuri slotted her own repair wand into place. "I thought you had hit that point weeks ago. I didn't want to bother you about it, but hearts practically burst out of your eyes when you look at him." She paused. "Okay, that sounded gross. But you get it. You understand my vision."

Nat cringed. Somehow, this realization made her want to turn tail and run far more than the confession about her potion mishap.

"It's that bad?" she squeaked. "Do you think he knows?"

"Oh, see, here's the great part." Zuri held up her hands and mimicked starburst shapes with them. "The hearts bursting out of *your* eyes are colliding with the hearts bursting out of *his* eyes, cancelling each other out and making you both..." She dropped her arms. "Complete idiots."

Fear and giddiness danced together in Nat's insides. "You really think he's got heart eyes?"

Zuri passed a hand over her face. "Oh my gods."

The door to the shop swung open. "Hello? Zuri, Nat? I'm here for the test."

Luka's voice nearly made Nat jump out of her skin. If only there was a way she could see his heart eyes, it would make all of this so much *easier*.

"Come on up!" She scrambled over to her pack and pulled out a bottle of wispy gray smoke. "We're ready to test the prototype!"

They gathered all their components together—the smoke, Zuri's disguise wands, and Luka's metal sieve. As Luka set out his sieve, he leaned over to Nat.

"How are your hands?" he asked quietly, his eyes darting down to her fingers.

Nat had to stifle a nonsensical giggle. It was just a look, there was nothing to a damn look—

"Fine, fine. Um, thank you." She cleared her throat, turned to Zuri, and spread out her arms. "Okay, let's start with the disguises. Make us look like old people."

Zuri waved three different wands, one for each of them. The air around Nat tingled and zipped, and after a moment, she opened her eyes and checked her hands.

She didn't feel any different—the magic was only a simple glamour, of course—but even her own eyes were tricked by the magic. She was wearing Ambrose's potion robes now, with his pale hands at the end of the cuffs.

Zuri—now Dawn-ified—held up a mirror, a proud glimmer of a smile on her face. "Trippy, huh?"

Nat laughed. The mirror showed just how high the glamour went, making up for Nat's lack of height to form the rest of Ambrose. She patted her ponytail, the sensation not at all matching the look of Ambrose's blue wave. It was perfect. She'd have to commission a few more of those wands from Zuri after all this was over. The opportunities for chaos in the shop...

"I'll have to practice walking like Banneker," Luka mumbled in Banneker's voice. He wore the artificer's likeness, but held himself like...well, himself. Stiff, polite, and unsure. Nat realized she herself was slouching and tried to pull her shoulders up. Ramrod straight like Ambrose, with arms behind her back. Chin held high, face slightly judgmental...

Luka glanced at her and reeled back in shock. "Oh, I don't like that. I don't like that at all."

Nat grinned far wider than Ambrose ever would. "Too close?"

"This is gonna give me nightmares." Zuri set aside the mirror. "Come on, let's get the smoke going."

Luka held out the sieve; Zuri held up her final wand. Nat took a deep breath and uncorked her bottle of smoke. All that was left to do was pour.

She carefully upended the bottle over Luka's device. As he had described, the dense smoke filtered right through the holes, forming the shape of a griffin just underneath. It floated there for a moment, its edges rippling and fading. Nat dared to run her hand—or, well, Ambrose's hand—through it. The texture was just what they wanted. Feathery soft and cool, ready to take flight with Zuri's final enchantment.

Nat stepped back, and Zuri raised her wand.

Green sparks shot out from the carved tip and landed directly inside the smoky griffin, briefly glowing like a beating heart. But rather than giving life to the wings, beak, and tail...the sparks only emitted more sparks. Then more and more, flashing and sputtering, until—

"Duck!" Zuri shouted, leaping for her reversal wand. Luka dove behind a straw target. Nat huddled under the table.

A second later, the griffin exploded into a burst of gray, melty goo and collapsed on the wooden floor in a sludgy pile.

Nat drooped. Great—just after they had cleaned the loft, too.

Luka popped up from behind the target. "Is everyone all right—?" He stopped at the sound of his own voice and slouched. "Oh."

Luka was suddenly back to looking like Luka. No more red hair or freckles or clashing waistcoat. Nat looked down at herself—her disguise had faded, too.

"But they were supposed to last," she said. "Zuri, I thought you had built them to stay on for—"

"For hours," Zuri grumbled, chewing her lip. "The backfiring sparks must have messed with the glamour. Hold on, let me check the wands..."

A minute of checking the wands turned into an hour of poring over her blueprints. Then inspecting every inch of the sieve, checking the remains of the smoke...

"It's gotta be the smoke." Nat plunked her forehead down on the table in disappointment and exhaustion. "We've ruled out everything else."

She ran through everything that could have gone wrong. Maybe she had diced the ash flower stem the wrong way, or set the wrong temperature when reducing the ice stone down to a syrup. With twenty steps in the recipe, there were at least forty ways she could have messed up.

"Why don't we test all of it one more time?" Nat gathered up her smoking bottle and the sieve, trying not to let her nerves show through in her voice. She just needed more information, that was all. "Zuri, you've got enough charge in the disguise wands, right?"

Zuri lifted one of the wands. "It won't last a while, but yeah. Enough for a test."

"Great." Nat wiped her sweaty palms against her pants. "And if it doesn't work, we can...pivot to something else! Or tell the mayor it failed and we can't show anything." She swallowed. "He...won't be too mad at us, right?"

"Only one way to find out, I guess." Zuri ran her three wands over each of them once more. "Just give these a second to set, then we'll pour the—"

The bell chimed over the front door. "Hello?"

Without thinking, Zuri disguised as Dawn turned to the front. "Sorry, we're closed!"

She clapped a hand over her mouth, but it was too late; Dawn's distinct voice floated through the shop.

"Ah, Miss Kerighin!" the newcomer responded. "Back in time for Spelltide. How was your trip?"

Nat froze, then dared a cautious glance over the railing. Mayor Rune and his daughter, Beatrice, stood in the shop, waving up at the loft.

"Um." Zuri blinked at him. "My trip was…"

Nat gently pushed on her back. Zuri cursed under her breath, then descended the steps in as Dawn-like of a manner as possible. "It was great! The trip was so great!"

She smoothed out her floral skirt and shot a brief glare back up the steps. Nat shook her head and gestured to herself—now very Ambrose in form—but it was no use. Rune had already caught sight of her.

"Ah, Master Beake and Banneker. You've all returned." He gave a short bow. "I'm sure your apprentices told you about the quakes rattling the city. I nearly required your assistance with them, but I'm relieved they went away before the festival."

Nat held her breath as she ventured down the steps with Luka, expecting Rune to squint and see through their disguises at any moment.

"Yes, the quakes," she said, straightening her back in her best imitation of Ambrose. "I—my apprentice did inform me of the quakes. But I am quite glad to have returned to a peaceful city with absolutely no problems whatsoever."

Zuri gave her a look, but Rune bought the lie.

"Good, good." His face brightened, while behind him, Beatrice wandered off to admire the display cases. "I must say, I was thrilled to hear that you're preparing something together for Spelltide. I even have—"

"Dad!" Beatrice pointed at a wand. "Can this one summon dragons?"

"No, my dear. As I was saying, I have associates from—"

"Dad!" Beatrice pointed at a staff. "How about this one?"

Rune's smile tightened. "Not that one, either. Why don't you... look for a purple one?"

"Okay!"

As she dashed off, Rune turned and sped up his words to finish them before his daughter's quest completed. "I have associates from other cities coming who can't wait to see your collective talent on display." He clasped his hands together and looked on them all with genuine warmth. "Now, I'm sure your clientele tells you this often, but allow me to echo them. The Scar is so very lucky to have each and every one of you on Rosemond Street."

His gaze landed on Nat, his eyes directed up to where Ambrose's illusioned face was. He wasn't talking to her, not really—but her pride swelled all the same.

She was a part of Rosemond Street now. She couldn't let any of them down.

"The apprentices insisted your project was a secret," Rune continued with a sparkle in his eye, "so it seems I must wait for the details like everyone else. Unless...?"

Nat's mouth opened of its own accord.

"Whirling winged griffins," she said in Ambrose's voice. "Named after our three shops. It's—"

A swift elbow strike from Zuri made her recall herself, and she cleared her throat.

"That's all we can say for now," she finished.

"All right. Well, thank you for the hint. I am satisfied." Rune gave a parting bow. "I must be off to survey the parade route for opening day. Have a good evening. Beatrice?"

Beatrice dashed back and looked up at Zuri. "Are you absolutely *sure* you don't have any big purple wands that summon dragons—?"

"All right." Rune took her hand. "Time to make sure the llamas in the parade know where they're going. Say goodbye, now."

The bell tinkled innocently to punctuate Beatrice's parting wave, and as soon as Rune disappeared down the street, Zuri rounded on Nat.

"Why'd you tell him?" she demanded, her disbelieving expression somehow worse when transposed onto Dawn's face. "We don't even have our spell working, and now we can't pivot—"

"I'll get it working!" Nat shot back, but not even Luka was satisfied.

"And our bosses?" he asked. "What do we tell them?"

Nat's voice was already fading back to her own, away from Ambrose's stiff cadence. "We...well, we don't have a working prototype yet, do we?" she said. "And we don't have to tell them until we do. That's exactly what I promised." She straightened. "And I *will* get it working."

The rest of the disguises faded until it was just the three apprentices left by the counter. Zuri let out a sigh and adjusted her glasses. "Are you absolutely sure you can get it to work?"

Luka stepped in before Nat could open her mouth.

"If she says she'll figure it out, she'll figure it out," he said confidently. "I trust her."

Then he smiled at her, his gaze both soft and sure—and in that moment, she desperately wanted to be whatever he saw her as.

"I'll do it." She stood. "I'll get it done by Spelltide."

TIP 20:

BREW CAREFULLY

Ambrose

IT WAS the night before Spelltide, and Ambrose's thoughts were nowhere near tomorrow's celebrations.

On the contrary, they were entirely focused on the embarrassment that was his makeshift workshop around Skipwallow's hearth. Banneker had helped rig him a fume pull, and he had commandeered an extra table to organize his equipment—but all told, it was a ramshackle setup in a ramshackle inn. Almost as much of a crime as his illegal brews down in Aphos.

He was quite lucky Xavion was staying upstairs, far away from the bards.

"You fought a bear, you say?" One of the bards had his lyre propped up on his knee, ready to immortalize the visiting adventurer's encounter in song. "Let's see, what rhymes with bear? Air, blare, chair..."

Ambrose moved his speaking stone as far away from the bard as he could.

"And you restocked the night vision potions?" he called to the stone, trying to make his voice heard over both the conversation and his bubbling cauldron. Over by the table, Banneker and Sherry played cards as they listened in.

"Sure did," Nat responded from the stone, her tone flat and distracted.

"And the healing potions?"

"Stocked them this morning."

Ambrose paused in his stirring and frowned. "And the…double-helix flying whirligig moon-destroying hair color potions?"

"Mm-hm."

He threw the stone a flat look. "Nat."

"What?" A pause on the other end. "Sorry, Mr. Ambrose. Just, uh—a lot of cleaning to get done before tomorrow."

Cleaning was never the most enjoyable part of the day for her, he knew that. But the task usually didn't take so much of her focus, nor make her sound so…taut.

"Are you sure everything's all right?" he asked. "Aphos hasn't made any moves, have they?"

"No, Rory hasn't heard anything."

"And you're not too overwhelmed with the brewing? The wisp guides will be leading us out of here right after Spelltide. I'll be back as soon as I can—"

"Everything's fine!" Nat said quickly. "I promise!"

Over by the hearth, Heckley crept up toward the flames under the cauldron. Ambrose immediately turned to shoo him off; his Heckley senses had greatly improved over the past two days. "No. *Down,* Heckley—!"

"I got 'im." Grim shuffled over, picked up the automaton, and set him in Banneker's lap. Banneker clapped with glee and rubbed the top of the stool.

"Who's a good boy? *Who's* a good boy—?"

In the light commotion, the cauldron began bubbling over; Ambrose stifled a curse and stirred the brew.

"Apologies, Nat, but I should go. We'll reach out to you tomorrow for Spelltide—"

"Sounds good! Bye, Mr. Ambrose!"

The stripes on the stone went dim far too quickly. Ambrose hummed in frustration and flipped through his potion notes. Normally, he'd try to reactivate the magic and talk to her further, but he had to complete the next step in four clockwise turns. Then, what, three counterclockwise? Heckley's shenanigans had smudged the fresh ink...

"Here, I got it." Eli picked up the notebook. "Four clockwise turns, then three and a half counterclockwise." He flipped the page. "Have you chopped up the heather yet?"

"No, it's over in that bottle—"

"I'll do it, then." Eli headed over to the cutting board. "Hey, Banneker, did you get that amplifier adjusted so I can join Ames in saying hi to Fio?"

"Should be ready to go tonight!"

"Great." Eli nudged Ambrose. "We can tell him all about how the potion is going."

Ambrose watched Eli set up the cutting board and chop the heather with a practiced hand, while he took the ingredients and slowly moved the potion forward. Their rhythm was both familiar and distant—an echo of how they once worked together on a commission years ago.

As he stared, Eli glanced over at him and paused. "What?"

Ambrose smiled. "Nothing."

They didn't brew alone. Banneker and Sherry continued chatting quietly at the nearby table, and as Ambrose reached the final steps of the recipe, Grim and Dawn arrived with plates of food.

"Okay, dudes of brew." Dawn hefted a thick slice of cornbread. "Eat."

Before Ambrose could protest, she stuffed a piece into his mouth. "*Dawn—*"

By the cutting board, Eli opened his mouth wide. "Throw it!"

"No." Dawn walked over and crammed another piece into his mouth.

"My dear, they are perfectly capable of sitting down for dinner."

Sherry stood to help Grim set up the plates. "Come take a break, you two."

"Almost done, Sherry." Ambrose rummaged through his pack for the last component of the potion—the sedative that would knock Fio out while Ambrose carried him to safety. He had packed it right in this pocket, but the bottle was...

He pulled out his hand with a sigh. The bottle was empty. He had used it all on Eli after the tower debacle.

"Wine's pouring!" Banneker called. Ambrose stared at the cauldron. He could try to brew up a replacement with the scant ingredients he had left. Or trudge back up to Xavion and beg a replacement off them...

He grimaced at the cauldron, a sour taste building in the back of his mouth. Beg or brew, it didn't matter. He'd still be knocking Fio out —a dragon that hadn't done anything wrong. He couldn't do it. Fio deserved a more dignified rescue than that.

"Ames?" Eli set a hand on his shoulder.

Ambrose gave the potion one last stir and stepped away. "Coming."

Together, they joined the others at the table, ready to eat cornbread like civilized people this time—but Dawn wasn't paying attention to the food. She had paper and a quill next to her plate and was poring over a chart layered with circles, scribbles, and stress.

"How's the seating arrangement going?" Ambrose asked, pointedly dropping a piece of cornbread on the plate by her hand. Dawn merely picked at the slice.

"Ames, why'd I invite so many people to this wedding?"

Grim gave her a half smile. "Would you really have settled for less than a hundred?"

Dawn groaned and set her face on the paper in defeat. "This is so *hard*. Sherry, how many people did you have at your wedding? You said yours was small, right?"

Ambrose could feel Eli glancing over at him, but he didn't return the gesture. He simply passed the empty breadbasket to Grim and poked at his salad, quietly bracing himself for the usual wedding chatter. The recitation of family members, the rituals...

Sherry laughed. "Oh, quite small. I had about seven people."

Dawn shot up. "*What?*"

"Oh, yes." Sherry stirred her soup. "It was a spur-of-the-moment decision. We were out near Elwig with a few friends and just...found the perfect spot. A willow tree, right by a pond. And we decided that was that."

"So what did you do?" Dawn pressed. "I mean, with no one there."

"What do you mean, no one there? We were with our friends. They handled the whole ceremony."

Ambrose stared at her. "What do you mean?"

"Exactly what I said." Sherry's smile went dreamy and distant. "They threw together the rituals, the flowers, the officiating. Iris plucked a few wildflowers from the meadow, Piper handled the witnessing. I'm fairly certain we got all the words in our vows wrong." She chuckled. "My Davis had to say his three times over before he got 'em right, he was laughing so much."

"But your family," Dawn spluttered. "Weren't they mad they weren't there?"

Sherry only grinned wider. "Oh, they were livid. My mother swore she wouldn't talk to me for a year. My aunt and uncle refused to visit for months. I even had second cousins writing in saying they were disappointed in me." She shrugged and blew on her soup. "But it didn't matter. Davis and I were married and that's what we wanted. We couldn't have asked for a more perfect wedding."

Ambrose blinked at his salad, something slowly coming unknotted in his stomach. If Sherry had done it—*Sherry*, of all people—

The clunk of heavy paper against metal pulled him from his thoughts, and a moment later, a mailbox by the front desk flashed white. Heckley leapt eagerly off Banneker's lap and scrambled over. As far as Ambrose had seen, no one had arrived to deliver letters—

but when Heckley's rope arms reached into the box, they pulled out an envelope marked with the outline of a wisp.

"Thank you for the help, Heckley." Chester took the envelope, now slightly crumpled from the automaton's excitement—but the news inside wasn't exciting in the slightest.

"Bad news, everyone," Chester called to the room at large. "The wisp guides are delayed."

Everyone groaned; Ambrose lost his appetite completely. He had promised Nat he'd be back before Spelltide, then revised his promise to be back the day after. At this rate, she'd never trust him again—if he even got out of the Driftwood, that was.

"How delayed?" he called back.

"Several days."

"Several days?" he repeated, his hands going cold. "But I'm making the potion right now—"

Grim turned to him. "Will the potion hold?"

Ambrose looked back at the cauldron. He was more concerned about Fio holding than the potion holding.

"If I bottle it tonight, it'll hold for at least a week before spoiling," he said reluctantly. "But Fio—"

"We're all right." Sherry reached forward and squeezed his wrist. "Fio is safe where he is, the apprentices have the street handled, and your potion won't spoil." She leaned back and happily whittled away at her cornbread. "Why don't we just enjoy Spelltide while we have it?"

"Hear, hear." Banneker raised his cider. "I know your aura's in knots right now, my dude, but we can take a day. It'll be all right."

Dawn nudged Ambrose's arm. "It'll be fun! I'll get my fireworks wands set up and everything."

If the bards were going to be a part of the festivities, Ambrose very much doubted that. But he didn't feel like arguing with the table now, not when there was no chance of leaving. He merely pushed away his dinner and returned to the cauldron, taking small comfort in the familiarity of brewing. The potion's viscosity was still as expected, as was the color. In another twenty minutes, he could have it bottled and cooled, then stored for however long he was stuck here for…

A pair of arms gently wrapped around his waist; Eli kissed his cheek from behind. "Hey, humbug."

"Hello, my dear."

He continued stirring, expecting another joke or comment. Only silence followed, and he twisted around to look at Eli. "What is it?"

Eli just stared at him softly for a moment. Ambrose knew that look—something weighed on his tongue, something important. But instead of releasing it, Eli gave him another kiss. "Will you come to Spelltide with me?"

Ambrose was certain that wasn't the burning topic Eli had in mind—but he found little use in trying to coax it out of him now, so surrounded by people. He turned back to the cauldron with a wry smile. "Will there be dancing?"

"No."

"Liar."

Eli set his chin on Ambrose's shoulder. "Please? Please please please—"

Ambrose gave a small laugh, then took one of Eli's hands and twined their fingers together. Standing in front of the fire was unbearably hot when cuddling, but he didn't dare push Eli away. He never could.

"All right, all right." He lifted Eli's hand and kissed his knuckles. "I'll go to Spelltide with you."

TIP 21:
ROLL FOR PERFORMANCE

Nat

NAT SPENT the day before Spelltide doing her best impression of a mad scientist.

She kept sprinting from the various shops to her workroom, taking every free moment between rotations to fix her smoke potion. She scribbled out recipe adjustments, brewed more smoke, tested it against Luka's sieve and Zuri's wand... Every now and then, Luka and Zuri would pop in with cookies, advice, and cleaning assistance.

But the brunt of the madness had to fall on her—and in the most maddening fashion, none of her solutions were working.

She had made progress, yes. She was no longer cleaning disastrous gray goo off the floor, and the griffins no longer exploded. But with every experiment, something else about the illusion would fail. In one test, the griffins had formed without wings. In the next, they hovered awkwardly like statues. Then they'd go invisible, or plop to the floor, or mutate into spiky blobs and dissipate...

By the time she poured out her twelfth batch of smoke—the one that, for sure, hopefully, fingers crossed, fixed all her problems—

hours had passed and The Griffin's Claw rose statue had filled with missed messages. Nat corked the bottle and finally opened the scroll.

Zuri: nat, you finished with the smoke?
Zuri: hey
Zuri: naaaaaaaat
Luka: Should I come over? Would you like to test it together?

Her stomach flipped at the thought of Luka visiting. She could show off the smoke to him. Run it through the sieve one last time. She had enough of that ash flower, didn't she—?

She rummaged around in the cabinet, and her heart fell. Between her Spelltide re-stocking and her endless test batches of smoke...she had nothing left. No ash flower, only a few shards of ice stone. If she tested it now, she'd have nothing to show tomorrow. The vial still cooling on the counter was her last chance at getting this right.

She held the quill above the rose statue's scroll, ink threatening to drip onto the paper. She could tell them it wouldn't work. Pull out of the demonstration somehow, make apologies to Rune without giving away the exact cause. He'd be disappointed, of course. So would all those people who had come to see Rosemond Street. And Zuri. And Luka.

With every name, bile churned in her stomach, until she scribbled out her response with a shaky hand.

Nat: all finished and ready to go! See you tomorrow!

The following day, Nat arrived at the government square with Zuri and Luka, her bottle of smoke tucked away in her pocket.

There wasn't any time for them to get there sooner. The shops needed to be open for the morning, then closed for the afternoon festivities. Then there was cleaning to do after, meals to catch up on, disguises to step into...

But stepping into the square made the day's effort worth it.

Mayor Rune's posters and advertisements couldn't quite capture the atmosphere of Spelltide in the middle of the city. Tourists and Scarrish folk alike filled every ramp and platform, teeming around food carts, flower stalls, and souvenir tents. Nat's neck hurt from trying to take it all in, whipping left, right, and up to catch all the color and excitement. And even then, she only caught snatches of entertainment further off: jugglers, puppeteers, bards. This wasn't even the entirety of it. Tomorrow, there would be a parade, and the day after, a whole stage of entertainers out in the lavender fields, if the migration itself wasn't enough of a show...

As they passed a violinist perched on the fountain, Zuri poked Luka, the flatness of her voice not at all matching Dawn's typical inflection. "Could be you, you know."

Luka-as-Banneker gave her a weak, nervous smile. "I'll pass, thank you."

He stuck close to Nat in the crowds, shoulders nearly hiked up to his ears.

"Hey." Nat gently nudged him. "Shoulders down, remember? You're Banneker. Banneker doesn't mind crowds."

"Banneker doesn't mind anything," Luka muttered, but he dutifully lowered his shoulders, just as commotion began to bubble on the stage opposite the fountain. An announcer hopped up onto the tall wooden platform, his cape and waistcoat both glittering in a rainbow of colors.

"And now!" he shouted. "An appreciation of magic from the Jovial Journeymen!"

Three adventurers clambered up on stage. The woman in the middle downed a fizzing strength potion, then shot the crowd a cheesy grin. "Thanks to magic, I can do this without blinking!"

She lifted both of her companions into the air, one perched on each arm. The gnome on her left juggled daggers; the elf on the right twirled flaming arrows. As oohs and aahs rippled through the crowd, Zuri tugged on Nat's arm.

"Come on, let's get checked in." She pointed to a table near the stage. "The sooner we get this demonstration over with, the sooner we can check out the food."

A lone secretary was present at the check-in table—a human boasting green hair, square glasses, and a thin veneer of a smile.

"Ah, Rosemond Street!" they said as soon as Nat—or, rather, Ambrose—appeared at the table. "Wonderful. If you're all ready, we can have you go on right after Bellz the Bard."

They lined up behind a bard wearing a truly astounding number of jingle bells on his clothing. Zuri stared at the giant bell hanging from his pointed hat and slowly began to reach for it. Luka quietly set a hand on her wrist and shook his head.

Once the Jovial Journeymen finally stopped juggling and left the stage, Bellz bounded in for his turn, the clanging almost hurting Nat's good ear. She was cringing before he even started playing—but Luka, for once, looked a smidgen relaxed.

"Look at the carvings on the side of his lute," he murmured to Nat, leaning close to her. "The wood's enchanted. I think the strings might be, too. You can see the colors if you watch them vibrate."

He pointed as Bellz began playing. Nat squinted at the strings, trying to spot the color change—but once the chorus began, she didn't need to try so hard. The music floated out of the lute in visible pastel swirls, delighting the children clustered at the front of the stage. They reached out with tiny hands, trying to catch the sparkles.

"Would you look at that!" Luka grinned, just as fascinated as the rest of the audience. "The strings are definitely enchanted. Some artificers try to get away with only enchanting the pegs, but to get that sort of amplification, you have to enchant the strings before installation. Do you think I could talk to him after the performance? I'd love to know if he enchants them himself."

As he spoke in excited, hushed tones, the back of his hand brushed hers. The touch betrayed their illusions a little—his hand was smaller than Banneker's, and hers was smaller than Ambrose's—but also sent another tingle shooting up her arm. She held herself very still, as if moving would shoo his touch away.

"If you talk to him," she whispered back, "could you get me one of his jingle bells? I want to sew one to the hem of Ambrose's potion robes to see how long it'll take him to find it—"

"Thank you, thank you!" Bellz finished playing and waved to the crowd. "Happy Spelltide! I'll be playing at The Rose & Crown all this week!"

Luka pulled his hand away to clap for the bard. Nat also gave some light applause, suddenly impatient for their demonstration to be over. Once they were free—and out of these disguises—the three of them could come back and enjoy the festival for real. Nat could accompany Luka to every stall and help him talk to all the bards and artificers about their work. Then join Zuri for drinks, stay up late, and maybe—and this was a very large, very scary *maybe*—hold Luka's hand at some point.

But they had an entire festival to dupe first.

"Thank you, Bellz!" The announcer gestured to the bard as he jingled his way down the stairs. "Next up are the merchants of Rosemond Street, showing their appreciation for the magic that shapes their livelihoods!"

He bowed to them as they ascended. Zuri floated up on stage with a wide smile, a near-perfect emulation of Dawn. Nat tried to look as unruffled as Ambrose always did. And behind her... Well, Luka managed to keep his shoulders down, at least.

The audience greeted them with eager applause—including Mayor Rune, who stood at the front with Beatrice, and Rory and Viola, who watched from the back. Viola whispered something to Rory, who frowned. Perhaps they knew that Nat had never actually said anything to Rosemond Street about this plan. Perhaps they'd be upset about it later.

Too late for all that now.

Nat nodded to Zuri to begin her short speech. Ambrose, after all, wouldn't be speaking in this scenario, and Luka most definitely couldn't.

So, Zuri it was.

"We call this," Zuri began in Dawn's voice, "the Whirling Winged Griffins."

She pulled her wand out of her sleeve in properly dramatic fashion; Luka and Nat revealed their devices with significantly less flair.

"Just a small gift of magic from us to you." Zuri nodded to them both. Nat held her breath, gripped the bottle tight, and poured the smoke through the sieve.

The gray mist slipped down at the perfect weight and speed, and below Luka's sieve, a dozen little griffins formed in the air. Zuri expertly flicked her wand at the creatures, and as sparks beat like tiny hearts in their chest, they took flight above the crowd. A few of the smaller ones looped around the children's hands, allowing them feel how soft and light they were before zooming up to join the others. As they twirled and flashed and gave soft cawing sounds, the audience clapped in awe.

Then the sparks began shimmering.

Nat went cold. Nothing was going to happen, she told herself. It was just a trick of the light, or a side effect of the griffins flying so high—

But then the sparks started expanding outward, as they had in Dawn's loft. Thinking it was just another part of the show, the crowd continued admiring the griffins, clapping at the increasingly dizzying display...

Until the griffins burst into flame.

Each wispy form morphed into miniature fireballs that rained down on the crowd. People shrieked and ducked a dozen different ways, while others frantically stamped out the heavy, flaming clouds with their boots. Zuri reached for her reversal wand, and Nat whipped around to look for water, or a cape, or anything that could help—

But just as the flames whiffed out on the ground, so did the disguises on stage.

It happened so fast that Nat almost felt undressed before the crowd. Within seconds, they were no longer the merchants of Rosemond Street, but three strangers, three kids, standing before a singed audience with frightened looks on their faces and smoke rising up around them. Zuri turned her stricken expression to Nat; Luka went as white as a sheet.

It was all Nat could do not to throw up right onto the stage.

"Well, that's all the time we have for...Rosemond Street!" the announcer called uncertainly, gesturing to the trio. Despite herself, Nat tried to spot Viola and Rory in the crowd, already flinching at what they would say to all this...

Instead, her gaze landed on Mayor Rune, who now stood unsmiling in the front row. As soon as she turned for the stairs, he turned as well and stalked over to the sign-up table.

"Quick," Zuri muttered. "Off the stage, get off the stage now—"

But there was nowhere to run. As soon as they descended the steps, the mayor's beleaguered secretary, Tiegan, stepped in front of them.

"Mayor Rune would like for me to direct you over here," they said, their smile now a cracked rictus grin. "Now, please."

Tiegan ushered the apprentices into a bakery behind the stage, one still open to cater to hungry festivalgoers. But Nat couldn't even glance at the pastries on offer; she still felt like she was going to throw up. In all honesty, she was surprised Luka hadn't already done so.

"Sit," Mayor Rune rumbled, directing them to a table with a cheerful bird-shaped vase in the corner. As they awkwardly took their seats, a friendly waiter strolled up to them.

"Happy Spelltide! May I interest you in a—?"

"No," Rune said.

"All righty, then!" The waiter breezed away just as quickly, leaving the mayor to stare at the trio with all the force of an overheated cauldron fire. Nat had been the victim of such stares in her old life—from Cassius, mostly. But somehow, this was worse.

"The merchants," Rune said. "The real ones. They're not here, are they?"

Nat fidgeted. "No."

"They have been gone for over a week now."

"They have, sir."

"Where are they, then?" he demanded. "I still haven't found the source of the earthquakes, and the alignment of their disappearance is not lost on me. If something has happened to them—"

"Nothing's happened to them!" Luka said quickly. "They're, um…"

The rest of his words caught in his throat; Rune's gaze narrowed.

"For the sake of your professional future, I recommend you not lie to me again."

Under the table, Luka's hands shook. Nat reached out and took one—then blurted out the truth.

"They're in the Driftwood," she said. "Getting ingredients for a potion."

"What sort of potion?"

"A shrinking potion. It's to save a dragon. One trapped under the city in Aphos. Their plan is to shrink him and take him somewhere safe."

Rune connected the dots far faster than Nat wanted him to.

"The quakes," he said. "Are they due to this dragon?"

Nat faltered. "Yes, but—but he can't escape. And our bosses have a plan. They're going to make sure the dragon is safe—"

"The *dragon*?" Rune repeated in disbelief. "I need to make sure my *city* is safe—"

Several of the bakery's patrons glanced over at him in concern. He cut off his own words and stared into the middle distance for a moment, a storm gathering over his face. Then he summoned Tiegan, who had been standing uncomfortably by the window the entire time.

"Get me a map of the city and the Guildhouse leader."

"But—!" Nat tried. A glare from Rune quickly silenced her until Tiegan hurried back with the map. Rune flattened it on the table and pushed it toward the trio.

"The dragon," he commanded. "Where is it?"

Everything inside Nat screamed for her to lie. That she was somehow giving Fio over to Rune, to his death, to pain he didn't deserve…

But under Rune's gaze, she took the accompanying quill with a shaky hand and marked an area in the fields just east of Rosemond Street.

"Here," she mumbled. "He's in Aphos territory, in a cavern. But—Mayor Rune, please don't hurt him. Mr. Ambrose and the others really can get him out without a fuss—"

"Seeing as they didn't bother to divulge their plan to me, I cannot trust it, nor can I trust your word in this moment." He took back the map and folded it up. "You are dismissed."

They stood to relinquish their seats to the Guildhouse leader: an older woman wearing a Spelltide boa, utterly confused as to why she had been summoned. A moment later, they found themselves standing in defeat in the alleyway beside the bakery, the jovial music of the festival souring the air around them.

None of them spoke or looked at each other for a moment—then Zuri broke the silence.

"You told us the smoke was ready to go, Nat," she said, each word uncharacteristically stony. "You lied to us."

"I didn't lie!" Nat shot back. "I really thought it was!"

Zuri rounded on her. "Did you check? Did you test it?"

"I..." Nat swallowed and stepped back. "I couldn't. I was out of ingredients. If I tested it and it didn't work, I couldn't have made another one, and then we'd be—"

"We'd be what?" Zuri glared, her expression a dozen times worse than Rune's. "Still in good standing with the mayor? Still employed? We could have just ditched the demonstration. Made up another lie, laid low. But you couldn't do it. You had to go set the crowd on fire and bring down all of Rosemond Street with you."

Shame washed over Nat in a cold, nauseating wave. "I didn't do it on purpose!"

"That doesn't matter now!" Zuri shouted—then ripped her gaze away, scuffing the ground with her boot. When she next spoke, it was hardly more than a monotone mumble. "I'm going back to the shop. Try to organize it or something before Dawn gets in trouble with the mayor."

"She won't!" Fear mixed with Nat's shame, fueling the words

spilling out of her. "It's—it's my fault, okay? I'm sorry. I'll take the fall, I'll talk to the mayor. I'll make sure he only punishes me—"

"And Fio?" Zuri snapped. "Is he gonna take the fall, too?"

Nat had no answer for that. Left with nothing but a wide, terrified stare to respond to, Zuri gave up and stormed out of the alleyway, melting into the loud, cheerful crowd.

"I didn't mean to mess everything up," Nat said to the air, to the one person who was left. "I won't let anyone get hurt. I won't." She turned to Luka, silently begging for reassurance, some scrap of hope. "I couldn't not make that potion. I had to, it was my job to—"

He gave a cold, breathy laugh.

"Your job," he repeated, and for the first time in minutes, he met her gaze. "Will any of us have jobs after this?"

And just like Zuri, he left, leaving Nat alone in the alleyway to choke on her own words.

She didn't leave the alley. She couldn't. She couldn't bring herself to join the throng of happy people, to even get close to Rosemond Street. Instead, she sat in the dust behind the crates, waiting for the music to drift away and for the air to get cold. And when the crowd had finally thinned, she walked back alone.

She took the long way back, trudging up ramps and across bridges just to delay her return. Her friends were only the first to yell at her. Rory and Viola would be next, then the rest of Rosemond Street... And the yelling was hardly the start of it. Fio was in danger now, and that wasn't going to change, no matter how much anyone shouted.

Her path took her by the elevators, and for a moment, she stopped and stared at them. These elevators led to the top of the chasm. Then the lavender fields, the roads, the world beyond. Part of her considered running back to the apprentices' house, grabbing her pack, and taking the elevator up and up and up, until she found a road to run down, a wagon to hitch a ride on. She'd find a different town, different people, a different job, and try to forget about all the damage she had just done—

The plan sounded stupid even as it was forming, and she abandoned it in favor of descending to the potion shop. She knew what she had to do. It would hurt, of course. It would make all the sharp knives in her stomach even sharper.

But there was no getting around it anymore.

She took the speaking stone off the shelf behind the counter and flipped it twice, her palm trembling.

"Mr. Ambrose?"

TIP 22:

ENJOY THE FESTIVAL

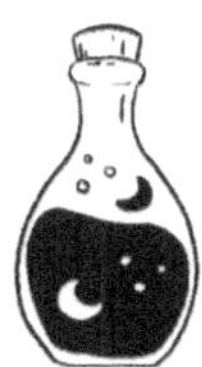

Ambrose

AMBROSE AND ELI decided that the night before Spelltide would be a nice time to try visiting Fio together—and given Fio's curiosity regarding the residents of Rosemond Street, Ambrose should have guessed that his questions would naturally extend to the festival.

And you celebrate magic for three days straight? Fio asked, one paw crossed over the other. Given his interrogative tone and the number of questions he had already asked Eli, he wouldn't have looked out of place with a very large pair of professorial glasses, staring down his long snout at the men in his lair.

"Every five years," Eli said.

And what is magic, exactly?

"Um." Eli turned to Ambrose, who set his hands behind his back.

"It's, well...a power that allows us to do things we otherwise couldn't." He nodded to Fio's wings. "Flight, for example."

Fio proudly flapped his wings, kicking up dust around their feet. *Does that mean I'm magical?*

Ambrose gave a small laugh. "I suppose it could."

Does that mean you should be celebrating me?

Eli grinned. "Absolutely, big guy."

The cavern dimmed; Ambrose's nap was coming to a close.

"I'm afraid we'll be disappearing soon," he said. "But I'll report back later. Perhaps with another, ah, guard of mine."

Tell me all about how you celebrated me later, Fio demanded. *Then celebrate me by getting me out.*

When the cave faded away and Ambrose woke in Eli's arms, he groaned into the man's chest. "What sort of Spelltide gift do you give a dragon?"

"A rescue." Eli kissed his forehead; Ambrose could feel the excited energy coursing through the gesture. "Hickory is gonna be so jealous I got to talk to Fio. And did you see the size of his claws?"

"I've been acutely aware of them for a while now, yes."

Eli hopped up and started to pull on his boots, his words growing faster. "I mean, he's unlike any other sub-species in the Scar. Unlike any other sub-species this side of the Deepriver. Marlin's gonna *faint* when he meets him."

"I very much hope not." Ambrose yawned and stretched. "He needs to take secret custody of a miniature giant dragon. We won't have any time for fainting."

Down in the courtyard, music tinkled. The sun hadn't yet set, but the residents of Skipwallow Inn had seen no reason not to start the Spelltide festivities early. Ambrose sighed and peeked through the curtains. "I suppose it's time to see what Chester's pulled together."

Eli raised a finger. "And Heckley."

"And Heckley."

Ambrose kept his expectations low as he descended the stairs. He anticipated a modest smattering of cheer. Some flowers, a table and chairs. An off-key bard using the courtyard bench as a stage.

But when he opened the door to the courtyard, he had to admit to being pleasantly surprised. Chester—and Heckley—had cleaned and repaired the decor torn apart by the mudmire. Lights strung from corner to corner of the little plaza warded off the growing darkness of the forest. The bards had indeed posted up by the platypus statue, but they were playing something that actually sounded like a song for once. While they strummed, the few merchants that were present had set out blankets and crates in an approximation of decorated festival stalls. The rest of the inn's guests milled about in subdued joy: clinking glasses, buying little trinkets, and accepting tiny appetizers from a plate Heckley was carrying around precariously with one arm.

"Why, *thank* you, Heckley." Sherry took a cheese bun off the platter and nodded to the automaton. Heckley whirled around soundlessly in response and skittered off toward the merchants.

"I daresay this isn't terrible at all," Sherry continued, admiring the cheese bun. "Dawn, did you find a gift for Rory?"

"Got these from the Elwig tinkerer!" Dawn pulled out a pair of earrings: clear studs that held tiny moving waves inside. "He says they're inspired by the actual Deepriver. She's gonna love them."

Ambrose dared a glance at the merchants' corner, wondering if he should find something for Eli. They had previously agreed to no gifts, but...well, it wouldn't hurt to look.

As he wandered over to the makeshift stalls, he tried not to think about what this sort of display would look like in the Scar. Despite Chester's best efforts, being here in the courtyard on the first day of Spelltide didn't feel right. He should be back on Rosemond Street, closing the shop and getting dinner with the others. He should be in his own city, his own home, with the apprentices. They hadn't called yet—should he call them—?

Eli gently tugged on his elbow. "Someone's thinking."

"At the risk of sounding full of myself, I'm always thinking."

Xavion floated by. "Oh, the things I could say to that."

Eli stuck out his tongue at Xavion, then pulled Ambrose in the opposite direction. "Come on. Less thinking, more enjoying. You said you'd have fun tonight."

Ambrose sighed. "I believe I said I would be present."

Despite it all, he did do his best to have fun. He admired the aurocs passing by overhead, then indulged in a few of the little cakes Heckley brought out. Once the sun set, he danced one—*one*—set with Eli, then sat back and watched as Banneker borrowed a lute and joined the bards. Not one to leave the dance floor unoccupied, Sherry danced with Grim and Eli as if she were Ambrose and Dawn's age. In turn, Dawn herself sat with Ambrose, drinking wine and making up stories about the other guests.

"Okay, so she's on a quest to find the long-lost...gibbering thrush." She pointed to an orc clapping along with the bards. "And *he's* on the quest so he can steal it from her as soon as she finds it. The thrush'll make him flush with cash."

Ambrose set a hand on his chest. "The betrayal."

"But"—Dawn held up a finger—"he falls in love with her three days in."

"*Egads.*"

"Yup. Scuttles his whole plan."

"I cannot wait for their thrilling fight that he cuts off with a love confession." Ambrose sipped his wine. "Shall you write it and shelve it at Widdershins', or shall I?"

Dawn giggled and rested her head on his shoulder. "You do it. I'm tired."

"Sleepy already?"

"It's the wine."

They fell into an amiable silence for a while, watching the bards and dancers twirl around the platypus statue. Dawn gave a hum.

"Wish Rory was here," she mumbled. "She's so good on the dance floor. I mean, she's bad. Really bad. So bad it's good." She smiled dreamily. "She's gonna be *such* an embarrassment at our wedding."

As she closed her eyes and daydreamed on his shoulder, Ambrose's gaze eventually settled back on Eli, who was still hopping about with Grim and Sherry. A Valenz wedding would have dancing. Hours of it, most likely. Ambrose hated the idea, of course, but... Eli deserved it. All the twirling with his family, all the joy.

Not for the first time, he felt his own confession teetering on his tongue. He could tell Dawn about it. About why he didn't dare imagine his own wedding. She would understand; she always did.

A dim white flash at his side drew his gaze—and thoughts—away from Eli. The speaking stone was still in his pocket, glowing against the fabric. He smiled. It must be the apprentices calling, wishing them a happy first day of Spelltide.

"One moment," he murmured to a sleepy Dawn. Not wishing to interrupt her or the dancers just yet, he slipped away to a quieter corner of the courtyard, where the crickets won out over the bards' warbling and Banneker's enthusiastic chords.

"Happy Spelltide," he said as he drew the stone from his pocket. "I'm afraid half the street is dancing right now, but I'll corral them as soon as—"

"I'm so sorry, Mr. Ambrose."

Nat's voice shook, tears pricking the edge of her words. The corner Ambrose stood in suddenly went frigid, and he tried to keep his own voice as steady as possible. "What's wrong? Are you all right?"

It all came out in one breathless, tearful run-on sentence from Nat. Mayor Rune investigating the earthquakes. The apprentices lying to cover Rosemond Street's absence and protect Fio. The lie deepening, a demonstration of magic, failed disguises at the festival...

Mayor Rune now hunting the dragon.

Ambrose couldn't move from the corner, rooted there in a cloud of anger and regret. He should have known Rune would investigate the quakes. He should have better prepared the apprentices, had some sort of back-up excuse written down. But a magic display at the festival? Disguising themselves as the merchants? If he'd had weeks to prepare, he couldn't have accounted for that sort of mess. What on earth had she been *thinking*—?

"Mr. Ambrose?" Nat's voice wavered. "Are you still there?"

He stared at the stone. He knew how Pearce would have reacted to such a lie. A torrent of anger, followed by a quick and final severance from the apprenticeship.

As soon as he imagined it, he instinctually recoiled from the thought. No, absolutely not. He couldn't. He instead turned his mind to the others, to Sherry and Grim. What would they do, what would they say...

He rubbed his eyes and took a deep breath. At least Nat had

called him directly about this. If it were him presenting this news to Pearce, he'd likely have up and left the city instead.

"I will..." He took another breath. "I will have a conversation with the group about how to handle the mayor. I trust you understand that you should have spoken to us earlier?"

"I know."

"And none of you are hurt?"

"No, we're...we're fine."

Ambrose nodded to himself. "This is fixable, then."

A long silence from the other end. "It is?"

"Of course it is. Nothing is lost yet."

"And...you're not going to kick me out?"

His stomach lurched at the mere thought of it. "What? No. Nat, you're—you're a part of the street. At this point, that's quite unconditional."

A very quiet, very sniffly "Oh" came back through the stone.

To work through his sudden nausea, Ambrose started pacing in the corner of the courtyard. He had to talk to the street, while Nat... Well, ideally she stayed firmly put in the shop, but in her deluge of fearful words, she had mentioned the other apprentices. Their anger, their storming off. Empathetic pain churned once more in his gut, and he looked over his shoulder at Eli and Dawn, who were now giggling at the table and clinking wineglasses together.

Yes, this was fixable, but Nat had several problems to address.

"You must talk to Luka and Zuri and apologize."

He could almost hear Nat recoiling on the other end. "But you didn't hear them! They hate me now. I should just"—he heard rustling from the other end as she looked around—"maybe I should just stay in the workroom tonight. I—I could check inventory and brew something—"

"*No.*"

The edge came out too sharp in his voice. He grimaced, wishing he could reach through the speaking stone and take her shoulders.

"Trust me." He forcibly softened his voice. "I've...I've tried that. It never works."

"But—"

"I cannot promise that it will get any easier, because it doesn't. But you need to at least start by talking to them. They are your friends, and they will forgive you."

"Will they?"

The words were hardened by years in Aphos—but she was no longer in Aphos.

"They will. I promise," he said. "And I don't make false promises."

"I know," Nat grumbled, then after a pause: "Thanks, Mr. Ambrose."

"Please stay safe."

"You, too."

He pocketed the stone and made his way back to the table, the news weighing heavily on his shoulders. Dawn could see the change right away—as soon as she turned to him, she sat up straight, wine-glass forgotten in her hand.

"Who was that?" She searched his face. "What's happened?"

Ambrose swallowed. "We need to talk," he said. "Inside."

***

Sherry sat down on Ambrose's bed. "Oh, by all the gods dead and alive. Rune knows?"

Ambrose stood stiffly before the group, who had all piled into his room. "I told Nat it was fixable. I didn't want to scare her—"

"You did the right thing," Grim interjected. "What's done is done."

"And we *can* fix this." Eli paced in a tiny open spot in front of the dresser. "We just have to think on it."

"So what, do we try to leave the forest now?" Dawn said.

Eli shook his head. "Not now. The forest is far too dangerous at night, even if we had a wisp guide and knew where we were going. We'll have to sort out a plan with the apprentices in the morning and leave right after."

Dawn slouched against the wall. "I can't believe Zuri didn't tell me."

Grim shrugged. "Kids knew it was a risk. Weren't going to tell their bosses about it."

"But we could've helped—!"

"*You* could have helped," Ambrose cut in. "I would have advised them not to do it."

Banneker raised a hand. "Do we know *what* they did, exactly? At the demonstration, I mean."

"I didn't catch all of Nat's description," Ambrose admitted. "She was talking too fast. Something about a three-part griffin illusion."

Banneker tapped his chin. "I mean...if Luka refines it, he could maybe turn that into a portfolio piece—"

Ambrose shot him a look. "Not the time, Banneker."

Eventually, everyone filtered out of the room in varying levels of dismay, all promising to meet downstairs at dawn to sort out the tangled mess. Once they were gone, Ambrose let out a long, slow breath, and Eli rubbed the spot between his shoulder blades.

"Don't be too mad at Nat," he said gently. "She was just trying to do the right thing."

Ambrose ran a hand through his hair. "I wish she had been honest about doing the right thing."

"She was, in the end."

Eli kissed his cheek, then started undressing for the night. Given that he had just come from Spelltide, said undressing involved picking flowers out of his hair and pockets, all gathered from the other celebrants. Outside, the bards played on, and he hummed a few notes along with them.

Given their impending meeting at dawn, Ambrose should have been undressing as well—but instead, he found himself just watching Eli, as he had in the courtyard before Nat reached out. He couldn't be angry with Nat for being dishonest. How could he? He hadn't been honest with Eli this entire time.

"Eli?" he ventured—but as soon as he spoke, his limbs felt weak and shaky, like he needed to sit down. To distract himself, he picked up one of the flowers Eli had placed on the dresser and stared hard at its bright yellow petals. "I...I'm afraid I have something to admit myself."

Eli frowned, his fingers still on his shirt buttons. "Yeah?"

Ambrose's throat went dry, and the urge to run out into the dark forest nearly overpowered him. But he had tried that sort of running once—well, many times—in the past. As he had told Nat, it never worked.

"It's about weddings." He swallowed against the hard knot in his throat, unable to look Eli in the eye. "I—I know you believe I don't want a wedding. But that isn't quite..." His vision blurred, the petals just smudges against his fingers. His own voice burned on his tongue. "That isn't quite true. I just don't have what's required for a wedding. I don't have a—a mother or a father or a..." The words lodged in his throat, sharp and painful. "Eli, I can't give you the wedding you want because I don't have a family. And I'm sorry, I'm *sorry* I don't—that I can't—"

Eli silently took the flower out of Ambrose's fingers and, with the gentlest of hands, tucked it behind his ear, a tiny patch of sunshine against his blue hair. Tears trickled down his own cheeks, but he smiled against them.

"Let's see," he said softly. "Do you have someone you want to marry?"

Desperately so, Ambrose wanted to say.

"Of course I do," he murmured instead.

Eli leaned forward and kissed him, a cool balm against the words that had pained him to say. "Then it sounds like you have all that's required for a wedding."

Tentative joy sparked in Ambrose's heart, just as it had when Sherry had described her wedding. It couldn't be that easy. It couldn't.

"But all your family's traditions," he tried. "You—you wouldn't get to have them. And everyone would be upset. You heard Sherry, even *her* parents were angry when she—"

Eli took both of Ambrose's hands in his. "I think you and I heard a different story, then. All I heard was that Sherry had the best day of her life showing off how much she loved her husband."

Ambrose choked on tears, though whether they were from sadness or happiness, he hardly knew. That was all he wanted. Gods, that was all he wanted—

Eli gathered him in his arms, his own voice hitched, his tears wetting Ambrose's hair. But he spoke through it regardless, just as loving and soft as ever.

"Our wedding can be whatever you want it to be," he said. "I don't care if it's a circle of ink drawn on your finger and a half-priced dinner at The Jumping Ogre."

Ambrose let out a broken laugh against his shoulder; Eli just held him tighter. "I just want to show people how much I love you." He finally released Ambrose and wiped a tear off his cheek. "Will you think about it?"

Ambrose silently decided he wouldn't stop thinking about it, and kissed Eli's palm in return.

"I will."

TIP 23:

SPLIT THE PARTY

Eli

ELI HAD BEEN adamant that his party be awake to discuss their escape at dawn—yet as the sun came up, he found himself packing his bags without a single thought as to how they could actually escape.

He secured his coil of rope to his pack, then sorted and unsorted his potions, hoping a solution would come to him as he worked. The wisp guides were delayed. They had no map, no teleportation device, no magic to help lead them out of the forest. And back in the Scar, Fio was being hunted by one supremely angry mayor.

He bit his lip and shoved his healing potions back into the bag. As the experienced adventurer here, he was supposed to keep everyone safe—and as far as he was concerned, that included Fio. Yet here he was, as helpful as a bard in a dragon fight...

"Eli?" Ambrose yawned across the room. "Are you almost ready?"

"Just about." Eli reached for the last bottle on the table: his proposal potion to Ambrose, safely hidden in an extra tunic. A pang of sadness cut in through his frustration. Tomorrow was the final day of Spelltide—the day he had planned to propose—but he hardly knew what the next few hours would look like.

With a suppressed sigh, he reluctantly tucked the vial into a side pouch. He'd find time to ask the question soon, when they were all safe at home.

Pack full and thoughts still empty, he joined the others on the main floor of the inn. Their speaking stones were already laid out on the table in front of them, neatly spaced between platters of biscuits and apple slices drizzled with honey. Together, they formed the Summoning Circle of Scoundrels, Eli liked to call it, made up of the street, the apprentices, and Marlin.

"I'm so sorry," Rory started off, the speaking stone closest to Dawn buzzing with her voice. "I thought they were going to tell you! I told them so many times—"

"I know, I know. You told me last night." Dawn passed a hand over her face. "*Gods*, this is such a mess."

"Didn't think Luka had it in him to dive into a fib like that." Banneker leaned away from the stones and lowered his voice. "Don't tell him, but I'm actually pretty impressed."

"All right." Grim cleared their throat and folded their arms. Both the participants at the table and in the stones quieted down. "Nat, Luka, Zuri. Afraid I can't say much that hasn't already been said by your mentors. I'm sure you understand the gravity of what you've done, and I'm sure we can expect honesty from you in the future."

A chorus of downtrodden, mumbled apologies fizzled from the stone. Eli rubbed Ambrose's shoulder. He couldn't say he would have done anything different in the apprentices' place—if anything, he would have failed at the first step of that three-in-one griffin illusion, then gone running to his mentor in defeat.

"Rory, you said you had an update for us," Grim continued, steering the conversation as if it were any other street meeting. Rory cleared her throat.

"I've been keeping tabs on Aphos," she said, her voice far more bleak than what Eli wanted to hear at such an early hour. "Rune's contacted them directly about the dragon. He's meeting with Madam Mila this morning to discuss how to get rid of him."

"And I'm *certain* they don't mean removing him to an accredited reservation," Marlin said bitterly.

"I still don't understand why the mayor contacted Aphos directly," Viola said. Judging by the clattering coming from the stone, she was passing out plates to the others with her. "Aren't they, you know... enemies?"

"A perpetual stalemate's a better word for it," Rory answered. "As a result, Rune can't just target something on their turf without giving some sort of heads-up. He won't make any moves until they meet. Which is in..." A pause and a rustle of fabric. "An hour."

Marlin gulped audibly. "How do we stop them?"

They all fell silent, and Eli's chest tightened. An hour was nothing —everyone stuck in the Skipwallow Inn was now useless to Fio.

"You all will have to delay Rune and Mila as much as you can. We'll get out of here right away."

"So you have a guide?" Viola asked eagerly. Eli shifted.

"Not exactly."

"A mount, then?"

"We, um..." He ran a hand through his hair. "Well, we've got..."

All eyes turned to him. *Nothing* was what he wanted to say. Nothing but a lopsided inn, a few bards, and a—

Distant cawing cut into his thoughts, and a few shadows flitted over the courtyard. Auroc calls, stronger and more vibrant than days past. More of them were migrating overhead now, joining the now-steady stream of birds all headed north for Titan's Nails...

Eli stopped and turned to the window. North. Where they needed to go.

"Hold on." He held up his hands, jumbled pieces of a plan falling into place in his head. "Hold on, hold on, hold on."

Banneker blinked. "We're holding."

Eli rushed over to the window. "We can get back to the Scar tomorrow—we just need to grab a few of those."

He pointed up at the sky just as a few sparkling feathers floated down through the canopy.

Dawn dropped the biscuit she was holding. "What, grab a few *aurocs*?"

"They're bigger than you think," Eli started to bounce on his heels. They could do this, they could *do* this. "Big enough to ride, if each of us caught one. They land every hour or so to rest. If we switch mounts every time they land to keep them from getting tired, we could—"

But Ambrose looked as shocked as Dawn.

"I beg your pardon?" he said. "Ride the aurocs without any sort of —of saddle? Or harness? Or anything from keeping us from falling to our deaths?"

Eli gestured to their bags. "You packed your whole shop in there, Ames. We've got floating potions and grounding potions and—"

"Hello?" Viola called from the abandoned speaking stone. "All I heard was 'falling to our deaths'!"

Eli ignored her—he had to get the others on board first. "Look, we don't have to do it if you all don't want to. But those birds are the fastest way out of here."

They all looked at each other—then Banneker shrugged. "I mean, we've already fought mimics and mudmires. What's a bird rodeo compared to that?"

"I...have always wanted to see them close up," Sherry added tentatively. Next to her, Grim rubbed their stubble.

"We already know their flight path goes directly over the Scar," they grunted. "If we plan this right, Valenz, we can get back by tomorrow morning."

Ambrose and Dawn turned to each other. When Dawn finally shrugged in defeat, Ambrose gave a long, tired sigh.

"Fine. *Fine.*" He threw up his hands. "We'll take the birds. What do we need?"

Eli grinned and turned to Banneker. "You still got the pieces for that tracking device?"

TIP 24:

KICK DOWN THE DOOR

Nat

NAT WATCHED the light on the speaking stone dim, wishing the magic connection in the stone could whisk her all the way to Skipwallow.

She'd rather take her chances with a bird rodeo than continue standing here in Viola's bakery. The sun hadn't even fully risen, and she had already been subject to disapproving stares (Viola), pointed words about honesty and disappointment (Rory), and a stale spinach puff (Viola again). Then she had only been able to stomach one bite of her spinach puff before learning that Fio was in danger, imminently, with no support from the rest of Rosemond Street.

And it was all her fault.

"Rory, come with me." Viola hurried toward her kitchen, sparkling midnight skirts flowing behind her. "I've got an idea about Rune, but I want to get your take on it." She paused and turned to the apprentices, all standing as far apart as possible by the counter. "We'll be right back. *Don't* any of you do anything."

In morose obedience, the apprentices continued to stand there even after the kitchen door swung closed, surrounded by deep purple curtains, weak sunlight, and terrible guilt. Nat stared at her breakfast, resisting the urge to dash back to into The Griffin's Claw and curl up inside a cauldron.

"I...talked to Ambrose last night." She didn't dare look at the others as she spoke. "Told him what happened. Did...did Dawn or Banneker—?"

"Dawn reached out last night." Zuri nodded to Luka. "You?"

Luka fiddled with his fork. "So did Banneker."

A tense silence blanketed them; Nat squeezed her eyes shut and ripped the bandage off.

"They didn't fire you, did they?" she blurted out. "Because if they did, I'll tell them it's all my fault. And if they don't listen, I'll—I'll fight them! I'll set cave spiders on them! With their hairy legs and all twenty-seven of their eyes—!"

"Okay, okay, hold the spiders," Zuri cut in. "I didn't get canned."

Luka immediately slouched in relief. "Oh, thank the gods. Me, neither." He swallowed. "Nat?"

They both looked at her; she suppressed a flinch. She should have been canned and kicked out. Or, at this point, just thrown into the cave with Fio.

"No." She quickly turned back to her plate. "Um, no. Not fired."

"Good," Luka said quietly. Next to him, Zuri gave a stiff nod. Nat pushed away her plate, the weight on her shoulders refusing to budge. Yes, their careers hadn't vanished—but their trust in her certainly had, and she knew what happened after that. She had seen it over and over in Aphos. The rapid distance, the silence. Soon, they wouldn't even acknowledge her presence, and she'd lose the one good thing, the *best* thing she had—

The kitchen door burst open, and Rory sprinted toward the street. Viola hurried close behind, a cloth-covered basket swinging from her arm.

"Come on!" She yanked open the door. "We're crashing Rune and Mila's party!"

Zuri and Luka scrambled out of their seats; Nat slid out more cautiously.

"We're going to see Madam Mila?" she asked. "Now?"

"Yes, now!"

The weight on her shoulders sank into her skin, into her lungs. She couldn't simply go see Madam Mila, the woman she had once served. Mila wouldn't know her from a roach, of course—but she never went anywhere without Cassius. And if *Cassius* saw her—

"I can't." Her breathing quickened. "*Rory* can't. Mila's her mom, they—they know who we are—"

"Oh, we know that." Viola flipped the cloth off the basket. "That's why I wanted to show Rory my disguise buns. They're a day-old test batch, but they should work just fine."

Zuri strode over and picked up one of the pastries, inspecting the plain yellow icing atop them. "All right. And once we're disguised?"

"I'll debrief everyone at the Guildhouse, where Rune and Mila are meeting." Rory met Nat's gaze. "I'm not going to pretend it isn't a risk. You don't have to go. But if you do..." Her eyes slid to the other apprentices. "You stay close and follow our lead. All right?"

Zuri immediately stepped forward. "Okay. Let's go."

Luka steeled himself and did the same. "I'm in." Then he turned to Nat, fear in his gaze. "Nat, you don't have to come with us. Really."

Nat's insides twisted. Of course she had to go. She had no idea how to fix a friendship—but Rory was handing her a tool to fix Fio, at least. She couldn't let the others go and wield it without her.

"All right," she said. "Let's go."

Rory split with them at the ramp, heading west, while Viola led them east.

"Reinforcements!" was all she yelled back as their paths diverged. "Keep going!"

Nat's nerves spiked as soon as Rory disappeared from view. Rory was the only one here who understood the risk. Who knew how to navigate around the people they were about to confront. If she didn't make it back in time...

But as soon as the Guildhouse's carved columns came into sight,

Rory reappeared around a bend, dashing across a bridge with several strangers trailing behind her. No, not strangers—*reporters*. Nat recognized them from past gatherings at The Jumping Ogre.

"So...we're not fighting them?" Nat asked Rory, looking pointedly at the notebooks in her friends' hands.

"Fighting? Who said anything about fighting?" Rory straightened her jacket and grinned at Nat. "Pulled in some favors from all my festival coverage. The *Scarrish Post* will handle this our way." She twisted around. "Gabriel, did you drop the hints?"

A journalist nodded behind her.

"Viola, the disguises?"

"Got 'em."

Viola dealt out the buns to everyone on Rosemond Street with the same ease as she handed out free samples. They weren't her strongest work—the edges of the buns were stale, and their flavor was a step above a plain cracker—but Nat could immediately feel the transformation ripple across her skin, far stronger than Zuri's disguise wands. The magic was coming from inside her, after all, forming an illusion all around her. Her gray skin remained the same, but her freckles faded, and a swath of thick, curly hair now weighed heavily against the back of her neck. She couldn't tell by touch alone if her face had changed drastically—but judging by the others, she would guess it had. Within seconds, she could only discern the others by their gait. Viola still clinked along with her prosthetic leg. Luka still hunched. And Rory and Zuri remained at the front, soldiering on like nothing had changed.

Nat wiped her sweaty palms on her shirt and tried to adopt their confidence. In this disguise, Cassius and Mila could look right at her and be none the wiser. She was perfectly safe...or as safe as one could be, given the circumstances.

By the time they reached the Guildhouse doors, she was ready to burst in and go along with Rory's plan—but the guard at the door had other ideas.

"Adventurers only," she grunted. Judging by the fur accoutrements on her armor, she was clearly an adventurer herself, brought on at the last minute to help with security. "No one else is allowed right now. If you're looking to post a quest, come back this afternoon."

Rory held up a hand. "We're actually—"

"No time!" Viola reached into her basket once more, grabbed a jar, and threw a pinch of rainbow sprinkles in the guard's face. Her features slackened, as if she were daydreaming leagues away.

"Come on, come on!" Without missing a beat, Viola yanked open the door and waved them in. "The enchantment won't last forever."

Rory stared at the guard. "Is she—?"

"Oh, she's fine. Won't remember a thing from the past twenty seconds or so." Viola giggled. "I've always wanted to try those out."

Zuri took the bottle and inspected the sprinkles. "Why do you have these?"

"Why not?" Viola blinked at her. "What if I eat something so good that I want to forget about it and eat it again for the first time—?"

"All right, stash the stun sprinkles and follow me." Rory ducked through the door. "My source told me Rune and Mila are in the reception hall."

But they weren't alone in the lobby. A line of adventurers had formed at the clerk's desk, where the slightly panicked woman was trying to answer their questions with very little information.

"Yes, the quest was posted by the mayor," she squeaked, "but the details are, um—well, the mayor will debrief you himself once he selects his adventurers!"

Nat picked up her pace and hurried past the line. If the adventurers had known that they were signing up for the biggest dragon hunt the Scar had seen in years, they'd be fighting each other over that paperwork.

"They should be just through here," Rory murmured as she led them into a hallway and cracked open a door. "Remember, follow my lead."

Nat peered over her shoulder and immediately understood why Rune and Mila had chosen this sinkhole-turned-gathering-hall for their meeting. Both leaders and their cadres stood in the middle of the vast space, triple-arm's-length apart. There would be no sudden moves or sneak attacks here in the sun-drenched open; they could discuss their dragon problem in relative safety.

"I won't pry into what the dragon is doing there," Rune said, pinching the bridge of his nose. "It just needs to be eliminated. For the safety of both our cities."

Madam Mila kept her head high and face carefully blank. She looked no different from whenever Nat had seen her in Aphos. Her robes flowed in endless layers, obfuscating her form with sparkles until she looked like one of the illusions she peddled to high-end buyers. Cassius stood next to her, his stark jacket and scowling expression as stormy as ever.

"Bold of you to believe we don't already have this problem handled," Mila countered.

"Trust me, I do not underestimate your rule." Rune's eyes narrowed. "If you truly had this problem handled, the dragon would be dead by now. What can the Scar provide to help with—?"

Rory slipped into the sinkhole, her now-blonde hair catching the light. Cassius caught her movement immediately and lurched forward; several of his cronies mirrored his movement on either side of him.

"Stop right there and state your business," he growled. An instinctive fear shot through Nat, and she whipped a shaky arm in front of Zuri and Luka.

"Get behind me," she said quietly.

Luka stiffened. "Is that—?"

"Cassius," was all she could manage. Luka's eyes went wide; Zuri whispered a curse under her breath. But before the three of them could move, Rory took over the conversation, not so much as batting an eye at Cassius' approach.

"Business?" she scoffed, as if it were obvious. "We're here for the press conference."

This threw Cassius off his wolflike posturing. "Press conference?" he repeated.

"Yes," Rory continued innocently, tapping her pen against her notebook. "To discuss renewed peace negotiations between the Scar and Aphos." She leaned around Cassius and grinned. "Fantastic timing, by the way. Can't wait to get this on the front page during Spelltide."

Rune's expression went slack, and all the color drained out of Mila's face. Cassius seemed to have taken all of Mila's color, for he rapidly turned a deep red.

"Miss, I don't know what you're on about, but there is no press conference." He snapped his fingers, and his fellow guards moved forward. "Escort them out at once."

One of the guards reached for Rory's elbow, and Nat's heart leapt into her throat. If Viola's disguise buns were anything like Zuri's wands, they wouldn't hold up to physical touch. The guard would catch the difference in body shapes, then they'd start questioning, and *Cassius* would start questioning—

Then another cluster of shadows burst through the door to the space.

"Oh gods dammit." An orc with a notepad groaned as soon as he saw the group. "The *Scarrish Post* beat us here."

The shadows—all journalists, with quills poking out from behind their ears—scurried forth into the light.

"Don't tell me you've started the press conference already," the orc continued as he arranged his team in front of Rune and Mila. "Damn *Post*, always getting to the story first..."

"Oh, darn," Rory said, grinning widely. "And here we thought we'd have this conference all to ourselves. Wonder who leaked it to the *Dragon Sun*?"

Behind Rory, the journalist named Gabriel squared his shoulders. A vein in Cassius' forehead started throbbing.

"I told you, there is no press conference! Now, get out or I'll—"

"*Chasm Gazette!*"

An elf rushed into the sinkhole, out of breath and stumbling over herself.

"*Chasm Gazette*," she repeated with a gasp. "If we haven't wrapped the questions, Rune, I must ask..." She caught sight of the other two teams and slouched. "Oh, hells, have you finished already?"

"No, no." Rory gestured proudly to the throng of reporters. "We're just getting started."

As the false press conference grew, every journalist began jostling for space at the front, while Rune exchanged befuddled looks with his associates and Madam Mila whispered furiously to Cassius. Rory grabbed Nat's hand and pulled her up toward the front.

"We can't let the others take over the questions," she whispered. "We have to keep controlling the narrative—"

"On it!" Viola nodded to Zuri and they both slipped away, corralling the other *Scarrish Post* journalists as if they were merely cookies sliding onto a cooling rack. "Come on, come on, up we go!"

Luka edged closer to Nat at the front; before them, Rune and Mila looked just as ready to flee. Rory quickly stepped forward and made a show of opening her notebook.

"Well, now that we're all here," she said loudly, "what exactly do these renewed peace negotiations entail?"

Every journalist followed suit with their notebooks, waiting eagerly. Rune looked at Mila; Mila blinked at Rune.

Rune cleared his throat.

"Well, um." He wiped his hands on his robes. "You see, they're... still...in the works."

"The negotiations are delicate," Mila added, her voice uncharacteristically high pitched. "We are not ready to—to reveal anything—"

Journalists shot their hands up and started shouting questions all at once.

"When did these conversations start?"

"What prompted this change?"

"Will this alter any current legislation?"

Nat tried to hide a grin as Rune and Mila fumbled every question, rapidly getting further and further away from their plot against Fio. Every bungled response bought Fio a few more minutes of life—

Then she caught sight of a newcomer standing nervously at the edge of the crowd: the beleaguered clerk from the lobby, holding a stack of adventurers' applications in her hands. Next to her, one of Rune's associates was flipping through the papers and pulling out applications, nodding at some and rapidly filing through others. Nat's relief instantly vanished. The quest—she had to stop Rune from sending out adventurers behind their backs.

She looked up at Rory. No impulse decisions—follow Rory's lead.

"Hey," she whispered and tugged on Rory's sleeve. "The Guild-house quest. Ask Rune about the quest he posted—"

Rory gave the barest hint of a nod and shot her hand up.

"Mayor Rune!" she called, her voice cutting through the others. "The urgent quest posted at the Guildhouse right now. I understand you posted that yourself, calling for no fewer than eight adventurers of the highest level. Is that related to these negotiations, or is there a danger the public should know about?"

Everyone over at the *Dragon Sun* started scribbling furiously.

"No danger!" Rune said quickly, his voice almost a panicked shout. "I, ah, I assure you. No danger at all. I'm hiring adventurers to…"

He caught sight of the clerk on the fringes and shooed them away with a glare and a hand wave.

"To increase security for the Spelltide festivities. Because…" He turned back to the reporters and pasted a false smile on his face. "Because Aphos is welcome to join the last two days of the festival, if its citizens so choose."

The elf from the *Chasm Gazette* barely suppressed a gasp, and so did Madam Mila. For her part, Nat nearly laughed in disbelief. As long as she had been in Aphos, they had never once mingled with Scarrish folk. Not for the Spelltide festival, not for anything.

More hands shot up, the shouting a cascade of fresh questions.

"Madam Mila, will you be attending the games this afternoon, then?"

"Mayor Rune, when was the last time you yourself visited Aphos? Will you be touring as part of the negotiations?"

With every question—most deftly guided by the *Scarrish Post*, others eagerly volunteered by the *Chasm Gazette* and the *Dragon Sun*

—Rune and Mila were roped into a new obligation, while Rune's associates and Cassius melted in confusion behind them. The two opposing leaders were now co-hosting the evening's games. Attending the parade together. Building a multi-day retreat to discuss actual terms for an actual peace negotiation, with an actual press conference at the end.

There could be no hunting Fio at this rate. The dragon hunters were now festival security, the masterminds were now going to be on a parade float together, and the threat of the dragon itself was firmly pushed under the rug. At one point, Rory nudged Nat and winked at her.

"Hey. Good work," she whispered. Nat stifled a giggle and continued pretending to take notes. They had bought Fio time, and with the rest of Rosemond Street on the way, that was all they needed.

The journalists had enough questions to easily last them until sundown, but an assistant hovering nervously by Rune's elbow finally shuffled forward.

"Apologies, but we must wrap this, ah...press conference. The mayor's very busy, you see, with both the festival and the negotiations. Any further questions can be directed to my desk."

The journalists scattered as quickly as they had converged, all of them eager to get this fresh story to the presses. But not all of the Aphosians had yet dashed off. While Madam Mila rushed away to safety underground, Cassius watched the reporters like a hawk, as if trying to determine by sight who had come up with the press conference lie. Who had known they'd be there, who had led the crash...

Rory pulled Nat and the others aside, briefly keeping them out of the flow of reporters. "I need to head back with the *Post* and make sure Aphos doesn't follow them. Viola, you stay near the Guildhouse door and watch for any sudden moves. And you three." She turned to Nat, Zuri, and Luka. "Get back to Rosemond Street, lock the doors, and stay away from the windows until one of us gets back. You understand?"

Nat understood better than most. Sweat trickled down the back of her neck as she made for the door, trying to both look casual and keep half her gaze on Cassius. Rory was right to be cautious on their exit. Neither Madam Mila nor Cassius knew what forgiving and forgetting meant. If they found out that Mila's daughter was behind this, or that Cassius' old servant was helping...

Cassius' gaze kept scanning the retreating crowd. Who was at fault, who could he pursue and punish—

His gaze narrowed on Luka.

Nat whipped her gaze to follow and nearly stumbled. Luka's disguise was fading, deep blue hair fading back to brown, and next to him, Zuri's glasses were beginning to show. She couldn't tell them to run, not without inciting a chase. Nor could she hide her changing hair and the freckles returning on her own skin.

But that didn't matter. That man wasn't going to touch her friends.

Without a flicker of hesitation, she stepped out of the crowd. That was all she had to do. Cassius was observant; Cassius was paranoid. Just one thing slightly out of place and—

"You there!" he called. Nat's steps slowed, as they always had when he'd summoned her. It was like she was back in the tunnels, every muscle tensed in preparation for getting yelled at or punished or both. But this was her problem, her fault, and no one else was going to get hurt. She'd only run as soon as Zuri and Luka were safe, and not a moment sooner—

Cassius' grip wrapped around her wrist and yanked backward. She turned, flinching, only to find him staring at the scars across her ear.

"*You*," he growled, fury building behind his eyes. She willed herself not to scream or punch or move. Her friends weren't out the door, they weren't safe yet.

And they weren't planning to be.

"Excuse me, sir!" Zuri's voice shot across Nat's shoulder. Within seconds, she was right up in Cassius' face, pen and paper in hand, Luka right beside her. "I understand you're a part of Madam Mila's staff. Do you have any insight into the curriculum for the peace retreat?"

Nat stopped breathing. No, Zuri, *no*—

Then Luka took a jar from her pocket and flung a rainbow of sprinkles into Cassius' face. His jaw slackened, his eyes glazed over. His grip fell from Nat's wrist.

And as Nat staggered back, Zuri grabbed her arm instead.

"*Run.*"

As soon as they left the Guildhouse, they sprinted. Down the ramps, across bridges, back to Rosemond Street, not stopping until they had slammed the workroom behind them. But before Nat could do anything—before she could scream or hide or wash her hands a thousand times to rid them of Cassius' grip—Luka pulled her into his arms.

"You're safe. You're all right." It didn't matter that he was shaking—his embrace was firm, keeping her grounded in the warm, familiar room. "They can't get you in here. He's never touching you ever again."

Behind him, Zuri shoved a chair in front of the door, then grabbed a cauldron lid and ladle. "What were you *thinking*? Don't scare us like that ever again. Gods and hells..."

She planted herself right in front of the door, hoisting her cauldron parts like weapons, while Luka's embrace acted as a shield between Nat and any assailants. The sight was so strange that Nat almost forgot about Cassius' angry voice in her ear.

This wasn't the silence or distance she had been expecting from former friends.

"Cassius was..." She gently extricated herself from Luka's arms, almost dazed in her confusion. "He was about to go after you. I couldn't let him."

Zuri huffed and tightened her grip on the ladle. "So you thought it was okay for him to go after *you* instead?"

"Yes," Nat said, the word so matter-of-fact that it dropped like a stone from her mouth. Both of them stared at her in disbelief.

But she wasn't done yet.

"I said I would take the fall," she continued, "and I meant it. I mean everything I say to you. Every word, I promise. So..." She swallowed and gripped the edge of the worktable for support, her hands trembling the more she spoke. "I'm sorry. I'm sorry I messed up the smoke, and I'm sorry I got us all into this. And I've never had friends like you before, and I"—her vision blurred—"please, I still want to be friends—"

Zuri dropped her ladle and yanked her into a hug. Moments later, Luka followed, wrapping both of them in his arms.

Nat burst into tears. Wet, salty, embarrassing tears that were absolutely ruining Zuri's shirt. But her friends didn't step away. On the contrary, Zuri's arms only latched on tighter.

"Come on, Luka," she commanded. "If we're not suffocating her, we're not doing our jobs."

"Yes, ma'am."

They both pressed in closer, until all thought of Aphos and Cassius was gone, and Nat was a sticky, laughing, safe puddle in their arms.

TIP 25:

TAKE FLIGHT

Ambrose

Rosemond Street had no time to second-guess Eli's escape plan or think too hard about the dangers of riding wild animals all the way to the Scar. While Ambrose was very much thinking about such things, the rest of his party was scrambling about the inn: gathering packs together, bartering helmets off a few adventurers, and bundling honey stalk into tempting piles for the birds.

"Today's the day, Heckley!" Chester practically bounded around the courtyard, scattering the bundles of honey stalk in every direction. "We're going to check in some auroc guests for the first time!"

Ambrose didn't have the heart to remind him that once they climbed on the aurocs' backs, his new guests would be checking out posthaste.

"Banneker?" He instead turned to the artificer, who was reassembling his reverse tracking device with more cheer and verve than anyone should have at dawn. "Are you quite sure that thing will be attracting the aurocs and nothing else?"

"I promise." With his tongue poked out, Banneker placed an

auroc feather on top of the lopsided structure. "Nothing but bird-brains in this courtyard soon."

Ambrose rolled his eyes. That much was already true.

While the gears steamed and whirred and Heckley made a few laps around the platypus statue, Ambrose returned to the porch, where Eli was handing out his potions like candy.

"The aurocs are friendly, but they're fragile now that they're shedding their protective feathers," he explained as he passed around invisibility vials. "Until they spend the next year building that ice back up in the mountains, they're vulnerable. We won't be able to approach any of them if we're visible."

The invisibility potions were only the start. Next were Grim's clip-on communication earrings, bright and dangly...

I think you'd look nice with your ears pierced, Eli said telepathically, nudging Ambrose. Ambrose rolled his eyes.

Our flat is only big enough for one person's earring collection, thank you.

And Banneker had one more experimental contraption of his own to add.

"Here," he said, pulling out a copper hand cannon. "All of you get together. Yeah, right there is good. Now say *anti-gravity!*"

The group hesitantly mumbled along with him as Banneker pulled the trigger. An iridescent bubble briefly warped over all of them, then silently popped.

Very slowly, Ambrose's feet began to lift off the ground.

"What the—?" He grabbed Eli's arm in a panic, but Eli wasn't about to keep him grounded; Eli was floating along with everyone else.

"Don't worry, you won't float higher than that," Banneker said, stashing his cannon even as his backpack started to drift away from him. "It'll make us a lighter load for the birds. And if you fall, you'll just feather your way to the ground."

"Oh," Ambrose said. "That's...a good idea, Banneker."

Banneker grinned and floated upside down. "All my ideas are good ideas."

Far above the canopy, aurocs screeched out a morning call. As the party donned their helmets and waited for the birds to land, a scattering of Skipwallow residents filtered onto the main floor and clustered around the windows. Ambrose glanced through them; Xavion had reclined back in the corner of the inn, near the hearth. When they caught Ambrose's gaze, they lifted their mug of tea, then went back to reading their magazine. Ambrose simply nodded back.

In terms of interactions with Xavion, they could rarely hope for something more positive than that.

"Well." Chester joined them one last time, his solemn expression sorely mismatched against his brightly checkered vest. "Before you all leave, I'd like to give you this." He held out his bird whistle to Eli. "Carved specifically for our auroc friends. I hope it helps you get home—and reminds you of your stay in the Skipwallow Inn."

Ambrose, for his part, wanted to remember very few things about his stay at the Skipwallow Inn—but Eli smiled and took the whistle.

"Appreciate it, Chester. You stay safe yourself, all right—?"

Behind Chester, one of the bards broke into song, his voice still raspy from sleep. "*Fly high with the birds, may we see you again—*"

Grim quickly reached for their invisibility potion. "Well, time to be off."

"*Disappear into the sky, take flight like a hen—*"

The aurocs cried out again, far louder this time. Chester shooed the bards back away from the windows.

"Everyone, get out your binoculars!" He scurried into the inn. "And don't disturb the birds! Don't worry, I'll call out some fun facts for us all as they land—"

As soon as the doors closed, Ambrose gave a sigh of relief, downed his own invisibility brew, and crouched in wait for the birds.

They didn't have to wait much longer—true to Banneker's promise, the aurocs all landed around his tracking device, cocking their heads and pecking at the gears in confusion. When it was apparent that the device itself meant them no harm, their attention gradually turned to the honey stalks scattered all over the courtyard, and they settled in to eat.

To Chester's credit, they were impressive birds. Each of them stood at about the height and breadth of a donkey, Ambrose surmised, with wings that were still shedding icy, glittering feathers. That ice would soon thaw and fall over the Scar, forming the natural show that everyone in the city gathered to watch. And to his surprise, the feathers betrayed a hint of color not typically seen from below. The one closest to the porch bore a few specks of pastel green, another a hazy purple...

I want the pink one! Dawn called. A moment later, the porch steps creaked, betraying her movement into the courtyard.

Dawn— Eli tried, but Banneker was already following her down.

It's not even that pink, and I called that one.

Get your own bird—!

One of the birds looked up from its honey stalk and turned its head toward them. They all froze.

After a few seconds, the bird rustled its feathers and turned back around.

Let's hold for a second, Eli cut in. *Check to make sure you have your extra honey stalk, then approach—but don't tackle them until I say so. Are we clear?*

Multiple agreements bounced around in Ambrose's head.

All right. Dawn, you take the pink one. Banneker, go for the one with the crest. Sherry, Grim, head for the ones on either side of it. Ames...

A hand reached out and tentatively brushed against his arm, then trailed down to take his wrist.

You take the one straight ahead. It'll be right next to mine. Don't worry, I'll be beside you the whole time.

Ambrose squeezed his hand back. *I know.*

They all crept—or rather, floated—along to their unsuspecting mounts, then crouched down beside them. Despite the cool breeze, Ambrose began to sweat. If they ruined their chance with these birds, there was no guarantee another flock would deign to visit. Then Fio would be trapped in the cave, and almost as tragically, Ambrose would be trapped in the inn with the bards and Xavion—

Now! Eli shouted.

Ambrose cast aside his worries and leapt onto the bird. He managed to wrap his arms around its smooth neck before floating slightly off its back.

I've got it—! he tried, but even his telepathic call was drowned out by the birds' surprised screeches. The rest of the birds who hadn't been mounted heeded their fellows' warning, quickly flapping on powerful wings to the clouds. Ambrose tried to count how many were left on the ground. The one next to him, that was Eli. Then the pinkish one, that was Dawn—

Then the auroc underneath him launched itself off the grass, trying to catch up with its brethren. Ambrose held on harder, trying to remember what Eli had said. The honey stalk, that was right—feed it the extra stalk and the bird might not send him to the earth with one good horizontal roll.

He fumbled around in his pocket, leaned forward, and held out the stalk.

"Here, bird," he tried. "Have a treat. Please don't kill me."

The bird turned and flinched at the sudden leaves waving in its face—and Ambrose started sliding off its back.

Oh no—Eli, I'm—!

Something bumped up against him—another bird, steered right into his bird's side, deftly nudging him back onto his feathery seat.

Thank you, Ambrose gasped and held out the stalk once more, slightly further away from its eyes. "Please, for the love of everything, eat the damn thing!"

The auroc gave one confused chomp, then another—then its eyes went wide, and it snapped at the entire stalk with its beak. A trill went through it, and it climbed higher into the sky, joining the other birds in the migration above. Ambrose closed his eyes, waiting for the creature to level out, to indicate it had chosen not to throw him off...

When the bird finally began to coast and wind whipped steadily past Ambrose's shoulders, he opened his eyes—and lost his breath again.

Thousands of birds stretching beyond and behind him, calling to each other and enjoying the steady northern air current. With all their glittering wings beating at once, they looked like a sunlit river moving through the clouds, just as beautiful as the real rivers they flew over. And his mount was merely a speck in the display: shedding icy feathers and munching in confusion on its favorite treat, all while wearing a wriggling, invisible, sentient coat.

Ambrose briefly wondered if he ever became this unthinking when someone fed him a cinnamon cookie.

All good? Eli called—and one by one, everyone else called back. Banneker gave a triumphant telepathic cheer; Sherry began waxing poetic about the birds' beauty. While Dawn claimed her mount to be the best at flying and Grim reminded Eli not to fly too high, Ambrose remained silent and let their chatter distract him from the dizzying heights below. They were out of the forest and headed to Fio—all they needed now was a steady wind, sunlight, and a straight path home.

And then he'd never so much as look at a single flying creature again in his life.

True to Eli's estimate, the aurocs rested every hour or so, balancing their immense speed with frequent rest. When they landed in a glade near a river, Ambrose and the others slid off their mounts, ready to renew their floating spells and find new mounts. But their initial birds had grown so accustomed to both the treats and the smell of their strange, sentient coats that a few of them chirped in indignation when they tried to leave.

"Guess we can take these guys the rest of the way." Eli scratched his head after they made their final landing for the evening. No longer minding that the humanoids were now visible, the aurocs searched their pockets for any extra honey stalks, then bedded down in tufts of long grass. "We can catch them again in the morning as long as we wake up early enough."

With yawns, bleary gazes, and sore muscles, they trudged to a cluster of lights on the next hill. Lights thankfully turned into a village, and the village thankfully had an inn. A normal inn, too—no floating tables, no automatons, and no rivals. Just plain bedrooms and some watery soup.

Ambrose sat in relief at the non-floating table, more than ready to fall asleep directly into his soup—but next to him, Dawn shook his arm in excitement.

"We get to see Fio tomorrow!" She clapped and passed a basket of bread, as if she were discussing a lunch date with friends and not a daring dragon rescue. "Do you think I could say hi to him tonight? I mean, he's heard of us, but we're still strangers to him. Well, all of us except for you and Eli."

Sherry brightened. "Why not all of us? Banneker, could you adjust the amplifier again?"

Ambrose's head already ached at the thought. "Perhaps we set a limit on the number of people entering my dreams," he tried, but Banneker was already stirring his soup in thought.

"Give me thirty," he finally said. "I think I can make it work."

So, thirty minutes and one sad bowl of soup later, Ambrose's room turned into a Rosemond Street slumber party.

The amplifier sat on the worn nightstand, its star projections covering the ceiling in a rainbow of shapes. Ambrose took the sliver of bed closest to the nightstand, with Eli curled up against him and Dawn hogging the spare pillows on his other side. Banneker, Grim, and Sherry had dragged in blankets and pillows from their rooms and set up a fortress around the bed, speckled with a few of the kitchen's day-old cookies and cups of tea.

"Good night, sleep tight." Sherry yawned. "Don't let the dragons bite."

Dawn hugged her pillow and set her forehead against Eli's back. "If you snore, I'm gonna kick you."

Eli snorted. "You kick me, I'll just push you off the bed."

"Then I'll drag *you* off the bed—"

"Please." Ambrose pulled a blanket over his head. "For the love of everything, go to sleep."

Part of him hoped that the amplifier wouldn't work, and he'd be allowed a full night of dreamless sleep for once. But those hopes fizzled out—and Fio couldn't have been more excited.

Is this—? He arched his neck high to gaze down upon them all at once. *Are these your guards? All of them together?*

Ambrose rubbed his eyes. "These are the people I've been telling you about, Fio. This is Sherry, and Grim, and—"

Fio didn't have the patience for introductions. He crouched low and shoved his snout in their faces, assessing them as he spoke.

You! He poked at Dawn. *You go to the cafe with Ambrose. You like pink. And flowers. And wine, whatever that is.*

"I mean." Dawn blinked. "Yeah, I—"

But Fio had already moved on to Banneker. *Ambrose said you give people their horoscopes.*

Banneker grinned. "Yeah, I do!"

What is mine, then?

Banneker's face fell. "Well, I don't have it with me, exactly."

Hm. Fio turned to Ambrose. *Your guards have come unprepared.*

When he faced Eli, Eli squared his shoulders and stared him down. "Come on, I'm ready—"

I know you, Fio said and moved on to Grim. Eli slouched.

"Hey, no fair! Come back, interrogate me, I'm ready for it—"

But the dragon continued on like this—assessing each member of Rosemond Street and passing judgment in turn. When he finally reached the end, he settled on his back haunches and peered down at them from above.

Sufficient, he said. *For two-legged creatures.*

But there was no mistaking the warmth hidden in his voice when he said it—and when Sherry sat down and patted his front claw, he made no attempt to pull away.

"You are a lovely dragon, Fio," she said, as if she were simply sitting down to tea with him. "Are you...still all right with us calling you by that name?"

Fio is fine. He paused. *Good. Fio is...good.*

Sherry beamed. "Then tell me, Fio. Have you seen all of the aurocs flying above your cave?"

He had indeed seen the aurocs—and naturally, he had opinions on them. Together, they spoke of the migration, then the lavender fields, then the Scarrish festival attractions, until Ambrose had lost track of how much time had passed within the dream. Not that Fio minded the long intrusion. As the conversation wore on, he settled lower and lower to listen, until he was sprawled comfortably on the floor in the middle of the group. Dawn idly scratched his nose, Banneker rubbed his shoulder—and a low purr vibrated the floor, steady and content.

Ambrose hid a smile. Sufficient for two-legged creatures, indeed.

Once the cave began to flicker—a sure sign the dream was fading around them—Banneker stood and stretched. "Think we'll be heading out soon, bud."

What? Fio stood up. *Now?*

"Well, the dream won't last forever." Banneker grinned. "But we'll see you in person tomorrow—with Marlin, too. He's gonna be stoked to meet you, big guy."

Fio briefly wilted, his ears falling to the sides of his head—then he straightened again.

Yes. Marlin, the one with the habitat. If you have assessed him, I am sure he is also sufficient. He paused. *Have you...seen the habitat yourself?*

Banneker hesitated and glanced at Sherry.

"We haven't seen it ourselves," she said. "But I'm sure it's just as wonderful as you are."

Fio didn't seem to be assuaged. *And...how far away is it from here?*

"Not far." Sherry's smile faltered, and she stepped forward. "You know, Fio... I appreciate Marlin's work as much as anyone. But if you wanted to stay in the Scar, in the caverns or the sinkholes... Well, I'm sure we can find a place for you." She bent down and patted Fio's claws once more, her voice firm. "You're a Scarrish dragon, my dear. You still belong here, whether your family is with you or not."

Something in Ambrose's heart tugged and cracked, and suddenly, he was too aware of Eli's shoulder leaning against him, Eli's fingers twined with his. Eli leaned over and kissed his cheek; Ambrose gently enclosed Eli's hand in both of his and squeezed.

Above, Fio tried to adopt his lofty tone once more, a weak attempt at distance.

I will think about it, he said.

But Ambrose knew Fio. Fio was not going to stop thinking about it.

TIP 26:
CALM EMOTIONS

Nat

THE NIGHT before the final day of Spelltide, Nat wandered aimlessly around the flat above the shop, unable to sleep.

Ambrose had insisted she make full use of the flat in his absence. The kitchen, the bedroom, the washroom—all of it had been tidied up for her. On her first day alone, she hadn't wanted to touch anything in case she ruined it.

But tonight, she moved freely about the place, making sure to clean as she went. After all, she knew Ambrose couldn't wait to be back here again. She had to make sure it was nice upon his return.

So long as he actually returned.

She tucked Tom into her spot on the couch—with a blanket and three pillows, of course—then settled in front of the stove and watched the kettle begin to steam, unblinking. She had, of course, always known that the plan to rescue a dragon from Aphos involved Ambrose going down *into* Aphos in some fashion.

But now that it was real—now that he was planning to do it tomorrow—the idea was like wrapping her insides in spiky metal.

Cassius was down there. Madam Mila was down there. They had

gotten too close to her that day, and tomorrow, Ambrose would be back in that cave, in their territory. Fair game to capture again, or worse.

She poured herself a cup of tea and dropped in a dollop of honey, then a spoonful of sugar. But rather than drinking it, she just kept adding things. First cinnamon, then nutmeg, then cloves... Then whatever she saw on the spice rack. Kolkean chili pepper flakes, sea salt from the coast, Elwig garlic powder—

She stared down at the abomination of a cup and laughed at herself. She wasn't making tea, she was making a potion. A completely useless and smelly Get Ambrose Back Safe potion.

She dumped the concoction into the sink and rubbed her face. There was no use trying to sleep in this state.

After turning out the lights, she aimlessly wandered down into the shop, her light footsteps a loud whisper in the emptiness of the place at night. Across the street, Viola's shop was dark, as was the wand emporium at the corner.

But not everyone had turned in for the night.

A shadow slipped past Banneker's shop. Nat squinted into the darkness. Who—? Oh. It was Luka, carrying a lute case and wandering out into the lamplight. She hurried over and opened the front door in confusion. "Luka?"

She kept her voice quiet, but that didn't matter in the empty street. Luka froze—then his shoulders relaxed.

"Nat," he whispered back. "You all right?"

She gave a shrug in response. "Where are you going?"

Instead of answering her question, Luka crossed the street, squinting back at her. "You don't look all right."

She shifted under his gaze, her cheeks growing warm at the attention.

"I'm worried," she admitted. The other words got stuck in her throat, but he understood the rest.

"About Ambrose?" he said. "He'll be all right. The rest of the street will be with him. They all know what they're doing."

She couldn't bring herself to do more than nod along; the words in her throat had formed a worried knot, and useless tears were pricking the back of her eyes. She should just go back inside, make a real cup of tea, climb into bed, and—

Luka held out his arm. "Would you like to see something?"

She immediately nodded and took his arm.

With unusual confidence, he led her toward the night market, a bustling jumble of carts and tents, musicians and street performers— then veered east, diving instead into one of the half-constructed tunnels on the third level.

"I found this place a few months ago," he said, his gentle voice bouncing smoothly against the rock walls. "I'm sure they'll finish construction eventually, but until then..."

He pulled aside a dusty tarp and ushered her into the next chamber.

Nat had seen many collapsed caves in her time, but none so pretty as this one. The fallen earth formed an amphitheater of sorts around a space cleared by the construction workers. Where the earth once reigned, the moon and stars now peeked through. And they were not the cave's only visitors: bioluminescent insects floated down from the lavender in curiosity, then buzzed up once more, creating a cozy, shifting curtain of lights.

Luka set his lute case down in the middle of the cave. "It might not look like much," he said, "but it's got the best sound I can find in the city, save for the expensive stages. Here, sit there. No, wait—over there."

He had her shift until he was satisfied with her spot, then finally opened up the lute case.

"I'd love to know what the harpsichord sounds like here, but I'm afraid this is a little more portable."

Nat set her chin on her palm and watched him tune the strings. "You come here a lot?"

He shrugged. "Maybe two days a week. At night, when the construction workers aren't here. Helps me think." Uncertainty crossed his face. "But—but if you're not interested, we could always head the night market—"

"No, no!" Nat smiled and leaned back. "Best sound in the Scar, right? I wanna hear it."

His cheeks went pink. "Well, maybe that was an exaggeration, but…" He settled onto a rock. "*I* think it sounds nice."

Unlike his other riffs, this melody was one he had played before. Nat recalled it from a prior late night in the apprentices' house. She had been studying, Zuri had been using a book as a pillow, and Luka had resorted to his lute just for something else to focus on. Nat had only been paying half attention to the melody then, but now she was able to absorb it fully—and she wasn't surprised to hear Luka's signature within it. Something soft and earnest and hopeful. Nothing nervous at all; with music, at least, he had no reason to be.

She was tempted to close her eyes to really drink in the sound, but that would mean tearing her gaze away from Luka. There was a stark difference between simply knowing someone was pretty and letting the sight have a home in her chest. The way his lashes hid his eyes while he strummed, the way his hands glided across the instrument… It was no wonder people tried to flirt with him at the market, and knowing him, it was no wonder he never flirted back.

She wished again that she could see those heart eyes Zuri was talking about. If she could just know for sure what he thought—if he wanted anything other than friendship—

Then the piece ended, and she tossed aside her thoughts.

"That was beautiful!" She clapped generously. "You were right— best sound in the Scar, hands down. We should get the others out to hear it when they're back."

Luka gave a small laugh as he put away his lute. "No, I don't think so."

"Why not?"

"I liked playing it just for you." The tips of his ears went red. "You see, I thought… I thought this song sounded a little like you."

Outwardly, Nat gave a nervous giggle; internally, she screamed. But before she could say anything further, Luka glanced up at the moon and stood.

"If the others really do make it back tomorrow, we should try to get some sleep tonight." He reached forward and helped her to her feet. "Thank you for listening. Are you feeling any better?"

"Much better." Nat took in the view of the stars and glowing insects one more time, committing it to memory. "I'm just...looking forward to everyone being home. Thanks for showing me all this. Really, it did help."

He smiled. "Happy to help. Always."

For the briefest of moments, his gaze darted to her lips... Then he lifted her hand and laid a gentle kiss on the back of it.

"Shall we go?" he asked softly.

Nat barely remembered walking out of the cave. It was taking all of her wherewithal to not giggle at every other step, or grin like a fool, or do something else embarrassing. She had to keep it together, at least until she reached the shop where she could scream and write to Zuri about—

"You sure Mila needs all of this?"

Her mind snapped back to herself. In a second, she had pinpointed the direction of the voice, found a nook in the opposite direction, and pulled Luka into its shadow.

"What is it?" Luka started; she pressed a hand over his mouth, the hand he had kissed not long ago, while her heart slammed against her ribs. Mila wasn't that rare of a name, she told herself, even as her fingers went cold. They could be talking about anyone in the city.

A moment later, two hunched figures trudged by, dragging a wheeled cart covered with canvas. She recognized those silhouettes: two cronies of Cassius', often sent to do his dirty work throughout the city. Not that they were any cleaner underground—they always stole from the kitchens and blamed it on servants like her.

"Don't move," she whispered to Luka, then held herself still. In the quiet night air, the henchmen's voices carried even while they spoke in low tones.

"She's gotta get through that tunnel, don't she?" the taller crony said. "Said the fastest way is to melt through all that rock. Can't go in from above, on account of all the picnickers."

"Why won't she just do it tonight?"

"Can't, you idiot. Dragon sight's too good in the dark for that. The hunters'll be at a dis...disad..." He waved a hand. "They won't do it. Dragon'll get got tomorrow, once they melt their way through."

Nat couldn't breathe. Mila and Rune were doing it anyway. Targeting Fio. Their ploy with the reporters had only bought them a single day.

She watched the cart roll by, anger and fear making it impossible to stay still. It would be so easy to leap out and knock out the stupid cronies. Or sabotage the cart, or tip it down into the chasm, or—

She took a breath and stopped herself, forcing her back further against the stone wall. That sort of reckless rush was how Rune had found out about Fio in the first place—was why those henchmen were even here.

She screwed her eyes shut and held her breath until the cronies disappeared, then released Luka, his face pale except for the slight imprint of her hand on his cheek.

"What do we do?" he whispered, his eyes wide in terror. "How do we stop them?"

Nat looked back in the direction of the shops. She was a part of Rosemond Street, and Rosemond Street never did anything alone.

"You go get Zuri. I'll wake up Rory and Viola," she said. "Meet back at The Griffin's Claw. We'll sort it out together."

TIP 27:

IT'S DANGEROUS TO GO ALONE

Eli

THERE WAS no rest for Rosemond Street after their long visit with Fio. Eli woke to the speaking stone flashing frantically, and Rory speaking equally frantically right after.

"I'm sorry! I thought we had bought more time!" her uncharacteristically nervous voice shot through the stone, while the merchants hurried out of the inn and into the hills. It had taken a few repetitions on Rory's part—and a few attempts to wake Grim—but she had eventually managed to relay the bad news.

Madam Mila and Rune had been conspiring in the dead of night, away from the nosy press and excited Spelltide crowds. Fio was still in danger.

"You still delayed them," Eli tried to encourage her as he scrambled up a hill. Once at the top, he blew Chester's bird whistle and waited. After a moment, the aurocs responded in kind, and he veered in their direction. "Look, if it wasn't for all of you, Fio would have been hunted down yesterday."

"And we're not far from the Scar," Sherry added, trying to keep up with Eli's brisk stride. "Only a few hours as the auroc flies, by the innkeeper's estimate."

"We'll land near the cave and get down there right away." Eli nodded. "Fio'll be out of there before anyone can melt their way through that tunnel."

"And us?" Nat cut in, her voice muffled, as if she were trying to lean around Rory. "Where do you want us?"

Eli paused to think as he skidded down a hill. Back in the Scar, everyone would be picnicking in the lavender fields above the city to watch the migration. Having allies positioned nearby couldn't hurt.

"Find a good spot to picnic close to the cave," he said. "We can wave you down from there."

"Already working on the picnic basket!" Viola called; somewhere behind her, cookie sheets clattered onto a countertop. "How about Marlin? He was going to meet you and Fio at the airfield, but if you think he should—"

Ambrose leaned forward, keeping up with Eli's pace far more easily than Sherry. "Keep Marlin at the airfield. We'll need to get Fio far away from the cave, no matter what."

"All right," Rory said. "I'll get myself down to Aphos, then. Keep an eye on their progress."

Dawn grabbed the speaking stone from Eli's hand. "Are you sure? What if they catch you?"

"Dawn, I'll be fine," Rory cut back in, more gently this time. "I'll arm myself with whatever Viola's got in the pantry. You should've seen what she did with just a handful of sprinkles the other day—"

Eli rounded a hill, and a few eager caws sliced through the air to greet him. Down in the long grass, the aurocs were shaking off their wings and looking to the skies, preparing to join the long trail of other birds overhead.

Eli slowed his pace and leaned toward Dawn so the stone would pick up his voice. "We have to catch our rides. If we take off now, we should get there in time. You got any other questions?"

A chorus of denials rang out of the stone.

"Be careful!" Nat called. "All of you!"

"Yes, Miss Nat." Ambrose tried to smile. "We'll see you soon."

When they descended into the cluster of aurocs, their mounts were happier to see them than Eli expected. They immediately tilted their heads and began shoving their beaks into pockets and packs, hunting for their favorite treats.

"All right, all right." Eli passed out the last of the honey stalks to the eager birds. "Just one more ride, okay, buddies? We'll leave you be when we get to the Scar."

They took to the skies once more, armed with mind-link earrings and another bubbly blast from Banneker's anti-gravity device. There was no need to bother with invisibility this time—according to Eli's plan, they'd be dismounting before anyone could spot them.

We'll land in the resting spot they use right on the edge of the fields, he explained to the others through the earrings. The wind would have stolen any words spoken aloud, and he didn't want to risk spooking any of the other birds in the migratory flow. *We won't be too far from Fio's cave.*

Then he settled in against the auroc's back, angling his helmet against the wind and keeping a constant eye on the changing landscape below. Typically, his return home from a quest had a bittersweet tinge to it. He loved being back in Ambrose's arms, of course, and returning to all of his friends. But it also meant the end of his adventure, and the start of waiting for the next journey to begin.

Today, however, there was no bitterness to his emotions. As soon as the Scar came into sight on the horizon, a great jagged tear in the earth surrounded by vibrant purple flowers, he practically melted against the bird's feathers underneath him.

Finally, they were home.

With some strategic uses of the bird whistle and some gentle nudging downward, their mounts all settled down in their next resting spot: a flattened patch of grass in the shade of a young cottonwood tree. As soon as the birds were seated and no longer begging for more honey stalks, Eli climbed up the lowest branch of the tree and squinted at the distant picnickers.

"Banneker, you got that scope—?"

"Sure do." Banneker handed up a long copper tube; at the press of a button on the side, it slid out into three sections, with one tiny lens popping out at the top. "Chester tried to buy it off me to watch the aurocs. Said I can't—I already named her, and I can't sell things I've named."

Eli gave him a flat look. "Is that why your shop is so full of stuff?"

Banneker looked from side to side. "No."

Eli shook his head and aimed the telescope at the crowd in the fields. All the expected Spelltide festivities were underway: the picnickers snacking on sandwiches, the entertainment stage in the distance. Even a few painters had set up in the lavender, trying to capture the beauty of the auroc migration on their canvas.

But that wasn't what Eli was looking for. He swung the scope to the closest picnic blanket—a slight outlier from the others, but not too far as to catch unwanted attention. As he had hoped, there were his allies: Nat, Zuri, and Luka clustered around a basket, and Viola presiding over them atop her floating chair. Banneker had built it for her years ago to easily traverse the lavender fields, and she had clearly added to it over time. Today, she had a black neck pillow speckled with cupcakes—a perfect match to her skirt, of course.

As she broke apart a cookie and handed one half to Luka, Eli grinned and pulled the speaking stone out of his pocket. "Save half of that for me, will you?"

Viola dropped the cookie in shock; all three apprentices reeled to their feet as if struck.

"Eli?" Nat whipped around, her gaze scanning the horizon. "Where are you?"

Other picnickers shot them confused looks. Viola gave an awkward laugh and waved to them.

"Just a bee!" she called. "Just an annoying little bee...that we named Eli..."

Once the strangers turned away, she bent over the speaking stone and rattled off her next question in a harsh whisper.

"When did you land? You haven't tried sneaking over to Fio yet, have you?"

Eli frowned. "We just landed a second ago, over by the tree. Why, what's—?"

"Just look in that direction."

He swung the scope to the left, where the entrance to Fio's cave created a dark divot in the earth—one of many dotting the landscape on this side of the Scar. Fio's cave, however, had company.

Three adventurers stood before it, hands clasped, eyes swiveling over the crowd in impatience and disinterest. They hardly looked different from any of the other peacekeepers wandering around the city as security—

But normal peacekeepers would never have three large ballistae standing at the ready behind them, pointed in the direction of the cave.

With a curse, Eli climbed back down the tree. "All right, slight change of plans."

As the others passed around the scope and cursed in turn, he paced around the base of the tree. Of course Rune had thought to cover Fio's only escape route. Sure, he was a former Fireball player, but the sport clearly hadn't knocked *all* the sense out of him.

"We can get around them." Dawn passed the scope back to Banneker, trying to sound positive. "Can't we just sneak past them with our invisibility potions?"

Behind her, Ambrose paled. "The ones we used to mount the aurocs, you mean?"

He reached into his pack and pulled out one bottle: the last invisibility potion he had packed, its half-full silvery liquid matching the ice on the aurocs' feathers.

Dawn gave a strained smile. "Maybe...Nat will have something!" She leaned down toward the stone in Eli's hand. "Nat, did you happen to bring any potions?"

"No, but I can run back and—"

Nat cut herself off and whipped to look at someone rushing up behind her. Dawn gasped and started slapping Eli's arm in excitement.

"There's Rory!" She squealed while Eli winced. "Rory, we're right over here! Look to your left! No, your other left!"

"You're back?" The tall silhouette—clearly Rory, judging by her purple hair—flopped onto the picnic blanket, out of breath. "Thank the gods. Look, Dawn, you have to get to Fio's cave now. Mila's guys have already started melting their way through the tunnel."

Echoes of dismay rose up around Eli, and while the others tossed out ideas—alternate paths, sending a fireball at the ballistae, dive-bombing the hole with the aurocs—he rummaged through his own pack. He had packed a dozen bottles, there *had* to be something...

Ambrose set a calming hand on his shoulder.

"We only have the one bottle left," he said quietly, underneath the others' shouts. "Let me use it."

Sherry, naturally, hated the idea.

"What, alone?" she said. "What if they hear you?"

"Oh, they won't hear him," Viola said. In the distance, she was already turning her chair in the direction of the guards. "Let us handle those guys."

Zuri stood with her. "You still got those sprinkles?"

"Oh, sure," Viola said cheerily. "I'm never leaving home without them again."

While Eli debated if he wanted to know what those sprinkles did, Grim took the telescope from Banneker and aimed it at the weapons behind the guards.

"Think you can disable those?" they nudged Banneker, who folded his arms and shrugged.

"Luka, you there?" he called.

"Yes, sir!"

"Bet you and I can sabotage those ballistae in thirty seconds flat," he said. "Consider this your final test."

"I—I don't think the guild will accept this as my final test—"

"Wait." Rustling sounded through the stone until Nat's voice came into focus. "There's three ballistae. Can I help?"

When Banneker hesitated, Luka piped up.

"She can do it," he said. "I trust her."

Banneker took the scope back and folded it up in one fluid motion. "Hey, the more the merrier. That's what they say about crimes."

Eli looked around, his nerves growing until his palms itched. Banneker had the ballistae, the picnickers had sprinkles—whatever that meant. But he had nothing to do himself. When he said as much aloud, Ambrose merely took the rope off Eli's pack and looped it around his arm, his face pale but determined.

"Stay here," Ambrose said. "I'll bring Fio back to you, and we can use the aurocs to get to Marlin at the airfield."

"We'll start as soon as you're ready, Ames," Viola called over the stone.

But Eli's nerves had seemed to spread. Dawn jumped to check Ambrose's pack with shaky hands.

"You've got the shrinking potion?" she asked.

Sherry tugged on the rope. "Let me double-check this just to be safe…"

"And you keep that earring clipped on." Grim gestured to their own ear. "Keep talking to us."

I am sending good vibes. Banneker set his hands to his temples. *Good vibes only—*

"That's quite enough." Ambrose extricated himself from their attentions and made his way to the tree next to Eli. He still looked pale, but he assessed the cave ahead and its security detail with his usual silent thoroughness, while the final invisibility potion dangled from his hand.

In a sudden, sweeping bout of admiration, Eli thought he looked like a true adventurer in that moment—but Ambrose would hate hearing that, so instead, he set a light hand on his back.

"You ready to head in?" he asked, shoving down the other words that popped into his head. Ready to jump into the cave, back into Aphos? Where they had already lost him once before?

Ambrose nodded and flicked the cork off the bottle. "Ready."

He raised the glass to his lips—but Eli couldn't let him go just yet.

He cradled Ambrose's face and pressed a kiss against his lips first, rougher and more nervous than he wanted.

"You be safe and bring him right back," he murmured. "We'll see you soon."

Ambrose's nerves wouldn't let him speak. He simply looked into Eli's eyes, as if memorizing everything he saw there—then he knocked back the potion, shoved his helmet onto his head, and disappeared.

TIP 28:

DOWN THE POTION

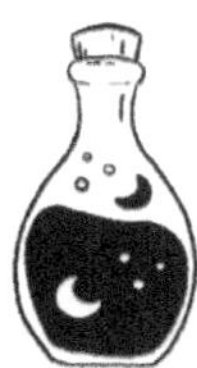

Ambrose

ELI MUST HAVE ALERTED the others to his departure, for as soon as Ambrose set off into the fields, the distant picnickers left the safety of their blanket.

He tried to keep one eye on them and one eye on the cave ahead, picking his way around bushes and brambles and wincing every time a plant rustled against his invisible legs. As soon as he grew close to the adventurers and their very large, very pointed ballistae, he slowed —but they didn't so much as glance in his direction. Rune's appointed security was too busy frowning at Viola and her cadre of apprentices.

"Happy Spelltide!" She floated up to them with all the cheer the festival had to offer, holding up a basket of cookies. "Want a celebratory cookie?"

She took out one of the bird-shaped sandwich cookies and shook it; bright sprinkles rattled in its clear middle. But its joyful shape and sound had no effect on the adventurers. One quietly settled their hand on the hilt of their sword.

Ambrose crouched down on instinct, resisting the urge to tell the others to run. Nat should be nowhere near that sword—what sort of awful mentor was he, dragging her into situations like this?

"This area's dangerous, ma'am," the adventurer said with a warning glower. "Lots of hazards here. Best get back to your picnic and enjoy the—"

In one synchronized motion, Nat, Zuri, and Viola tossed something into the guards' faces—something not all that different from the sprinkles inside the cookie. Ambrose froze, expecting the guards to stagger backward or fall to the ground. But they sort of...crumpled, like puppets slack on their strings. Their heads tilted strangely, their shoulders rounded down.

Thoroughly disturbed, Ambrose rushed forward and skidded to the edge of the cave entrance. Behind him, Banneker came shooting out from his hiding spot near the aurocs.

"Luka, you take the ballista on the left!" He stage-whispered across the field. "I'll take the one on the right! Nat, you follow along with what Luka does for the middle one!"

Nat quickly knelt by the ballista, but her focus was instead on the hole, scanning its edge for any sign of movement. "Mr. Ambrose? Please tell me you're—"

"I'm here!" He reached out to touch her shoulder. She jumped with a relieved grin.

"Good! Now go get Fio!"

"I'm trying. You be careful—"

"No, *you* be careful!"

As she ducked to deal with the ballista, Ambrose slid the length of rope off his shoulder and swallowed. He had only ever seen Eli do this in the practice pits, and his motions were always too smooth and fast to truly catch...

With a grimace, he held one end of the rope against the ground and threw the other end into the cave. As soon as the rope went slack, the enchanted knot at the top quickly sunk into the earth. Ambrose gave it a tentative tug—it remained anchored, as if firmly tied to a rock.

Which left only the descent remaining.

Holding his breath, Ambrose slipped down the rope, clumsy and constantly bumping against the stone wall. Gods, he should have let Eli do this. *He* was the adventurer, *he* was the hero…

Then his feet hit the earth, and he straightened his jerkin in relief.

"Hello." He tried to smile at Fio. "I'm here. Don't mind—"

You're here! Fio shoved his snout into Ambrose's face—but rather than snuffling or purring, he pushed him back toward the wall until the moss cushioned his back.

It only took Ambrose a second to understand why. Fio was no longer alone in the cave, not truly—across from them, shouts and footsteps bounced through the rock-filled tunnel. They were muffled now, but grew louder with every passing second.

They're here, they're coming for me, Fio said, then turned back to Ambrose in confusion. *What's on your face?*

"Oh." Ambrose tugged off his helmet and set it on the ground, then reached and scratched Fio's snout with both hands. "See, it's just me. Are you ready to take the potion?"

Yes. Fio shifted on his paws, every spine raised. *Yes, get me out of here.*

More shouting filled the tunnel. The cave itself reeked of caustic acid now, bubbling sounds accompanying the not-so-distant voices. But clearly, the acid wasn't working fast enough for them: a sharp pop soon rattled the stones and sent Fio's spines flaring again.

"Set them up again!" someone ordered. "One explosive there, another over here!"

The next blast shook the earth under Ambrose's feet, almost covering Banneker's call.

Ballistae are down, get away, go—

But the artificer's order wasn't to Ambrose. A second later, one of the guards up above gave a confused groan.

"What?" A pause. "Who are you—?"

"Hey!" Viola called too loudly, her voice echoing in a veiled panic down to Ambrose. "Happy Spelltide! Would you like a cookie?"

"No—? Look, ma'am, there's, um—hazards over this way, and—"

As the adventurer began to shoo off the others, Ambrose scrambled for the shrinking potion from his belt. They had far less time than he'd initially hoped.

"I cannot promise that this will taste good," he murmured to Fio, "but it's the most concentrated brew I could make. It'll shrink you enough for me to carry you out of the cave, all right?"

Another explosion from the tunnel; Fio set his wide, scared golden eyes on him. *All right.*

The dragon opened his mouth, his long, sharp teeth gleaming in the sunlight. After sending up a silent apology to his own scientific field, Ambrose violently shook the bottle, shoved his hand past the teeth, and began to pour.

"Let 'er rip!" another voice shouted in the tunnel. "One, two..."

Ambrose steeled himself—but it wasn't enough. The explosion jolted the entire cave, throwing him sideways. His arm barely missed Fio's teeth as it whipped away, his hands losing their grip on the bottle—

It flew out of his hand and shattered on the ground.

"No!" He knelt and tried to grab the pieces. "No, no, no..."

But the rest of the green liquid was already melting into the earth. He looked up at Fio, who had already begun to shrink. Perhaps the drops he had consumed were enough. If he just kept shrinking, Ambrose could—

Then Fio stopped getting smaller, spread his wings, and looked at himself. *Can you...carry me like this?*

Ambrose just stared.

Fio was about the size of a griffin now, far too large for him to carry. Not even Eli and Grim combined could hoist him out like this. There was no way to hide Fio anymore. He couldn't be shrunk anymore, or hidden, or—or made to seem like he was never here—

Anger bubbled up inside him, and he threw aside the glass shard in his hand. And why *should* he be hidden? Fio had been a part of the Scar before the city had even existed. Why did *he* need to shrink, or hide, or pretend like he didn't belong—?

As the fallen piece of glass winked against the wet, green patch of earth, something else caught the sunlight beyond him—his borrowed riding helmet.

Your potion, Fio sniffed the puddle in a panic. *I can help. I'll—I'll lick it off the ground—*

He lowered his snout; Ambrose set a hand on his muzzle.

"No," he said quietly. "No, you won't."

He picked up his helmet and looked up the hole above him—thanks to the few drops Fio had consumed, it was just big enough now. *Eli?*

Ames! Eli's relieved voice flooded his head. *How'd the potion go? Are you on your way back with—?*

Ambrose shoved the helmet onto his head. *Get back on the birds.*

What?

Ambrose didn't have time to respond nor even think about what he was doing. Something was scratching at the rocks just beyond the tunnel, and torchlight leaked through the cracks. But he could do this. Fio could do this. He rushed over to the dragon's side, searching for handholds. Yes, there was a spine he could hold on to here. And if he climbed up this way...

He stopped and looked Fio in the eye.

"Fio," he said. "How would you like to fly out of here?"

Fio looked at the tunnel, then turned silently to the sun, the golden light burnishing his eyes until they glowed.

Then he flapped his wings once and lowered to all four haunches. *Get on.*

Ambrose clambered up the scales and spines—clumsily, but he managed. He ran through Eli's past instructions as he sat. Shoulders over hips, don't grip too hard with his legs...

Rock debris flew into the cave; torchlight spilled onto the floor. Ambrose held his breath and grabbed the spines in front of him. "Fio, it's up to you now."

Fio hunched, every muscle coiled tight—then he leapt into the air.

TIP 29:

DEFEND

Eli

"Get back on the birds?" Sherry repeated. "What on earth does that mean?"

Eli was already scrambling up the tree for a better view of the cave, the aurocs behind him squawking in confusion. They had all been flinching at muffled booms for the past few minutes—Mila's team trying to get through the tunnel, surely—and his hands had been sweating waiting for Ambrose to report back. But to get back a riddle in response...

Ambrose, what's going on? he called again. *What are you—?*

Then a brilliant green dragon hurtled out of the earth.

Even having seen Fio in his dreams, he couldn't have fathomed the sight of him in the sunlight. His wings stretched wide, his scales a thousand studded emeralds in the sunlight. His roar, wild and angry and loud and free, should have broken apart the clouds. And above him, fireworks cascaded from a wand in a frantic flurry of color: blue, green, silver, all fighting to be seen against the sky.

Eli grinned so wide his cheeks ached. Ambrose was on the dragon's back.

"Get back on the birds!" He leapt off the tree branch. "Up in the air, *now!*"

The aurocs had no time to react or even think—as soon as the humans scrambled up on their backs, they screeched and flew off into the air, joining their brethren on instinct.

But the other birds were just as confused as they were—for they had a new, un-feathery companion in their midst.

It was our only way out! Ambrose shouted from the back of the dragon, his voice ringing in fear. *The shrinking potion, it spilled!*

It's all right! Eli called back and checked their surroundings. Ahead of him, Ambrose clung to Fio for dear life, while below, picnickers leapt to their feet in shock. Over by the cave, the adventurers rushed to their ballistae—

Which fell apart like matchsticks at their touch.

Final test passed! Banneker whooped. *Let's go!*

"Please stop saying that's my final test, sir," Luka called. "I can do better than that—"

Eli ignored their chatter and focused on Fio's motion ahead of him. After years of disuse, his wings still held impressive power, but they wouldn't carry him far. He'd have to maneuver carefully if they wanted to get to the airfield.

Eli directed his auroc to hover above the dragon. *Sherry, Grim, you stick to the dragon's left and right. Dawn, swing below it. Ames, I'm coming to help you!*

How? Ambrose whipped around, looking for Eli—then he craned his neck upward. *What in the hells are you doing?*

Eli drew his legs up with a grin and balanced himself. *Joining you!*

WHAT?

Make sure Fio keeps a steady pace!

Shouting telepathically was no longer enough for Ambrose. "If you miss, Eli Valenz, I swear to every single god I'll—"

Eli jumped.

His untethered moment in the air was both terrifying and freeing. Nothing was around, above, or below him. Just pure air, the shadow of the auroc, and the rapidly approaching scales of the dragon—

He landed with a thud on Fio's back. Not daring to grab Ambrose and knock him off-balance, he grabbed the nearest spikes and anchored himself. With any other dragon, this may have thrown them all off—but Fio's bulk hardly moved. With a long sigh of relief, Eli shifted forward and eagerly wrapped his arms around Ambrose. *His* Ambrose. The Ambrose who was riding an extinct dragon out of Aphos. Who was heroic, and beautiful, and—and who couldn't possibly be more perfect than he was this very instant—

"Oh, thank the gods." Ambrose clutched one of Eli's hands, his own fingers clammy. "If you had fallen, I don't know what I—"

The words spilled out of Eli's mouth. "Will you marry me?"

Ambrose almost let go of the dragon. "*What?*"

"I said, will you—?"

"Eli!" Ambrose shouted—but it came out as a laugh, betraying the foolish grin that crinkled the corners of his eyes. "I am on a *dragon!*"

"I know!" Eli beamed. "And you've never been more attractive than you are right now!"

"*Eli!*"

"Will you, though?"

Ambrose let out a single, wild, teary laugh. "Yes, of course I'll marry you!"

As Eli laughed and squeezed the life out of him in response, Grim navigated their auroc to fly level with Fio's wing. *Got company up ahead!*

Eli reluctantly set his hands back on the dragon and set his gaze forward. The migration was splitting in one smooth motion, making way for three large hunters on griffins: dragon hunters, judging by the large crossbows on their backs.

Eli immediately regretted voting for Mayor Rune.

"All right, we can do this," he started, assessing every angle of the aerial encounter. "Sherry, Grim, and Dawn can fly ahead and distract them with their wands. If we maneuver into the clouds, we can hide in the upper layer and—"

But Ambrose wasn't looking at the clouds; he was leaning over Fio's shoulder, his gaze on the lavender fields. "No. We're landing."

"But the airfield is over—"

"We're not going to the airfield. We're not hiding and we're not running." Ambrose pointed down. "We're landing there."

Eli followed his gesture down to a brown wooden rectangle in the fields: an empty stage erected for Spelltide. "What, right in the middle of the—?"

"Exactly."

Eli blinked. He was typically the one with the bad ideas. With the roles reversed, he hardly knew what to do with himself.

But he trusted his future husband—so he nodded and held tight to Ambrose's waist.

Change of plans—we're landing on that stage, he called to the others. *Flank us and circle Fio as best you can.*

In confusion, the others spiraled downward right behind Fio. Even the dragon hunters above shouted in befuddlement as they shot right over their prey, aurocs scattering to avoid them.

"Can we shoot at him?"

"Not down at the people, you ninny—!"

Eli silently urged Fio to land faster. This was good, this could *work*. If the others landed just right and he signaled to the others—

But he didn't need to worry about his allies. When Fio landed with a heavy thud on the stage, amidst a thousand shrieking picnickers, his friends were there. Sherry settled on his left flank, Grim on his right. Dawn landed right at the tail and slid off her auroc immediately, waving excitedly to more newcomers: Rory, Viola, Banneker, and the apprentices, all sprinting up to the stage while everyone else staggered back. Without hesitation, they clambered up onto the boards to greet the others and further surround Fio.

Fio, however, slunk back against the backdrop, staring wide-eyed at the onslaught of two-legged creatures.

"It's all right!" Ambrose slid down to the boards and reached for Fio's snout with a shaky smile. "Fio, you remember everyone in the dream, don't you? And everyone we talked about? Look, they're all here for you. See, this is my apprentice, Na—"

He didn't have time to finish her name. She pummeled him with a hug, knocking the rest of the word out of him, then turned to Fio with tears in her eyes.

"Fio, I'm Nat," she said with a wide smile. "I was stuck down in Aphos like you for years and years. I've been keeping a notebook with Mr.—"

But Fio knew. Both of his ears flew up to point to the sky, and he bent his great head to snuffle her. Ambrose laughed at something no one else could hear.

"Yes, this is her. And look—over here is Rory, and Zuri, and—"

Eli glanced out at the scattered crowd and set a warning hand on Ambrose's wrist.

"And Mayor Rune."

Rune effortlessly parted the onlookers, his dark green robes flapping in the wind as he stalked forward with a corp of adventurers behind him. "Everyone, get away from the dragon."

The crowd didn't need to be told twice, but everyone on Rosemond Street did the opposite. They scrambled to get in front of Fio, shielding every exposed scale and limb.

But within seconds, it became a fruitless task—because Fio was rapidly un-shrinking.

Eli could only watch as the dragon quickly expanded back to his full, regal size. His tail slipped off the edge of the stage. His claws scraped the boards as they lengthened and curled. By the time he settled, his head towering above the flimsy backdrop, and Rosemond Street could barely fit on the stage with him.

Rune stopped in the dragon's shadow and glared up at his defiant citizens.

"Master Beake," he said, while the rest of the Spelltide crowd watched fearfully from behind him. "All of you. Step away from the dragon."

Fio growled, his ears flat and spines raised. Eli maintained his hold on Ambrose's wrist. On Ambrose's other side, Dawn held onto his arm with one hand and Rory's with the other.

But Ambrose slipped out of their grasp and stepped forward.

"Fio isn't going to hurt anyone," he said. "And you're not going to hurt him."

Disbelief flashed across the mayor's face. "He's dangerous, son—"

"And so are you!" Ambrose shouted. "So are you all, if that's how you greet him!"

He gestured sharply to the adventurers and their crossbows; a few of them hesitantly lowered their weapons.

"And what has he done?" Ambrose continued. "Has he hurt you? Has he done anything except remain trapped underground for years on end? Are you so afraid of him that you won't let him see sunlight again? Let him live here as his family once did for hundreds of years?"

Rune's face darkened. "His family is no longer here. He doesn't belong—"

Ambrose's voice broke. "*That doesn't matter!*"

For a moment, the entire field was silent, with nothing to accompany the wind but the quiet fall of ice feathers behind the stage.

Then Ambrose took another step forward.

"This is Spelltide, is it not?" He threw his arm toward the sky. "Fio belongs here as much as the aurocs do. Is he no less magical, simply because he frightens you? Does he not deserve to fly as free as they do?"

A few of the picnickers began to whisper, their curious words hardly louder than the breeze sifting through the fields. But it was enough to unsettle Rune; he looked around, then squared his shoulders and nodded sharply to his guards.

"Get them off stage," he ordered. "Then—"

A purple blur shot past his legs.

"A dragon!" Beatrice, swathed in a sparkling purple dress and shoes, rushed forward with a wide grin. "Dad, you brought a real *dragon!*"

All of the color drained out of Rune's face.

"Beatrice, *no!*" He swept a hand out toward the adventurers, then rushed forward himself. "Guards, hold—"

Not even Eli had time to intercept Rune's daughter—with all

the eagerness of a nine-year-old, she clambered up on stage and stood before Fio in wonder, her hands clasped in front of her. Fio, on the other hand, reeled back in confusion, his golden eyes gone wide.

"It's all right!" Ambrose set a hand on his front leg. "Fio, it's all right. She's a..." He smiled and looked at Beatrice. "She's a youngling."

Fio's countenance shifted at once. His ears perked up, his spines flattened. Slowly, tentatively, he lowered his head toward Beatrice. She stepped back to give him room until his head was nearly on the boards of the stage, his golden eyes level with her.

Everyone on the stage froze, their breath held—but after a moment, Ambrose gave a gentle laugh.

"You're right, she is quite small. Here." He knelt beside Beatrice. "Place your hand right there."

He pointed to the scales in the middle of Fio's snout. She set both of her tiny hands on the scales and waited.

Then Fio closed his eyes and began to purr: a great, constant thrum vibrating the floorboards, radiating a delight that Eli didn't need an astral connection to understand.

And before the dragon, Beatrice giggled.

"He's so warm!" She twisted toward the stairs. "Dad, look!"

Rune took the stairs two at a time, face panicked, breath heaving. "Beatrice, you—you can't..."

His fears collapsed into confusion, leaving him standing on the stage while Beatrice happily set her cheek on Fio's scales and tried to hug his entire head with her tiny arms.

"Thank you, Dad," she said. "This is the best Spelltide ever."

"I..." Rune stared—first at her, then the rest of Rosemond Street. All of the people who were distinctly not getting eaten by the frightening dragon. "I...Well. Um."

His hesitation only further spurred curiosity in the crowd. Slowly, more and more of his own citizens edged closer to the stage, their gossip now buzzing loudly amidst the lavender. Two of the painters ventured back to their canvases and began digging for their green paints. One intrepid picnicker shrugged, crouched back down on her blanket, and reached for her half-eaten sandwich.

And in the middle of the field, Rune's adventurers shifted awkwardly, their weapons hanging down at their sides.

"Sir?" One of the guards cleared his throat. Rune just stared back at them, then turned to Ambrose in defeat.

"What do we do with him, then?"

"I'll *tell* you what we do with him!"

Everyone on stage looked toward the voice—Marlin was running toward them with all the speed he could muster, his bald head shining in the sun and his dragon-handling gloves flapping in his pockets.

"By order four hundred and thirty of the Scarrish environmental code!" Out of breath, he skidded to a halt by the stage, one hand on the boards and the other holding up a single, authoritative finger. "This dragon is a critically endangered species! By my authority as a dragonkeeper, he shall remain unharmed, and he must be taken away to—"

As he pointed away from the Scar, Fio opened his eyes and uttered one short, corrective growl. Marlin swallowed.

"He must," he began again, "be allowed a...place where he chooses—?"

Fio firmly set his head between Beatrice and Ambrose and closed his eyes in finality. Marlin nodded, straightened, and turned to Rune.

"For environmental rehabilitation purposes," he said, "this dragon must remain in the Scar."

TIP 30:

REAP THE REWARDS

Nat

After Marlin's arrival, Nat refused to leave Fio's side.

It didn't matter that they weren't connected like Ambrose and Fio were. Once Beatrice had been scooped up by Mayor Rune, Nat planted herself right by the dragon's head and began to talk to him.

She told him of everything. Of her former role in Aphos, of her meeting Ambrose and escaping with him. Of her notebook—which he sniffed with great curiosity—and all of her guesses about his wingspan, his size, his scale color...

She had never seen him before, and some of her guesses were wrong. But she still felt like she had known him for years.

So, when the other dragonkeepers arrived and scuttled around Fio in excitement, she didn't move. She watched them write endless notes on his wings and teeth. She helped them feed him an array of meats (he liked fish) and fruits (he hated cantaloupe). And all throughout the health inspections and greetings of keeper after keeper, Fio kept his head right next to Nat.

"He understands," Ambrose said once, while the keepers were taking away a bowl of untouched cucumber. "About you."

Nat looked up at him. "He does?"

"I told him about you, of course." Ambrose bit back a smile. "Though I'm finding it difficult to convince him you're not a youngling to guard."

"But I'm not—!"

Fio huffed, his eyes closed. Ambrose laughed. "He says you get into too much trouble."

Nat shifted against his scales. She had no good counterargument for that.

Another hour passed of her describing the Scar to Fio—the markets, the shops, the streets—and eventually, the dragon fell asleep beside her, his purr melting into a deep murmur that cycled with his long, slow breaths. She must have caught his exhaustion, for at some point, she fell asleep curled against his warm scales.

When she woke, the dusky lavender fields had nearly emptied out. Most of the crowd had packed up their picnic blankets and headed back into the Scar for their evening festivities. Most of Rosemond Street had, too: save for Luka, kneeling in front of her.

"Hey." He tilted his head sideways and grinned. "Are you hungry?"

Nat quickly pushed herself up off Fio's scales. In that moment, she was many things—confused, happy, starving, stupidly giddy at his smile—but she tried to play it cool and focus on just one for now. "Where'd everyone else go?"

"They went to set up dinner at Sherry's. Mr. Ambrose didn't want to wake you, so I said I'd bring you down once you were ready." He held out a hand. "Eli said he had something to tell everyone, but I told him he couldn't say a thing until you got there."

Gods bless this man.

"Good." Nat tried to stand, though her legs had lost all feeling and gone all fuzzy during her nap. "Because if he starts talking about the mudmire encounter and I'm not there to hear all the details, I'll—"

One of her still-fuzzy legs wobbled, but she didn't need to reach out for Luka. He had already caught her and was guiding her down the stage steps with a suppressed laugh.

"Thanks," she mumbled, her cheeks blazing with heat. Partially as an excuse to turn away from him, she twisted back toward Fio. "But who's going to stay with—?"

Luka nodded to the dragonkeepers. "Don't worry. Marlin won't be leaving Fio's side anytime soon." He paused. "Possibly never."

True to form, Marlin was at the other end of the stage, directing the other dragonkeepers like his own small army. "We can set up a space in the construction zone by the night markets," he said, sending keepers this way and that. "Send Rosemord Street a map of it at once. The place doesn't have a waterfall yet, but I will not rest until I see one installed!"

Someone mumbled a question.

"Permits? Who needs permits, we have a *dragon!*"

After giving a sleeping Fio one last pat and promising to come visit tomorrow—and every day after that—Nat took Luka's arm, and together they made their way over to the elevators leading into the chasm. With the crowd already gone, the wait for the creaky old elevator was...peaceful. The lavender bushes tickled her legs; the breeze gently wiped the sleep from her eyes. She took in a deep, relieved breath. Fio was safe, Ambrose was safe, everyone was *safe*.

But next to her, against the subdued pinks and purples of the sunset, Luka was fidgeting.

"I, um...I meant to talk to you. After the music in the sinkhole. After..." He glanced back at the stage. "All this."

Giddiness and nerves suddenly whisked away Nat's hunger. She carefully kept silent, giving him the space to continue—but he had trouble filling it.

"I really enjoyed playing for you," he said. "I mean—I *always* enjoy playing for you. And the others. But—but especially you. Because you're..." His voice shook. "Because I—"

Someone had to save this poor man from himself, and there was no one else around to do it. So, Nat gently took his hand, lifted it, and kissed his knuckles.

His words fell away at once. He stared at her like he didn't have a single coherent thought in his head, and the blush that bloomed across his face was fierce, a deep, lovely pink. "Oh," he said, so soft she almost missed it. "Really?"

He met her gaze, and Nat almost laughed. She could practically see the hearts coming from his eyes, soft and loving and surprised. They were so obvious, it was a wonder she had ever missed them.

"Really," she said.

He took a breath, then carefully leaned forward and brushed his lips against hers. She was surprised at how warm he was, like his blush was radiating outward to draw her in. But she wasn't surprised at how gentle he was, nor how the simple gesture sent a shock from her head to her toes. Her legs went fuzzy and numb once more, but it didn't matter. Luka was holding her and grounding her all at once, keeping her from floating away on the lavender-scented breeze—

Then the elevator creaked to a halt before them, and someone sighed. "Thank the gods."

They sprang apart; Zuri stood there in the elevator, one of Viola's sprinkle cookies in her hand.

"Zuri!" Luka's blush turned tomato-red. "Hi, Zuri. Hello. We were just—"

"Yeah, I have eyes. Congrats." She stepped back to make space for them in the elevator. "Come on, dinner's almost ready. Just don't make out in here or whatever."

"Yes, ma'am." Luka shot Nat a sheepish smile, then shuffled into the elevator, still holding on to her hand. But Nat wasn't ready to leave the fields or the sunset behind just yet.

"Wait!" She slipped out of his grasp, plucked a lavender stalk from the nearest bush, then hurried into the elevator. Once cramped inside between Zuri and Luka, she tucked the flower into a buttonhole on his waistcoat. The muted purple still wasn't her style—but it certainly was his. He took one look at it, and it was like the entire sunset was shining out of his face.

"Thank you." He bent and kissed her forehead. "Very kind of you."

TIP 31:

TIE THE KNOT

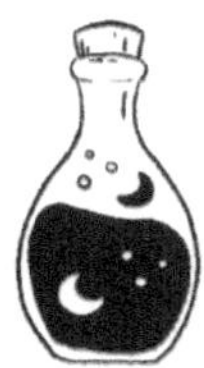

Ambrose

ELI LEANED out the door to The Griffin's Claw. "You got the lights, Banneker?"

"Yep. You sent someone out for the flowers?"

"Rory's picking them up now!" Dawn shouted from down the road.

It was the morning of Ambrose's and Eli's wedding, and despite being closed for the day, Rosemond Street bustled as if it were Spelltide all over again.

"Outfits? Check." Eli hefted up his bag, then patted his pocket. "Ring? Check." He pointed at Ambrose. "Fiancé? Check." He grinned and kissed Ambrose's cheek as he passed by. "You about ready to go?"

"Almost." Ambrose picked up his bag, then gestured wearily to the stack of packages on the front counter. "My dear, what do we do with all this?"

Eli blinked. "They're gifts. We open them after the wedding."

The gifts were all quite unnecessary, Ambrose wanted to grumble —but there was no giving them back. As soon as news of their engagement had spread, gifts began pouring in from all over. From customers, Potion Con friends, Eli's family members and fellow adventurers...

"They're far too generous," Ambrose mumbled, sorting the packages in cubbies under the counter. "It'll take us days to—"

He picked up a package and frowned at the label. The sender's name had been written in shimmering gold ink, the letters far larger and more elegant than the recipient's name on the package. Ambrose held it up.

"Eli, why has Xavion Demachel sent me a wedding gift?"

Eli froze, his hand halfway to the door. "Um."

Ambrose snorted and made to shove it into a corner. "Well, I'm not opening it. It's likely to be an explosive made of glitter. Or a copy of their damned magazine—"

"You have to."

Ambrose looked up. "What?"

Eli scrunched up his face. "I maybe sort of told them they could you send you one."

"I *beg* your pardon?"

"Come on, just open it."

Ambrose reluctantly opened the package and reached inside. No glitter yet. Just shreds of packing paper and...

He pulled out a mug. A simple, white coffee mug—with Xavion Demachel's face painted on both sides.

A grin slowly spread across Eli's face. "I love it. Put it on the shelf."

Ambrose shot a glare at him. "Absolutely not."

"Top shelf, right over your shoulder behind the counter—"

"I am destroying this in a fire. I am melting it in a cauldron."

Eli leapt for the mug, laughing the entire time. "You can't!"

Ambrose held it out of his reach. "I can and I will!"

"Please, please, *please* put it on the shelf—"

A knock sounded on the bay window.

"Ambrose!" Sherry waved through the glass. "We'll be ready to leave in just a moment!" She turned to Grim behind her and lowered her voice. "Should I bring my shield? Just in case?"

Grim sighed. "It's a wedding, Sherry."

Ambrose huffed and stashed the mug in a cubby; he had no time to argue with his imminent husband. "I still have to change. Go on up to the venue with your family—I'll head up after I talk to Fio and finish getting ready."

Still stretched out across the counter, Eli grabbed his hand and kissed it. "Okay. Love you!"

He rushed out at once; Ambrose followed at a more leisurely pace. Fio's new home wasn't exactly neat. He wasn't going to stand and chat there in his wedding suit.

He passed by Viola's bakery, where the apprentices were counting cupcakes and marking lists. Luka kept glancing over at Nat and blushing.

"You look very nice, Nat," he finally murmured.

"Yeah?" Nat grinned and spun around in the suit Sherry and Rory had bought for her. "So do you."

"Kill me," Zuri muttered, hiding a smile behind her baking list. Ambrose tried to pass by and let them continue their cupcake count in peace—but Nat spotted him and scuttled out, her list still in hand.

"Mr. Ambrose!" she called, following him toward the ramp. "Did you see all the stock I brewed last night?"

"Of course I did."

"And the price list, did you read over that?"

Ambrose bit back a smile. "Signed off on it this morning."

"And the shopping list, did you—?"

He stopped and turned before reaching the ramp. "Nat, I'll only be gone for a week."

"I know—"

"And there is no dragon hiding under the city, nor other shops to cover, nor a festival flooding the city with tourists." He set his hands behind his back. "Compared to last time, this should be quite easy for you."

"I *know*, but..." Nat glanced nervously back at the potion shop. "It's your honeymoon. I don't want you to worry."

Down the street, Zuri poked her head out of the bakery. "Nat!" she shouted. "Viola's letting us taste-test!"

Nat hesitated, but didn't move; Ambrose reached out and straightened her cravat.

"I am not worried in the slightest," he said. He had no reason to be. She was as much a part of the shop as he was. In a blink, she'd be mastering her six level potions. Another blink, and she'd be gaining her master's certification. And in another...she'd have the shop key pressed into her hand, just as he once had.

The Griffin's Claw was in good hands, now and forever.

He stepped back and cleared his throat. "As my apprentice, could you please go ensure Viola isn't trying to poison the wedding party?"

Nat grinned in relief. "On it!"

As she dashed back to the bakery, Ambrose continued up the ramp, toward Fio's domain on the fourth level. The tunnels that had once been under constant, slow construction had been scrapped in favor of a very large dragon's nest. It didn't matter that it was a decent walk from the ground floor of Rosemond Street; the merchants made time to visit almost every day.

Not that Fio needed their visits to remain occupied. Every day brought more people, Scarrish and otherwise, who had ventured to admire both the dragon and his nest. True to his word, Marlin had crowned the open sinkhole with a line of elegant waterfalls. As the weather grew hotter, both children and pigeons would splash around the pools without fear—and when Fio was absent from his nest, the little ones would wave as he flew by. Soon, Fio's shadow passing overhead was said to be good luck—a superstition that Banneker abided by immediately—and his visitors often left him coins, feathers, and trinkets in thanks. Such shiny things, naturally, were put to good use by the dragon. Whenever Ambrose visited, he had woven another new trinket into his gargantuan nest.

And today, he had a special guest supplying him an offering.

"Hi, Fio!" A young woman with long black hair bowed to him and laid a dainty necklace at his claws. "I'm Lily, Eli's sister. He's probably mentioned me. But he probably hasn't mentioned that I'm far cooler than him, so please keep that in mind—"

Ambrose cleared his throat. "Lily."

She whirled around and grinned, that same Valenz grin that Eli sported every day. "Ambrose! I was just saying hi to Fio—"

"And spreading your own propaganda, I see."

"Obviously."

She had grown in the years since their first meeting—much like Nat, she held herself with the self-assurance of a fresh adult—but she stubbornly held on to that mischievous glint in her eye.

"I was gonna convince him to fly me back to Kolkea next," she said airily. "You know, take a small vacation while you're on your honeymoon—"

"Not a chance, Lily."

Honeymoon? Fio asked, his voice appearing in Ambrose's head alone. *What's that?*

Ambrose bit back a smile. Fio had vastly improved at picking up the language of the two-legged creatures around him—which meant that Ambrose had to take on the role of dictionary more frequently.

In a moment, he said, then turned to Lily. "I believe Eli's ready to head up with your parents. If you don't mind ensuring he doesn't get lost?"

She snorted. "He's been talking my ear off about this wedding since I got here. He's probably already sprinted there." She squeezed his arm. "But yeah. For my new brother, I'll make sure none of them get lost."

As she ran off to join the rest of her family, Ambrose turned to Fio, his chest unbearably warm at the sound of *new brother*.

The honeymoon's just a short trip. He patted Fio's claw, careful not to venture too deep into the puddles around the nest. *Eli and I will be back in a week. Rosemond Street and Marlin will take good care of you in the meantime, all right? And who knows—perhaps I'll appear now and then.*

Now that Ambrose was no longer chugging catnap potions, his

dream visits with Fio had become increasingly rare and unpredictable—but every now and then, he'd find himself standing by the nest in the moonlight, chatting with the dragon for a few minutes before the visit faded. Not that he minded. The dreams had become quite relaxing.

But he had little time to chat now. He glanced over at the platform leading back to the street, where his wedding suit was waiting. *I should get going—*

Wait! Fio turned around, his steps shaking the earth a little, and rummaged in the back of his nest. When he turned back, he gently dropped something sparkling at Ambrose's feet. *A wedding gift,* he said proudly. *Eli said you've been getting them, and I wanted to get you one, too.*

Ambrose blinked. It was a potion bottle.

I filled it with my favorite things. Fio nudged it with his nose. *Or, rather, the not-youngling helped fill it. You know, the tall one who assists you.*

Ambrose picked up the bottle. The simple thing had been filled to the brim with shiny rocks. Some taken from the Scar, some clearly dug up from the surrounding plains. And some weren't rocks at all, but glass gems bought from the markets, all in a rainbow of colors.

A knot formed in his throat. He'd have to thank Nat for this later.

Thank you, Fio. He patted the dragon's snout, warmed by the bright sun, quietly resolving to give the gift a place of honor on his lucky shelf. *It's perfect.*

You're welcome. And don't worry, I'll keep everyone safe while you're on your trip.

With that, he snuggled deeper into his sunlit nest, with his waterfalls, his birds, and the entirety of the Scar to guard.

Ambrose and Eli had settled on the lavender fields for their wedding.

The process was far easier than Ambrose had expected. The day after they'd decided, Grim spoke to The Jumping Ogre, who reached out to their favorite winery, who promptly booked them a little venue they had built in the fields. Ambrose had been horrified to see the price and even more horrified to learn that Rosemond Street and the Valenzes had paid for the place. *And* volunteered to bake the cake, assemble the flowers, decorate the arch...

And he couldn't even *help*. He was informed in no uncertain terms that on the day of the ceremony, he had to lounge with Sherry, Dawn, and Rory, while Eli stayed with his family and the others set up his own *wedding* for him—

"That's how it should work." Dawn patted his hand. "You just sit and look pretty."

Yes, well, she had done a magnificent job of that at her wedding. She had looked like a wand-wielding angel. He merely grumbled, straightened his coat, and paced around the shop. "I have never sat and looked pretty in my entire life."

Eventually he was allowed into the venue—sort of. He had to remain behind a partition that separated the wedding feast from the ceremony space, hiding him from Eli and the others. He patted his left pocket; yes, his part of it was all still there. And tucked into his coat, Eli's proposal potion was safely hidden. His engagement ring was no longer tied to it, of course, but the green liquid remained, still bearing hints of the memories Eli had infused into it.

He took it out now and wrapped a hand around the warm glass. The memories were different each time he touched it, and softer now that the magic was fading. He caught hints of them in a cave this time, in a sinkhole drenched in moonlight. It was the night they had first kissed, after going off and harvesting dangerous magical ingredients like fools.

Funny how some things never changed.

As he smiled and tucked away the potion, Sherry lightly touched his arm.

"What are you thinking about, dear?" she asked. It was nearly time for the ceremony to begin. Dawn and Rory had already gone ahead, leaving them alone by the partitions in wait for the music to start. Music provided by Luka, of course. With flowers bought by

Dawn, a whole feast paid for by Grim and Sherry...all to celebrate him and Eli, and the memories tucked right next to his heart.

Ambrose shook his head. "That you all do far too much for us."

Sherry beamed and adjusted the half-cape at his shoulder. Her blue dress matched the navy elements of his own coat, gold sparkling in subtle accents on both of them. "It's no more than you deserve, my dear. You have everything ready?"

Gentle murmurs rose and fell from the other side of the partition. He swallowed and set back his shoulders. "Yes."

"It's all right to be nervous."

He gave a weak laugh. "What, about marrying him? Gods, never."

As she squeezed his hand, the music started. Luka's playing—Nat had coached him on it, even up to the night before, when he had convinced himself he was a hack and would ruin the whole thing. But Nat had been right; it sounded lovely. Enticing, almost, telling him it would be all right to walk down the aisle in view of those he loved.

Then Sherry took his arm and linked it with hers, her eyes already welling.

"All right," she said in her firm, smile-tinged voice. "Let's go get you married."

As Ambrose had expected, the others had outdone themselves with decorating the little ceremony space. Lights and garlands stretched over the wide pergola. Flower petals were scattered in little piles over the center walkway, set there by Tom, who still had flower petals sticking onto her fork hands. And the archway ahead framed Eli and their officiant Grim in a wreath of pastel blue and yellow, a harmonized song with the lavender fields beyond.

It would be perfect, Ambrose thought—if it weren't for everyone shedding tears before he even reached the altar.

Sherry didn't last long, of course. Several steps in, she was already crying. Up at the end of the aisle, Dawn waited next to the space Ambrose would occupy, also dabbing at her eyes while Grim supplied her with handkerchiefs. The only person who didn't seem to be on the verge of sobbing was Nat, who sat on his side of the aisle and was throwing him an excited double thumbs-up.

And she wasn't the only one on his side. The Valenzes clustered on Eli's side, of course, right in front of his adventuring party. But all of Rosemond Street had taken up space on Ambrose's side. The apprentices on one bench. Rory close to Dawn, supplying her with additional handkerchiefs. Viola, one cheek still dusted with the tiniest bit of blue frosting.

But Ambrose could no longer focus on them: Eli was just ahead of him. Dressed in scarlet and gold, grinning from ear to ear while trying to wipe tears from his face. Ambrose steeled himself and held back his own—gods, *someone* in this place had to keep it together.

When they finally reached Eli, Sherry kissed Ambrose's cheek, did the same for Eli, then scurried to sit at the front row beside Rory. Behind him, Dawn sniffled and adjusted his half-cape.

"You're so handsome," she stage-whispered.

"Thank you," he whispered back. Keep it together, keep it *together*—

Grim cleared their throat, and just like with every Rosemond Street meeting, the group settled down into silence.

"We're gathered here," they began, "to witness the union of..."

At Ambrose's request, he and Eli had given the jeweler a very *short* statement to recite. Sentiments loosely translated from Kolkean, all delivered in Grim's stoic, professional fashion. At least, Ambrose assumed so. With Eli holding both of his hands, he could hardly pay attention to things like words.

"Now," Grim closed their notebook and lowered their voice. "Eli, you have the ring?"

Ambrose took a steadying breath and redoubled his focus on Eli's touch. They had pared down all of the Scarrish and Kolkean traditions to something simple: a statement and an exchange of rings.

(Eli had assured him that his family in Kolkea would make up for the brevity in their own way when they visited. Ambrose decided that as long as they bribed him with plenty of Kolkean food, he'd allow it.)

Eli pulled the requested ring out of his pocket: a simple gold band cradling a cluster of blue and white gems. He lifted Ambrose's hand and opened his mouth to say his vows. "I—"

He broke immediately. Ambrose held back a loving grin.

"It's all right," he murmured. Eli wiped his cheeks.

"I'm *trying*," he said through his weepy smile. His family and fellow adventurers laughed.

"You got this, Valenz!" one of them called. Eli shook his head, then set his shoulders back and took a breath.

"I've been waiting to give you this ring for my entire life." His voice trembled, but he soldiered on. "And you should know that no matter what quest I go on—no matter where it is or what I'm doing—there is no more worthy quest than the one we're going on together. With this ring, I swear to always love you, honor you, and take care of you for as long as I live."

As soon as he slipped the ring on, he turned back to the others on his side of the aisle. "See, I did it."

More easy laughter from the audience.

Grim nodded to Ambrose, signaling his turn. He pulled the ring out of his pocket: a red gem wreathed in tiny, delicate lines of gold, and shimmering with the strongest shield enchantments he had ever seen.

"I once gave you something like this as a peace offering," he began. Eli's face crumpled all over again. Grim quietly handed him another handkerchief.

"And now I offer this as a symbol of my affection," Ambrose continued, braving his way forward despite his heart crashing against his ribcage. "Mine and the..."

Tears pricked at his eyes. No, he *had* to hold on.

"Mine and that of the family you're marrying into. Because the whole street contributed to enchanting this so—so that you'd stay safe no matter where you are—"

He failed to hold on; tears rolled down his cheeks despite himself. Dawn sniffled and squeezed his shoulder. He briefly covered her hand with his and took a shaky breath.

"With this"—he slipped the ring onto Eli's finger—"I swear to always love you, honor you, and take care of you. For as long as I live."

Grim nodded, their eyes glimmering with pride. "Mr. Valenz, Mr. Beake. You may now—"

There was no need to wait for the end of that sentence. As the crowd cheered, Eli had Ambrose in his arms instantly, his kiss salty with tears and sweet with love and a symbol of what Ambrose wanted every day for the rest of his life.

His husband, his family, and his shop.

WANT MORE?

Did you enjoy *A Draught for a Dragon*?

Spread the word and leave a review!

Want more cozy fantasy romance?

Sign up for my newsletter to get free stories, art, and release updates:

https://rkashwick.com/newsletter/

THE SIDE QUEST ROW SERIES

A Rival Most Vial

A Captured Cauldron

A Draught for a Dragon

THE LUTESONG SERIES

The Stray Spirit

The Spirit Well

The Spirit's Curse

ACKNOWLEDGMENTS

Well, I suppose it's time to flip Rosemond Street's shop sign to *Closed*.

At this point, I struggle to recall what it was like before Ambrose and Eli. It feels like they've always been with me, whether they're bickering or yearning or adventuring together. And as always, I have a lot of people to thank for their help in getting those boys out of my head—not for just one book, but three.

First, to my beta and sensitivity readers: Joe, Emma, Kalynn, Lila, Jenna, and Tessa. Without your help, this book would still be a tangled mess in Scrivener, and I'd probably be a tanged mess on the floor.

To my editor Kim Halstead, who has guided me through six books now. Six! Can you believe she's put up with me for that long? Incredible. Thank you so, so, so much.

To CoverKitchen for making book 3's cover the perfect little green bookend to the series. Thank you so much for your artistry!

To my family, friends, and writing groups who heard me complain, whine, lament, and self-doubt my way through this entire series, and countered all of that with positivity and encouragement: this book wouldn't be here without you.

And finally, to Rosemond Street. To Ambrose, Eli, Dawn, and their many loved ones. I love you very much. I'll come by for a shopping spree soon.

ABOUT THE AUTHOR

By day, R.K. Ashwick herds cats in the animation industry. By night, she writes, bakes, and herds her literal cat around her living room. She lives with her husband (and said cat) in California.

For more information, visit https://rkashwick.com/.